The Iron Tongue of Midnight

Books by Beverle Graves Myers

Interrupted Aria
Painted Veil
Cruel Music
The Iron Tongue of Midnight

The Iron Tongue
of Midnight

The Fourth Baroque Mystery

Beverle Graves Myers

Poisoned Pen Press

*Poisoned
Pen
Press*

Copyright © 2008 by Beverle Graves Myers

First Edition 2008

10 9 8 7 6 5 4 3 2 1

Library of Congress Catalog Card Number: 2007935726

ISBN: 978-1-59058-232-9   Hardcover

Poisoned Pen Press
6962 E. First Ave., Ste. 103
Scottsdale, AZ 85251
www.poisonedpenpress.com
info@poisonedpenpress.com

Printed in the United States of America

Characters

Tito Amato	well-known singer
Annetta Amato Rumbolt	His sister
Augustus(Gussie)Rumbolt	Her husband, an artist

The opera company

Karl Johann Weber	A German composer
Gabrielle Fouquet	French soprano
Jean-Louis Fouquet	Her husband and manager
Emilio Strada	A castrato
Romeo Battaglia	A basso
Carmela Costa	A soprano
Mario and Lucca Gecco	Accompanists

The Villa Dolfini and environs

Vincenzo Dolfini	The master
Octavia Dolfini	His wife
Nita	The housekeeper
Giovanni and others	Footmen
Alphonso	Vincenzo's valet
Ernesto Verdi	The steward
Pia Verdi	His wife
Manuel and Basilio	Their sons
Signor Luvisi	The nearest neighbor
Captain Forti	The high constable
Mayor Bartoli, Padre Romano	Local officials

Constantinople

Alessandro Amato	Tito's brother
Zuhal	His wife
Yusuf Ali Muhammad	His father-in-law
Sebboy	A white eunuch
Yanus	Proprietor of a brothel
Sefa, Danika	Women of the brothel
Count Vladimir Paninovich	A Russian nobleman

Part One

"And into the midnight we galloped abreast."

—Robert Browning

Chapter One

My eyes smoldered. My brow wrinkled. Curling my lip in a sneer, I raised my chin and crossed my arms in a gesture of implacable fury.

Gussie turned his gaze from the autumn landscape speeding past the carriage window and regarded me with the bemused grin he usually reserved for Matteo and Titolino's childish capers. The light carriage we'd hired after disembarking from the river barge at Padua was so cramped that our knees nearly touched.

"Tito?" he asked. "What the deuce are you doing?"

"Practicing," I replied across the small space. "If I'm going to make a convincing Tamerlano, I must cultivate a fierce demeanor."

"Will you be able to sing with that scowl on your face?"

I cleared my throat, took a deep breath, and attempted a run that ended in a high C. The demands of technique pulled my lips into an angelic oval of silvery sound. "It's no use." I sighed in disgust. "I'll have to convey the tyrant's cruel nature by gesture alone."

"I'm sure you will manage. But I must say, this Tamerlano fellow isn't really in your line. You sang a splendid Apollo in your last opera at the San Marco, and no one can touch you as a noble prince. But Tito Amato as a lustful, pillaging Mongol conqueror?" Gussie shook his head, releasing a lock of wayward blond hair from its queue at the back of his neck. "I can't quite twist my brain around it. Why do you think Maestro Weber is so insistent that you sing the part?"

In his frank, good-humored way, my friend and brother-in-law had given voice to the very question I'd been trying to avoid. Ever since I'd received the invitation to sing the lead role in a new opera by Karl Johann Weber, I'd been wondering why the German had chosen me. I'd barely heard of the man, and what little I knew gave me pause. Italian opera was the rage of Europe, and composers of all nations flocked to our musical capitals to imbibe the art from its source. If memory served, this Weber was a Saxon who had come to grief over a duel with a fellow composer. At the Teatro Ducale in Milan. Or had it been Torino? Whichever, Maestro Weber had scampered back over the Alps and gone to ground for several years. Now, it appeared, he was making a comeback.

That was another odd thing. Venice was fertile ground for relaunching a career, but a man who wanted to make a splash should be calling on theater managers, engaging practice rooms, making the rounds of coffee houses that cater to musicians, in short, conducting himself in a manner that would whet the public's appetite for his new opera. Maestro Weber had taken the opposite tack. Instead of displaying himself about town, he was completing the score for *Il Gran Tamerlano* deep in the countryside.

Octavia Dolfini, the wife of a wealthy Venetian iron merchant, was playing Lady Bountiful to Weber's production. Like every other household that could afford to quit our mosquito-ridden island for the warm months, Octavia and her husband kept a villa on Terrafirma, the mainland. It was a note from Signora Dolfini that had summoned me to begin rehearsal, and I had agreed mainly because the signora had also been eager to hire my brother-in-law.

Vincenzo Dolfini, the master of the villa, had conceived a fancy for a series of scenic views of his rural property: picturesque gardens, a groom holding the reins of a prize stallion, grinning peasants bringing in the grape harvest. The sort of fashionable daubs Gussie could toss off in his sleep. As Signora Dolfini's flowery letter of invitation had put it: What a happy coincidence that the painter Augustus Rumbolt is married to the sister of Venice's most renowned singer.

Gussie and I had debated the matter for several days My first inclination had been to refuse; I could easily find more suitable work that did not involve traveling to such an out-of-the-way spot. Gussie's excitement overcame my reluctance. For once, he did not have a string of commissions waiting, and since my unorthodox marriage, our shared house on the Campo dei Polli was not a pleasant place to be at liberty. My darling, but stubborn wife Liya and my sweet sister Annetta differed considerably in their philosophy concerning household management. I'm being gracious. In truth, the female members of our household were at each other like a cat and dog stuffed in a knapsack.

Signora Dolfini had also sweetened her invitation with liberal financial arrangements. Thanks to the public's insatiable appetite for male sopranos, my career had advanced nicely over the years. Even so, the pay offered for *Tamerlano* nearly made me blush. It was enough to offset the inconvenience of travel and still provide a tidy sum to put toward the purchase of a large home for my new family. Gussie, too, was quite happy with his promised compensation. Thus contracts were exchanged, and we found ourselves jolting along a rutted lane toward a villa situated in the first risings of the Euganean Hills south of Padua.

On this mellow, late September afternoon, the fields spread out in a harlequin patchwork of amber and gold. Wooded streams and single files of sentinel elms separated the barley from the wheat. In the distance, a range of dark hills folded into billowing white clouds. Gussie had just raised his hand to point out a flock of sheep when an ominous crack burst forth from the undercarriage. The top-heavy vehicle lurched violently, throwing me into the corner and upending Gussie on top of me. Above the pounding of hooves and squealing of the brake, I heard the driver calming his team with deep, caressing tones. He knew his business. After a skid of only a moment's duration, the carriage rattled to a halt.

A fog of road dust filled the interior. Groaning, I struggled to free my right arm. "Are you hurt?" I cried.

Gussie braced himself against the sharply-tilted carriage frame and inched his bulk back onto the slick leather cushion. Once upright, he gave his nose an exploratory pinch and wiggle, then withdrew his hand, tentatively, as if he expected to find it covered in blood. No trace of crimson was in evidence. "I'll do." He shrugged. "You?"

I probed my ribs. They were tender, perhaps bruised, but a deep intake of breath told me I would still be able to sing. I nodded. "What happened?"

Before he could hazard a guess, the driver's goggle-eyed face popped through the window that framed the tips of the trees across the road. "Are you injured, Signori?"

"We're all right," I replied. "Did we lose a wheel?"

"*Si*, we snapped a linch-pin. The wheel shot off and skittered clean away."

"Can you fix it?"

"Not without the wheel. And not without some help."

"We can—"

The carriage creaked in another lurch. Gussie and I grabbed for a handhold. "Stay put," the driver said. "I must see to the horses."

He jumped away. I heard his feet hit the ground and the sounds of horses being soothed and unhitched. Then, proceeding with care, Gussie and I clambered out to view the damage for ourselves.

The carriage was skewed across the lane with its right front axle dug into the soft dirt. The wheel that should have capped it was nowhere to be seen. It could have been worse; at least, the axle hadn't snapped. Yet I feared we were in for either a long walk or a long wait.

Gussie's immediate concern was his paint and canvases. If they were ruined, replacements could not easily be found in this rustic paradise. With a leg up from a tall back wheel, he pawed among the trunks and boxes lashed to the top of the carriage.

After testing ropes and retying several loose knots, he climbed down and planted himself in the middle of the lane. I could sense his mounting frustration as he peered down the tree-canopied corridor and slapped his tricorne against his thigh.

With his haystack of fair hair and his ruddy English cheeks, Gussie could have been any one of the droves of young Englishmen who made Italy the highlight of their Grand Tours. In fact, he had landed in our ancient, decaying republic on just such an edifying journey some years ago. He always said he decided to stay in Venice the minute he saw the jade waters of the lagoon meet the shimmery blue of the sky. Perhaps. I chose to believe that my sister was more instrumental in seducing Gussie away from the country of his birth than our watery landscape.

"Any idea how far it is to the villa?" My brother-in-law directed this question to the driver who had returned from tying his horses under a gold-leafed elm.

"The Dolfini place is three miles. The village of Molina Mori another mile beyond, more or less. You two young fellows could walk, but with some luck, you won't have to." The driver opened a trunk bolted to the undercarriage and rummaged in its depths. Several tools hit the dirt with a clang. "Yes, here we have it." With a wide grin, he produced a new linch-pin.

"Don't suppose you have a spare wheel hiding in there, too?" I asked.

"Our wheel must be somewhere." He raised his eyebrows and searched the air with the expectant look of a confirmed optimist. Dame Fortune answered his call in a surprisingly deep voice.

"Here's your wheel. Still serviceable it is—not a spoke broken." A compact, broad-shouldered man of fifty or so spoke from the top of the bank that defined the lane's right-hand boundary. His weather-beaten face and loden jacket marked him as a countryman, but his pose outlined by the slanting rays of the afternoon sun was as regal as the towering elms that surrounded us. Guiding the wheel with one hand, he descended the mossy slope and cleared the drainage ditch with a sure-footed leap.

"We'll have you back on your way in no time. Then maybe the villa will go off the boil for a bit." He transferred his burden to the driver, but spoke to me. Doffing his wide-brimmed hat, he inclined from the waist and continued, "The mistress won't rest until her company of singers is complete, and the master is champing at the bit to have his vineyard painted while the grapes are still on the vine."

"You know who we are?"

His mouth pursed in a twitch as he ran his gaze over my beardless face and gangly limbs: the tell-tale signs of the surgery that had prevented my angelic voice from deepening with maturity. Of course. This confirmed rustic handled animals of all kinds. He might not know me by sight, but he would recognize a gelding when he saw one.

"Up at the house, the names of Signor Amato and Signor Rumbolt are on everyone's lips. They expected you would arrive today."

Gussie came around the back of the carriage. "This must be Dolfini land, then. Who are you?"

"Ah, *scusi*. I am Ernesto Verdi, Signor Dolfini's steward." The newcomer sketched another bow, then waved his hat toward the top of the bank. "But you are mistaken in thinking that this is Signor Dolfini's meadow. My master's estate lies a mile distant as the crow flies, more by way of the road. It is Signor Luvisi who owns this land."

Our driver's craggy face registered surprise. "You're either very brave or outright foolhardy to tramp over Luvisi land."

The steward replied smoothly, "Signor Luvisi won't mind—we have an understanding. We've been chasing Bettina. If she gets loose this time of year, she always runs straight for his grove of oaks."

It transpired that Bettina was an old sow with a long memory and a keen appetite for acorns. She had been duly captured before damage had come to the neighbor's grove, and the search party had been heading back across the fields when they saw our wheel bounce over the bank.

After a brief conversation with the driver, Ernesto called to a sturdy boy atop the bank. "Manuel, take Bettina back to her pen."

"But Papa…" Cheeks flushing, he ran a hand through crisp dark curls and answered with the obstinacy of a youth ripe for any distraction from everyday chores. "She's bucking and digging in with her feet. Send Santini back with Bettina. I can help you fix the gentlemen's carriage."

Ernesto squared his shoulders impatiently. "Do as I say, boy. Keep a tight grip on the sow's lead and Zuzu will drive her along."

A shaggy mountain of a dog with white fur and bright black eyes appeared at the boy's side.

"Eh, Zuzu." Ernesto grinned. "Run them both home. There's a good girl."

At her name, the dog gave a few deep barks and butted the boy's thigh with her muzzle.

Manuel was outgunned and he knew it. After a subdued "*Sì, Papa,*" the boy slunk away with a rebellious pout. Zuzu made a fluffy white shadow.

Beside the sagging carriage, our driver had knelt to run his hands over the scarred wheel and test the new linch-pin. Gussie shrugged out of his jacket and hung it on a handy branch, eager to add his strength to the task of lifting the axle.

Ernesto stopped him. "I must not allow it, Signor Rumbolt. The master would never forgive me if I allowed you to risk your gifted hands in such labor. Leave this to Santini and me."

Santini turned out to be an elongated gawk with dirt on his chin and a matted mane of graying brown hair. His slack-jawed expression and ungainly scramble down the bank did little to inspire confidence, but he and Ernesto made a good team. With the ease of long association, they bent to their repairs as skillfully as a pair of cartwrights.

Leaving the countrymen to their work, Gussie and I crossed the lane and rested our backsides on a wooden fence. The neat trellis posts of a vineyard stretched behind us, bearing a sea of leaves and tendrils. We remained silent for a while, inhaling the perfume of ripening grapes and listening to the rustle of their foliage in the dry breeze. Eventually, I was moved to speak about another problem that our journey was allowing us to avoid.

"Do you think we did the right thing, Gussie? Not telling Annetta before we left?"

He recrossed his legs and shot me an uncomfortable glance. "Circumstances left us no choice. Annetta hasn't been herself since Isabella's birth."

A familiar wave of guilt washed over me. "It was a poor time for me to bring Liya and her son into our household. Two women with opposing temperaments, a new baby, three boisterous children. What could I have been thinking?"

"You were thinking that your years of loneliness were over and that you'd found the family you always wanted." Gussie raised a shadow of a smile. "You can't blame yourself for Annetta's moody ways."

I wasn't convinced. "And to top it off, I return from Rome with an injured manservant who requires a servant to wait on him."

"Time will smooth the rough edges, Tito. Benito will heal. Annetta will find a way out of her doldrums, and she and Liya will find a way to get along. I predict that by the time we return to Venice, Annetta will be in a fit state to receive bad news."

"How will we ever find the right words?"

He shook his head, rubbing his jaw. "She will want to read the letter for herself, of course. But we must prepare her carefully. Here…" he extended his hand. "Let me see it again."

I removed a calfskin wallet from an inside pocket, opened the clasp, and handed over the folded sheets that had arrived a few days ago. Their edges were already crinkled from repeated reading.

The letter was from Alessandro, our seafaring brother who had embraced Islam and now called Constantinople home. His defection to such an alien land still perturbed us. We had become accustomed to his long absences; Alessandro was a merchant trader, after all. But we always knew he would return. With no warning, he would appear at the door shipworn and weary, his duffle cloak slung across his shoulders, his tanned face split by a huge grin. He always insisted on distributing presents before he even cleaned up. From his travel bag would come a gold chain or bright length of silk that he had spotted at an eastern bazaar, a paisley shawl bought straight off a camel caravan, or some such exotic trinket for each of us.

Our older brother might travel half a world away, but he never forgot his family. That is until Zuhal, the Turkish woman who became his wife, stole his heart away from us.

Alessandro's new loyalty to Constantinople provided only one benefit as far as Annetta and I were concerned. It put him in a convenient spot to search for Grisella, the sister who had sailed out of our lives so many years ago. The Turkish capital had been her last known port of call. In the dappled sunlight of the country lane, Gussie perused the letter that recounted Alessandro's efforts. I had learned the words by heart:

Constantinople, 21st August 1740

My dear family,

As you see, I have kept my word and pushed balance sheets and ledgers aside. My darling Zuhal accused me of setting her on the shelf as well, so assiduous I have been in executing the mission I was charged with. I only wish I had better news to impart. But more of that later. So you will learn the fate of our sister as I did, in small steps, I will begin at the beginning.

Grisella left us as a naïve young girl enticed away by the attentions of a rogue. In consequence of the local strictures which tend to keep the lives of women hidden, I thought it best to start searching for, and it pains me to even write his name, Domenico Viviani. My father-in-law was most helpful in this regard. As a merchant, Yusuf Ali has many ties to the foreign communities that make up a good part of Constantinople. He put me in touch with a certain Halim Talat, an apostate like myself, but with one difference. Halim turned Turk out of fear, intent on escaping disgrace in his homeland, while I embraced Islam to honor the people I have come to love. Before assuming his current name and manner of living, Halim had been a nobleman of Rovigo, but since his personal history has no bearing on my search, I will not test your patience by recounting it.

Halim took a keen interest in the train of events which put Grisella in Constantinople with Viviani, and I was overjoyed when he claimed knowledge of the vile libertine. On advance of a small sum, he took me to a likely tavern in Pera, a hilltop quarter known as a veritable stewpot of Armenians, Italians, Frenchmen, and Russians. Since the Turks avoid alcohol as a strict sin, a Greek tended the drinking establishment. I was disappointed to see that my companion failed to take the Koran's proscription to heart. Halim downed three glasses of Montepulciano while we waited for Viviani to make his appearance.

I was losing patience when a gaunt man with spectacles entered the tavern and threaded a timid path through the tables. Halim astonished me by pointing in his direction. "There's Viviani," he said.

I'd been hoodwinked. The newcomer's elbows had rubbed through his silk coat and the fraying tail of a cheap wig ran down his bowed back. He looked like a bookworm who had acquired a gentleman's suit from the rag man, hardly a terror to women and surely not the audacious scoundrel that I had been warned to approach warily.

I bunched the front of Halim's loose robe in my fist.

"No, no. You will see," said he, beckoning the ramshackle figure with two fingers. He shook me off and continued in a shout, "Signor Viviani, join us. I have someone who wishes to buy you a drink."

I will dispense with lengthy explanation. It wasn't Domenico Viviani who sat down to abuse my generosity in the matter of Montepulciano, but his elder brother Carlo. At close range, he cut an even sorrier figure. Snuff encrusted the rim of one nostril, his wet blue eyes seemed to have lost the will to focus, and his odor told me he did not avail himself of the public baths. Since he seemed willing to talk as long as I was willing to fill his glass, I sent Halim away and proceeded to learn much.

Domenico Viviani is dead. After the Doge ran the three Viviani brothers out of Venice, they arrived in Constantinople with chests of gold coins and all the riches they had managed to strip from their *palazzo*. As usual, Domenico was at the helm. He set them up in a house on the water, a splendid *yali* that served as both residence and center of their business dealings. Yes, Grisella was with them. Without shame, Carlo recounted how Domenico had forced her to serve as wife to all three brothers. You can imagine my difficulty in controlling my outrage.

Once Domenico had pledged his service to Sultan Mahmud and furnished the Turkish navy with his expertise in the latest Venetian shipbuilding techniques, the fortunes of the renegade brothers seemed limitless. They acquired a flotilla of trading vessels, and for several years they lived in a luxury few European men can imagine. More women joined Grisella on the *haremlik* side of the *yali*.

There was, however, one favor that the sultan could not bestow: protection from the dreaded plague that languishes and revives but never totally disappears from our shores. Claudio was stricken first, then Domenico. They suffered many days of fever and swelling before succumbing. May Allah strike me down, I wish their agonies had been tenfold. It still wouldn't have been as much as they deserved. Carlo was spared, possibly because his role as keeper of accounts did not take him to the docks where the pest seems particularly virulent.

"How have you come to your current sorry pass?" I asked, hoping to goad Carlo's story along.

"I am not the man of business that my brothers were," he replied dolefully. "I lost the *yali* sometime ago, and now I exist on the small wages I earn by tending the books of a Turkish gentleman who desires a European library."

"And where have you stashed my sister?" My tone would have sent most men running, but Carlo had indulged in too much wine to take that precaution.

"Ah, our pretty Grisella," he replied with his chin lolling on his chest. "A Russian took the house. Took her, too. Shame to lose her like that."

"Where is your former *yali*?"

"Doesn't matter." Closing his eyes, he yawned and murmured, "The Russian is gone. A Dutchman lives there now."

Since my informant was nearly unconscious from drink, I feared the rest of the story would remain a mystery. (Family, I know you hold my new beliefs in slight regard, but truly the Prophet was wise in commanding us to abstain from a substance that can so addle the senses.) I unsheathed my dagger and dug it into the filthy damask of Carlo's waistcoat. When I saw his eyes widen, I asked the Russian's name.

"Oh, do stop poking me," he answered in a fussy, old woman's voice. "It's one of those odd mouthfuls that shouldn't be a name at all. Pan-something-vich."

I extended my knife a bit farther and felt the point pop through the fabric.

"Paninovich. Yes, that's it. Count Vladimir Paninovich."

That was all the man knew. With great relish, I slammed his face into the table and left the tavern.

The day after my interview with the surviving Viviani, we received a caravan of cured tobacco which necessitated many days of picking and sorting. It was a full week before our weed had been rebaled, but you may be sure that the moment our cargo was loaded onto the outgoing lighters, I went to find this Count Paninovich.

A few questions in the right ears started me out. Though not attached to the Russian Embassy, Paninovich had been received by the Grand Vizier and was a staple at the concerts and balls where Turks mixed with the foreign ambassadors and their courts. When I pressed, several recalled that the Russian often spent his evenings in the company of military men. Apparently, he was generous in standing new stakes for young officers who bet too rashly at the faro table.

For several days, that remained the sum total of my investigation. Then a customer who keeps his snuffbox filled with our blend stopped in with one more remembered detail. Paninovich sometimes escorted a young woman admired on two counts: her stunning red hair and her talented rendition of Italian arias. Ah, Grisella! And where could Count Paninovich be found? Alas, my customer hadn't seen him for a year or more. Perhaps he had been recalled to the court of Empress Anna Ivanova at St. Petersburg.

The trail quickly grew cold. Count Paninovich seemed to be a topic that most people wished to avoid. Try as I might, I managed to discover nothing more about the circumstances or business dealings which had brought him to Constantinople, still less about his women. It was time for my sweet Zuhal to take the reins.

My new city has vast marble temples that are unlike any Venice knows. I speak of the *hamam*, the baths, the temples of personal cleanliness. Well-born women visit the *hamam* every few days and spend hours in grooming and visiting with each other. Behind their veils, Turkish women are no different from Italian. The air is heavy with gossip whenever they get together. In the *hamam*, no news or scandal can exist without being picked over as thoroughly as my bales of tobacco.

And that, dear family, is how I came to learn our sister's fate. Zuhal discovered that Grisella and her count both died just over a year ago, in a fire at a new *yali* he had purchased farther up the Bosphorus. Some say that he jumped from a window but went back in a vain attempt to rescue Grisella. Others say the roof collapsed before either of them could escape. I hope the former is true, only because it would mean that our little sister was loved, at least at the end.

We located her burial place just yesterday, in a Christian cemetery near a beautiful Greek church dedicated to St. Anthony. Without benefit of gossip from the *hamam*, we would never have found it. Grisella was buried under the name Viviani, you see, not Amato. The sexton had no record of who made the arrangements. Perhaps it was one of the count's countrymen from the embassy. I am sorry to report that her stone was spattered with mud and surrounded by brambles. Zuhal helped me clear it, and we laid a sheaf of lilies on the marble slab. It will go untended no longer.

Continue in good health, my dear ones, and don't let grief overtake you. With great sorrow we must admit that our sister bears some blame for the path she chose. I will always remember her as a laughing, willful child, her beautiful red gold hair flying in the breeze as she chased a ball across our campo, not as the hardened woman she must have become. Pray for her soul, as I do in my own way, and light a candle every Sunday.

As always your loving,
Alessandro

"Tito?" Gussie repeated insistently, "Tito?"

I blinked my eyes, trying to rid myself of the image of a weedy grave overshadowed by the onion-shaped domes and minarets of a distant, pestilential city. I drew in a lungful of good Italian air as my brother-in-law pressed the letter into my hand.

"Tito, Ernesto says the wheel is ready. We must go."

Chapter Two

We caught our first glimpse of the Villa Dolfini as our carriage rattled through the iron gates at the bottom of the curving drive. The main house stood on a slight rise. Its central mass, clad in cream-colored stucco, rose to a perfectly proportioned dome topped by a spire that glinted in the rays of the lowering sun. From each side of the house, identical wings swept out to open colonnades, which in turn led to structures I took to have an agricultural function. Fields of standing grain, separated by low stone walls, stretched toward the olive orchard beyond. A lovely scene, though I was surprised to see the walls between the fields collapsing in several places.

After the carriage had come to a halt, Gussie jumped out without bothering to unfold the stairs. He claimed his paintbox while I followed more slowly, still caught up in the melancholy produced by recalling Alessandro's letter. I gave my head a vehement shake. Time to put family matters aside and go to work. I had a new opera to learn.

Wide stone steps conducted us to a covered portico encircled by pots of red geraniums. Before us loomed an ancient wooden door with a most unusual knocker, a gauntleted hand clenched in a fist. The door swung inward before I had a chance to knock.

A bulky, not-so-young maid greeted us. "I'm Nita," she said in a flat tone. "This way if you please. The boys will bring your bags."

Our footsteps resonated on terra-cotta tiles as we followed Nita across the shadowy foyer. To our right and left stretched long corridors walled with frescos and mirrors. Ahead, through an entrance framed by two fluted columns, was the grand salon. I listened for sounds of a rehearsal in progress. Hearing none, I applied my attention to the layout of the house.

In much the way of the grander *palazzi* in town, the level that we traversed contained the villa's public rooms. The ground floor below would be given over to working rooms: kitchen, wine cellar, larders, and other storerooms. Bed chambers and the family's private suites would fill the second level, and the servants would make do with attic quarters.

Nita huffed and puffed as she led us up a staircase that looped upwards from the right-hand corridor. "The mistress has put you together," she called over her shoulder. "It's not the best room, but the only one left. If anyone else shows up, he'll have to bed down on a sack of potatoes in a larder."

"Are other guests still expected?" I asked as we reached the long, nearly empty second-floor hall that spanned the villa from front to back. Here the tiled floor was hyphenated by a narrow scrap of Persian carpet, and the only furniture was a mammoth armoire on the rear wall and a tall clock standing between two windows at the front. "I thought the rest of the opera company would have already arrived."

"Ah, *si*. By God's grace, Signore, I pray you are correct." After a barely concealed sigh, she pointed to the various doors. "The Frenchwoman and her husband are there, with the little Italian soprano just across. Then we have the two gentlemen—the one who sings so high and the one who sings so low. Here is your room, right across from them. The others are farther along, opposite the back stairs."

"The others?" Gussie asked.

"Those brothers that play the fiddles and such." She shook her head, then continued in prolonged syllables, "The musical accompanists, I'm supposed to say."

I gave the maid a closer look. A kerchief of unbleached linen contained her silver-streaked hair, and her freckled cheeks were brown as a biscuit. A thumbprint of flour decorated her jaw. The exotic performers who had been thrust into her midst must be causing her a great deal of extra work. The resentful set to her well-padded shoulders told me exactly what Nita thought of that.

"Where is Maestro Weber's room?" I asked.

"Oh, him." She pressed her lips in a thin line, then jerked her chin toward the narrower corridor that crossed along the front of the house. "He's around there, in the first room of the west wing. The German was the first to arrive, so he got the pick of the lot. The rooms overlooking the drive are bigger by half than these here."

"I suppose our hosts have rooms on that corridor then."

She nodded.

"And the others in the family?"

"There are no others."

"No children?"

"None. And not likely to be, with the master and mistress married almost twenty years." As if disposing of the topic of the Dolfini family, Nita briskly dusted her palms and opened the nearest door.

Our room was certainly nothing to complain about. Several lamps lent a welcoming glow to the plastered walls which had been washed the color of a pale lettuce leaf. Simple iron bedsteads and armchairs with tapestry cushions stood ready to welcome road-weary bodies. Gussie chose the bed nearest the door by depositing his paintbox on its faded crimson coverlet. I plopped down on the other and sank into feather-filled heaven.

After a pointed reminder that the household's dinner had been put off until our arrival, Nita withdrew. A footman in plum-blue livery, probably imported from the Dolfini house in town, appeared with warm water for the wash bowls. Another brought our trunks and cases. After the footmen had unpacked, Gussie and I made hasty work of dressing. The ministrations of my manservant Benito were sorely missed, as well as his steady stream of irreverent banter, but I trusted that Gussie and I made ourselves presentable.

We were descending the front stairs under the blank gazes of classical busts set in wall niches when a furious string of Italian obscenities emanated from somewhere above. The feminine screech continued: "You bastard! I won't take any more of your orders, do you hear? You're the cause of all our troubles."

A man's guttural rumble followed, difficult to fathom as it bounced off the turns of the stairwell.

We halted, listening, questioning each other with our eyes.

"You've been warned. I won't go on like this," the woman's voice replied, even shriller than before.

"Harpy!" We understood that readily enough, as well as the smack of palm on flesh that followed.

Gussie flinched. "You singers are an emotional lot."

I shrugged. "It could be members of the household. Or servants."

"Well, whoever it is, they're not happy."

♫♫♫

We found the company on the first-floor loggia, the recessed porch that overlooked the rear lawn. Its velvety carpet of green sloped away to a man-made lake crossed by an arched footbridge. On the far side, a farmer's cottage nestled in a ring of feathery cypress trees. Shadows were gathering, and in the eastern sky, a single star glimmered. Near at hand, a tray of wine glasses stood on a marble-topped credenza. Our hostess was holding court across the tiles, expounding on the merits of the Teatro San Marco for mounting her production of *Tamerlano*.

Propped up by the loose pillows of a long chair, Octavia Dolfini was attended by several men who appeared to be hanging on her every word. The masculine half of our cast, I presumed. Though opera was one of Venice's ruling passions, there were always more singers than good roles to support them. A patron willing to sink a fortune into producing an opera could be assured of any number of fawning admirers.

The moment Octavia caught sight of Gussie and me, she broke off in mid-sentence and extended a hand. Her onlookers bumped against each other in their zeal to assist her to her feet.

"Signor Amato," she exclaimed, sailing across the tiles with her arms spread in an expansive gesture. "Our final treasure has arrived."

Our hostess appeared to be sliding into her middle years, but not without digging her heels in for all she was worth. The gingery hue of her brittle curls had come from a dye pot, and every crevice on her square-jawed face was chinked with paint and powder. Her gown, indigo blue over canary yellow petticoats, was padded with wide panniers. A shallow bosom dripping stones of golden topaz and aquamarine completed the picture. The excess sent a chuckle to my lips, but Octavia's hawk-like gaze stopped it at my teeth. Despite her almost comical appearance, this was a woman who took life very seriously indeed.

Octavia didn't halt her progress until her toes nearly touched mine; then she reached up to press my cheeks between her hands. I smiled weakly. Her rings made cold dimples in my skin.

"So tall, and even handsomer than I remember. Yes, Signor Amato, I've seen you before—on the stage. But you wouldn't remember. To you, I was simply one of those adoring faces in the crowd. Ah me, what a sublime addition to our opera you will make." She raised her voice, spraying my chin with a mist of spittle. "Karl, stop brooding. Come and meet your Tamerlano."

A slight man in a blue coat stood alone at the balcony rail. He looked to be around thirty, with a pale complexion and deeply set eyes capped by prominent brows. Tilting his head to let the gentle breeze ruffle the sandy hair that dusted his shoulders, he gave the impression of being consumed with altogether higher matters. His lofty thoughts, however, did not prevent him from sending me a brief, curious glance from under half-lowered lids.

The composer aimed a faint nod in my direction but stayed where he was.

Octavia plowed on, seemingly oblivious to Maestro Weber's want of manners. "You wouldn't know, of course, but I'm more than a simple music lover. I've been singing since I was a girl. Before I married, I was often encouraged to put my voice to advantage and take to the stage. Despite my obvious gifts, Mama and Papa wouldn't hear of it." She heaved a sigh. "Like a dutiful daughter, I abandoned my divine calling. But I still vocalize a bit... in my own home... when I'm asked most particularly..."

Never one to miss a cue, I replied gallantly, "Is it too much to hope that you might favor us with a few songs after dinner?"

"Well, perhaps, if you insist." She smiled and fluttered her eyelashes in a caricature of coy acceptance.

Gussie had been waiting patiently throughout this exchange. Now he cleared his throat. Several times.

I made introductions.

"Ah yes, the painter," our hostess replied vacantly. "Delighted."

If Octavia's delight left something to be desired, there was one person who seemed to find Gussie as enchanting as a carnival regatta and fireworks display rolled into one. Vincenzo Dolfini emerged from behind a potted palm where he had evidently been sitting alone. Broad shoulders dominated a rangy, six-foot frame. Bright eyes glittered from a smoothly hewn, pleasant face. "My painter? He's arrived?"

Octavia's husband looked the prosperous iron merchant from his neatly folded neckcloth to his sensible buckled shoes. Let others ape the silks and embroidery and laces of fashion, his appearance proclaimed, I'll wear sturdy broadcloth and worsted stockings and be proud of them. He advanced in long-legged, bouncing strides.

"Signor Rumbolt! At last. You've brought your canvases, I hope."

Gussie acknowledged our host with a deep bow, then replied, "I have a number stretched and ready, but first I'll need to do some preliminary sketches."

"Good man." Vincenzo clapped Gussie on the shoulder. "Come along to my study. I want to show you a map of the estate."

"Don't be silly, Vincenzo." Octavia's tone rumbled like distant thunder. "Dinner will be served any moment."

The master of the villa dug into his waistcoat and consulted a large watch. He shrugged his shoulders, saying, "We'll have trays in the study, my dear. Inform Nita."

Ignoring his wife's stormy gaze, Vincenzo steered Gussie across the loggia and chattered on: "In the morning, I thought you might start with the vineyard. And when you're ready to move indoors, I've had Ernesto clear out the *barchessa* that usually houses some cattle and wagons and whatnot. It has several high windows. You'll have to tell me if the light is sufficient. That's what you painters reckon of prime importance, I believe."

Gussie smiled his agreement and asked several questions as the pair passed into the salon. By benefit of our long association, I could tell that my brother-in-law had taken an immediate liking to Vincenzo Dolfini.

Beside me, the climate wasn't nearly so pleasant. Octavia was still simmering, and I wondered if my presence had forestalled the tempest that would usually rage over such an ill-timed desertion. Then again, our hostess might simply be holding her forces in reserve. I didn't envy her husband their next tête-à-tête.

After shifting her stare toward Maestro Weber, Octavia transformed the mood with a bright smile. Like a child eager to show off a new toy, she called the composer and my fellow musicians to gather around. Weber must have heard her, but he remained at the rail, leaning over at a precarious angle, almost as if he meant to throw himself on the breeze to swoop and dive with the evening swallows.

Octavia stretched up to whisper near my ear, "Don't mind Karl. He'll be over directly. When he's tinkering with a melody, he can think of nothing else. Karl is a poppet, really. I'm certain you will become fast friends."

I nodded, though in truth, I had no ambition to make a friend of the composer. All I wanted from the moody German was a satisfactory score and sensible direction.

Octavia gave my arm a motherly pat and gestured to a tall man in a neat bob wig. "Ah, here is someone I think you must already be acquainted with."

Indeed, the first man to make his bow was Emilio Strada, a fellow castrato with whom I'd often shared the stage. His face was as smooth as my own, of course, barely capable of raising a single whisker, and he had the wispy, attenuated stature that many of us are left with. There our resemblance ended. Emilio's nose was a squashed lump of dough—I had always wondered how it afforded the breath necessary for song—and his mouth was narrow and wrinkled. Despite these physical drawbacks, Emilio had worked hard at his craft and developed a precise soprano with an appealing silvery quality. Emilio was also ambitious. Though he welcomed me with light banter and spoke proudly of his role of Andronicus, Tamerlano's rival in love, he didn't fool me. Emilio coveted my title role with the relentless greed of a Barbary corsair.

Octavia then introduced a man who had just come onto the loggia, the basso Romeo Battaglia. I fear my jaw dropped when Romeo announced that he was singing Bazajet, the Ottoman sultan defeated and humiliated by Tamerlano. Bazajet was a tragic figure who was allotted almost as many arias as my character. In scoring the role for a low voice, Maestro Weber had made an audacious choice.

I could see that the mellow depth and power of Romeo's basso would serve the drama well. But what would Venice make of it? The Venice that reveled in the acrobatic roulades and endless trills of the castrati? I had only to hit high C to bring the box holders to their feet with wild applause, while a poor basso could sing his heart out and be ignored by those who couldn't be bothered to raise their heads from their card games or their socializing. I glanced toward the composer. Maestro Karl Weber must have a stiffer backbone than it appeared.

If Romeo Battaglia had any qualms, he didn't show them. He planted himself before me with feet spread wide, took frequent swallows of wine, and discussed his role with the heedless enthusiasm of a puppy chasing a ball—a very large puppy of the sheep-herding variety. The loose curls of his formal wig hung to his shoulders, and his waistcoat swelled over a well-padded belly that jiggled whenever he laughed, which seemed to be a frequent occurrence. I put his age at a callow twenty-five.

Romeo didn't strike me as the sort of fellow who would carry on like the man we had overheard as we came downstairs, but I couldn't help noticing that he was the only male of the company to follow Gussie and me onto the loggia. After the young basso had invoked the names of some mutual acquaintances and praised the musical taste of our hostess, he retreated so that Octavia could present the accompanists.

I had worked with Mario and Lucca Gecco several times before. They were short, weasel-thin fiddlers who had been making the rounds of theater orchestras since long before I made my stage debut. As competent, but uninspired players, they fulfilled menial roles in the spectacles where musicians of greater talent achieved sublime heights. To them, the opera was merely a way to put bread on the table. I found it difficult to appreciate their philosophy. Though my vocation had been forced upon me, I always gave it my best and experienced boundless joy in using the amazing voice that the knife had bestowed. To do otherwise would make a mockery of my sacrifice. I exchanged only a few words with Mario and Lucca before they retreated to down another glass of wine before dinner.

"But where are the ladies?" I asked my hostess. The cast contained two female characters. Asteria was Bajazet's daughter, a Turkish beauty who would inflame my lust, and Princess Irene was my faithful betrothed. I had yet to see a sign of either.

Octavia rolled her eyes. "Madame Fouquet is in her room, battling an attack of migraine."

"That would be our prima donna, the French soprano?"

Octavia nodded. "Our Asteria."

"I am most anxious to meet her. I hear Madame Fouquet has captivated the Parisian audiences to the point of provoking them to riot if she refuses to give encores."

"I can well believe it, but you will have to wait until tomorrow to be caught in her snare. I doubt that she or her husband will join us tonight."

I cocked my head at the bitterness of her tone.

"It's her régime, you see. Madame Fouquet takes exquisite care of herself. She has a time to eat, a time to rest, a time to gargle and spray her tonsils. And if she comes down with one of her headaches, rehearsals must grind to a halt until she feels ready to continue."

I chuckled. "True prima donna behavior. I know some castrati who are equally guilty. I suppose a certain amount of temperament goes with the territory."

Octavia snorted. "Gabrielle Fouquet can cosset her pretty throat on her own time. I'm funding this opera, not only the singers, but every last inch of canvas and drop of paint once we take it to the theater. Now that you've arrived to complete the company, there will be no more time wasted." She smiled broadly, exposing healthy teeth and a glistening expanse of pink gum. "One way or another, Madame Fouquet will be brought to heel."

The appearance of Nita at the doorway, apron showing evidence of a kitchen catastrophe, took my hostess away.

I was drifting toward the rail to attempt to shift Maestro Weber's attention away from his latest melody when I felt a tug at my sleeve. "Tito?" The voice was soft, almost intimate.

I spun around, then had to lower my chin to meet Carmela Costa's eyes. Petite, compact, with an intelligent gaze that seemed at odds with her loose, pink mouth, Carmela was a soprano I had often appeared with. Tonight, a simple chignon confined her lightly powdered hair, and a sprinkling of Alençon lace ornamented her rose satin gown. The effect was a delicate spring flower peeking through an unexpected April frost. Octavia Dolfini could use a few fashion lessons from Carmela.

"Hello, old friend." The soprano smiled, then gabbled on, "I've been dawdling tonight. I just came down. What a treat to find that you've arrived. I was so pleased when I heard you had joined the cast, but surprised, too. I'd heard you were in Rome."

"I was for a while, but happy to be back. The pope's hand rests a little too heavily on the Roman opera houses for my taste." I detected a speculative look in Carmela's gray eyes. "Was there another reason why you were surprised?"

She pulled on one of the teardrop pearls that hung from her ear lobes. "Well…"

"Speak freely. I doubt you could tell me anything I haven't thought of myself."

"All right, if you like. Since your role contains so many bravura arias, I expected that Maestro Weber would engage a singer with a sustained fortissimo, someone who can raise the roof, as they say. Your excellence lies in other directions."

"You don't think my expressive style is up to the task?"

"Let's just say that rehearsals are likely to be… interesting. Our maestro doesn't stint his criticism. You may want to gird yourself in mental armor."

I shrugged, then glanced toward the German. He had moved to converse with Romeo and Emilio, but he was still well out of earshot. "Maestro Weber must think I can sing Tamerlano. He cast me, after all."

When Carmela narrowed her eyes, I remembered what an avid collector of backstage intrigue she was. And how much she enjoyed springing her information on unsuspecting innocents.

"What do you know, my lovely friend? Out with it, or I'll make sure I stumble over your entrance in each of our duets." Not certain whether I was joking or not, I smiled to make Carmela think I was.

"Only this, Tito dear. Maestro Weber didn't want you for the part. The French songbird was the one who insisted."

"Madame Fouquet?"

"Umm." She rolled the sound on her tongue like a mouthful of chocolate. "Gabrielle Fouquet refused to join the cast unless you were engaged for the title role. Absolutely adamant, they tell me. Maestro Weber and Signora Dolfini were so determined to have the new French sensation sing Asteria, they finally agreed. At some point, you must have impressed her most satisfactorily." She finished with a questioning eyebrow and a knowing pout.

"But I've never met the lady," I replied, well aware of Carmela's titillating implication. Many women were enchanted by my kind. During performances, they cheered, moaned, and swooned. They threw flowers. Once the curtain came down, they fought like tigresses to get backstage. It was not true, as many thought, that we castrati were unable to complete the act of love. Some of us were quite able to fulfill our admirers' desires, though none of us were able to plant the seed that would lead to pregnancy. Most women deemed this another point in our favor.

"Really, Carmela," I continued. "I don't think I had even heard of Madame Fouquet until a few months ago when she burst on the scene at the Italian Opera in Paris. Has she been to Venice, do you know?"

"Her husband says she has sung only in France and Germany. He should know. He has managed her career from the beginning."

"Is he a singer, as well?"

"No, he's rather close-mouthed about both their backgrounds, but I gather that he's been knocking around several countries as an impresario."

"What's his name?"

"Jean-Louis Fouquet."

I shook my head. "I don't believe I've ever heard of the man."

She responded with an impish grin. "You wouldn't have. The type of talent he engages runs more to ridottos and masquerades, the sort that gentlemen frequent."

"I wonder how he came to hook a soprano of his wife's caliber," I murmured.

She shrugged. "Even the worst fisherman gets lucky sometimes."

Carmela's words heightened my curiosity about Gabrielle Fouquet, but as it appeared I would not set eyes on the lady until the morrow, I changed the subject. "What about you? You must have been on an extended tour. Now that I recall, our last opera together was over two years ago."

She looked out at the darkening sky, again pulling on her earring. "Yes, quite an extended tour."

"Where did you sing?"

"Last month I sang at the Italian Opera in Paris. That's where I made the acquaintance of the Fouquets, not that they mix with other singers any more than is necessary. "

"And before that?"

"Oh, here and there. We're all such vagabonds, aren't we? Singing for our suppers wherever they'll have us."

"I'm surprised our paths haven't crossed more often. There are only so many opera houses, after all. Before Rome, I spent some months in Dresden—a very congenial city for musicians. Did your tour take you there, by any—"

"Oh, look," Carmela interrupted, pointing excitedly. "A shooting star. Did you see it?"

I hadn't.

The soprano squeezed her eyes shut and brought fingertips to her lips. "I must make a wish. Quiet now, while I think."

Before I could question her further, a bell summoned us to dinner. I offered Carmela my arm, and Octavia bustled onto the loggia to claim Maestro Weber. The other men straggled across the salon and into the dining room.

Dinner had come straight from the farm to the table. Freshly caught trout, pork cutlets drizzled with a sauce of golden raisins, polenta with wild mushrooms, wine bottled in the estate's own cantina: these delicacies and more absorbed the guests' attention and hampered conversation.

The meal held only one incident of note, an embarrassing one that I would rather forget. During the soup course, I was dipping my spoon when a sudden pair of blasts shook the room like an artillery discharge. I jumped and my little finger upended the flat rim of my soup plate. It was pumpkin soup, unfortunately. Bright orange flooded the white linen cloth.

Everyone except Karl guffawed at the top of their lungs. Looking back, I believe they had all been waiting for just such an occurrence.

"Oh, Tito, don't worry. Sit back." Octavia spoke through her giggles as I mopped frantically with my napkin. "The boys will take care of it." She motioned to one of the young footmen stationed on each end of the marquetry sideboard. "Bring Signor Amato another bowl."

"What is that infernal racket?" I asked, for the banging continued, coursing through the villa in rhythmic volleys, now very close, now diminishing in the distance.

"The shutters," Octavia exclaimed, cheeks red from laughter. "Every night Ernesto closes the shutters, and every morning before breakfast he opens them. Fortunately, the morning operation is not as noisy."

"How many shutters do you have?" I asked, struggling to regain my dignity.

"Oh, I don't know," she answered. "I can't be bothered with the details of this place."

"I know," said Emilio. "It's thirty-eight pairs. Every slam is burned into my brain."

I looked around the dining room. It was an inside room; the walls were covered in moss green damask punctuated by mirrors instead of windows. Apparently I would not witness the procedure until another night.

Carmela was no longer laughing. She ran her fingers nervously up and down the stem of her wine glass. "Why do you go to such trouble to secure the house? Is this part of the country infested with bandits?"

Octavia dismissed Carmela's worry with a wave of her fork. "No bandits around here. It's quite peaceful, really. Trespassing and filching poultry are the only crimes that keep the self-styled *Capitano della Compagna* from his interminable riding and hunting."

"Who is he?" asked Carmela.

"Captain Forti, the high constable posted at Molina Mori. He was in the army once, the hero of some battle or other, so he insists on being called Captain. As an officer of the law, he leaves much to be desired, but he's all we have."

"If the country isn't crime-ridden, then why do we endure this nightly fusillade?" Emilio looked up and down the table, perhaps seeking support for a request that the shutters remain open.

"My husband has already fought that battle with Ernesto," Octavia replied. "The shutters must be closed at night because they have always been closed at night. Ernesto's father closed and latched them when he was steward, and his father before him. It's useless to argue with the man. If he's not begging money to repair a fence or purchase a new plow, he's lecturing Vincenzo on the history of the estate."

Karl had been listening with a nasty frown. He touched his napkin to his lips, then cocked his thin face toward Octavia. The composer spoke the first words I'd heard from him with a noticeable German accent: "But Vincenzo is master, now. His word should be law."

Octavia narrowed her eyes and nodded thoughtfully.

Pretending to dab at a spot of soup on my sleeve, Carmela leaned close and whispered, "Karl shouldn't complain. If Vincenzo were truly the master, he would apply his boot to the seat of some German breeches and Karl would find himself on the public road with his bags flying past his head."

Chapter Three

Later, in our room, after enduring a round of Octavia's wavering arias sung at an alarming volume, I sat up to read through Alessandro's letter one more time. Gussie's gentle snores and the muted chimes of the long-case clock in the hall were my only company. At home, I would have heard the soft dip of oars on the canal beside our house, the warning cries of the boatmen as they navigated around corners, perhaps a burst of revelry from a distant square. Compared to Venice, the countryside around the villa was unnervingly quiet. At one point, a dog let fly with a cascade of barks. Otherwise, silence reigned. I didn't get very far into the letter. I missed Liya. This trip marked the first time we had been apart since our marriage. Though I knew she would welcome the pay I earned for *Tamerlano*, being away from her made me feel oddly out of joint. I burrowed back into the cushions, rubbed my ribs where they'd been bruised in the carriage accident, and let images of my beautiful Jewess run through my mind: her warm skin, her sweet-smelling hair, the notch at the base of her neck that seemed perfect for bestowing kisses.

The candle burned itself out on my reverie, but I didn't bother to relight it. Closing heavy eyelids, I let Alessandro's letter slip from my fingers and allowed sleep to claim me inch by inch. I remained in its silent cocoon until, just outside our door, a woman screamed.

The terrified yelps had me on my feet in an instant, heart racing and eyes straining. Our room was as black as the inside of a tar barrel.

"By Jove!" Gussie exclaimed, feet hitting the floor an instant after mine. He swore as he crashed into something hard. I echoed him as I tripped over the shoes I'd left forgotten by my chair. By the time we'd fumbled our way through the door, the screams had diluted to stuttering sobs.

Carmela Costa was standing in the center of the dark hall, surrounded by a nimbus of yellow light. She held a candlestick aloft with a firm hand, but her chin was trembling and so was the hand that clutched her nightshift. As our fellow guests spilled out of their rooms, exclaiming loudly and bearing more candles, the cause of Carmela's distress became obvious.

A man lay at her feet. He was dressed for outdoors in dark clothing and boots of black leather that laced up to his knees. His head was turned sharply, so that he seemed to be staring directly at Carmela's shapely ankle. He wasn't moving.

"Is he dead?" Gussie asked.

I took in the chestnut hair, loosened from its ribbon, spreading across the patterned carpet. Blood caked a concave patch at his temple and matted the flowing locks.

"It would seem so." I was amazed at how steady my voice sounded. My heart was pounding against my ribs as if I'd just run a foot-race.

"We must see." Gussie knelt and curled his long fingers around the man's wrist.

Carmela shuffled back, still sobbing in noisy gulps. By common consent, the rest of the company formed a shield around her, patting her shoulders, whispering questions, and casting horrified looks at the body.

Gussie shook his head. "No pulse. And he's not breathing."

"Are you sure?" Emilio's high voice sliced through the general murmur.

"Quite sure. He's not stone cold, but he's most certainly dead."

How could it be otherwise, I thought. Someone had bashed his head in. The instrument of his demise still lay beside him: a shiny brass disk attached to a thin rod of duller metal. The brass was smeared with dried blood, forming an obscene caricature of a rose.

I stooped beside Gussie and studied the object. It looked so familiar, glinting in the shifting candlelight. Yet I couldn't place it.

"What is this thing?" I asked.

Thanks to his keen artist's eye, my brother-in-law had the answer immediately. Gussie pointed, and everyone's gaze followed his outstretched finger toward the long-case clock that overlooked the intersecting corridors like a stoic, unflagging sentinel. This soldier of time had sustained a wound. Its regular ticking had ceased, and the narrow door of its case hung open. The brass hands on its enamel-white dial were nearly vertical. Two minutes to midnight: the exact time that the pendulum had been jerked from its case to do murder.

"For God's sake! What's happened?" Octavia burst out of the west wing to interrupt our stricken tableau.

I expected fits and hysterics, but our hostess was made of sterner stuff. She took the situation in at a glance, made a solemn sign of the cross, and sent one of the Gecco brothers to fetch her husband. I noticed that he sprinted down the corridor to the east wing; the Dolfinis must sleep as far apart from each other as the confines of the villa would allow.

Octavia prowled the length of the hall while we waited for Vincenzo. The ruffles of her loose dressing gown swirled like foam on the crest of a wave. "Who is this man?" she asked. "Surely one of you must know him."

The assembled company murmured negatively, shook their heads.

She set on her husband as soon as he rounded the corner. "This man is dead, Vincenzo, and no one seems to know him. Tell me who he is immediately."

Vincenzo knelt by the body. Removing his velvet nightcap and twisting it in his hands, the master of the villa studied the dead man's face for a long moment. Slowly, calmly, he asked, "What makes you think I know him, Octavia?"

"You ride out on the estate all the time. And visit the neighbors, too. You know all the laborers for miles around."

Vincenzo shoved his nightcap in the pocket of his dressing gown. He reached for the lifeless hand. After a moment's examination, he said, "This poor unfortunate is plainly dressed, to be sure, but he is no working man. His palms are smooth as silk. And look at these nails. Clean, neatly trimmed, buffed to a shine. The man is a gentleman, but not one of my acquaintance."

I agreed with his assessment. The corpse was that of a youngish man with high cheekbones and slender features which would have been quite handsome in life. His dark breeches were finely woven cord, and his snug, waist-length jacket was the sort worn for dancing or fencing lessons. An adept fencer, I guessed, for rather than the lithe limbs of a dancer, he displayed the well-muscled form of a sportsman with a midsection just beginning to expand.

"Search his pockets," Octavia ordered.

Vincenzo complied. "They are empty."

"Totally empty?" Octavia drew an exasperated breath. "No purse? No tobacco?"

"Not so much as a coin or flake of snuff, my dear."

Octavia moved to stand over the body. She stared straight down into its wax-like face. Her nostrils flared, her hands balled into fists, and the toe of one satin slipper jogged up and down. I half-expected her to kick the corpse in frustration.

"Who *can* he be?" she finally asked again.

"I know," said Karl Weber. The composer had slunk from the west wing a few moments before, barefoot and wrapped in a banyan of paislied silk. Above the riotous blues and oranges, his face was pale as a sheet of parchment. "He's a thief who broke in to steal my music."

Vincenzo's knees cracked as he stood, and his voice thickened with anger. "You know this man who invaded my home?"

Karl shook his head. "He's a complete stranger. But my score must surely be the most valuable thing in the villa. I've taken great pains with *Il Gran Tamerlano* and created an entirely new entertainment, a thoroughly human drama, with flesh and blood characters instead of pasteboard gods and heroes. *Tamerlano* will take Venice by storm, then the rest of Europe. This man must be a rival composer out to steal my thunder."

Doubtful glances passed between the singers. The Gecco brothers laughed outright.

Vincenzo answered, "That would give you an excellent reason to hit him over the head."

"No, no." The composer's eyebrows shot up. "I haven't been in this corridor since I retired for the night. I only meant... I can see why a jealous composer might be skulking around."

A tallish man stood apart from the group, holding his candle to one side, casting his face into shadow. As he stepped forward, the dancing flame illuminated a beaked nose and cool, detached stare. His wide triangular jawline was taut with an emotion I couldn't identify. I assumed this must be Jean-Louis Fouquet, the Frenchman who had missed dinner to tend to his wife's headache. In the general confusion following Carmela's panicked screams, I'd barely been aware of him coming from his room with his wife clinging to his side. She had immediately gasped and threatened to be sick, giving me only a glimpse of a violet-sprigged nightshift and blond locks tumbling from a lavender nightcap as her husband thrust her back through the door. Since then, the Frenchman had been watching quietly, but now he spoke up as if he could restrain himself no longer.

"It's perfectly obvious. Our mystery man is a handsome devil, dressed for stealth. He was meeting someone in secret." Jean-Louis turned his pointed gaze on the only unattached woman of the company. "For a lover's tryst."

Carmela had been sheltering against Romeo's stalwart chest—a tiny nightingale in the branches of a great oak. At the Frenchman's accusation, she dropped her fragile persona, flung Romeo's arm away, and rounded on Jean-Louis. "Well, aren't you the slimy, stinking frog-eater? I'll have you know that I never saw this man until I tripped over him ten minutes ago.

If he was keeping an assignation with anyone, it would be your sluttish wife who pushes her tits about like peaches for sale to any man who relishes a bite."

Jean-Louis reddened, but refused to give ground. "Certainly not my Gabrielle. Frenchwomen see no reason to hide their beauty, but her honor is above reproach. Besides, we arrived only days ago and know no one in Italy outside this villa. If not you, this man must have been visiting one of the maids." A stamp from his booted heel underscored his theory.

I glanced toward the group of servants gathered in a tight knot by the back stairs. Three young footmen watched quietly, faces aflame with curiosity, while Nita made an unsuccessful attempt to shield two maids from the grisly sight on the carpet. Determined not to miss a crumb of excitement, the girls craned over and around her flannel-clad bulk. One was plump with greasy, spotty skin. The other was a lank collection of bones with a gap the size of my thumb between her front teeth.

"Nonsense," Octavia spoke to Jean-Louis, but echoed my thought. She then swung around to Carmela. "But you *were* the one who discovered him. What were you doing out in the hall?"

"Well…" Carmela hesitated a moment. "I was on my way down to the laundry. I gave Nita some things I needed washed and pressed for tomorrow, but she never brought them back up. I couldn't sleep, so I thought I'd fetch them myself."

"Then you must have heard something," I responded quickly.

"Yes," Vincenzo took a stern, official tone. "This man must have cried out as he was struck. Perhaps there was a scuffle."

"I was reading." Carmela knit her brows. "I started a novel that Gabrielle loaned me, but it was too silly for words. I eventually dozed off for a bit. Something did wake me, but it wasn't a cry. That was when I decided to go down to the laundry."

"What did you hear?" Emilio's soprano rose to a squeak.

"Footsteps. Very light, like someone running on his toes. I assumed it was—" She started to glance to her right, toward Karl, I thought. Then she checked herself. "Well, I supposed it must be one of us, but now I see it couldn't have been. It must have been the killer."

Heads swiveled right and left. Nightclothes rustled as they were drawn tightly over hunched shoulders. An errant draft extinguished several candles, and the gray shadows deepened to black. They seemed to expand with a life of their own, creeping toward the edge of the carpet, clouding vision. For the first time, Carmela's candlestick began to tremble.

The soprano drifted back toward Romeo, but his attention was trained on the huge armoire at the rear of the corridor.

With a sudden bellow, the big basso knocked his fellow singers aside and charged the hulking piece of furniture. His body hit the wood with a smack, and he twisted the handles with fists that might have bent an iron bar. The doors wouldn't budge.

"*Scusi*, Signore." With a deft move, one of the footmen jiggled the handles, then stepped away. "The latch tends to catch."

Romeo threw the doors open, and bounced back, shoulders braced for a fight. I got to my feet and squeezed between the Gecco brothers to catch a closer look. Neatly folded quilts and blankets made a colorful ladder on one side of the armoire; the other was stuffed with Turkish toweling.

Romeo turned, cheeks blazing red. He shrugged. "It seemed like a perfect place for someone to hide."

Relief rippled through the corridor in the form of sighs and nervous chuckles. The singers and musicians were recovering their usual aplomb. Those with flickering tapers touched them to dead wicks. One by one, the added lights forced the shadows to retreat. Competing opinions on what should be done next sounded from every corner.

Fortunately, Vincenzo was ready to take charge. He lifted his chin and sucked in his cheeks. It seemed as if he'd suddenly grown two inches. "Adamo, Tullio," he ordered the footmen. "Search the attics. Shine your lights in every place big enough for a man to hide and report anything that looks uncommon. And for God's sake, see where Alphonso has gotten to."

"Alphonso?" I whispered.

Gussie muttered near my ear, "Vincenzo's valet, older than God and hard of hearing. I met him earlier this evening."

Vincenzo gestured toward the third footman. "Giovanni, you come downstairs with me."

A look passed between Octavia and Karl. "I'll come, too," the composer announced. "Three sets of eyes are worth more than two." He started forward, but Vincenzo shot a hand to his chest.

"I can't sort this out with a pack of music makers running all over the house. I'll thank you to return to your room and stay there." Our host sent a dark look around the company. Vincenzo recognized what Carmela apparently hadn't: there was no reason why the killer wasn't one of our own.

"All of you," he continued, "shut yourselves in and leave your chambers on no account. I must send for the constable. He will want to question everyone."

There was a brief moment of absolute stillness.

Emilio was the first to break it. "You do us a disservice, Signore, treating us like common criminals. It's positively offensive."

The rest of the company leapt in at once, defending themselves loudly, stridently, shrilly. Everyone except Jean-Louis, that is. In a tone as icy and sharp as an alpine peak, he raised his voice and said, "Signor Dolfini is right. An organized investigation must commence. We can help clear ourselves of suspicion by obeying his orders."

As Vincenzo bowed in the Frenchman's direction, Gussie and I nodded at each other and headed for our room. With lingering glances divided between the corpse and the silent clock, the others slowly followed our lead. I closed the door of our chamber on a last glimpse of Karl and Octavia in deep, whispered conversation.

♪♪♪

Once Gussie had every candle and lamp in our room aflame, he threw himself in a chair and exhaled through pursed lips. "It's like a bad dream. We were expecting a few quiet weeks in the countryside, and now we're faced with a murder."

"We do seem to have a knack for finding trouble of this sort." I crossed to the window, opened it, and unlatched the shutter. The two halves swung apart and hit the side of the building with a thud.

I leaned out and took a deep breath. The odor of dying vegetation and wood smoke laced the crisp night air. All was dark except for a glowing window in the cottage beyond the cypress trees. Turning back to Gussie, I asked, "Did you hear the shutters slamming earlier this evening?"

He nodded. "Vincenzo and I were in his study on the first floor. I nearly jumped out of my skin. I thought we were under attack until he explained the procedure."

"Which is?"

"Ernesto, the steward who helped us with the carriage wheel, closes them every night. His time is eleven o'clock in the summer and nine once September comes. He starts with the rooms in the west wing and moves through the central part of the villa and on to the east wing. When all the shutters are latched and the ones on the ground floor secured with steel bars, he and Vincenzo meet at the front entrance for an amusing little ceremony."

"You saw it?"

Gussie nodded. "I went to the foyer with Vincenzo. The poor man kept me talking for hours. He seemed pitifully glad of the company—I don't think people around here listen to him very much. He immerses himself in books with titles like *The Complete Farmer* and *Observations on Modern Agriculture*. Believe me, I learned more about the theory and practice of four-field rotation than I ever thought possible. Vincenzo made his fortune making anchors and other iron fittings, but it's this estate that he dotes on now."

"He's playing lord of the manor."

"Exactly. If you didn't know that Vincenzo acquired the Villa Dolfini only months ago, you would think he was the last of a noble family that has held the estate for centuries."

"Tell me about this ceremony at the front door."

"Vincenzo handed his steward an ancient key that looked like something Doge Pisani might use to lock his palace doors—" Gussie's forehead creased thoughtfully "—if the Doge would ever stoop to such a menial task. And then Ernesto responded with a solemn recitation about being the guardian of the land and the villa. Can't remember every word, but it seemed to end with him wishing a healthy, happy life to the master of the estate."

"That's all?"

"Almost." Gussie smiled quizzically. "Vincenzo responded with a regal nod, then Ernesto crossed the threshold, tugged the door shut, and shot the bolt with the heavy key."

"I wonder what happens in the morning."

"Vincenzo said that Ernesto lets himself in at cock's crow, goes through the rooms opening shutters, and returns the key. Whether they perform another little drama, I don't know."

"It all sounds very pretty—the vassal paying homage to his liege lord."

"I think that's probably how Vincenzo likes to think of himself."

"So with all the windows and the door secure, how did our corpse get inside the house?"

"Surely there are other doors," Gussie responded. "On the ground floor, for instance, giving access to the cantina and kitchens. And the loggia—a set of double doors from there opened right onto the salon."

I nodded. Of course the Villa Dolfini would have many entrances; it was the hub of a working farm. The buildings that capped the east and west wings would house stores and equipment, even animals. They would also connect to the house in some way. Then I had another thought. "This is a big place. Our man could have entered in the daytime and hid in a cupboard or unused room until everyone went to bed."

Gussie sat forward. "But Nita said that all the rooms are full, and with so much activity about—" He cocked his head. "What's that?"

I heard it, too. Clumping steps in the hall. I crossed the room and put my ear to the door. "Someone's out there."

Barely breathing, I turned the door handle.

Gussie sprinted to my side and imprisoned my hand in his strong grasp. "What are you doing?" he whispered, pressing my fingers into the cold metal. "Vincenzo said to—"

"Vincenzo be damned. We need to find out what's going on."

Gussie clapped his hands on my shoulders and twisted me round to face him. "Tito, I'm here to paint and you're here to sing. This murder is not a matter for us. Let's stay out of it for once and leave it in the hands of the constable."

"You'll excuse me if I don't find the thought of the local law very comforting."

Gussie nodded, mouth twisted in a grimace. We'd had a recent adventure in Rome where a misguided magistrate had almost been the death of me.

"I know. But this is a different case, and it is simply not our business."

"The body of a perfect stranger, murdered on an errand of mystery. Every person in the villa, even you and me, under suspicion. Admit it, Gussie, you want to open this door as much as I do."

He sighed, but dropped his hands and stepped away to collect a candlestick. As I clicked the door open, I heard him murmur, "As sure as night follows day, we're going to live to regret this."

We stepped into the hall. Ernesto and Santini were unfurling a length of canvas beside the body.

The steward turned and cleared his throat apologetically. "We expected to find you in your room, Signor Amato. Is there something I can get for you?"

"Signor Rumbolt and I thought we might be of some help."

"No need. We can take care of this."

"Where are you taking him?" That was Gussie. He spoke in whispers, as we all did. There is something about the dead that inspires hushed tones.

"Signor Dolfini directed us to put the body in the ice house until Captain Forti arrives."

"And then?" I asked.

Ernesto shrugged his broad shoulders. "Then the churchyard, I suppose, to a pauper's grave. Unless someone comes forward to claim it."

"Have you ever seen this man before? In the village perhaps?"

He shook his head. "Strangers stand out in Molina Mori. If he's been staying nearby, I'll wager it would be in Padua. Unfamiliar faces cause no comment in a town with a university and a pilgrim shrine. But Padua is over ten miles away—I don't often get up there."

"Is Captain Forti coming from Molina Mori?"

"That's where the constable's house is. I've sent my boys to fetch him, but I doubt he will be arriving anytime soon."

Santini nodded knowingly, mouth hanging open. He looked as if he'd been sleeping in the wild. His hair was matted with remnants of leaves and twigs.

Ernesto continued, "Gaspare Forti is an avid hunter, and it's perfect weather for boar. I'd wager the grape harvest that right now he's headed to Monte Rosso with a hunting party."

I was astonished. "Then he could be gone a week or more. How can he neglect his duties for so long?"

Santini and Ernesto both chuckled. "This isn't Venice," the steward replied. "We don't have hordes of people out to rob and maim each other."

"Until now," I answered, stepping closer. Gussie was right behind me.

Ernesto clenched his jaw. He was clearly itching to tell us to go back to our room, but a steward was not in the habit of giving orders to his master's guests. Instead, he turned and nodded to Santini. Both men squatted. With no flinching that I could detect, Ernesto slid his hands under the corpse's shoulders and Santini took hold of the legs. They rolled the dead stranger onto the canvas and began to fold the ends of the heavy fabric around him.

"Wait," I cried. "What's that?" Now that the body was lying face down, it was evident that the man's short jacket stretched over a bulge at the small of his back.

Voicing a grunt of surprise, Ernesto quickly pulled the jacket up to reveal the butt of a pistol. Before the steward could object, I bent over and jerked it from the stranger's waistband.

It was a small pistol, uncocked. I took a sniff of the pan. "Doesn't seem to have been fired recently."

"Let's have a good look." Gussie brought his light and we all clustered round the object on my outstretched palm.

"A costly item, that," Ernesto said. "I can't say I've ever seen a piece quite like it. Look how the lock sits atop the frame instead of sticking out from the side."

"A clever design," Gussie added. "Makes the pistol much less likely to catch on clothing when it's needed in a hurry."

Santini nodded. A rumbled "Hmm" escaped his lips. Did the man never speak?

I ran my finger over the inlaid scrollwork of gold wire that ornamented the handle. "It's certainly not of Italian make," I observed.

"What's that image outlined there? A bird?" Gussie reached for the pistol and scrutinized it through narrowed eyelids. "A two-headed eagle with a crown. I've seen this crest before— the Imperial Russian eagle."

I looked down at the stranger. His still form mocked us with its anonymity. "Then our man is a long way from home."

Gussie shrugged. "Just because he carries a Russian pistol doesn't mean he's from Russia."

My brother-in-law was right, of course. I was getting ahead of myself.

"Maybe there's something else we missed," I said. I started to bend over again, but Ernesto had reached his limit.

The steward swiped the pistol out of Gussie's hand and fell to his knees with a thump. "Signor Dolfini will want to see this. I'll give it to the master once we've seen to the body."

Ernesto and his helper made short work of trussing the corpse into its canvas cocoon. With a few grunts, they hoisted the bulky burden and started toward the rear of the hall. The steward halted at the top of the enclosed staircase. "Please Signori, tell me that I can assure Signor Dolfini that all the guests are in their proper places up here."

There was really no reason to make Ernesto's job more difficult. "Don't worry, we'll go straight back to our room," I assured him.

Gussie nodded in agreement. "We'll pull our covers over our heads and you won't hear a peep out of us until morning."

Chapter Four

I'm generally quite a reliable fellow, and there's no one more trustworthy than my brother-in-law. We were doing just as we'd promised; the door to our room was actually giving beneath my hand when a flash of metal caught my eye. It was the pendulum that had felled our mysterious friend, glinting in the rays of Gussie's candle. Someone had propped it up beside the timepiece that had supplied it.

Gussie cocked an eyebrow. I knew what he was thinking. Ernesto and Santini had disappeared down the stairwell; Vincenzo and the footmen were in distant parts of the house; our fellow guests remained behind closed doors. We sprinted across the hall.

"This makes a curious weapon," I whispered, after contemplating the bloodied disk for a moment.

"But a very effective one." Gussie shuddered a bit.

"If you were going to kill someone in this hall, is this the weapon you would choose?"

He looked around. "There isn't much here. If someone was forced to defend himself, the pendulum might have been the only possibility."

"Defend against what? The pistol was in the stranger's waistband. And see here…" I ran my palm over the polished surface of the clock's case, then moved the door back and forth on its hinges. "This is solid oak, not glass. It's not as if the killer could have caught sight of the pendulum and thought, 'here's my salvation.' No, the killer must have removed the pendulum and been lying in wait."

"You're talking about planned murder."

"It makes more sense than a chance meeting."

"Then Jean-Louis must be on the right track. There was an assignation of some sort. Someone was expecting the stranger to be here at midnight."

"But it makes no sense. If you intended to do murder, you'd furnish yourself with a stiletto or a garrote."

Gussie drummed a finger on his lips. "Unless you had a specific reason to use the pendulum," he said.

"What earthly reason could there be?"

"Hmm… sending a message of sorts?"

We both stepped back to view the timepiece with fresh eyes. I creaked the narrow door open as far as it would go and poked my head inside. With Gussie maneuvering his light at my shoulder, I swept the chain that supported the weights aside and squinted into the bowels of the mechanism. A miniature stirrup dangled right above me.

I freed an arm and thrust it behind me. "Hand me that pendulum, will you?"

A small steel block at the proximal end of the pendulum fit the stirrup exactly. I hooked and unhooked the pendulum several times.

"This is fairly easy—doesn't take as much strength as I would have thought," I said.

"What about swinging it?"

I made several experimental swipes. The brass disk whooshed through the air. "Not so difficult."

"Could a woman heft it?"

"I think so. Especially if rage or hatred fueled her strength." I handed him the implement. "See what you think."

While Gussie wielded the pendulum like a mercenary's battle-ax, I held the candle close to the clock's face. The brass hands were pointing straight up, almost on top of each other. Above the face, a lunette was painted with a full moon rising over a woodland copse. The scrolling letters of a motto arched above the lovely scene, but I couldn't read them.

"Gussie, is this an English clock?" I pointed to the words.

Huffing a bit, he deposited the pendulum where we'd found it and stretched on tiptoe. "Yes, it's a quote. From Shakespeare, I think."

"What does it say?"

Slowly and distinctly, he translated the words of the great English playwright so that I could understand. "The iron tongue of midnight hath told twelve. Lovers, to bed; 'tis almost fairy time."

"Iron tongue? Is he speaking of a church bell?"

Gussie nodded. "Tolling midnight."

"This is very curious. A clock that speaks of midnight pillaged for a weapon to commit a midnight murder. I wonder—"

Gussie shook his head in warning and darted his eyes toward the door across from ours. Its stealthy click had also met my ears.

"You're right," I said in a louder tone. "Perhaps it *is* time to seek our beds."

Bowing toward Romeo and Emilio's room, I made a motion as if I were tipping a hat to our unseen observer, then followed my brother-in-law back into our chamber.

♫♫♫

The next morning I awoke to find Giovanni, one of the young footmen, depositing a pitcher by the wash basin. Steam curled off the warm water, forming a gauzy ribbon in a slanting bar of light. The washstand sat by the far window, not the one I had opened last night. Ernesto must have been in to open the shutter without waking me.

"*Scusi*, Signore. I'm to make sure everyone is out of bed." Giovanni placed some folded towels by the pitcher.

"What time is it?"

"Just past eight, Signore. We're all getting a late start this morning. Nita will lay out some breakfast in a few minutes."

Gussie's blond haystack emerged from his covers. He gazed around with one eye shut and the other in a squint. "Did the constable come?" he asked in a hoarse voice.

The footman shook his head. "Signora Forti told Manuel and Basilio that her husband has gone hunting—he won't be back for many days. Until then, the master says we're all to go on with our work as if nothing unusual happened."

Gussie emitted a gravelly groan and folded the pillow around his head, but I felt strangely exhilarated. I had a new opera to sing and an intriguing mystery to ponder, two things that always made my blood flow more swiftly. I sent Giovanni on his way and dressed in haste. Gussie gave me a grumpy send-off. It was always thus. Though the reverse would have better suited our professions, my brother-in-law was the night owl, I the lark.

The rest of the household straggled down to the dining room in small groups. The Gecco brothers were already at table, gulping large cups of coffee laced with milk. Plates coated with jam and buttery crumbs sat at their elbows. As I filled my own plate, Romeo and Carmela entered together, murmuring little jokes to each other and appearing none the worse for the night's adventure. Emilio followed, bleary-eyed and out-of-sorts.

"I don't know if I will even be able to sing today," he announced as he reached toward an epergne heaped with pears and apples and grapes.

"Why is that?" I asked.

Before answering, my fellow castrato pinched each piece of fruit, selected an apple, and made a face when the first bite was not to his liking. Some castrati took the loss of their manhood in stride, devoting themselves to music and enjoying the riches it could bring. Others harbored a grudge against the world for the rest of their lives. Emilio belonged to the latter group, and I'd never known him to stint his complaints about anything that displeased him.

"Well," Emilio finally replied, "up at all hours. Exposed to unconscionable violence. Ordered about by a puffed-up ironmonger. How do you like it? This surely wasn't what you expected."

I shrugged, making short work of my own apple. Between bites, I replied, "Last night was a shock, but I'm eager to get started on *Tamerlano*. Work is the best antidote, I say. I've also been itching to meet this prima donna I've heard so much about." I turned to the Gecco brothers. "Has Madame Fouquet made an appearance?"

Mario stopped slurping from his cup long enough to answer, "She was the first down. She took her coffee out to the loggia."

I bowed to the company and made my way there.

My first glimpse of Madame Fouquet was of her feet as she reclined on the same long chair that Octavia had graced the night before. The Frenchwoman's face was hidden by the red-marbled covers of an open book that seemed to absorb every bit of her attention. She did not lower it so much as an inch as I approached, so I took the opportunity to admire the Louis-style heels that emphasized the arch of her dainty feet and the newly fashionable *robe à la Polonaise* with the coquettish hemline that stopped several inches north of her neatly crossed ankles.

Neither her husband nor anyone else was around to make introductions, so I cleared my throat. "Madame Fouquet, allow me to present myself. I am Tito Amato."

She plopped the book in her lap and answered with a pert grin. "Good morning, Tito."

That simple act robbed me of speech. As I stared at the woman before me, my knees went soft as mush and wings fluttered over my heart.

Bleach had washed the red from the hair that now shown brassy yellow under her lace cap, and her once sylph-like form had widened into the body of a woman. As Carmela had so rudely observed, her corseted bodice did push her pink breasts up like ripe peaches spilling from a basket. But some things hadn't changed. I would recognize that impudent mouth and the striking angles of her cheekbones anywhere. Yes, I knew the woman laughing at me from behind brilliant dark eyes. I knew her well.

"Come, sit." She patted a footstool beside the divan.

I complied stiffly, still without words.

She sent me a challenging smile. "Nothing to say? The Tito I remember rarely shut his mouth."

"Grisella," I whispered. The fluttering had moved from my heart to my stomach and was now at war with the sensation of a cherry pit lodged in my throat. My sister who was supposed to be buried in Turkish soil was draped over the divan cushions like a long-legged cat relaxing in a splash of sun. Not dead, no, very much alive.

She straightened her back and reached out to place a forefinger on my lips. "Not Grisella. As welcome as my real Christian name sounds, I'm Gabrielle Fouquet now, and if I value my safety, must always be."

"I don't understand. We thought you were dead."

"Did you now?" She reclined again. Her nostrils flared and her eyes grew round. For the first time, I noticed the bluish smudges beneath them. "Is that why no one ever came looking for me?"

"No…I mean, we didn't know. Alessandro just recently found your grave…" I stammered, then fell silent, beset by disturbing memories.

Grisella had entered the world on a tide of tragedy. Our mother died giving birth to her, and our father never allowed her to forget it. One of my earliest memories was playing with my toy soldiers on the floor of our sitting room. Annetta was at the harpsichord, playing a childish version of a sonata under Father's formidable supervision, and Alessandro was doing his lessons. When Berta, Grisella's old nurse, brought her into the room warmed by the fire and bright with lamplight, Father turned his gimlet eye on the toddling child and ordered her taken away. I had cried at his harsh words and even more at the thought of my little sister alone in the darkened nursery, away from the rest of the family. Though she was never really alone, of course. Berta was her one champion, and that good woman fussed over Grisella like an old hen with her last chick.

Berta's influence was not all positive, unfortunately. She could never deny Grisella anything that was in her power to give, and a child without limits knows no peace, always wanting more and more. By the time Grisella had turned five, she had perfected crocodile tears and foot stamping to a high art. By seven, her tantrums took a more serious turn. The mildest frustration would cause one shoulder to roll and her head to jerk, seemingly beyond her control. I was away at the *conservatorio* during the worst of her sufferings, but I remembered Annetta's despairing letters about Grisella's odd behavior, especially her tendency to explode in oaths that would make a sailor blush.

Her shoulder was twitching now, and she clenched her teeth so hard that her jaw muscles bulged. I steeled myself for an outburst, but Grisella merely took a deep breath, brushed her fingers over the striped silk of her gown as if she were removing a fallen hair, and gave her head a small shake.

"As you can see, I'm very much alive. And thriving, thanks to Jean-Louis."

I nodded slowly. It had been almost ten years since I'd last seen my sister. Where should I start? I blurted out the first thing that came to mind. "Why is there a tombstone with your name on it in Constantinople?"

"There is someone in that city who thinks I belong to him. It is much better that he believes I'm dead."

"Count Vladimir Paninovich?"

"You're very well informed." She raised an eyebrow.

"Before he found your grave, Alessandro heard about the Russian and the fire that supposedly killed you both. Perhaps Count Paninovich's death was as much of a sham as yours."

She gave a pretty shrug. "Vladimir's body is in his coffin, while mine holds only a bag of sand. Jean-Louis arranged my... burial. In the fire, the smoke overcame Vladimir quickly, but I wrapped myself in a wet shawl and managed to crawl to a window. I kicked through the lattice and jumped into a fig tree."

"With the Russian dead, who is left to lay claim to you?"

She dropped her gaze and fanned the pages of her book. The flutter made a breeze against my clasped hands. "Vladimir had grown tired of Constantinople. He was homesick for St. Petersburg but could hardly return with an Italian paramour in tow."

"According to Alessandro, Count Paninovich was wealthy enough to do as he pleased."

"Vladimir had a wife in St. Petersburg. He was married to the Czarina's cousin, both of them particular favorites of Anna Ivanova." Her rouged lips formed a salacious sneer. "There was no room for me in that ménage, so Vladimir promised me to a friend. A Turk who had admired me."

"Just like that?"

"Constantinople is a different world, Tito. Without a family to protect her, a woman can simply vanish behind veils and locked doors, entirely at the mercy of the man who keeps her. The more powerful the man, the deeper the dungeon."

"This Turk is powerful?"

"Let's just say that I was very fortunate to make Jean-Louis' acquaintance when I did. If he hadn't come along, I would have disappeared behind the walls of the Sublime Porte forever." She suddenly looked very tired. "Or found myself in a sack at the bottom of the Bosphorus."

I frowned thoughtfully, still barely able to get over the fact that I was talking with the sister I hadn't seen in years. I said, "Carmela told me that Jean-Louis is an impresario."

"Jean-Louis has been in the theater since he was a boy. He began as a sceneshifter in Marseille. His star was made one night when the troupe on the bill failed to appear. Marseille isn't Paris—it's a rough-and-tumble port full of sailors from all parts of the Mediterranean. If the show disappoints, they don't throw rotten fruit, they start firing pistols." She paused to chuckle. "Have you ever played there?"

I shook my head.

She narrowed her eyes. "Of course not, Marseille doesn't possess an opera house that matches your renown."

I didn't like her tone, so I turned the conversation back to her husband. "What happened that night?"

"Ah, with the management cowering in the wings, my Jean-Louis raised the curtain and rushed onstage. He sang, he danced, he declaimed scenes from popular plays, doing first a man's part, then a woman's. The sailors were amused, and from that night forward, Jean-Louis was on the bill. Since then, he's done a little bit of everything."

"What was he doing in Constantinople?"

"Searching for oriental entertainers. You know the sort—rope dancers, fire walkers, fakirs who pierce their cheeks and lips with needles. But when he heard me sing at one of Vladimir's musical soirées, he found a way to send me a message. If I could only get away from Vladimir, he would take me back to Europe and put me on the opera stage. My talent could make us both rich."

"Then the fire was a godsend for you."

Frowning, she tossed her book aside and crossed her arms. "Yes, I suppose you could call it that. I'm happy singing and the stage suits me well. And I'm home… well, almost. Venice is only a day or two away."

A smile broke over her face, and I couldn't help smiling back. Here was my little sister, snatched from the grave. Our shattered family whole at long last. My heart swelled as I slid to my knees and threw my arms around her in an awkward embrace.

"Oh, Tito," she whispered, burying her face in my shoulder. "All those terrible years… you have no idea. You won't tell anyone who I really am, will you? Especially Jean-Louis. He has no idea that you're my brother."

"If you wish," I replied, my nose full of musky French scent, my eyes full of tears.

We heard the step on the tiles at the same time. Someone had come onto the loggia. Grisella pulled back in alarm and snatched up her book. I sprang to my feet.

Carmela moved out of a deep shadow thrown by one of the massive columns that supported the ceiling and the stories above.

"Maestro Weber is ready to begin," she announced, giving us each a penetrating look.

"Thank you, Carmela." Grisella rose, tucked her book under her arm, and collected her handkerchief and fan. She swept toward the salon doors without a backward glance.

I attempted to follow, but Carmela laid a detaining hand on my arm. "You seem very friendly with our prima donna."

"It's fitting to get to know your fellow singers as individuals, not just voices, don't you think?" I cringed inwardly. Couldn't I have come up with a less inane excuse for embracing Grisella?

Carmela snorted. "You've made fast work of it, even for a celebrated singer that half the women of Venice would welcome to their beds. Are you still going to claim that you've never met her?"

My mouth went dry and I willed myself to meet Carmela's gray eyes without flinching. I didn't fully understand why Grisella was so intent on hiding her true identity, but I was willing to keep her secret until I could learn more. With a broad smile I answered, "Madame Fouquet is a lady completely new to me."

♫♫♫

Karl met us with a preoccupied frown. He was in his shirtsleeves with his waistcoat hanging open. I couldn't help noticing his bloodshot eyes and wine-soaked breath as he directed Carmela and me to take a seat in a ring of sofas and chairs around the harpsichord.

"We'll begin with Gabrielle and Emilio," he said, his German accent seeming even heavier than last night. "The duet from Act Three that we worked on yesterday. But take careful note, Carmela, your aria follows."

A sunny corner of the vast cream and gilt salon had been given over to music. A fresco of cherubs bearing mandolins and garlands of flowers made a fitting background for a handsome harpsichord in a richly carved case. Potted palms and vases of end-of-season rose cuttings created the atmosphere of a garden pavilion much more conducive to singing than a dusty rehearsal hall. I could easily become accustomed to this.

At one side of the harpsichord, the Gecco brothers were coaxing their instruments into proper tune. Mario notched his violin under his chin and drew his bow across the A string, which was just enough off pitch to set my teeth on edge. After tightening the peg, he played a snippet of a popular tune. Lucca's violoncello echoed him in lower tones.

Karl handed us our scores for the day's rehearsal, assured me that I would catch up in no time, then settled himself at the keyboard. He took a deep breath; on exhalation, his shoulders sank away from his ears and he began to smile like a man reaching home after a long journey.

Grisella and Emilio were already studying their parts. I hoped their scores were neater than mine. My paper held staves of tilting, ragged notes looking as if they had been set down at breakneck speed. When I withdrew my thumb, it was smudged.

Leaning close, I whispered to Carmela, "I can't believe it—our maestro wrote these out this morning. He must have been up for hours. Why in Heaven's name didn't he have his original manuscript copied into parts before he came to the villa?"

Touching the satin ribbon that circled her throat, she threw a nervous glance toward Karl and shook her head.

Romeo was not so prudent. He'd been leaning against a nearby pillar, unashamedly listening. He lumbered over and threw himself on a delicate chair that responded with an ominous creak. "For the same reason he assumed that the man who got his brains bashed in came to steal his music." Romeo winked and circled his ear with a forefinger. "Our maestro is a genius at composition, but a few tiles seem to have slid off the roof, if you catch my meaning."

"He actually believes a copyist would dare publish a composer's score under his own name?" I was astounded. In our tight-knit world of music, such a crime would be swiftly discovered and that copyist would never work again.

Romeo shrugged. He started to elaborate, but changed course when Karl sent him a glare from the keyboard. The basso jerked his chin toward Emilio. "Poor fellow. You've made him so nervous, it'll be a wonder if he can get through the song."

Emilio did appear ill at ease. Grisella stood by the harpsichord, idly twisting a lock of hair as she waited. But Emilio couldn't seem to stand still, and his complexion resembled the flesh of a peeled potato.

"What's all that about?" I asked Romeo in a whisper. "I'm not doing a thing."

"You don't have to," he answered in his deep, carrying voice. "Just knowing that everyone will soon compare his voice to yours is enough to make Emilio sweat."

Looking alarmed at hearing his name mentioned, my fellow castrato paled even more. I sent him a nod, encouragingly, I hoped.

"All right, we go?" Karl raised his right hand high, his first two fingers ready to mark the tempo.

Emilio muttered an indistinguishable reply, chin on his chest.

The composer's arm sank. "I know we've all had a difficult night, but it is time to put that unpleasantness aside. You are all professionals, so give me professional work."

"Of course, Maestro." Grisella assumed an expression she had inherited from our father, a smile at once virtuous and deprecating to those around her. She then directed a nod toward the entrance, and I turned to see Jean-Louis reply with a tight-lipped grimace. The Frenchman was dressed in a suit tailored to fit his frame like a second skin. He crossed the salon with a courtier's glide and settled in a wing chair with a stack of news-gazettes.

"Emilio?" The composer's question held a note of impatience.

The castrato steadied himself and managed a gracious nod.

"Good, we go. One, two, three—" Karl introduced a swaying meter of three-quarter time. Over the strings and the *continuo* provided by the harpsichord, Grisella's voice took flight like a falcon rising on sleek wings.

All the worries my sister had caused us over the years had made me forget what a truly fine singer she was. Her clear soprano was capable of the most elegant trills and divisions, but that was technique. Above the schooling she'd had as a girl, her singing flowed with a loveliness born of pure instinct.

I sat forward with my elbows on my knees, drinking it all in and thinking back to the days right before she had disappeared from our lives. Father often set her to vocalizing scales at the battered harpsichord in our sitting room. Under his direction, she sang endless rounds of ascending and descending notes, striving to link them like a string of perfectly matched glass beads. But once her stern taskmaster was out of earshot, she would launch into lilting songs she had heard only from the gondoliers on the canal. She sang them by ear with joyous gusto, never missing a note. I couldn't have done as well at thirteen, even with my *conservatorio* training.

Karl appeared as delighted as I was. Grisella seemed particularly sensitive to the directions he gave with his right hand while he played the *continuo* with his left. A hint of Karl's flattened palm and she extended her note; a precise wiggle of his fingers and she adjusted her phrasing accordingly. They made an excellent team: a skilled director and a talented soprano.

Glancing around to see what Jean-Louis made of Grisella's performance, I was surprised to see his beaked nose buried in a news-sheet. He must be so accustomed to her singing that it made little impression.

Now it was Emilio's entrance, and the castrato didn't fare so well. Early on, he snatched a breath in the wrong place that threw him off tempo for several measures.

Karl abruptly stopped playing and the Gecco brothers followed suit. "You know where you went wrong," the maestro observed in a level tone.

Emilio nodded, cheeks flushing.

"That's all right. Let's have it again." Karl sounded a chord and Emilio returned to the beginning. Better this time, I thought. With proper breathing, Emilio's small mouth was able to produce tones of mellow, bell-like timbre. Just the thing for his role of Andronicus, the lovesick prince.

He and Grisella were blending their voices in an energetic cadenza when Octavia joined us. She wore a loosely draped morning gown of screaming yellow dotted with red bouquets. If any of our eyes were still bleary from sleep, they were jolted to full wakefulness by one glimpse of our hostess.

"Oh, don't mind me," she called gaily as she crossed to a settee near the open loggia doors. "I'll listen while I work on my stitching over here in the good light. I promise to stay quiet as a mouse."

Nita followed her mistress, bearing a floor stand topped with an oval tapestry frame. Rehearsal continued over Octavia's increasingly strident commands: "Set it here. No, not there, you fool. I'll be too warm. Put it over here. No, this is the spot to catch the breeze—you must move the settee."

The duet concluded on a subdued note. Before dismissing Grisella and Emilio, Karl mumbled a few obvious corrections. I expected him to mention several others, but something had happened to the composer. As Carmela took her place, Karl leafed through his score distractedly. The adroit master of the company was once more the moody artiste.

At least Carmela was in good voice, and seasoned enough to handle her aria without much direction from Karl. Her bold, vivid soprano was the perfect instrument to convey the frustrations of Irene, the princess of Trebizond who had been callously rejected by Tamerlano. She also showed herself an accomplished actress with artful expressions and sweeping gestures that could have given a deaf man the sense of her words. I rubbed my chin thoughtfully; holding my own would not be easy when I shared the stage with Carmela.

Several times I glanced across the salon toward our hostess. Octavia plied her needle with an air of rampant gentility, but her promise to imitate the house mouse didn't last long. The concluding note of the aria had barely faded when she popped off the settee.

Octavia's heels tapped a staccato beat across the floor. "Karl, my lamb, you know I don't like to interfere, but must Signora Costa be so loud?"

The composer cleared his throat. "It's an impassioned aria, expressing the anger of a wronged woman."

"Yes, but for female singers, the common vogue favors more… restraint. The public wants their lovely nightingales to chirp, not shriek. Don't you agree?"

"I'm afraid I don't."

"Charm, Karl, feminine grace."

The composer steeled himself like a schoolboy expecting to be boxed on the ear. "Carmela is delivering the aria exactly as I asked."

"Really, now. I understand Venetian audiences just a bit better than you. Vincenzo keeps a box at both the Teatro San Marco and the San Moise. I've had my eye on the nobility for years, and I know what will win their approval."

"*Il Gran Tamerlano* is not just for Venice. It will open there, to be sure, but soon it will play in London and Paris. They expect fire from all Italian singers, men or women."

Octavia tapped a furious toe. "London and Paris are nothing to me. I'm mounting this opera for Venice's benefit. Above all, I'm lending my name to it. Think how humiliated I'll be if people say Signora Dolfini's soprano trumpets like an elephant and spreads her jaws as wide as an Egyptian crocodile."

Carmela had been following this exchange with one hand on the rim of the harpsichord. Octavia's comparison to wild beasts propelled her away from the instrument. "I'll have you know that my singing has been praised from Lisbon to St. Petersburg."

"Perhaps by moonstruck students or rabble who know no better," Octavia snapped.

"By the Czarina, herself. I was a favorite at her court for months. When I left Russia last spring, Anna Ivanova presented me with a pair of pearl-studded garters and a purse full of rubles."

The women continued to bicker, yowling like angry cats, Octavia towering over Carmela by a head. Karl's melancholy face sank lower and lower behind the harpsichord's music stand, and the rest of the company began to stretch and chat as players tend to do during any rehearsal interruption, however contentious. Jean-Louis left his gazettes and spoke with Grisella in low, intense tones. Was he giving her a personal critique?

I didn't join in any of their conversations. Carmela's mention of St. Petersburg forced me to confront something I'd been trying to ignore. I strolled over to the loggia doors and gazed toward the lawn dozing under the gentle autumn sun. The lake beyond twinkled as if diamonds floated on its lazy waters, and the tops of the cypresses waved in the breeze. An idyllic scene. But last night, violence worthy of the most turbulent city had forced its way into this quiet paradise.

We were sure of only one thing concerning the murdered stranger. By virtue of his unique pistol, he had a connection to Russia. Within the space of the morning, I'd heard two women mention their own ties to that distant, northbound country. And one of them was my sister.

Chapter Five

After several more hours, we were released from one of the most grueling rehearsals I had ever endured. Octavia had been called away to tend to household affairs, and Karl had resumed his mantle of director with a vengeance.

Our maestro demanded perfection, not with the strident commands or biting sarcasm of some composers, but with steady encouragement to shift focus and imbue the music with the true expression of the poetry we sang. He was most insistent that the drama not be stifled by ornamentation. An interesting stance, I thought. Usually I was asked to invent as many flowery embellishments as possible.

I taxed my voice to meet Karl's new challenges and was feeling exceedingly proud of my performance when the composer rose from the harpsichord.

"Very pretty," he said with a small sigh. "You could easily carry their hearts away."

I allowed myself no more than a modest nod. Emilio had been watching from the ring of chairs, trying to appear aloof and detached, but his flared jaw revealed his true state of mind. No need to further inflame his jealousy by basking in the composer's praise.

Karl came to stand in front of me. He thumped on my chest as if he were knocking on a door. "A beautiful instrument you have here. But you forget, Tito. You're playing a tyrant who has sacked villages and murdered thousands. You've callously abandoned your betrothed Irene, and you're trying to force Asteria to marry you by offering to free her imprisoned father. If she doesn't comply, you have every intention of cutting off both their heads. I want the audience to hate you—I want you to make them wish they could storm the stage and tear you to bits with their bare hands."

Emilio broke into a broad grin. Romeo and Carmela traded appalled looks. I couldn't see Grisella's reaction; Karl blocked my view.

After a stunned moment I realized that the composer was absolutely correct. In my zeal to make beautiful music, I had sung Tamerlano as a light, roguish villain. I had not yet found the truth of his ruthless character. I gulped and mumbled, "*Sì*, Maestro Weber."

"Drink deep of Tamerlano," the composer continued. "Come to know his barbarity, his blood lust—and show these to me after dinner. We will break for now." After a decisive nod, Karl headed toward the loggia, where Nita was arranging a tray of lemonade and glasses.

I didn't follow my fellow singers out to partake of refreshment. Karl's criticism stung all the more for being well-considered, and I needed a moment to soothe my battered pride. I went to our room, hoping to find Gussie, but he wasn't there. Vincenzo had probably installed him in the vineyard to begin sketching.

I rang for a footman. Giovanni answered my call and didn't seem surprised when I requested a pot of tea.

"That Maestro Weber, he's written a throat-scorcher for sure."

"Indeed," I replied baldly, then asked, "Giovanni, does the Post stop in the village?"

He nodded. "There's a Post house and station at the bottom of the hill, just past the church."

"When you come back with the tea, I'll have a letter ready. I'd like you to take it into Molina Mori for me."

A dubious look came over his handsome, young face. "I don't know if I can get away, Signore. The mistress keeps us all very busy."

Fortunately, my travels had taught me a thing a two about busy young footmen. "There's a *zecchino* in it for you."

"I'll manage, then. Happy to be of service, Signore." Giovanni bowed and withdrew.

I retrieved my writing case from the chest of drawers. I would ponder Tamerlano later; just then I was bursting to write to Alessandro. I scribbled the news of our sister with a stubby quill and enclosed my brother's letter in a short note addressed to Benito. My manservant would take charge of sending the longer missive on its way to Constantinople. Barring bad weather, it should reach Alessandro in three weeks. I only wished I could be there to see my brother's face when he realized he'd been fooled over the matter of Grisella's grave.

Giovanni returned as I was heating wax for the seal. After I'd impressed my ring in the soft blob, the footman took charge of my letter as promised. I bathed my throat with several quick cups of tea and headed for the vineyard to deliver the news to Gussie.

♫♫♫

"By Jove, but this is wonderful—Grisella alive! Nothing could please Annetta more." Gussie's sketching pad lay abandoned on the stone wall that overlooked the vine rows. His blue eyes danced with glee. "You *are* sure? I mean, this prima donna couldn't be some sort of imposter, could she? I wouldn't want to tell Annetta and then have to disappointment her."

"I'm absolutely certain that Gabrielle Fouquet is my sister Grisella. Beyond that, I'm not sure of anything." I spoke in low, unforced tones, resting my throat.

Gussie gathered his sticks of chalk into a leather portfolio. "I'll start a letter immediately. I've accomplished enough for the day."

"Whoa, don't be so hasty. I've already written to Alessandro, but no one in Venice or here at the villa must know."

Gussie gave me a perturbed stare.

"Grisella made me promise. Apparently this new husband of hers smuggled her out of Turkey one step ahead of a pasha who considers her a stolen piece of personal property. If he suspected she survived the fire and was appearing on the stage, he would be most anxious for her return."

"Constantinople is a long way away, Tito. And your Grisella is now a married woman. She should have no reason to fear."

The vineyard was hot; the afternoon sun bore down on men and vines more like July than September. I removed my hat and mopped my forehead with my sleeve. "If Grisella was being truthful, the pasha she fears may be from the Sultan's inner circle."

Gussie whistled under his breath. "Your little sister disappeared long before I came to Venice, but I've heard all the stories. Never does anything by halves, does she?"

"No, and I don't suppose she's much changed. Where this need for secrecy is concerned, I'd like to think her harsh experiences have made her overly cautious and her fears are unfounded, but… I don't know. The Sultan's empire stretches from Persia to Algiers and north across the mountains into Europe. Even the eastern coast of the Adriatic is now in Turkish hands. The Ottoman arm has a long reach when you look at it that way."

"The man with the Russian pistol—you don't think he could've been after Grisella, do you?"

"I can't imagine that a Turk would send a European to do his dirty work. Or that any gentleman with an ounce of honor would take it on. Besides, we concluded that the stranger must have been expected. That hardly fits the picture of someone snatching Grisella to drag her back to Constantinople."

Gussie nodded. "It's more likely that this pasha forgot about your sister once he heard of her death. After all, she's only one woman, and not exactly fresh—" He stopped short when he caught sight of my dark look. "I'm sorry, I don't mean to disparage her. My unbridled tongue is getting me in trouble, as usual."

"Don't worry. You're only speaking the truth." I sighed. "But let's keep this to ourselves. Not even her husband knows her true origin, and that's the way she wants it for now. We'll explain to Annetta in good time, after I've wrung a few more details out of Grisella."

"Gabrielle," he replied, nodding.

"Eh?"

"You had better start thinking of her as Gabrielle, lest you slip and give the game away."

I put a finger to my lips. I'd heard voices in the distance, and now they were coming closer. Two men rounded the end of the nearest trellis.

"If you would just let me explain, Signore." Ernesto spoke in plodding, patient tones, but his shoulders balled in tense mounds under his loose, open-weave shirt.

Vincenzo grimaced impatiently. Rivulets of sweat coursed down his cheeks. His muscular chest was buttoned into a snug waistcoat topped by a neckcloth that was already half-sodden. He'd slung his jacket over his arm. "All right, tell me again."

"Spring was unusually warm this year, and the buds broke through early. Then we had a hot summer, putting the crop ahead of schedule. These berries have wonderful color, but the flavor lags behind." The steward plucked several grapes from the bulging purple clusters and offered them to his master. "You try a taste. You must chew the skin thoroughly—the skin tells the tale. These tell me they need to stay on the vine a bit longer."

They walked toward us, Vincenzo chewing dutifully, Ernesto clasping his hands behind his back. Santini, the peasant who had helped put our carriage back on the road, loped into view and caught up with them in a few strides of his spindly, scarecrow legs.

Vincenzo paused to spit out grape skins. "All right, they could be sweeter. But next door, Luvisi has already started his harvest."

"Signor Luvisi's vines are a different variety," Ernesto explained. "His berries are ready, yours are not. We must remain patient— that's the key to unlocking the full flavor of any vintage."

Behind him, Santini nodded his long chin.

Vincenzo mopped his cheeks with a cloth. "But Luvisi is getting ahead of us—"

"With all due respect, Signore." Ernesto bobbed his head. "The harvesting of grapes is not a race. And if I might be allowed to venture a prediction, I believe we're in for a cool spell, perhaps even some rain that will delay the harvest even further."

Santini licked a finger and held it up to catch the breeze. He nodded again.

"Mercy me." Vincenzo chewed at his lower lip. "Signora Dolfini won't stand for that. The grapes will have to be in well before her concert. She's planning a musical evening to show her opera off to the entire neighborhood. She wants the front steps of the villa planked over to make a temporary stage and benches set up in the drive. She won't appreciate any competition from farm work."

"And when does the signora plan on holding this concert?"

Vincenzo frowned uncertainly. "She's told me, but I'm damned if I can recall the date now. I'll have her speak to you about the arrangements."

"*Si*, Signore." Ernesto bowed stiffly. "Now if you'll excuse me, the boys are cutting hemp in the north field, and I must make sure that the stalks are properly retted."

"Yes, I was going to speak to you about that. I rode out that way this morning, and they seemed to be making a fearful mess of it. The crop was still on the ground, lying every which way. That big white dog was walking all over the cut hemp."

Ernesto cleared his throat, and I caught Santini rolling his eyes before he dipped his gaze to the ground. The man's tongue might be impaired, but his natural reason was clearly intact.

The steward replied, "The hemp stalks are left in the field for the dew and rain to start breaking down the fibers, but they must be stacked just so or rot will set in."

"Oh yes, of course. Decidedly so." Vincenzo nodded as if he had learned the vagaries of hemp farming at his father's knee. "Go on, Ernesto and see to that, ah… retting."

As the steward and his silent shadow left the vineyard by a gate in the stone wall, Vincenzo walked over to Gussie and me. "I hope both of you have had a more profitable day than I have."

Gussie responded by opening his portfolio and spreading his sketches on the sun-drenched wall. In his modest manner, he said, "Mind you, these are only a start. I've been working my way around the vineyard, taking in several viewpoints so you could have your choice."

"Yes. Very nice." Vincenzo nodded as he inspected each drawing, then picked up several sheets by the corners. "I want you to paint both of these. This one with the hills stretching into the distance and this other that shows the lawn and the north side of the house in the background." He sighed deeply, raising his gaze to the golden landscape that had inspired Gussie's pen and chalk. "It will soon be time to return to the city, and I tell you, Signori, I dread it. This is the very meat of existence, living on the land as men were meant to."

"You prefer the country to the city?" I asked.

Our host nodded vigorously, gesturing to the shimmering fields, the remote hills flaming orange and yellow. "Venice can hardly compare with this. There's purity and virility in nature, while the city is smelly, dirty, and full of strangers on the prowl for who knows what. It's not like the old days when the Arsenale was turning out three boats a day and the dock workers were never idle. Now a new vice lurks down every alleyway."

Vincenzo had a point. I was a confirmed Venetian, never quite comfortable unless the undulating waters of the lagoon were a short walk away, but I had to admit that my city had changed in recent years. Venice's abiding tragedy was the shift of trade to Atlantic routes just as she was losing her territories in the eastern Mediterranean. Now England and Spain ruled the waves, and Venice, once the mighty queen of the seas, had become a tawdry harlot, surviving on tourists lured to her nearly endless Carnevale.

"At least you will have my scenes of the estate hanging on your walls in town." That was Gussie, ever able to find the patch of blue among the storm clouds.

"Ah, yes. Your paintings will be a comfort, but it won't be like living at the villa. By the middle of October, I'll have to leave my beloved farm for that den of thieves and murderers."

Vincenzo seemed determined to ignore the murder that had invaded his Arcadia only the night before, but I couldn't be so indifferent. "Signor Dolfini, I hope you won't think me impertinent if I ask a question about the man who was killed here last night."

His shoulders stiffened, but he inclined his head.

"Has any progress been made in identifying the unfortunate victim?"

"No, and I don't expect there will be."

"Why is that?"

"Ernesto had all the workers on the estate file past the body in the ice house. No one recognized him."

"Did Ernesto give you his pistol? It's of a rather unusual make."

"Yes, it's in my study, awaiting Captain Forti. But I don't see how it will be of help. It's obvious what happened."

"Is it?"

He shrugged and handed the sketches back to Gussie. "When the boys and I went downstairs, we found one of the long windows in the front corridor open. The shutters stood wide apart, the bar undone. All the intruder had to do was step over a low sill from the porch. One of your company must have let him in."

"But why do you suspect one of the musicians?" Gussie asked quickly. "There are others living in the house."

Vincenzo shrugged. "My valet Alphonso and the other servants from our house in town have been with us for some time. All perfectly trustworthy, I assure you. Then we have Nita and the maids, but they are simple country people. Intrigue and scandal are quite beyond their comprehension.

"No." He shook his head. "This… er… unfortunate incident has nothing to do with my household. It must relate to some trouble among you singers, some vulgar exchange that no one wants to own up to and I'd rather not even speculate about. I mean…" He interrupted himself to send me an abashed smile. "You two seem decent enough, but the rest of your lot impress me as living one step from the gutter. As my good wife is determined to have you, I can only hope your squabbles won't result in further violence."

I was at a loss for words as Vincenzo excused himself and ambled off in the direction of the villa. Unbelievable! He was content to pass the murder off as a petty quarrel among theatrical riff-raff. Our host might be aping the life of a noble estate holder, but he was nothing but a bourgeois iron merchant at heart. Dull, narrow, and utterly devoid of imagination.

♫♫♫

Dinner was served at the normal hour of half past three. Several more hours of rehearsal followed. I had hoped for an opportunity to have Grisella to myself, but Jean-Louis hovered like an anxious chaperone and bore her upstairs to rest as soon as she had sung her pieces. My sister did look tired, and it was clear that the palsies that had afflicted her girlhood were still with her. Though she concealed it well, her eyes blinked when she became excited and her left shoulder seemed to roll without her volition. I wondered if she still took her calming elixir.

I found it much easier to question Carmela Costa. Since she had boasted of her presents from the Czarina, Carmela was no longer shy about recounting her Russian adventure.

"Consider yourself fortunate if you've never performed in Russia, Tito. I've never been so cold in my life as I was last winter. I had to cover myself with a mountain of furs just for the short trip from my lodging to the theater." Carmela and I were sitting on the loggia just beyond the double doors to the salon. A breeze had picked up. The soprano drew a lacy shawl around her shoulders.

Inside, Maestro Weber was putting Romeo and Emilio through their paces. Intriguing snatches of airs and duets floated through the door. Emilio's clear, keen soprano complemented Romeo's thick basso like mustard on roasted beef.

"The management in St. Petersburg were tyrants," Carmela continued. "Just imagine, if we were late to rehearsal we were fined for every minute. Double fines once full dress rehearsals commenced."

"That must have been hard on your purse," I replied with a smile. I was well aware how Carmela tended to dawdle in her dressing room.

"Other, more pleasant things made up for it."

"Oh?"

"It was the vogue to end each performance with a rendition of the Preobrajensky March, a stirring military hymn. I was chosen for that honor and had to learn it in Russian. No small feat, believe me. Both the men and women of that country are a bloodthirsty lot. When I reached the part about going abroad to vanquish the enemies of the fatherland, they would jump to their feet, yell 'Huzza' with all the force of their lungs, and fling flowers until I was knee-deep. Every night, the stage manager had to rescue me from a mountain of blossoms. So exhausting." Carmela finished on a sigh, twining her fingers in the fringe of her shawl.

"You can't fool me," I teased, "you were loving every minute."

Her mouth turned down in a solemn frown. "We must enjoy our triumphs when we can, Tito. They make up for... the bad times."

"Were there bad times in St. Petersburg?"

She reached into her skirts for her fan. Keeping it closed, she tapped it on her lips thoughtfully. Finally she said, "The theater had a backstage lounge where the artists of the company and the audience mingled for long, sociable intermissions. Only the best people were allowed backstage, of course. That's where I met Nikolai."

"Nikolai." I encouraged her with a nod.

"He was one of those tall, fair-haired Russians with eyes like blue ice. As so many of his countrymen, he wore a mustache, a bushy caterpillar that he treated with wax before he dressed for the evening. At first I thought it very comical—facial hair is so out of fashion everywhere else. But apparently these were made popular by their late emperor. Anyway…" She trailed off, staring over her shoulder at the evening swallows wheeling and diving. "The day after we met, Nikolai sent a troika filled with yellow hothouse roses, the color of my costume on that fateful night."

"The expense must have been huge."

"Everything is done on a grandiose scale in Russia. When we would dine in his apartments, the table was covered with enough fine dishes to feed an army and the champagne truly flowed like water. The servants poured your glass and you never saw the same bottle return. Every glass was poured from a bottle newly opened."

"What happened to this charming Nikolai?"

"He was a widower, not as young as I had first thought. In fact his eldest son was very near my age." Carmela's voice grew husky, and she tugged at one of the pearl earrings that I hadn't seen her without since I'd arrived at the villa. "Nikolai wanted to marry me. It was a serious proposal, not an empty promise made in the heat of passion. He introduced me to a priest of the Orthodox Church who was going to tutor me in their beliefs. Nikolai even made me a present of these earrings to celebrate our engagement."

I gazed at the lustrous gems hanging from delicate wires that pierced her earlobes. As large as the tip of my little finger, with a slight golden cast, Carmela's pearls were fit for a queen, or at least a duchess. I told her so in admiring tones.

"Yes," she answered with the smile of a cat who'd had an uninterrupted session with a cream pitcher. "They once belonged to his grandmother, and I believe she was a duchess. My gems have traveled far and wide. Nikky said they were retrieved from oyster beds off the shores of Ceylon and set by a jeweler to the imperial court. Now they'll tour the opera houses of Europe on my ears."

She paused for a moment and we sat quietly, listening to Romeo sing of Bajazet's tragic defeat. When she resumed, the sorrowful aria made a perfect background for her tale's denouement. "Nikolai's children were much against the marriage. A foreigner, an opera singer, what should I have expected?"

"I once knew a count who married a rope dancer from Constantinople," I observed.

"In Venice?"

"Yes."

"Ah, but that is La Serenissima, city of masking and romance, and I was in St. Petersburg, the very seat of darkness and gloom. My lover's son marshaled the troops—Nikolai's elderly mother, brothers, cousins, uncles, friends. They all lined up against me. I fought hard, but I lost."

"I'm sorry, Carmela," I said, reaching for her small, white hand.

As I squeezed it, she pressed her lips together and shook her head so hard that her pearls swung back and forth like a chandelier in a windstorm. I had never seen Carmela so full of unfeigned emotion. At least it seemed genuine. I had to remind myself that the soprano was, after all, an accomplished actress.

Watching her face closely, I said, "I believe the man who was killed last night may have been Russian."

"What?" She paled and grew still.

"Yes. Gussie and I were helping to move him when we discovered a pistol of Russian make in his waistband. Are you quite sure you didn't recognize him?"

She snatched her hand from my grasp. "As I said last night—he's a complete stranger."

"I'm not accusing you of whacking him on the head, my dear, just trying to uncover the truth. It might be awkward to admit you know him, but if you do, you should say."

Carmela jumped up. Two dots of color had sprung to her cheeks. "Now I realize all the gossip I've heard about you must be true."

"People are talking about me? Behind my back?" I sat up tall, ears wide open.

"Oh, there's plenty of talk. You didn't leave Rome of your own accord like you said—a magistrate ran you out for being involved in the murder of a serving girl. Then you installed your Hebrew mistress and her bastard brat in your house in Venice, practically cheek by jowl with her humiliated parents. But the worst thing…" Carmela paused her tirade to draw a breath and shove her fan into a pocket. "You've become a damned, nosy busybody, Tito Amato."

I had to smile as Carmela made a regal, angry exit. She was correct on one charge: I was a busybody. Even Liya would've agreed with that.

♪♪♪

Later that evening, as blue-black shadows descended over the fields and woods of the estate, the company and its hosts assembled in the salon. A fire crackled under the marble mantelpiece, providing just enough warmth to counter the slight chill in the air. Lamps and candles splashed the frescoed walls with golden light. It was a lovely, harmonious room, but everyone in it seemed bored, peevish, or somehow out-of-sorts. It was the awkward hour, the limbo of the evening. Rehearsals were over for the day, and supper wouldn't be served for an hour or more.

At a card table, Romeo and Carmela were playing a desultory game of three-hand Tarocco with Jean-Louis. Bright kings, queens, devils, and monks shuffled through their hands. Grisella—I couldn't think of her as Gabrielle no matter what Gussie advised—sat reading her book nearby. Octavia's settee had been moved near the fire, but her needlework lay idle as she and Karl chatted quietly, heads only inches apart. Vincenzo was also reading, alone, in a far corner. One of his treatises on farming, no doubt. Emilio and the Gecco brothers slouched at the loggia doors, arguing about an opera that had lately been performed in Venice.

Gussie caught my eye and raised his voice. "Care to stretch your legs, old fellow?"

I forced a mammoth yawn and replied lazily, "I suppose I could do with a circuit or two around the house." Actually, I was doubly glad that Gussie had proposed a walk. Understandably curious, he'd been observing Grisella with such intensity that people were bound to notice.

Carmela was the only one to acknowledge our departure. She fluttered her fingers in a wave, and her gray eyes followed us all the way through the foyer to the front door.

"You must stop staring at my sister," I said as soon as we stepped onto the circular drive. As Ernesto had predicted, the air had turned cooler. An almost full moon shone above, shrouded in mist.

"Just can't stop myself, Tito. Every time I catch sight of her, I think she looks like a hardened version of Annetta. Only with that brassy hair, of course. Then I start thinking of the life Grisella must have led in Constantinople." He shook his head. "But you're right, I must be more careful."

After a judicious nod, I asked, "Did you find the ice house?" Earlier, Gussie had offered to use his freedom to roam the estate to locate the murdered stranger's current resting place.

"Yes, it's not far. We can go through the garden."

Strolling as if we had no definite destination, mutually aware of the prying eyes that could be watching from the villa's dark windows, we rounded the house and crossed the back lawn. The garden path stood out as a pale ribbon winding through umber foliage. Tendrils of fog roped our ankles as we trod its graveled surface.

We had just rounded a bend graced by a marble nymph that seemed to hover like a luminous phantom when Gussie paused. "This way," he whispered, turning onto a side path that was little more than a cleft in the shrubbery. "Mind the stair."

I followed him onto a sunken path defined by stone retaining walls that came up to our knees. It was darker here, and dominated by the smell of dampness and leaf mold. I slipped once or twice; my slick-soled dress shoes weren't meant for traipsing this country path. Just as I thought we would have to go back to the villa for a lantern, I spotted a thin wedge of yellow light spilling from a door some distance ahead.

"That's it," Gussie said near my ear.

We drew closer, and I saw that the ice house was really just a façade of masonry built over the sloping bank. From within, a flurry of movement met our ears and a shadow blocked the light.

"Carissimo?" The question was a caress bestowed by a deep feminine alto. Not receiving a reply, the alto turned harsh. "Who's there?"

Chapter Six

"Friends," I cried. "From the villa."

The door opened wide, framing the silhouette of a large woman outlined by candlelight. After a brief moment, she bobbed a curtsy and stepped aside.

With Gussie on my heels, I entered a small cave with a hard dirt floor and reinforced walls. My head barely cleared the ceiling rafters as I shuffled around the pit that contained blocks of ice transported from nearby mountains. Carcasses of birds and rabbits hung from hooks suspended over the pit. An odor of stale meat and blood permeated the cool air.

"We... came to pay our respects," I said, noting signs of a vigil in progress.

The stranger's corpse rested on a shelf that would normally have held foodstuffs. The rough wood planks had been covered with a threadbare Persian carpet, the sort of thing that the lady of the villa would offer to a tenant once its usefulness was over. Candles burned at the dead man's head and feet. His hair had been washed of gore, and his hands were crossed neatly over a winding sheet that covered him from foot to chin.

"I was beginning to think I would be the only one to keep the watch." The woman spoke softly, dark eyes liquid in the flickering light, black curls escaping her kerchief of snow white linen and falling to the shoulders of her short, red cape. Her face was too round and her skin too brown from the sun to be considered beautiful. But there was something about this peasant that compelled attention. An aura of calmness clung to her, like the mist encircling the moon outside.

She continued, "Last night, after my husband and Santini brought him in, I washed and dressed him for burial. I've kept the candles going since, but I haven't been able to sit with him for a proper vigil."

"You must be Ernesto's wife," I observed.

She nodded. "I'm Pia Verdi."

"I'm Signor Amato and this is Signor Rumbolt."

Gussie favored Pia with a warm smile.

She nodded again, grinning shyly. "I know. I saw your carriage arrive yesterday, and I asked Nita who you were. I heard the singing earlier today, and…" She paused to gesture toward Gussie. "While I was on my way to feed the pigs, I saw you out in the vineyard, drawing the grapes."

"I didn't realize we were so interesting," I replied lightly.

"Oh, Signore, anything new is interesting in a place where one day is exactly like the next. Some may complain, but I'm glad the mistress brought the opera to the villa. I never heard such beautiful music before in all my life."

"I suppose we create a great deal of extra work, though."

She shrugged within her red cape. "I don't mind. And Nita shouldn't either, not since I've been helping her with the laundry and cooking."

I cocked an eyebrow at the body on the makeshift bier. "Then it's doubly good of you to take so much care with someone you don't know. You could have let his body stay as it was. No one would have faulted you."

"That wouldn't be right. The poor man may be a stranger to me, but he has a mother somewhere, perhaps a wife and children. If one of my boys should ever chance to die in foreign parts, I hope someone will do the same."

"We saw one of your boys," Gussie put in. "He wanted to help fix our carriage wheel, but Ernesto sent him back with the pig."

"That was Manuel. He's fourteen. Basilio is just a year older. They've been working in the hemp all day." She bit her lip and looked toward the door. "I really should be seeing to their supper."

"Go on, then. We'll say a few prayers for the unfortunate stranger."

"God be praised," she answered, keeping her eyes on the door and touching the small crucifix that hung in the hollow of her throat. I noticed that her fingers slid down to caress the shadowy cleft between her breasts as she ducked her head to clear the lintel and pass into the night.

Pia's breadth and height had taken up a good deal of space, but somehow, after she'd gone, the ice house seemed even smaller.

Gussie also seemed affected by the change in the atmosphere. He shook his head like a dog emerging from a stream. "What an amazing woman. I'd love to paint her."

"A portrait? Of a peasant woman?"

"I'd seat her on a throne in a field of ripe wheat, as naked as the day she was born, with her black hair streaming over her shoulders. I'd crown her with a wreath of red and yellow grapes and call it… Harvest. No… The Bounty of the Harvest."

I chuckled. "Somehow I don't think that's what Vincenzo had in mind when he asked you to paint the estate."

"Nevertheless, think how impressive that could be. Something to make the Academy sit up and take notice."

My poor brother-in-law. Though Gussie's talent was obvious and his pictures sold well, the Venetian painters' guild had turned down his request for admittance for four years running. The tradition-bound Academy was not about to sully its register with the name of an Englishman, even one who had adopted Venice as his permanent home.

I grasped his shoulder. "The Devil take the Academy. Let's see what we can make of this corpse."

Our mysterious friend had been dead almost twenty-four hours. Long enough for his limbs to stiffen and his skin to mottle where it met the rug-covered shelf, but not long enough for the stench of corruption to take hold. Nevertheless, we made haste, mindful of the passing time and wanting to avoid any awkward questions our late arrival at supper would provoke. Gussie helped me undo the linen winding sheet, but the stranger's pale, pitiful nakedness had no stories to tell. He was simply a well-cared for, virile male in his early middle years.

We wrapped him back up, and I bent over his face. Very lightly, I ran my fingertips over his upper lip.

"What are you looking for?" asked Gussie.

"Does it seem that this patch of skin under his nose is lighter than the rest of his face?"

"Yes, now that you mention it. But what does that signify?"

"It tells me he's a Russian, not just a man with a Russian pistol." I elaborated after Gussie shot me a fish-eyed stare. "Carmela gave me an account of her adventures in St. Petersburg. She mentioned that the men of a certain class wear mustaches in honor of their late Czar."

"Yes, I saw a Russian delegation in London once, all bushy mustaches and tall sealskin hats. The only other man you might see with facial hair would be a Mohammedan of some sort, and our examination proves that our poor fellow doesn't follow their tenets. But he doesn't have…" Gussie shook his head, then broke into an eye-crinkling grin. "Oh, I see what you mean. He had a mustache and shaved it off. Quite recently."

I nodded. "His cheeks are lightly tanned and toughened like a man who spent at least a few hours a day in the open, but his upper lip is as pale and soft as an infant's."

"You think he didn't want to be recognized?"

"Perhaps," I answered, as I used both hands to part the hair over his shattered temple. "It's also possible that he shaved because he didn't want to stand out or call attention to himself. Hmm, this is odd…"

"What is it, Tito?"

I frowned. I'm not unduly squeamish, but probing a dead man's skull isn't high on my list of preferred activities. Above the

Russian's left ear, at the center of the concave depression that I expected to find, my forefinger encountered a deep, narrow well of flesh, bone, and a yielding substance that I didn't even want to name. "*Dio mio*! He has a hole in his skull. The clock pendulum couldn't have caused this."

"Are you sure?"

I stepped back and ransacked my jacket for a handkerchief. Wiping my hands more times than was strictly necessary, I replied, "You take a look."

Gussie traded places with me. With a greenish cast to his complexion, he gingerly repeated my examination, then straightened with a solemn frown. He reached for his own handkerchief and brought something else out of his pocket. Candlelight glinted off a metal blade: the slender knife that he used to sharpen his drawing pencils and chalks.

I closed my eyes as Gussie probed the Russian's skull, but opened them when I heard his sharp exhalation. With the tip of his knife, he rolled something on the cambric square that covered his outstretched palm. I stepped close and peered over his shoulder at a ball of lead shot.

♫♫♫

We escaped to our room after a tedious supper dominated by Octavia's cooing attempts to coax Karl from a melancholy silence. Ernesto, this time accompanied by his silent shadow Santini, had already made his rounds and closed the shutters. In the enclosed space, the air felt heavy and the pale green walls seemed as bleak as the stones of a prison cell.

"This is a damned rotten business," Gussie muttered.

"What? The composer who's set himself up as Octavia's plaything while her husband looks the other way? Or someone arranging the body to look as if the Russian was killed by the pendulum instead of a gunshot?"

My brother-in-law threw off his jacket and slowly unbuttoned his waistcoat. "Both, I suppose."

"I can sympathize with Maestro Weber's position," I replied. "Few composers can afford to mount productions loaded with the best singers and the lavish scenic effects that audiences expect. That leaves a lot of talented fellows scrambling to find a patron with a deep purse and an itch for speculation."

"Don't the backers make money? Everyone from the humblest gondolier to Doge Pisani goes to the opera."

"Some backers succeed royally. Domenico Viviani, for instance, when he owned the Teatro San Stefano. But most lose their shirts. So many things can go wrong—the fickle public takes an instant dislike to the prima donna, a visiting star cancels at the last moment, a fire destroys the scenery. Expecting an opera to make you rich is sheer lunacy."

"Then why do so many of the wealthy gamble their fortunes?"

"Some are genuine music lovers. Some are simply mad for the stage and relish being a part of its inside workings. Others, like our hostess I suspect, seek to raise their stock in society by becoming connoisseurs who discover hidden genius. Maestro Weber is lucky to have attracted Octavia's interest."

Gussie snorted. "That's debatable. I have a feeling that the formidable Octavia forces the poor chap to earn every *zecchino* two times over. Vincenzo is hardly an idiot. I keep wondering why he allows such a flagrant affair right under his nose."

"Saintly forbearance?"

"I doubt it. I believe that Vincenzo simply grew weary of arguing years ago and finds life a good deal pleasanter if he lets Octavia have her head."

I threw my jacket on the bed, poured some water in the basin, and grinned as I splashed my face. "I bow to your wisdom, my sage elder. Can you also supply as easy an explanation for that bullet that now resides in your pocket?"

"I'll have to think on that one a bit." He produced the lead ball and gave it a quizzical squint. "Obviously, the Russian wasn't killed inside the villa—someone would have heard the shot."

"His body must have been carried in from the outside," I replied as I toweled dry. "The only one of our company who has the strength to accomplish that on his own is Romeo Battaglia."

"Oh, I don't know. What about Jean-Louis? I saw him taking some sun with his shirtsleeves rolled back. Under his fancy clothing, the Frenchman is all muscle and sinew."

"No, not Jean-Louis." I shook my head firmly.

"Why not? When we discovered the body, did you not notice that he wore his outside shoes while everyone else in the corridor was in slippers or barefoot?"

"I noticed, but it means nothing. A pair of shoes can be changed in the twinkling of an eye." I added hastily, "It's much more likely that two people acted together."

Gussie pulled his chin back. Concern flickered in his blue eyes. "Tito, I'm surprised at you. You act as if you're afraid to even speculate that Grisella's husband might be involved. It's not like you to shy away from the obvious, even if it's not to your liking."

A light knock forestalled my reply, and Giovanni's boyish face appeared around the door. "Your letter is on its way, Signor Amato."

"Oh, yes." Our foray to the ice house had almost made me forget the footman's errand. I fetched my jacket to find the *zecchino* I'd promised.

"There's more," he said, fanning a fistful of letters like a winning hand of cards.

"You found those waiting for me?"

"Just this one." He handed over the thickest missive. "These others are addressed to the German."

I raised my eyebrows at the letters in his hand. They all bore the same curlicued, feminine hand. "Maestro Weber must be quite the correspondent."

Giovanni shook his head. "Oh, he doesn't answer them. He doesn't even read them, just tears them to bits or feeds them to the fire the minute I give them over. Doesn't even seem to appreciate the trouble I go to fetching them from the Post." The footman presented his palm with a smile, obviously hoping I would place a suitable value on his efforts.

I added a few small coins to Giovanni's *zecchino* and sent him on his way. Gussie hurried over, the mystery of the murdered stranger put aside. "Is the letter from Liya? Is there some trouble at home?"

"It's Benito's writing." I broke the red seal and removed a short note wrapped around another sealed packet. "He says this letter from Alessandro arrived soon after we left the house. He thought it might be important so he posted it at once."

"Let's see it, then." Gussie lit the table lamp with a wax-tipped spill and we both drew up chairs. I slid my thumb under Alessandro's seal and spread his pages out in the circle of lamplight.

Constantinople, 28th August 1740

Dear family,

Excuse my scrawl. I write in haste, eager that you should know my good news as soon as possible. Grisella may yet be alive!

Gussie gave a low whistle and drummed his fingers on the table-top. "I say, Tito. For once you're a nose ahead of Alessandro."

"Shush. This isn't a horse race. Let's see what he's found out."

Pray don't blame me for leaping to conclusions. What else is a man to think when he stands over a grave with his sister's name carved on the tombstone? I'm still not certain, but I'll set my roundabout tale down as best I can, and you can come to your own conclusions.

It began with my sulking around the warehouse, the thought of our sister held as a virtual prisoner gnawing at my vitals like the fox in the old fable. Grisella's actions disgraced us, it is true, but while I conducted business only a few miles away, she was sinned against by a procession of brutes. After my esteemed father-in-law's efforts to draw me out of my black mood failed, he insisted that I put work aside, follow Grisella's trail through our city, and do whatever could be done to restore honor.

I decided to start at the site of the *yali* that was consumed in the fire. It didn't take long to find. Many people on the western shore of the Bosphorus remembered the blaze. Like the mythical phoenix, another *yali* has risen from the ruins, an imposing mansion with a bay that juts out over the rolling blue water and, on its landward side, well-tended gardens enclosed by a high wall. By design, I arrived at the hottest hour of the day. The inhabitants of the house would be within, taking their rest behind the shutters that admitted the delicious breeze. I hoped to find a servant who had been around long enough to provide some useful information.

I was in luck. As I paused at the gate, only one sound carried: the rasp of a rake on the pebbled drive. My entrance startled a peacock into uttering a shrill cry and spreading his sapphire train. A giant came to investigate. He carried a rake and wore an immaculate caftan and neatly folded green turban. A eunuch, of course, a white eunuch.

Tito, you cannot imagine how many altered men walk the streets of Constantinople. They are not mutilated in a quest for heavenly voices as in Italy. Evil, unvarnished greed is the only explanation. The poor creatures are captured as boys in Wallachia and the Balkans and carried back to Turkey to be turned into tractable slaves and servants. And Tito, I shudder to report that their surgery is even worse than what you were forced to undergo. Their entire generative organs are cut away so that the needs of nature must be accomplished through a hollow straw. If I could change just one feature of my adopted homeland it would be this barbaric practice.

But I digress. Sebboy, for that was his name, told me he has worked on this shore for thirty of his forty years and that Count Paninovich was once his master. In our language, Sebboy would be called Gillyflower. All the young eunuchs, black and white, are given these ridiculous names. There are Daisies and Hyacinths on every corner.

So, this Sebboy claimed to remember Grisella well, as he had served as her companion when not occupied with other duties. Such relationships are common here, especially in wealthy households where several wives or concubines compete for their husband's attention. These eunuchs fill the hours with music and witty conversation, fend off annoyances, and supply news from the outside. I suppose it is natural for women shuttered away from the world to make a bond with men removed from society by their cruel mutilation. I sincerely hope I never give Zuhal any cause to wish for such a companion.

I am sorry, dear ones, your patience must be wearing thin. I can see Annetta's red cheeks and Gussie about to bite his pipe stem in two. Without further meanderings, I will set our conversation down exactly as it happened.

I identified myself as Grisella's brother, and Sebboy immediately fell on my neck, babbling and weeping.

"Where is my sweet mistress?" he asked. "Does she go well?"

I scratched my head. Didn't the fellow know? "But she died in the fire," I replied.

"That is what some believe, but Sebboy knows better."

"Some?"

"The master's countrymen. When Paninovich Effendi burned up in the fire, five men came from the embassy. They were very angry. They herded all the servants into the cookhouse that sat away from the ruined *yali* and asked many questions."

"About what?"

"How the fire started. What had we done to fight the blaze. Where the master kept his valuables. They kept us in there all night and part of the next day without food or water, even the old ones. If they thought we weren't telling the truth they beat us."

"What was the truth?"

He shrugged. "Only Allah knows the truth. I just know that my mistress and Paninovich Effendi were upstairs. All the servants were downstairs eating the evening meal. It was windy that night and the window draperies were blowing in the breeze. Some thought the fabric caught fire from a lamp…" A deep crease formed between his eyebrows, and he shrugged again.

"What did the men from the embassy do then?"

"They took Paninovich Effendi's body away. To send back to their country, I believe. The other body they left. To them it was no more than the furniture and carpets that had burned to ashes."

"The other body? But you said my sister did not die."

"No, while the others were dipping buckets in the fountain and running to throw water on the raging fire, I saw my mistress run away into the trees." He pointed toward a cypress grove that stood beside the wall on the other side of the garden.

"In all the panic, could you have been mistaken?"

He propped his chin on his rake and thought a moment. "No, it could only have been my mistress. The glow from the flames shone on the red hair streaming down her back. I know her hair… I brushed it often."

"Did you go after her?"

"Not right away. The roof fell in and showered sparks everywhere. By the time we had the small fires put out, the cypress grove was empty."

"Then who was the other body?"

"It is a mystery. When the ashes had cooled, the embassy men locked the doors of the cookhouse and went to sort through the rubble. The other sillies were weeping and chattering like a flock of chickens, but I kept my head. I got on a stool and unhinged a stove pipe so that I could watch through the hole. I was amazed to see them lay the body of a woman beside that of my master's. She was badly burned, but enough of her hair remained to show its red color. I have no idea who this woman was or how she came to be in the house."

"Could she have been one of the female servants?"

"No, they were all in the cookhouse. And none of them had red hair."

"You didn't tell the Russians about Grisella escaping the fire?"

"No, the men were very angry. When I saw that they accepted the woman's body as my mistress, I thought, Allah wills it. My mistress is well away, and who is Sebboy to upset the will of Allah?"

"Someone arranged for the woman's burial, though. I've seen the tombstone."

"It was the Frankish man." By this he meant French, dear family. Apparently this man arrived just after the Russians had gone. Telling the servants that he had admired Grisella's singing at European gatherings in Pera, he volunteered to take charge of her body and see that she received a proper Christian burial. Bewildered and frightened, no one, not even Sebboy, thought to ask his name. The Frenchman loaded the woman's corpse onto a cart and disappeared as quickly as he had come.

Falling silent, Sebboy began to toy with his rake. The afternoon was wearing on. The music of a *ney* came from the house, piping strains that rose and fell but never quite resolved into a melody.

"I must go," I said. Sebboy nodded, then begged me to wait another moment. He leaned his rake against the wall and sped off with his loose robe flapping like wings.

When he returned, he thrust a small box at me. It was rosewood inlaid with mother-of-pearl. A beautiful thing despite the charred edges.

"It was hers," said the big eunuch. "Now it should be yours."

I lifted the lid and saw a nest of women's sundries: garters, a broken string of beads, an almost empty scent bottle, several mismatched earrings. There was only one thing I wanted, a visiting card engraved with a French name. I pocketed the card and insisted that Sebboy keep the box and its contents. He couldn't have been more pleased if I'd granted him one of Aladdin's treasure chests.

Before I left, Sebboy took my hands and kissed them on the palms, a Turkish gesture that signifies intense devotion. "Find my mistress," he said. "She tries to disguise it, but she is often ill and cannot care for herself. Take her into the bosom of your family and keep her safe and well. Tell her that her poor Sebboy thinks of her every day."

Do I believe him? That is hard to say. As I discussed the matter with Zuhal, we wavered between hope and incredulity. Many things dull the blade of truth: fear, envy, and especially greed. I saw none of these in Sebboy's face as he told his fantastic story, but yet, it is hardly imaginable that a European woman could make her way through Constantinople on her own, especially if she is ill. Then I remember how our little sister always did have more lives than a cat. Tito, you're too young, but surely Annetta recalls how Grisella crawled out on the ledge over the canal before she could even walk. Berta nearly had heart failure.

One trail remains. As I write this letter, the visiting card from Grisella's box sits on my desk. It's smudged with smoke, but the name is still clear. Louis Chevrier. On the back, there is a terse sentence written in western script, Italian. Contact me at The Red Tulip, the rogue writes. I say rogue because there is no club more notorious in Pera. It's a gathering place for European gentlemen who have a yen to explore their very distorted and debauched view of the harem. One cannot pass through its doors without the patronage of someone known to the management. It may take a few days, but I'll breach those doors and discover all that Monsieur Chevrier knows about our sister.

Addio, my dear ones. Expect another letter soon. As you are well aware, I never give up without a fight.

Your most affectionate brother,
Alessandro

Gussie and I stared at Alessandro's bold signature for several breaths. Then my brother-in-law leaned back in his seat. His cheeks had gone quite flushed. "A second red-haired girl?

Buried in Grisella's place? Didn't she tell you that her husband had buried—"

"A bag of sand. Yes." I chewed at a knuckle, tongue-tied for the moment. Finally I continued, "There must be some explanation. Alessandro speaks of a Monsieur Chevrier. He's not necessarily the same person as Jean-Louis Fouquet."

"Oh, Tito." Gussie shook his head in dismay. "Surely you must see—"

"Don't say it," I cut him off again. "I'll question Grisella tomorrow. Clearly the girl has been the victim of some vicious intrigue. When I'm able to talk to her alone, I'm sure she will make sense of it. You'll see."

"Talk to her tonight."

I shook my head. "Tomorrow. I'll ask her to walk with me during a break in rehearsal. Just now I want to look into something else while the opportunity presents itself. And I need your help."

Part Two

*"Midnight shout and revelry,
Tipsy dance and jollity."*

—John Milton

Chapter Seven

"I won't do it. Absolutely not," said Gussie, emphasizing his refusal by marching over to his bed and pulling back the covers as if he meant to dive between the sheets fully clothed. "It's late, I'm tired, and what you ask is not... the work of a gentleman."

"Since when does murder require gentlemanly behavior?" I countered quickly.

He jerked out of his waistcoat and started untying his shirt. "I'd oblige you, Tito, I truly would. *If* we had learned anything that made it absolutely necessary for you to search Carmela's room. After reading Alessandro's letter, I'm more inclined to think you ought to search Grisella and Jean-Louis' room."

"Let's not pick through that again." I shook my head stubbornly. We'd been arguing over my plan for some minutes, and the evening was wearing on.

I had just returned from creeping down the stairs to investigate the whereabouts of the rest of the villa's inhabitants. From behind a column that separated the salon from the foyer, I'd observed everyone except Vincenzo amusing themselves with a lively game of blind man's bluff. The furniture had been pushed to the perimeter of the salon. First Emilio, and then Romeo, tied a folded handkerchief over their eyes, allowed themselves to be spun around, then blundered about with outstretched arms. The object was to lay hands on one of the ladies.

Karl awaited his turn, elbow on the mantelpiece, cheeks rouged by the fire's warmth. For once, his thin features seemed untroubled by worry or suffering. The composer actually lifted his chin and laughed when Carmela and Octavia tried to outfox their blindfolded pursuer by diving under the same table.

The Gecco brothers had stationed themselves near the brandy decanter and urged the players on with slightly slurred calls of "be quick, to your right" or "damn it, man, she's ducked under your arm." A pair of footmen was on hand to keep the decanter filled and to help raise the players to their feet when an errant ottoman or misplaced foot resulted in misfortune.

The game was apparently too boisterous for my sister. After twirling away from Romeo's persistent grabs, Grisella pleaded dizziness, stumbled out of the way, and curled herself into a corner of the settee. With the back of her hand massaging her forehead, she was a picture of loveliness in a bottle-green gown that made her artfully arranged ringlets seem more golden than brassy.

Jean-Louis had been lounging in a nearby armchair, legs stretched long and crossed at the ankles. Now he heaved to his feet. "Good. We can go up."

"Oh, no, not yet," Grisella pleaded. "I want to watch them having fun. Please, Jean-Louis." She gave a peevish shrug. "I'm too wound up to sleep, anyway."

Her husband responded with a look that made me think sleep had been the last thing on his mind, but he did sink back down in the chair. The last thing I'd seen before ascending the stairs was his frowning, hawk-like face.

"Gussie," I started into my plea again. "It's already past ten. They'll start drifting off to bed soon. Take your sketchbook downstairs and plant yourself in that big chair by the fireplace. Start with a caricature of Octavia—not too wicked, mind you. The company will cluster round, and they'll all want you to draw them. Please, if you love me as a brother, do this."

Gussie answered by slowly pulling his shirt back over his head and donning his waistcoat. He frowned as he slipped his sketchbook from his portfolio. When he reached the door, he paused with a hand on the knob. "Carmela seems a very unlikely murderer, but I suppose you won't rest until you've searched her things for a pistol."

"And Romeo's," I whispered.

Gussie's eyebrows shot up. "Now you're proposing to rummage through two of your colleagues' rooms?"

"I must, don't you see? Romeo follows Carmela around like a big puppy. He's little more than a boy, hardly the picture of tasteful charm and elegance that usually turns her head, yet she encourages him."

"Perhaps she's just lonely."

"I think she wants his protection. I think she's been expecting trouble to follow her from St. Petersburg. Perhaps that was her reason for agreeing to rehearse this opera in the middle of nowhere—she may have found it safer to be out of sight for a time."

"And why did this *trouble* follow her all the way from Russia?"

"The earrings—surely you've noticed them—they're pearls of exquisite quality. Most women would keep such beauties in a lockbox except on special occasions, but they never leave Carmela's ears. She says they were a gift from a Russian admirer that she hoped to marry. I have a feeling that his family feels otherwise."

Gussie dropped his hand from the doorknob. "You think the dead Russian was sent to retrieve the earrings?"

I nodded. "Not just for the value. Carmela described the family as highly distinguished. Can you imagine their indignation, their wrath? A common stage performer absconding with family heirlooms?"

"But would a delicate little woman like Carmela fight to the death over earrings? Sentiment is all very fine, but when confronted by a man with a pistol, I'd expect her to hand them over to be conveyed back to the rightful owners."

"Carmela does set great store by those earrings, but she values her life more," I agreed. "I think perhaps the stranger didn't give her the option of simply slipping the earrings off and walking away."

"His mission included revenge?"

"It seems likely—everyone knows the Russians are a particularly haughty and barbaric race. Let's say that Carmela had received some communication from the stranger. Knowing she'd have to face him sooner or later and wanting to avoid the embarrassment of a public confrontation, she would have requested a secret meeting." I continued, warming to my theory, "Carmela unbarred the window shutter from the inside to leave the house and keep that appointment. Perhaps she was intending to return the earrings quietly, but the Russian jumped her by surprise and she used her pistol to defend herself."

"Then why fetch Romeo to carry him back into the house?"

"She probably had Romeo following at a discreet distance. Perhaps he actually took the shot."

"All right, but if it happened as you say, why not dispose of the body as far away from the house as possible? Bury it in the woods, for instance."

"It is a puzzle," I said after some reflection. "But you have to remember that neither Carmela nor Romeo knows the estate. They just arrived a few days ago and have been kept inside rehearsing. Doubting that they could make a proper job of concealing the murder, they may have decided to take the opposite tack and place the body right in the middle of a large group of possible suspects."

"Meaning to stand by while an innocent party took the blame?" Gussie sounded more than a little vexed. "From what you've told me of Carmela, I could just barely believe that. But Romeo seems like a more decent sort—hard to believe that she could push him into such a black deed."

"Perhaps the deed was not as black as all that. What if Carmela's plan was simply to confound the authorities? Rural constables aren't known for thoroughness, especially when a wealthy landowner is involved. This Captain Forti seems particularly lax in his duties."

"We know that now, but Carmela and Romeo had no clue about the constable's proclivities until he was summoned and found to be on a boar hunt."

"They did, though. If you'd been at dinner last night, you would have heard Octavia make quite a point about Captain Forti's lack of attention to duty."

"You don't say?" Gussie scratched his chin thoughtfully.

"Yes! The more I think on it, I believe Carmela and Romeo were hoping that the dead man's anonymity and the lack of motive in the opera company or the Dolfini household would stir up enough confusion to prevent any arrests."

"But what a chance to take. They might have been seen."

"Not through the shutters. The villa was shut up tight as a drum. And everyone was in bed."

"Why the clock?"

"To make it appear that he was killed inside the house. As you said, a shot would have been heard. But a blow to the head, probably not. Besides, a midnight murder would be just the sort of dramatic scenario that Carmela would devise."

"I suppose it's possible..." he answered haltingly. "Then the murder would remain a mystery and pass into the lore of the villa... a story to tell around the fire... merely something to give future guests a little shiver before they turn in for the night." He looked me over with some misgiving. "Perhaps you should leave it at that, Tito."

"You know I cannot."

"Oh, yes. I understand that readily enough. I've known you for a long time, my friend." Gussie smiled ruefully as he once again reached for the doorknob. "If I'm going to do this, I must hurry."

I smiled my thanks. "Yes, I've kept you too long. Hurry down to the salon before they finish their nonsensical game."

"I'll do my best, but a party's fascination with my drawings usually doesn't last over thirty minutes or so."

"It will be enough," I replied, pushing him through the door.

♫♫♫

I let several minutes pass before lighting a three-taper candlestick and bounding soft-footed across the corridor. I started with Romeo and Emilio's room. My hastily worked-up plan was to identify Romeo's possessions by virtue of his large-sized clothing and examine all neatly but thoroughly. If I didn't find a pistol, perhaps I would be rewarded by an overlooked or partially removed bloodstain. Wielding my light, I made a quick survey of the chamber. It was similar to ours, comfortably but plainly furnished, the windows shuttered tight.

I found the wardrobe packed to capacity. Even if Romeo's clothing had not eclipsed Emilio's in yardage, I would have been able to identify his garments by smell. My fellow castrato favored cologne-water that created a pleasing hint of orange and bergamot. Romeo showed no more taste in his scent than he did his wigs. His jackets and waistcoats assaulted my nose with a cloying stew of vanilla, jasmine, and musk. Quickly I patted down pockets and linings; my fingers probed shoes to the tips, and I didn't slight his shirt tails. Nothing. His trunk and the empty bags stacked atop the wardrobe were similarly unfruitful.

I proceeded to Romeo's bed. Kneeling on the thin carpet, I started from the headboard, working my long arm between the feather-stuffed mattress and the straps that supported it. During my boyhood at the Conservatorio San Remo, this had been my favorite hiding place for tins of candy and other forbidden treats that eased the boredom of endless vocal exercises. Some things don't change. Exactly in the spot I would have chosen, Romeo had secreted a package wrapped in cloth. I tugged it loose.

I hoped to find a case containing a pair of pistols but saw at once that the package was too small. It was a book that slipped out of the linen sleeve. And not just any book. I was holding the scandal of the decade: *The Postures of Aretino*.

Everyone was whispering about these copper-plate engravings of naked men and women entwined in every conceivable position and the bawdy sonnets that accompanied them. New editions were printed in secret as quickly as popes and bishops ordered the book to be tossed on bonfires. One look told me why these pages had caused such a stir. I itched to study them further, but almost half of my precious thirty minutes had already passed.

Aretino would have to wait.

I stuffed the book back under the mattress and moved to search Romeo's neckcloths, linen, and other bits and pieces of masculine dress stored in the chest of drawers. Again I found nothing to suggest that he was involved in the Russian's murder.

I let myself out. Treading quietly, I eased across the corridor and paused at the top of the front stairs. Exclamations of admiration met my ears. The guests in the salon were still entranced by Gussie's ability to capture a person's essence with a few, well-placed lines of charcoal.

I was at Carmela's door when I heard furtive footsteps coming up the stairs at the back of the corridor. One of the servants? Since they wouldn't be allowed to retire until the guests were snug in their beds and the salon had been returned to its usual orderly condition, I hadn't expected to be caught by a maid or footman ascending to the attic.

I managed to blow out only one of my candles before a shadowy form separated itself from the blackness of the stairwell.

"Tito?" said a male voice in a carrying whisper. "What are you doing? I thought everyone was downstairs."

The figure crossed the tiles, glancing back once or twice as if worried he was being followed. Vincenzo! His evening clothing was covered with a dark cloak that sparkled with droplets of mist or light rain. He regarded me with a puzzled frown.

"Ah, Signor Dolfini. You see… Carmela…" I furiously racked my brain for some plausible reason to be entering Carmela's room. Before I could think of anything, Vincenzo leapt to his own conclusion. Amusement transformed his expression, and he gave a conspiratorial chuckle.

"Going to wait for her between the sheets, eh? Can't blame you. Signora Costa is a cute little filly who always seems ready for the race."

I cringed as he punctuated his words with an exaggerated wink, but I knew I had to play along. "Yes," I whispered. "She should be coming up any minute now."

"I wager she won't dawdle." He chuckled again, taking an altogether more relaxed view of our company's affairs than he had earlier in the day. "Surely you suit her better than that oversize young man who is constantly making calf's eyes at her."

"That would be Romeo, the basso who plays Bazajet."

"Of course. Hard to keep you singers and your roles straight. I'm not musical, you know. It's Octavia that lives and dies for the opera. She tells me that even though you're missing a thing or two, women chase you down the street merely to touch your sleeve or snip a lock of your hair."

"It has happened, Signore. I really don't understand it. Sincere applause for my singing is all I've ever asked for."

"Hmm…" Vincenzo looked me up and down, his innate respectability at war with natural curiosity. "And she says that some particularly shameless creatures actually keep their stockings up with garters adorned with your likeness."

"So I've heard." I shifted from foot to foot, silently entreating all the saints of heaven to send Vincenzo on his way.

One of the elect who wasn't particularly busy that night must have taken pity on me and granted a small miracle. After another wink, my host trotted off toward the east wing humming a gay tune under his breath.

Moving like the wind, I slipped through the door and went to work. My search of Carmela's wardrobe and chest was not accomplished as easily as Romeo's. The soprano had more garments than Romeo, Emilio, Gussie, and I put together. In one drawer, I counted seven nightshifts alone. Then there was the dressing alcove where she'd stored little trunks filled with jars of lotions and face paints and hampers containing yards of ribbons, lace fichus and other folderol. I wasn't able to make the business as methodical as I'd planned, but once I crept back across the corridor, I was reasonably sure that Carmela did not possess a pistol.

Almost as soon as I'd closed my door, I heard voices in the corridor calling good night. Suddenly weak-kneed, I sank into the chair and mopped my forehead with the towel I'd left on its arm. I'd cut it fine, much too fine for comfort.

Gussie returned a moment later. "You're back. Thank the good Lord." He sighed heavily, then brightened to ask, "Did you find anything?"

My voice sounded as glum as my mood. "I have no reason to suspect that Romeo harbors any secrets beyond a book of erotica or that Carmela has any worries besides keeping the years at bay."

Gussie nodded with pursed lips. He could have said, I told you so, but those words were not in my brother-in-law's lexicon. Instead, he opened his sketchbook and tore a sheet off the top. "Here, Grisella wouldn't take this. I thought you might like to have it."

"She didn't want her portrait?"

Gussie shrugged. "She glanced at it, and then returned it to me with a cold shake of her head. Jean-Louis laughed outright and said it looked no more like her than he did."

Studying the drawing, I thought I saw why Grisella had rejected it. Her lips were upturned and her cheeks dimpled, but like a magic mirror, Gussie's sketch also revealed a pitiful longing beneath the smile. Grisella would never want to admit to such naked vulnerability. Though I'd renewed our acquaintance only that morning, I already understood that my sister made a virtue of self-control. Gussie had caught something else, too. In her narrowed eyes, I detected something hard and merciless that gave me a hollow feeling in the pit of my stomach.

We both sought our beds. Gussie's day in the open air of the vineyard must have worn him out. Within minutes, he was snoring softly. I didn't fare as well.

Two women involved in scandals that tied them to Russia, and when I weighed my night's activities in the balance, the scales dipped toward my wayward sister. Rearranging my pillow for the tenth time, I pondered how Grisella had artfully induced our reluctant maestro to include me in the cast of *Tamerlano*. My sister was obviously interested in more than renewing family ties: I felt that down to the meat of my bones. Grisella's daring leap from Count Paninovich's burning *yali* had been only the beginning of a long journey. With mounting anxiety, I wondered if I was the end point or merely a stop along the way.

Before I found my desperately needed repose, another matter which probably had no bearing on either Grisella or the Russian stranger floated to the top of my mind: Why did the master of the villa feel the need to skulk about his own house like a thief in the night? And what had Vincenzo been up to that put him in such a mellow mood?

♫♫♫

The next morning Maestro Weber set us to rehearsing recitatives. For me, this was a necessary evil at the best of times. Accompanied by only a few supporting chords from harpsichord and strings, passages of recitative moved the story along in great chunks of repetitive, sing-song dialogue. Give me an aria that combined a musical challenge with an inspired melody, and I could scale sublime heights, but singing recitatives made me feel like an Arabian steed forced to drag a plow over a muddy field. What torture!

Bored, and distracted by family concerns which perforce must remain secret, I'm afraid I delivered my tuneless bits with scant grace. Maestro Weber dismissed me with a frown, but voiced no overt criticism. When he called Emilio up, I retreated to a comfortable wing chair in a distant corner of the salon. This turned out to be a fortuitous choice, as my position offered an unobstructed view of the front door that soon resounded with the metallic clang of the knocker.

A footman should have answered immediately. Instead, another series of increasingly impatient knocks brought Nita from the depths of the house drying her hands on her apron. She opened the door on a draft of chilly air. Three men waited on the portico, the first a sober personage whose ample stomach was spanned by a gold chain bearing a medal of office.

Nita dropped a dutiful curtsy and greeted him by name. Unfortunately, I couldn't quite make it out.

The maid curtsied even lower to the second visitor, a middle-aged man of distinguished bearing with a shock of tawny hair that put me in mind of a lion's mane. His roving gaze took in every corner of the foyer and the salon beyond, sweeping over me as if I were invisible. His attention lingered on the furnishings and décor, and he did not appear to appreciate what he saw.

"Signor Luvisi," Nita announced grandly, "we make you welcome."

Ah, I'd heard that name mentioned several times. Luvisi was the neighboring estate owner who had stolen a march on Vincenzo with the grape harvest.

A twinkle sprang to Luvisi's eyes as he handed Nita his cloak and tricorne. Calling her by name, he said, "I hope that welcome goes for your master as well."

She answered by pressing her lips into a tight line and giving a small shake of her head.

The third man needed no introduction. His rusty black cassock and wooden cross marked him as the parish priest. The expression on his lined face would have suited one of the gloomier Old Testament prophets. Nita avoided his eyes as he handed over his broad-brimmed hat.

Before the maid could show the callers to an anteroom, Vincenzo came down the corridor that held his study. He entered the foyer with the usual pleasantries, but his polite phrases were woven with threads of tension that stood out like gilt embroidery on a black suit.

Hoping to escape notice, I pressed myself into the well-padded chair and focused my gaze on the harpsichord as if Emilio's recitative was the most amazing performance I had ever witnessed. My ears were not trained on his droning soprano, however, but on the increasingly animated conversation among Vincenzo and his visitors.

It transpired that Agostino Bartoli, the mayor of Molina Mori, headed the small delegation. Rumors concerning the villa's midnight tragedy had penetrated every corner of the village, and its good people feared being murdered in their beds. In the constable Captain Forti's absence, Mayor Bartoli had been forced to make inquiries himself. Signor Luvisi had been included because of the proximity of his estate. Padre Romano had joined the group to ensure that the murdered man received the proper rites of burial.

Vincenzo obviously resented the delegation's intrusion. Perhaps it was because he was accustomed to holding unopposed sway over everyone at the Dolfini Ironworks. Or perhaps it was the bustling air of pomp and ceremony that enveloped Mayor Bartoli like an invisible cloud. Whichever the case, Vincenzo announced his intention to keep the stranger's body in the ice house until Monte Rosso ran out of boar and Captain Forti returned to Molina Mori. Though Forti was giving his official duties short shrift, he was, after all, the only judicial authority in the region.

Vincenzo's visitors were just as determined that the body be released, advising that it could reach an unconscionable state of deterioration before the constable came away from his hunting. Mayor Bartoli also wanted to question everyone who was staying at the Villa Dolfini or lived on the estate. Luvisi had already allowed the mayor to question his tenants. None of them had noticed anything unusual on the night in question, but then, Luvisi's estate lay several miles away. Surely a man couldn't have been bludgeoned to death in the second floor corridor of a house without someone in that very house seeing or hearing something. The mayor's tone bristled with suspicion at Vincenzo's assurances that he had already put these questions to his household without any light shed on the mystery.

As they disputed all the way down the hall, I strained my ears to catch their fading voices. I couldn't help noticing that Vincenzo directed most of his comments to Mayor Bartoli or Padre Romano, as though he disdained to acknowledge his neighbor any more than was absolutely necessary.

The slam of a door put an end to my eavesdropping, but not my curiosity. At the harpsichord, Grisella had replaced Emilio and was trilling her way through her recitative like a gay woodland bird. Her bright efforts had captured everyone's attention. Silently, I eased myself from my chair and slunk into the foyer.

Nita was visible through the half-open door of the cloak room, tossing the priest's broad-brim on a peg beside the mayor's gilt-edged tricorne. When she came to Signor Luvisi's headgear, she smoothed its spray of white plumes and dusted its crown for any sign of lint.

"A fine man—Signor Luvisi," I said as I stepped through the doorway.

Startled, Nita jerked around with a tiny jump. On seeing my pleasant smile, she hung up the hat and replied in her flat tone, "That he is, Signore. A fine man from a family of the highest station. You'll not find anyone here that would breathe a word against a Luvisi."

"He seems quite concerned about our recent tragedy."

"He would be. Not like some," she finished sotto voce.

"I noticed that he called you by name. Did you once work for him?"

She shook her head. "I worked for his cousin, Signor Annibale Luvisi. We all did. This was his villa."

I nodded. Many noble families owned great country estates, but it had not always been thus. Our island republic was founded on one guiding dictum: *Cultivate the sea, let the land be.* The discovery of the new continent across the Atlantic forced Venice to reconsider that proverbial wisdom. With their maritime fortunes diminishing, patricians scrambled to purchase land on Terrafirma and exploit its luxuriant soil. The intervening years had seen the huge tracts split up to accommodate younger sons, but it was rare for an estate to pass out of family hands entirely.

From some deep recess, Nita heaved a sigh that trailed memories in its wake. "Signor Annibale was the mildest of masters, never out of sorts. His wife, also. You should have seen the villa then. When they were in residence, we had parties that went on all night with hundreds of candles burning, luncheons served in the open air by the lake, carriages streaming through the gate to pay afternoon calls. Everyone loved the young master and mistress." Her freckled cheeks bunched into a rare smile.

"Did Annibale Luvisi also take an interest in agriculture?"

"He took pride in the estate, but he was a child of the city at heart. The ways of the country didn't come naturally to him. Just as Signora Francesca left the housekeeping to me, Signor Annibale allowed Ernesto to see to the farming."

"Ernesto seems very capable in that regard."

"Indeed so. Ernesto was born on this estate. He worked alongside his father from the time he could toddle. Thanks to Signor Annibale's open hand, Ernesto was able to plant a new vineyard, build a new threshing barn, and refurbish all the walls and fences. The more improvements he made, the more lucrative the estate became. Signor Annibale was the envy of all the neighboring landowners."

"How did it happen that the villa passed into Dolfini hands?"

Nita shook her head and flapped her apron. "Oh, Signore. It was enough to make you doubt the Lord's goodness. One day Signora Francesca woke up looking as white as bread dough and complaining of a pain in her side. By afternoon, she was burning up with fever and her little belly was as hard as slate. The doctor from the village was useless. She died the next morning in a torment I never hope to see the likes of again. Signor Annibale changed forever that day. He truly loved his wife and couldn't accept that she'd been taken in such a cruel fashion. For a week, he shut himself up in the chamber where she died. Then he took off for Venice where they say he meant to drink himself to death."

"He's dead, too?"

"No, he still lives, but while he was in his cups he gambled everything away. Some foreign count won the house and land and turned around and sold it before the rest of the family even knew what was happening."

"Vincenzo Dolfini was the buyer?"

She nodded solemnly.

"What happened to Signor Annibale?"

"When he came to himself, he tried to undo the sale. He even took it to court, but Signor Dolfini is a good man of business. He'd insisted that all the papers be drawn up in the proper way. The sale was held to be valid, so that was that."

"The rest of the Luvisi family must have been livid."

"Yes, especially the current signore." She threw a longing glance at the plumed tricorne. "His fields surround this estate like the arms of a crescent moon. Signor Annibale's land was scooped out from the whole centuries ago, a bequest from a Luvisi long past. If it was to be sold, it should have been offered to his cousin."

"You said Signor Annibale is still living. Is he in Venice?"

"No, my poor master had no taste for society, and he bore his family's displeasure like a millstone on his back. He left Venice and withdrew to the Capuchin monastery on Monte Rosso. As hard as it is to imagine, my proud young master is shut behind stone walls living a monk's life of solitude and hardship."

I shook my head slowly. "What a sad tale. I had no idea the Villa Dolfini possessed such a regrettable history."

"There's no reason why you should. Signora Dolfini got you and the others here to put on her opera, not stir up the past." Nita fell silent, then smoothed her apron and clasped her hands over her rounded belly, as if to signal an end to the subject. I formed the vague impression that she regretted having talked so freely. "Is there anything else I can do for you, Signore?" she asked.

"As a matter of fact…" I paused to clear my throat. "I meant to ask you in the first place—where is Giovanni? I thought he would be on duty somewhere hereabout."

"You require a footman?"

"Ah, yes. I may want him to run into the village—to the Post." I thought of all the people who expected news from me: Liya, Benito, and of course, Alessandro.

"You can leave your letters on the round table," she said, pointing into the foyer. "Old Alphonso is taking a cart into Molina Mori later this afternoon. He'll stop at the Post. All the other male servants have been drafted to help with the grape harvest."

"Grape harvest? In this weather? It's much too damp and cool."

The maid cocked her head. "You are an expert on grapes, Signore?"

"No, no. I just heard Ernesto say…" I trailed off, backing nimbly through the door of the cloakroom. Nita was clearly anxious to return to her duties and she looked quite capable of flattening me like a pancake if I blocked her path to the kitchen.

"Damp or no, the mistress wants the grapes in and the wine-making under way before her concert. The master was up at dawn giving orders and—" She paused and raised an eyebrow. "I believe you're wanted."

I heard Karl, as well. Impossible not to. He was bellowing my name like a German officer drilling his troops on the parade ground. And I'd just made a misstep.

Chapter Eight

"Think of yourselves as operatic ambassadors. After all, one has a duty to bring vocal art to these backward areas." Octavia was addressing the singers and musicians who had ranged themselves in front of the harpsichord.

Karl was the only one not staring at our hostess in wary fascination. Clutching his hands behind his back, the composer was pacing back and forth before the company with an air of a herd dog guarding his flock. "My opera simply isn't ready," he said. "Rehearsal has barely begun." He stopped directly in front of Octavia, and his eyes shifted with the look of a man in pain. "We've barely touched the third act. Why not make your neighbors wait until they return to Venice? When the opera opens, they can enjoy *Il Gran Tamerlano* as it's meant to be played, with costumes and full stage effects."

Octavia snapped her reply. "The landowners will be closing up their villas soon, yes. But where they are concerned, presenting a concert now can only work to our advantage. Consider the excitement it will generate. Signor and Signora Luvisi, the Sansovino household, and the Reniers farther down the road, they'll all return to town chattering about our amazing Turkish spectacle. I'll make sure to remind everyone that *Tamerlano* will mark Madame Fouquet's first appearance in Venice, and they'll spread the word about that, too. By the time the opera opens, people will be fighting to purchase tickets."

"Will the estate owners make up the bulk of the concert audience?" Karl asked.

Octavia gave a chuckling snort. "How many estates do you think there are in the near vicinity? The people of Molina Mori will fill most of the seats, and I can just imagine how grateful they will be to hear snatches of an opera that is quite beyond their reach. I'm told that even now my husband is receiving Mayor Bartoli—an estimable man, though his good wife dresses years behind the fashion—I'll make sure he knows about my concert before he leaves the house."

As Octavia paused for breath, her expansive smile mimicked Juno or some other ancient goddess favoring mere mortals with her noble generosity. Then her gaze lit on me, and she was once again the commander marshalling the troops for her assault on Society. "Ah, Tito, there you are. I must say, you're certainly one for wandering off. I've put you down for several arias and a duet with Madame Fouquet. Yesterday, I thought you two sang very prettily together. Let me see..." She shuffled through a clutch of papers scrawled with lists.

Fixing a mutinous eye on Octavia's lists, Karl said, "I agree that our principals complement each other. In fact, their voices blend like a braid woven from matching ribbons. Their stage mannerisms, as well. If Gabriele weren't a Frenchwoman, I would almost think she and Tito were sister and brother. But that still doesn't make *Il Gran Tamerlano* ready for performance."

A flush sprang to Grisella's wide-eyed face, and I had to clear my throat to mask a breath of surprise. Karl's impromptu remark seemed to waver in the air like a banner proclaiming news of the greatest import, but no one beside my sister and me seemed to see it. The others were all focusing on our hostess.

"Fiddle-faddle," said Octavia, actually shaking her finger at the composer. "The parts you've been rehearsing sound wonderful. You're just afraid that someone in the audience will take a liking to one of your tunes, rush back to town, and publish it as his own."

"It has happened." Karl's sepulchral tone reverberated through the salon.

"A hazard of the trade, *mio caro*. Surely, those who follow the occupation of music must learn to take such things in stride."

Several of the company gasped. The Gecco brothers traded popeyed looks.

Veins began to bulge on Karl's forehead. "Is it possible you don't understand? After all I've suffered through? Presenting another man's achievement is theft of the basest sort—"

Finally realizing she'd pushed too far, Octavia bit her lip in distress.

"My work is my life and my love," Karl flew on. "I'd rather have them take my last penny than pirate my music. Just thinking about it rips my heart in two." As if to underscore this sentiment, the composer tore his waistcoat open and beat his breast. Gold buttons ricocheted off the unyielding floor tiles.

"*Santo Dio*," Octavia exclaimed, hurrying to Karl's side. "Calm yourself, my poppet, I spoke without thinking. But you truly have nothing to get so worked up about. Not one person of my rural acquaintance possesses the skill to set down a nursery tune, much less one of your inspired scores."

All this was said as she hauled her protégé to the opposite end of the salon. They stopped at the loggia doors where Karl buried his face in his hands and swayed on his feet. Though it was scarcely past noon, the outdoor vista was as dusky as twilight. Gray clouds scudded across the piece of sky that was visible through the glass; the cheery sunlight of yesterday might never have existed.

As I watched Octavia console the composer with clumsy caresses and numerous thimble-sized glasses of cordial-water, I thought it prudent to refresh my memory about the duel that had forced our maestro to leave Italy in the first place. Naturally, I approached Carmela. While I drank at the font of all operatic gossip, the rest of the company milled about the salon, quietly speculating, gloating, or joking about the latest delay in rehearsal.

"Don't you remember, Tito?" Carmela grinned like a she-wolf drooling over a fat grouse. "The duel took place in Milan during the theater's Easter season. Maestro Weber's popularity had been gradually growing over a span of months, but when the theaters reopened after being dark for Lent, opera fever gripped the town. People went wild over his new production set on the exploits of Alexander the Great. The gazettes took to calling him the new Handel."

"How long ago was this?"

She counted on her fingers. "Must have been over six years now."

I racked my memory, not really surprised when details failed to emerge. I'd been more than a little preoccupied with murderous doings at my own opera house in Venice at the time. "Did they fight with swords or pistols?" I asked.

"Pistols."

"What led up to it?"

"Well, people were literally tripping over themselves to get into Karl's performances—the manager of the Teatro Ducale was able to auction tickets for two or three times the price printed on the playbill. Karl's success seemed assured until one evening when he jumped up from the audience and accused a rival composer of quarrying melodies from one of his productions from the previous season."

"In the middle of a performance?"

"Yes! It was one of the few nights that another composer's opera was on the bill. The Duke and his retinue were in attendance, as well as the cream of Milan aristocracy. In front of everyone, our maestro stormed the orchestra pit and dragged the offending composer from the harpsichord by the scruff of his neck. Urged on by the Milanese—you know they love a good fight even more than a good opera—the two faced each other in the open market directly in front of the theater. Their affair of honor might have passed off as a one-night wonder if they had fired pistols over each others' heads—"

"I remember now," I broke in excitedly. "It was a tragic scandal. Karl's bullet pierced his rival's chest. He staggered to the steps and collapsed under a poster advertising his opera, then bled to death affirming that every note was his and no other's. He was another German—a mere youth who had already made a name for himself as a child violinist. Pindor. No, Lindor."

"That's right. Lindor was at the beginning of his career as a composer, untried and somewhat raw, but popular. He was accustomed to traveling in aristocratic circles, and his good looks counterbalanced his musical flaws."

"Had he copied from Karl's score or not? Seems rather foolhardy to steal from a composer whose work is being staged at the same theater."

Carmela shrugged. "I wasn't there, but rumor has it that our maestro took exception to only one aria. You know how melodies stay in your head and eventually you begin to forget where they came from—it would be easy to duplicate a few phrases and not even realize it."

"Happens all the time." I nodded. "Some composers take offense, but I've never known one to become so incensed that he assassinated his rival."

"I've always liked to think that Karl was trying to aim safely above Lindor—just to make his point, you understand—and as music makers are not the best of shots, the bullet went unintentionally awry. They do say Karl fainted when he realized he'd killed the poor fellow. His supporters roused him just in time to flee and escape arrest."

"And now he's returned to Italy."

She broke into her wolf-smile one more time. "Our hostess may have managed to tempt him into Venetian territory, but I'll wager he won't take one step inside the Duchy of Milan. Some people have long memories."

"I've been wondering…" I said, casting a pointed glance across the room toward Octavia and Karl. "How did those two happen to join forces?"

Carmela fingered one of her exquisite earrings, suddenly hesitant. Then she spoke slowly, as if the words were revealing themselves through a dim mist. "I believe Karl told me they met in Switzerland, at the spa in Baden…"

"That's all?" I prodded when no elaboration was forthcoming.

Carmela lowered her voice and spoke quickly; Romeo was striding across the salon in our direction, lank wig flapping on his shoulders. "Octavia had gone to bathe in the sulfur spring, and Karl was providing musical entertainment in the pleasure garden. That's all I know for certain, though you can probably fill in the rest of their story as easily as I."

Of course. A matron with the energy of a whirling dervish, childless, largely ignored, or at best, airily placated by a husband whose passions were reserved for his factory and his farm: Octavia would not be the first to throw herself into a love affair with a moody, young artiste. How convenient that her lover also happened to possess talents that could farther her social aspirations.

And Karl: a disgraced composer reduced to competing with illuminated fountains, games of chance, fireworks displays, and other typical spa amusements. He must have died a thousand deaths dribbling his music away before the holiday makers who lent him half an ear at best. And then Lady Bountiful appeared, her purse weighed down with the profits from tons and tons of ironwork. He need only act the part of an attentive lover to gain another opportunity to stun the world, or at least Venice, with a new opera. If he was successful, doors that had been firmly shut would fly open. Impresarios would race to offer contracts.

Across the salon, a sheaf of light piercing a hole in the clouds turned the door panes to liquid gold. Octavia and Karl stood illuminated. Their story should have been as easily perceived as his sulky pout and her overweening concern. Why did I feel that I was overlooking something?

♫♫♫

A few minutes later, Vincenzo entered the salon to find us receiving our marching orders for the concert. When no one paid him the slightest attention, he crossed to the fireplace, selected a poker, and nudged the waning flames back to life. He then took up a position before the fire, warming his backside and observing the company as if we were exotic beasts rounded up for exhibition.

With scant reference to Octavia's lists, Karl assigned me two arias, one sentimental and one exceedingly florid, as well as a duet with my sister. Romeo seemed pleased with his two arias, but Emilio flushed when he received only one in addition to a duet with Carmela. As that soprano was nodding over her assigned pieces, Octavia could hold her tongue no longer.

"Why are you allowing Signora Costa to sing that lovesick aria? The mood calls for a sorrowful, lyrical touch. Her blistering plaints could melt an alpine snow. People will find it vulgar."

"I know what the mood calls for. I wrote the piece, after all."

"Well, she makes a mess of it," Octavia retorted.

Karl squeezed his eyes shut in distress, apparently tongue-tied for the moment. Romeo was not.

"The hell you say," the basso rumbled from his barrel chest. "I'll hear no words against our Carmela. There's not a finer soprano in all of Italy."

As her protector glowered, the soprano in question darted toward Octavia, shoulders hunched, airs and graces thrown aside. "You're off your head if you think I'll stand by and let you go on about my singing. What do you know? You're just a tattered old crow trying to pass herself off as a nightingale."

Romeo nodded decisively.

Octavia's chin shot out at a menacing angle, but she took a step or two backward.

Finally coming to life, Karl stepped between the women and barred the soprano's way with an outflung arm. "I'll thank you to hold your tongue, Carmela. You too, Romeo."

"I will not," Carmela flung back. "The future of your career may be dangling between your legs, but mine isn't. I could set out for Venice this minute and find another position by the end of the week. In a better production. At a better theater."

"No one wants you to leave," Karl answered more gently. "I cast you as Irene, and I would be desolated if anyone else sang that role in Venice. I need you." He gripped both of her hands in his. "But you must let me handle this. Please."

Carmela shook her head, anger still obvious, but she quickly cooled. After a few seconds' thought, she sauntered the length of the salon to a sofa where she plopped down and stared fixedly toward the loggia which was now bathed in weak sunlight. Romeo's gaze swiveled between our maestro and Carmela. I thought the big basso might join her in exile, but he stayed where he was.

Karl turned back to Octavia. Except for a twitch in his left eye, the composer's face could have been sculpted from granite. He said, "Not over ten minutes ago you promised that you wouldn't interfere."

"Do you call it interfering if someone merely makes suggestions?"

"Yes."

"Then that merely proves how much you need my guidance," she replied breezily.

Karl squeezed his eyes shut again. Perhaps he was counting to ten. I reckoned time enough to count that far and beyond before he blinked them open to say, "You've set the time and place for your concert. If I'm to direct it, I will select the pieces. And who sings them."

A cough from the fireplace forestalled Octavia's reply. Vincenzo pocketed the large watch he had been fingering and strode in among us. "Ah, my dear. I think Maestro Weber is dispensing wise counsel. If a window shatters, we call in a glazier, yes? And if a key breaks off in a lock, we seek out the locksmith."

Octavia rounded on her husband. "Vincenzo, what are you rattling on about?"

"You keep telling me you've hired a first-rate composer and musical director. Maestro Weber is the expert, *the one you chose*, so let the man get on with what he's meant to do. There are plenty of other details that require your touch. Once the grapes are in, you must organize the construction of a stage, procure seating, write out invitations…"

"Invitations!" Octavia threw up her hands and waggled her fingers in the air. "You've not let our visitors leave, have you? Oh, Vincenzo. I wanted to speak with the mayor. I'm sure I told you."

"Mayor Bartoli left some time ago, my dear. Signor Luvisi and Padre Romano, too," Vincenzo answered in his patient, good-humored way. "I saw them out through the *barchessa*. I wanted them to see the studio I've set up for Augustus."

"You and your painter," his wife retorted. "As usual, your head is too full of your own schemes to attend to my wishes."

Vincenzo stared down at his boots, calmly raising one to inspect some mud clinging to the instep. "I did put my *schemes*, as you call them, aside long enough to have one hell of a dust-up with Ernesto over the grapes. But I am sorry about the mayor. Perhaps you could write to him."

"Yes, of course. Written invitations are in order. I must make a list." Octavia's voice sank and her gaze turned inward. "No one of quality must be left out. Besides the mayor, there's Doctor Gennari and…" Her words trailed off as she bustled away.

Her new fixation did not preclude one last shot aimed at her husband, however. Pausing half-turned in the doorway, she said, "You forgot to clean your boots on the scraper, Vincenzo. That's the third time this week. Please do try and remember. The servants have more important work to do than trailing after you with a brush and dustpan." She completed her scolding with a sharp nod and was gone.

Vincenzo left, too. But not before he approached Carmela's sofa. Smiling down at the soprano, he said, "If you'll accept the opinion of a man whose ears might as well be made of flannel where music is concerned…"

She looked up, dimpling. "Please go on, Signore."

"I think you're a fine songstress—much more spirited than those whey-faced ladies who think all it takes to display passion is a bit of eyelash fluttering."

Much mollified, Carmela returned to the group at the harpsichord and declared herself "positively itching" to get on with rehearsal. With the Dolfinis out of the way, Karl was of like mind. Handing scores around, he directed the Gecco brothers to their instruments and announced Emilio and Carmela's duet that opened Act Three. "We will take some time with this," our maestro advised. "The rest of you are at liberty until after dinner."

Perhaps feeling that Carmela still required his bracing presence, Romeo threw her a moist glance of approval, seated himself at the card table, and laid out a game of solitaire. All without a word to Grisella or me.

This was the opportunity I'd been waiting for, my chance to have my sister to myself. We both had several hours free, and I'd not laid eyes on Jean-Louis all morning. To my surprise, Grisella did not immediately fall in with my suggestion of a walk.

"I'm not feeling well, Tito. It's better that I rest." She held up her book and ruffled its creamy pages. "I'm almost finished with my novel. I'll read for a bit and perhaps take a nap."

I had escorted her into the foyer. During the scene in the salon, she had held herself aloof: a silent, but fretful observer. I had noticed her left shoulder twitching and her mouth also drawing in that direction. Those signs were still in evidence, worse if anything.

"I promise I won't take you far. The sun has come out, and you may find a bit of air soothing."

She gazed up the stairs, her hands clenching the slim volume.

"Please, Grisella," I whispered. "We must talk."

"I know, but not now. Later, I promise." With an apologetic shrug, she started for the stairs.

I couldn't let her slip away so easily. Who knows when we would have this chance again? I lifted my voice a notch. "If you won't walk with me, perhaps I should ask Madame Chevrier."

"Madame Chevrier?" she echoed on a tremor.

I nodded grimly.

"Let me fetch my shawl." Ducking her chin, Grisella sped up the stairs.

Realizing that my hat and walking stick were in my room, I followed at a more leisurely pace. I retrieved those items, emerged into the second floor hall, and waited for my sister.

And waited.

Either the shawl was buried deep in her trunk or she also had some other feminine rite to perform. As I rocked back and forth on my heels, I became aware that each second of each minute was literally ticking away. The tall clock at the front of the corridor was in operation again.

I strolled over to gaze on its enameled face and the charming moonlit scene depicted in the lunette above. As a man who prided himself on his powers of observation, it piqued me that I couldn't say if it had been chiming the hours that morning or not.

"Is the old girl keeping good time?" asked a wheezy voice.

It was Alphonso, Vincenzo's valet, creeping along the strip of carpet that bisected the corridor to the east wing. I'd seen him in the halls of the villa but had not yet engaged him in conversation. He was elderly, but spry, with skin like vellum softened for binding and hooded dark eyes.

I consulted my watch. "Ten of one. Yes, we match."

He nodded appreciatively.

"Who fixed it?" I asked.

"Eh?"

I repeated my question more loudly.

"Oh, I did, Signore. This morning, while the master was busy in the vineyard. Not much to do really. The movement hadn't been harmed."

I smiled. "When did you turn from clockmaking to valeting?"

Alphonso cackled at that. "I was footman at twelve and valet at twenty-four. Never been a clockmaker but I did serve one. Andrea Cametti, in town, on the Mercerie. Do you know his shop?"

"I'm afraid I don't."

He shook his head. "You're too young to remember it, of course. Signor Cametti died twenty years back and had no son to carry on."

"Have you been with Signor Dolfini since then?"

"*Sì*, Signore. And what I don't know about anchors and ships' fittings could be written on the head of a pin." He nodded slowly. "You pick things up, can't help not to. Anchors and clocks—that's what I know."

"Are you in charge of the clock, then? Winding it as well as repairing it?"

His eyes rolled under their bulging lids. "I very well could. This old girl's a thirty-hour clock. I could wind her up every morning tight as a drum, but Ernesto claims that job by right."

From my first dinner at the villa, I remembered Octavia's diatribe on the ritual of the shutters.

"Let me guess," I said, "Ernesto winds the clock because he's always wound the clock. Ernesto's father wound it, and his father before him."

Alphonso gave a wheezy chuckle and shot me a jab of his elbow. Somehow, he managed to turn that gesture into a very proper bow as he caught sight of Grisella.

She had changed her dress. Her silk morning gown had perhaps been too flimsy for the cooler weather, even if covered by a shawl, but I couldn't stop myself noticing how the scarlet riding habit she'd exchanged it for showed off her figure to even better advantage. She had also contained her curls in a low, netted chignon. A small velvet tricorne balanced at a fetching angle completed her headgear.

As we descended to the foyer, I noticed one other thing. A purple smudge lined her upper lip. "Here." I paused at the bottom of the stairs and took out my handkerchief. "There's something on your lip, let me get it."

Grisella stood very still while I completed my operation, then turned her attention to drawing on a pair of kidskin gloves. A manufactured sneeze allowed me to turn away and take a good whiff of the purple stain before I returned my handkerchief to its pocket. I knew that smell. How could I ever forget it? When we were still all together in our house on the Campo dei Polli, I had taken many turns at spooning Grisella's elixir into her unwilling little mouth. I'd always turned up my nose at the peculiar smell, somehow sweet and acrid at the same time.

At least the medicine was doing its job. Grisella's shoulder had relaxed, and her mouth turned up only when she smiled, which she was doing now, in a languid way. Her mood seemed to have changed completely, the tensions of rehearsal conquered. My sister and I chatted about the coming concert until we had left the house, crossed the porch, and started down the drive. Then her smile took on an air of entreaty.

"So, Tito," she said. "Are you going to tell me how you found out about Louis Chevrier?"

Chapter Nine

The day was growing fair. The sun had gained enough strength to warm my cheeks, and above us, drifting clouds made an ever-changing backdrop of white on vivid cornflower blue. I paused and leaned on my stick. In the middle of the drive, with the columned façade of the villa rising behind us, I pondered how to respond to Grisella's question. Alessandro would probably advise caution, but he wasn't standing in my shoes, facing our little sister with her upturned gaze begging for an answer.

"I've had another letter from Alessandro," I replied. "He's been doing some digging. A servant who used to work for your Russian count mentioned Chevrier."

"I see." Her tone took on a hint of tartness. "Don't you mean that you and Signor Rumbolt had a letter?"

"Well…" Suddenly on the defensive, I stirred up the gravel of the drive with my stick. "Yes. Gussie is family, and also my closest friend. I would as soon keep anything from him as Annetta or Alessandro. You've felt him staring, I take it."

She nodded. "I'm accustomed to male gazes of a certain type, but your… Gussie… he's been studying me in quite a different way. Oh, Tito!" Her hand darted out to squeeze my arm. "Is he a good husband to Annetta? Is she happy? Are there children? There is so much I want to know."

I covered her softly gloved hand with my own. "Gussie is the finest husband and papa I know. He and Annetta have three children. The latest, Isabella, is still a babe in arms. Her birth was rather difficult and laid Annetta low, but she's rallying. Slowly. At least she has plenty of help at home."

Grisella's grasp tightened on my forearm. "Are you speaking of Berta?"

I looked away and found my gaze focusing on the iron gates at the bottom of the drive. My shoulders slumped as though the weight of passing years was accumulating one by one. To me, it seemed like Grisella's childhood nurse had been gone for ages, but of course, my sister had no way of knowing.

"Berta died the winter after you went away," I told her gently. "Inflammation of the lungs. She didn't suffer, if that's any comfort."

"I see," she replied dully. "I shouldn't be surprised. Berta was quite old, wasn't she?"

I nodded.

"I did hear about Papa."

"How?"

"Domenico kept some ties with Venice. He heard the news of Papa's death from one of his cronies—I don't know who—and he reported it to me with glee. Domenico never had any use for Papa." Now it was Grisella's turn to stare into the middle distance.

I shook my head dolefully as I recalled several very specific ways in which Domenico Viviani had used my father, but I kept my mouth shut. Sometimes old hurts are best not mentioned.

"What about Alessandro?" Grisella continued on a sharper note. "Did he marry or is he still the carefree sailor?"

"Alessandro surprised us all. He found a most unlikely patron, a merchant of status in Constantinople. Yusuf Ali not only took our brother into his business, but also married him to his daughter."

She dropped my arm, wide-eyed. "Alessandro turned Turk?"

"Yes. It's taken quite some getting used to, especially for Annetta. She still refuses to speak about it with anyone outside the family."

"And Alessandro has been living in Constantinople?"

I nodded. "For several years, now."

A series of emotions flashed across Grisella's countenance: doubt, puzzlement, regret, and finally annoyance.

I continued, "He used his new family's circle of acquaintances to find your grave… which in reality is someone else's grave, I suppose."

"No, I told you." She shook her head adamantly. "My grave is empty. It was meant for show only."

I stepped close and tipped her chin back so I could look directly into her eyes. This was one question that needed an answer. "Then where is the red-haired woman who died in the fire buried?"

She twisted away and began to stride toward the gates. Moving quickly, I went around her and planted myself in her path. "I truly want to help you, Grisella, but in return, I must have your full honesty."

"Who says I want your help?"

"It's obvious. You're the only reason I'm here. You refused to join the company unless Maestro Weber hired me, as well."

She stood still a moment, breathing hard and cheeks flushing. Then she said quietly, "Yes, you're right—I could never lie to you, Tito. I brought you here for a purpose."

At least she admitted it. Somewhat mollified, I spotted a bench farther down the drive, under a stand of bronzing shade trees. "Come. Let's sit. Explain what you want of me."

Dry foliage crunched under our feet as we stepped onto the lawn. I swept curling leaves from the flat stone of the bench only to find it pitted and covered with scales of ash-colored lichen. Grisella flinched away, but I took off my jacket and folded it into a cushion to protect her skirt. "Where do you want me to start?" she asked, sinking down with a ramrod straight back.

"Let's start with your husband. Is Jean-Louis actually Louis Chevrier?"

"Yes, he was born a Chevrier, in a little town in Burgundy a few miles from Dijon. You see, I'm giving you all the details. I don't want to hide anything. When my husband smuggled me out of Turkey, he thought it prudent to revert to the surname of his mother's family."

"This was necessary," I put in, "because of this Turk you told me about, the influential pasha who thinks you belong to him?"

She nodded solemnly. "Jean-Louis already had plans to put me on the stage. If my career took off as he expected, my name would become known far and wide. Using Viviani, the name I went by then, was unthinkable. Even performing as Madame Chevrier might attract some dangerous attention. Jean-Louis thought it best that we start absolutely fresh. Given all I had suffered, he wanted to make certain I would not be subjected to any further... complications."

"He thinks ahead, your Jean-Louis."

"Yes. It was he who suggested telling people I hailed from the south of France. I'd picked up some French from one of Domenico's other girls, and later, since I had no Russian, Vladimir and I spoke French almost all the time. But still, Jean-Louis insisted that the fastidious Parisians would find my command of the language lacking. If asked, I'm to say that my father was French, my mother Italian, and I grew up speaking the one tongue over the other."

"Clever as he is, Jean-Louis must be giving you some problems."

She lowered her eyes. "Have you spotted some of my bruises, then? I thought I'd covered them rather well."

"No, *cara*. Our first evening at the villa, Gussie and I overheard a couple in a violent quarrel. Since they were arguing in Italian rather than French, I thought it must be Romeo and Carmela. But now I see it must have been you and Jean-Louis. When did he turn from rescuer to tyrant?"

Her face crumpled into a mask of tragedy. "Oh, Tito, at first Jean-Louis seemed like an agent of the divinity I had practically given up praying to. Seclusion is such cruel torment. You who are free to do as you please have no idea. Time scarcely seems to move at all, and each day seems like a month. When I was with Vladimir, he at least allowed me to have music lessons and took me to European gatherings on occasion, but I knew that once I was shut up in a Turk's household, I could well spend the rest of my life behind the same four walls." She held a fist to her brow as if to drive away the very thought.

"And once you had escaped…"

"I've learned that Jean-Louis never takes a step or utters a word which will not bring him profit. Since he risked his neck to get me out of Constantinople, he is determined that my voice will make his fortune. He seems to forget that I am flesh and blood. He's become a demon who controls my every move—a greedy, insatiable demon. If it were possible, he'd have me singing every hour of the day and night."

"Your freedom was dearly bought."

She nodded, and then leaned so close that I could feel the heat from her body. Her shadowed eyes seemed to take over her pale face. "Do you remember the fits that plagued my childhood?"

"Yes. I've noticed your shoulder twitching. It doesn't seem to happen while you're singing."

"No, music is my release. When I'm well-rested and able to focus, it sinks into my skin and my sinews and limbs like a magical balm. Only then am I at peace."

I nodded, understanding. For singer and audience alike, music is a potent charm. It has cured me of despair many a time.

She continued, "Otherwise, if I'm to keep the fits in bounds, I need my elixir. And to sing well, I need to take proper care of my voice. But Jean-Louis won't allow it. In Paris, he arranged subscription concerts for every night I wasn't performing at the Opera. In the afternoons he dragged me to fashionable salons where he hoped my songs would be rewarded with nice presents—which he promptly sold."

"I'm surprised he allowed you to come to the villa."

"*Il Gran Tamerlano* fits perfectly into Jean-Louis' plans. It is only the luck of the wretched that it fits into mine. Jean-Louis is determined to keep on the move. He believes Paris will eventually grow tired of me. He plans to conquer Venice, Milan, Naples. Then on to London. But, Tito, I'll never make it." She touched her throat with the tips of her fingers. "The more exhausted I become, the harder it is to control my spasms. And my voice will never hold up under this wear and tear. There've been times already when I've strained my vocal cords and can't sing a note. Jean-Louis' answer to that is to beat me with his cane and lock me in our bedroom until I'm fit to go back to the stage."

I'd seen it many times: young singers and dancers forced to perform by stage-mad mothers, women driven by husband-managers whose greed knew no bounds. If you wanted to avoid rifts with your fellow singers, you learned to ignore it. But this was my sister who was being abused.

"What do you want me to do?" I asked quietly.

Pretty head cocked to one side, my sister studied me in silence for several minutes. A breeze rustled the dying foliage above us, and leaves began to float down. Some traveled in pairs, others alone. As they hit ground, they mimicked the sound of a light rain.

All at once Grisella threw herself onto my chest. On a sob, she murmured, "Take me home, Tito."

I heard her words, but I made her repeat them.

"Home, Tito." She took my hand and bathed it with her tears. "More than anything in the world, I want us all to be together in Venice like we used to be."

Women's tears have always cast a spell on me. Sitting on that bench with the breeze ruffling my hair and Grisella's French fragrance in my nostrils, I had only to close my eyes to be transported to our sitting room in Venice.

In my beautiful vision, both our wanderers were home. Annetta, Alessandro, Grisella and I talked happily before the crackling stove. Our mother's kind smile beamed down on us from the portrait above the harpsichord, and in the background, Liya and Gussie stood together nodding.

Though my doubts on certain matters were by no means assuaged, I returned my sister's hug. "There now," I whispered. "Everything will be all right. Trust yourself to me. I'll find a way to bring you home."

She pushed away, and a smile fought its way through her tears. "I have your word?"

"You may depend on it," I replied, placing my hand on my heart. "Consider me your champion."

"You'll stand up to Jean-Louis?"

I sighed. Considering the difficulties that lay ahead, I'd uttered brave words. Though Grisella had left Venice almost ten years ago, the scandal that surrounded her and Domenico Viviani had not been forgotten. But first things first. "As far as Jean-Louis is concerned," I finally replied, "he is your husband and the law gives him certain rights."

"Not really." She gave me a perky glance.

"What are you saying?"

"Jean-Louis and I never married. We intended to, but after leaving Turkey we kept on the move for several months. Once we reached Paris, the proper occasion never seemed to present itself. Though I call him husband, I'm not really a wife, merely a mistress. So—" she finished lightly, "there's another secret I'm asking you to keep. At least for now."

I nodded unhappily. Grisella's secrets were piling up almost as quickly as my questions about her recent past. I glanced around. As we were still quite alone in the far-reaching autumn landscape, it seemed like a good time to return to those questions. But my sister had grown restless. She stood up and shook the leaves from her skirts, saying, "I must get back to the house. Jean-Louis will be returning soon."

"Where did he go?"

"He went into Molina Mori to conduct some business."

I cocked an eyebrow. What business could he have in such an insignificant, out-of-the-way village where he knew no one?

Grisella took my meaning and shrugged. "I don't know, but he'll have my head if he sees me walking out in the cool air." Then she flashed a smile that could have lit up the top tier of the San Marco opera house. "But not for long. You'll soon send him packing, won't you, Tito? Today, I've gone from the most wretched to the happiest of women. I knew I did right by coming here. I knew my wonderful brother would save me."

I stood up, too. "You can surely make time to answer one question, Grisella."

She retrieved my folded jacket, wiped away the bits of debris, and handed it to me with a sidelong glance. "Of course," she said. "Ask it while we walk."

Her little feet moved quickly. After throwing on my jacket, I was forced to break into a trot to overtake her. "The other red-haired girl at the *yali* in Constantinople—who was she?" I asked.

"I don't know who you're talking about, Tito. I was the only woman in Vladimir's household."

"Alessandro talked to a servant named Sebboy. Do you remember him?"

"Yes," she replied, forging toward the house, staring straight ahead.

I briefly summarized what Sebboy had reported to Alessandro.

That news stopped my sister in her tracks. She turned abruptly, and a gruff voice I hadn't heard for many years rumbled from her throat. "Did Sebboy tell the Russians I escaped the fire?"

"No."

She gave a barely audible sigh. "Well, then there's no cause for worry."

"Sebboy's story suggests that a girl who could have been your double died in the fire. Doesn't that raise a few worries for you?"

She didn't answer, but started walking again, more slowly this time. I kept silent. When we reached the wide, stone steps leading up to the portico, she paused and faced me with one hand to her forehead. Shading her eyes as if the sun that only peeked from behind the clouds were blinding her, she said, "I only know what Jean-Louis told me. When I ran from the *yali*, the fire was still raging. Searching that strange city for Jean-Louis was my final bid for freedom, and I can assure you it was no easy matter. By the time I found him, I was nearly perished with fear and exhaustion."

She bit her lip, and then continued, "He handed me over to his landlady, a sweet, dutiful Christian woman. She tended to me while he hurried to make arrangements. When we sailed out of the Golden Horn a day or two later, I was in such a state of collapse, I barely knew my own name. If there was any deception over the grave, put it down to Jean-Louis, not me."

Imagining the terrors my sister must have faced raised my protective instincts to new heights, but a further, disconcerting thought rapidly followed. "Sebboy said that the Russians who came to the *yali* were interested in where Count Paninovich stored his valuables. What do you suppose—"

Grisella stopped me with a violent shake of her head. Her tears had begun to flow again. "Oh, Tito, don't ask. It's all such a blur. If you knew everything I've endured, you would understand. Please don't press me for answers I don't have." She stroked my cheek and whispered, "Now I must compose myself before Jean-Louis returns. *Adieu* for now, dear brother. You know how much I'm counting on you."

She kissed her gloved fingertips and, after touching them to my lips in a feather-light caress, hurried into the house.

♫♫♫

I would have welcomed a glass of brandy. But getting a drink meant going back into the increasingly contentious confines of the villa. I could stomach only so much of Octavia's musical pretensions, our maestro's moods, and the wall of indifference concerning the murder in our midst. Body? What body? If we ignore it, perhaps it will go away, had become the unspoken rule.

Preferring the open air, I again set off down the drive. I'd made a sacred promise, given Grisella my word. Now I had to assess what I'd let myself in for.

The world at large held the women of my city in low repute, and I had to admit that many of Venice's fair daughters did behave very badly. There was no arguing that my city's famed courtesans were among the prime attractions for the foreign visitor. Behind the dazzling façade of our prolonged Carnevale, however, there existed legions of respectable wives and widows who functioned as exacting judges in the court of public opinion. The irregular marriage I'd forged with Liya had already run afoul of their standard-bearers. Once I brought the infamous Grisella home, it would be a wonder if our neighbors ever spoke to any of us again.

I reckoned that Annetta could weather the storm. When she realized that our little sister was safe and well, she would be beside herself with a joy that no amount of social embarrassment could dampen. A new spring came into my steps as I imagined Gussie and me ushering Grisella through our door. Her miraculous return might be just the tonic that would restore Annetta to her old self.

My steps slowed again when I thought of Jean-Louis. One look at the Frenchman would tell you that he was not a man to be trifled with. Though he had no advantage of breeding or education, he clearly possessed animal cunning backed by an uncompromising will. Jean-Louis had invested a great deal in Grisella. Once he realized she meant to return to her family, he would fight tooth and nail to keep her.

I paused in the middle of the drive, drawing in a deep breath of crisp September air, and suddenly realized that I was headed the wrong way. What I needed above all was to talk the whole business over with Gussie, and he was in the vineyard making sketches of the workers bringing in the grapes. I swung right and left, trying to figure the shortest route across the fields, until the sight of an unexpected onlooker gave me a start.

The front gates lay fifty strides away, curving stanchions of wrought iron set into a five-foot stone wall. The gates were closed, but at this time of day, probably not locked. The woman standing in the public road on the other side could hardly have been described as menacing. Short and slim, she seemed hardly larger than a child. She wore a short brown cloak over a plain blue gown, and a lank coil of yellow hair dusted one shoulder.

It must have been the suddenness of her appearance that unnerved me. Or perhaps the intensity of her gaze. Beneath her unseasonable straw hat, dark eyes shone above a blunt nose and meager, unsmiling mouth.

Curious, I started forward only to see her turn and hasten away. Her boots kicked up her skirt as she passed from sight. Who was this solemn little creature? Not a peasant. And certainly not a Venetian. If my brief moment of observation was at all telling, she could have been a companion or governess of the sort English or German families always seemed to have in tow. Perhaps she was a guest at a neighboring estate and was merely taking a walk. Word of the murder had spread; she might have been curious to view the site of the grisly deed. Whoever she was, she had nothing to do with me.

I decided to skirt the east side of the villa and take the garden path that led to the bridge over the ornamental lake. Once on the other side, beyond the cypress trees, I passed a rambling cottage. Its walls were washed a pale corn yellow, and its red roof wasn't missing a single tile. A lovingly tended vegetable plot crowned with drooping sunflowers spread out to one side. Ernesto's house, I'd been told. Except for several chickens scratching in the dirt, it was deserted.

Ten more minutes of brisk walking took me past a few tenant houses and then to the vineyard. While the rest of the estate drowsed in the afternoon sun, these trellised rows hummed with activity. Ernesto had obviously hired extra labor. A bevy of harvesters moved along the vines, bending and stooping. Knife blades flashed, and shallow, oval baskets received dusky clusters of blue-black grapes. A festive atmosphere reigned. Many of the men and woman were singing in unison, a sprightly old tune to make the work go faster.

I spotted Ernesto's son Manuel picking at the end of one row. Now that I had met Pia, I could see where his soft, brown eyes and swelling cheeks came from. The curly haired boy beside him could only be his brother Basilio; he was the spitting image of their father, right down to his broad shoulders and proud carriage. Zuzu, the big white dog who was never far from her two young masters, padded up and down the row snapping at the bees swarming to taste the sweet, fragrant produce. Manuel saw me watching and waved.

I returned his greeting and moved along to find Gussie sketching an ox-cart bearing a large, open container. Ernesto was on the ground, Santini astride the bed of the cart. Balancing heaping baskets on their heads, the workers conveyed their loads to the steward for inspection. Ernesto tossed any clusters that didn't meet his exacting standards on a waste pile. At his nod, the workers then handed their baskets up to Santini who tipped shining streams of grapes into the container. His stained shirt clung to his back and chest, and the sticky juice rolling down his forearms and cheeks made it appear as if his sweat had turned to purple.

Gussie was also hard at work: all concentration, tongue between his teeth, gaze flicking up and down. I peered over his shoulder at the gray page. In animated strokes of red and white chalk, he captured the rough-coated, muscular oxen as they patiently waited to haul the precious cargo to the house. Then he traded his chalk for a pencil and jotted some notes in the corner.

"What are you writing?" I asked.

"Measurements. Notes on color for when I start painting."

"When will that be?"

"Soon, I hope. Vincenzo has settled on twelve different scenes."

"Can you finish them all before the opera is ready for Venice?"

"Probably not, but I can get them to the point where I can finish up in my studio at home." As he spoke, Gussie tore the top sheet off his sketching block and slipped it in his portfolio. Only then did he give me his full attention. "What have you been up to this morning, Tito? You look as if you're about to burst."

"There are a few things I'd like to talk to you about," I said carefully, watching the grape pickers line up for Ernesto's inspection. Giovanni and the other footmen were joking with the farm workers in easy familiarity as they waited. The harvest must provide a welcome distraction from their regular duties. "Are you coming in to dinner?"

Gussie shook his head. "Can't. I need to do some figure studies. Vincenzo is most particular that nothing is missed."

"You must eat."

"Have you ever known me to go hungry?" He smiled and patted his sturdy mid-section. "I'll eat with the workers. I'm told they have quite a spread when the day's work is done."

"Where is Vincenzo anyway? I'd expect him to be right in the middle of all this."

"He's at the house, in the cantina. The crushing of his grapes seems to interest him more than the picking." Gussie finished with a knowing wink that told me he'd say more if we were alone.

"What?" I whispered.

He shook his head a fraction of an inch. "Just stop by the cantina before dinner. I'll be interested to hear your impressions."

I returned to the villa on the rutted dirt path employed by the ox-cart. It led around the west side of the great lawn and skirted the stable yard and kitchen garden before bringing me to the house. The cantina was on the ground floor, down a gently sloping ramp. I had to mind my footing; many years of rolling barrels had formed a trough-like depression down the center.

At the bottom of the ramp, a planked door stood invitingly open. I stepped inside. Scores of lamps and candles illuminated a red-brick chamber. Vaulted bays stacked with oak casks pierced the walls, and containers of grapes waited to be added to the stomping vat at the opposite end of the cantina. As I crossed the flagstones coated with purple juice, the soles of my shoes stuck with each step.

Vincenzo acknowledged me with a nod as I joined him at the raised, knee-high vat. Romeo and Jean-Louis had also come down to watch the stomping. The Frenchman must have returned from his mysterious errand while I was in the vineyard. I itched to ask him where he'd been, but the look he sent me over his beaked nose discouraged questions. Though I knew it to be impossible, it was almost as if he'd found out that I was planning to carry his breadwinner off to Venice.

I took a deep breath. The cantina air was cool and damp, concentrating the scent of the fruit until it was almost overpowering. A slurry of grapes, juice, stems, and skins filled the vat to within two handbreadths of the top. Everyone was watching Pia move through the cloying stew in slow, continuous circles. She raised her knees high and brought her feet down with mindful intensity. Several other stompers had removed their shoes and were awaiting their turns.

Despite the hard work Pia seemed to be enjoying herself. Her cheeks glowed, and curls of black hair escaped her kerchief and plastered themselves to her neck. To free her legs, she'd pulled the back hem of her bright green skirt to the front and tucked it firmly into her waistband. The pliant flesh of her bare thighs emerged from the folds of cloth around her hips and gleamed with sweat. The graceful curves of her calves were stained a reddish-purple.

Now I knew what Gussie had meant me to see. Not Pia, but Vincenzo watching Pia. Our host was positively drooling.

♫♫♫

It was late that evening before Gussie and I had a chance to talk. He had thrown himself on his bed in our room, boots crossed at the ankle and hands behind his head.

"It's as plain as that crack on the ceiling, Tito. Vincenzo loves playing the country gentleman, but if it weren't for Pia he would be content to return to Venice when all the other landowners leave their villas for the cold season."

"She does present a certain earthy charm," I replied. I was at the table attempting to darn the toe of a stocking by flickering lamplight. Saying that Benito's presence was sorely missed would be a gross understatement.

Gussie rose up on one elbow. "A certain charm? Upon my word, is that all you can say? I find her nothing short of magnificent. I wonder if Vincenzo has bedded her. Would he dare…?" He sank back into the pillow and stared meditatively at the ceiling.

"Dare Octavia's wrath, you mean? I think he's accustomed to that. What complaint could she make, after all, while she dangles Karl like a fish on her line for everyone to admire?"

"Actually, it was Ernesto's wrath I had in mind. I've been watching him. Though each crop demands a different set of skills and knowledge, he manages them all quite competently. He must also cope with the motley collection of workers attached to the estate. I talked to one poor fellow who sneezes whenever he gets near hay, whether in the field or stable. Ernesto has put him in charge of the olives. When there are no duties in the olive grove, he picks mushrooms in the forest. I could give you a hundred other examples. My point is that despite Vincenzo's bumbling interference, Ernesto has this estate running like a piece of finely tuned clockwork. Quite proud of it all, is our Ernesto."

I nodded, stretching the stocking over my fingers to check my needlework. "Yet he is never impertinent," I said. "Though he must be seething over the early grape harvest, he's carrying out Vincenzo's orders to the letter."

"So far Ernesto's patience seems to outweigh his frustrations," Gussie agreed, "but if the steward caught the master of the villa with his wife, I'd hate to witness the result."

"You believe Ernesto is capable of violence?"

Gussie thought for a long moment. "Who knows? Let's just hope we never have the occasion to find out."

I was thinking, too, remembering the evening Vincenzo had stolen into the villa while the others were playing blind man's bluff. Had an assignation with Pia been the cause of his uncommonly jaunty mood? By the time Gussie and I had calculated the potential consequences of such a mismatched romance in all its ribald and tragic permutations, the clock in the corridor was striking eleven.

"Where did the time go?" I exclaimed. "I still need to tell you about Grisella."

Gussie sat up and swung his legs down to the floor. I tossed my darning aside to perch on the opposite bed and recount all. In the main, my brother-in-law reacted to the idea of installing

Grisella on the Campo dei Polli much better than I'd hoped. His first concern was any negative effect her presence might have on our houseful of youngsters. As a new father to Liya's son, I'm ashamed to say that I hadn't so much as considered that question. In the end, it was the possibility of raising Annetta's spirits that carried the day.

"All right." Gussie made a rueful face. "I agree that Grisella has a rightful place in our home… as long as she behaves herself. Now tell me how you propose to handle Jean-Louis."

"Honestly," I answered, slapping my hands on my knees. "Grisella's life in Turkey was fraught with falsehood and deception. If she's to start a new life with us, she'll have to agree to truth and plain speaking. We'll begin by facing Jean-Louis together, with Grisella admitting that I'm her brother."

Gussie rubbed his jaw. With a frown, he said, "A noble plan, Tito, but I don't know if it's the best way to handle that canny Frenchman. Jean-Louis wouldn't respect the truth if it jumped up and bit him in the nose."

"Well, what do you advise?" I countered.

Instead of answering, Gussie tipped his head back to study the crack in the ceiling once again. I didn't press my question, and we soon readied ourselves for sleep and extinguished the lamp.

Thus passed the last day of relative calm at the Villa Dolfini. When we awoke early the next morning, the fire was dead and Ernesto had not yet made his rounds. To quell the darkness, Gussie opened our shutters himself. Swathed in quilted dressing gowns that barely kept the room's chill at bay, we gazed out on a mist-shrouded landscape. Across the sloping fields, the trees I knew to be dressed in their red and gold finery were hulking gray shapes. All was still. The villa could have been a galleon sailing through a sea of fog, far from any civilized shore.

Neither of us had slept well or long enough. We moved about our room with heavy-lidded eyes, barely speaking, seeing to small personal tasks while we waited for a footman to bring hot water. Five or ten minutes must have passed when we were startled to full wakefulness by a loud exclamation of surprise. We streaked into the corridor to find Alphonso, Vincenzo's valet, planted open-mouthed before the long-case clock.

The timepiece had again stopped ticking. The door to its case was ajar, and a quick glance told me the aperture was empty. Above, the brass hands pointed straight to heaven, a double-tipped arrow poised in flight.

Midnight.

Chapter Ten

"Is this someone's poor idea of a joke?" asked Alphonso, gazing at the clock in bewilderment.

"I pray that it is," I replied.

The valet threw me a puzzled look.

"Consider the alternative." I jerked my chin toward the patch of carpet where the Russian had been dumped. A cold queasiness rippled through my empty stomach.

"*Dio mio*," Alphonso exclaimed, quickly making the sign of the cross.

"Has your master risen?" Gussie asked.

The elderly man shook his head. "No one is up and about besides the servants."

"Get him," Gussie ordered. "We'll wake the others."

We pounded on doors, Gussie taking the east side of the corridor and I the west.

In an eerie encore of the scene from the night Carmela's screams had awakened us, the villa's inhabitants poured from their rooms with candles held aloft. Half-clothed or shrugging into dressing gowns, they demanded to be told what was going on, some in hushed whispers, some in rampant bluster.

"The clock has stopped," I cried.

Emilio tied the sash of his wrinkled banyan with a peevish shrug. "Is that any reason to make such a racket? I'd hoped to catch a few winks before that bear comes through to open the shutters."

"See for yourself," I replied. "The clock reads midnight and the pendulum is missing."

Looks of dismay were traded around as Alphonso returned with a strained-looking Vincenzo. While the master of the villa examined the clock, Romeo realized that our company was one member short. "Where is Carmela?" he loudly demanded.

Our collective attention immediately shifted to the soprano's closed door.

Romeo took two long steps and flattened his palm against the stout oak. Over his resounding smacks, he called, "Carmela, *carissima*, open up."

The door remained shut.

"Go in," someone urged.

Romeo put his hand to the knob, then reddened. "Perhaps I shouldn't. She might be in her bath… or indisposed."

"A fine time for delicacy," Mario Gecco said with a laugh. "She's given you a noisy romp in her bed practically every night we've been here."

His brother Lucca poked him in the ribs, and Grisella started to giggle. The others joined in, grateful for some small release from the growing tension.

"This is ridiculous," Octavia exclaimed, pushing her sleeves up as she strode forward. "Signora Costa isn't in her bath. The footmen haven't brought the water or stirred up the fires. Stand aside."

She threw the door open and passed through. Romeo stepped in behind her, and I pushed Emilio aside to be next. The others followed or congregated in the doorway.

"She's not here," Octavia said shakily.

"We need more light," cried Romeo as he opened windows and threw back the shutters. The early morning sun filtering through the mist bathed the furniture and bed hangings in an opalescent glow, but there was still no Carmela.

I could detect no overt signs of struggle. The pier-glass hanging between the windows, as well as all the other smaller mirrors, was unbroken. A slender brass candlestick sat unmolested on a light tripod table that a hearty sneeze could have overturned.

And not one jar on the crowded dressing table had spilled its contents.

It also appeared that the soprano had left the room before retiring for the night. Her counterpane was drawn up tightly under the bolster at the bed's carved headboard. Neatly draped across it lay her ruffled nightshift. The muslin gaily sprigged with yellow rosebuds lent a personal touch to the austere four-poster.

Even as my eyes swept the contents of Carmela's chamber, I took careful note of my companions' reactions. Romeo was beside himself. His cheeks shone bright red, and he had lost his nightcap so that his short brown hair stood on end like a dome of needles. He was gripping Vincenzo's arm, demanding that a search party be organized at once.

Jean-Louis' emotions occupied the opposite end of the scale. The Frenchman slouched against the doorjamb, shoeless but clad in stockings, breeches, and a full-sleeved shirt of expensive linen. Like the other men who had been waiting on their shaving water, his chin was dark with stubble. He was rubbing a thumb back and forth through his whiskers and observing the proceedings in a detached manner, as though solving a riddle or adding a column of figures in his head. Grisella's huge eyes peered around his shoulder. Curious, but not frightened, I thought.

My gaze slid to Emilio, who was unsuccessfully attempting to calm Romeo. The castrato seemed more worried over his roommate's distress than Carmela's disappearance. The Gecco brothers had pasted grim expressions on their faces, but as they whispered between themselves, I nevertheless formed the impression that they were speculating on how long breakfast would be delayed.

As usual, Karl held himself aloof from his fellow musicians. Under his riotously patterned banyan and nightcap, the composer was pale and trembling. Octavia hovered at a discreet distance, casting glances that seemed to confer a steadying influence. Just once, she reached out so that her fingertips barely brushed his shoulder; an inscrutable quaver passed over Karl's thin face.

Vincenzo occupied the center of the room. A heavy frown creased his brow and he was staring at the floor. Just as I concluded that he lacked the will to confront this new crisis, Vincenzo raised his chin, dusted his palms, and briskly assured Romeo that Carmela would be found. Then he called to Alphonso in the corridor, "Are all the other servants downstairs?"

"Yes, Signore."

"Right then, we must proceed in a logical fashion. We'll split our forces and search every—"

Before Vincenzo could finish, the sounds of running feet sounded in the corridor. Giovanni and another footman burst into the room, terror on their faces. "Ernesto says you must come, Signore! Right away!"

"What is it?" Octavia and Vincenzo cried in tandem.

Giovanni shook his head wildly. "Something in the cantina. Ernesto wouldn't let us go down. He sent us to fetch you."

Vincenzo rushed for the stairs, motioning the footmen to accompany him. To everyone else, he threw over his shoulder, "Stay up here, all of you. Go to your rooms."

"I'll be damned," said Romeo and broke into a sprint.

The rest of us followed like a herd of startled sheep—down the stairwell so low its ceiling brushed the top of my head, across an uncarpeted hallway, and into another tight stairwell. A right turn, and a left, and then a blast of warm air met my face as we entered the kitchen. Copper pots bubbled on a hearth set before a huge fireplace, and the long worktable was covered with stoneware bowls, heaps of vegetables, the skinned carcasses of several rabbits.

Across the room, a brick arch framed Nita and the two young maids. The girls were gabbling in whispers and twisting their aprons, one with tears running down her face. "Stop your foolishness, Bettina," Nita was saying. "I know no more than you do, so it's no good going on with your questions." The nervous trio scurried back at the sight of their master and his motley entourage.

Beyond the arch, a passageway with a short flight of steps led down to the cantina. After a heartbeat of hesitation, Vincenzo plunged ahead. In my haste to keep up, I tripped over the hem of my dressing gown and tumbled into Emilio.

He shoved me back on balance with a rough hand. "You don't always have to be first, Amato. We'll all see soon enough."

See we did, and it was a sight I won't soon forget. Carmela lay half-submerged in the stomping vat, her shoulders propped against the far rim and her head lolling to one side. Long tendrils of her unbound hair floated on the surface of the grape slurry, and the discolored fabric of her skirt billowed in violet hillocks. By virtue of a trio of bows that decorated her sleeves, I recognized the dress as one of her loose morning gowns.

The juice had stained the soprano's face with livid purple blotches so that I didn't at first notice the dark, reddened pulp where her hairline met her forehead. Had a bash on the head felled her? Her mouth was agape in a circle of surprise, and her eyes seemed frozen in the desperate gaze of a drowning woman.

I looked away, sickened, but an urgent memory forced me to look right back. Yes, they were still there: a beautiful pearl gleamed at each ear.

"Get her out!" Vincenzo ordered. "You, Giovanni. And you, Adamo." The footmen shuffled toward the vat. Neither seemed to want to be the first to touch the corpse.

Ernesto stepped over the rim with a look that clearly asked, Must I do everything myself? The footmen reluctantly followed, staining their white stockings as dark as their blue livery. After much slipping and sliding, the three of them lifted Carmela from her ghastly bath and laid her on the flagstoned floor.

Sobbing unabashedly, Romeo bent on one knee and tried to wipe his lover's face clean with the hem of his nightshirt. I'd never seen the big fellow so moved. The other musicians gathered close behind him, frightened, astonished, whispering among themselves. I noted that Octavia had the presence of mind to test the door to the outside ramp. It was locked from the inside.

Meanwhile, Ernesto had returned to the brick platform that supported the stomping vat. Bending at a sharp angle, he plunged his arm into the liquid mixture and raked it back and forth. "Ah," he said, "I thought my foot slipped on something that shouldn't be in a wine vat."

He brought up the clock pendulum and held it aloft. In the flickering candlelight, the horrified company gazed at the juice sluicing off the brass disk and hitting the floor in noisy plops.

Giovanni had noticed something else. "*Scusi*, Signore," he said to Vincenzo. "But what is that?" The footman pointed to a chink in the bricks at the foot of the vat. A paper folded into quarters and splotched with purple stood up from the crack.

Vincenzo bent to retrieve the paper, carefully peeled the corners back, and studied it for a long moment. I was close enough to see some sort of message written there, not formed in a running hand, but in the blocky letters of a child or the barely educated.

Vincenzo looked up and gazed at us in uneasy amazement. In a quiet, but forceful voice, he ordered, "Get dressed. We'll gather in the salon in half an hour."

♫♫♫

"I must speak with you. Meet me in the cantina at midnight."

Vincenzo's ominous tones filled the salon as he read the missive found by the stomping vat. Then, he sliced the paper through the air like a battle flag. "Someone connected with the villa lured Carmela to her death with this note, and I mean to find out who. Captain Forti may hunt boar until Judgment Day, but that doesn't force me to shelter a murderer on my land. I'll deliver the guilty culprit to justice myself."

If Vincenzo's response to the Russian's murder had been a bit tepid, the discovery of Carmela's body had raised his indignation to a white-hot heat. This mild man who tended to avoid conflict at all costs seemed personally affronted that a killer's violent passion had once again invaded his well-ordered estate. In our own way, each of us was similarly affected. For me, it was the difference between tripping over the body of a stranger and coming face to face with the gruesome death of someone you've come to know and admire.

Nita had served coffee. It was an excellent brew, but the ten of us gathered under Vincenzo's gimlet stare sipped at our cups with little enthusiasm.

As we watched from a semi-circle of sofas and chairs, Vincenzo paced before the unlit fireplace. He said, "Ernesto has told me that he rose before sunrise. After seeing to a few duties connected with the harvest, he entered the front door of the villa at a quarter past seven. Instead of immediately opening the shutters in his usual ritual, he went down to inspect the cantina."

Vincenzo paused and rocked back on his heels. "We know what Ernesto found. What I want to learn is who last saw Carmela alive."

All eyes turned toward Romeo. The basso was the only one among us who had not dressed. He made a pitiful figure as he slumped in his chair with his dressing gown hanging open and his nightshirt streaked with purple and red.

"Carmela and I came up together last night," he said hoarsely. "Around ten o'clock. We passed a few words and then said goodnight at her door."

"Are you certain?"

"Yes, the clock was striking ten."

"I mean to say, are you certain that you stopped at her door?"

Romeo eyed Vincenzo coldly. "Absolutely certain. Carmela insisted. She was feeling tired and meant to go straight to bed. She was going to call a maid to unlace her gown. So you see, I wasn't the last person in the villa to see her alive. You had better talk to the maids."

"I intend to," Vincenzo replied. "Nita is gathering the indoor servants downstairs, and Ernesto is rounding up everyone from around the estate. All will be questioned in due time." He surveyed our group with a lifted brow. "Now, did anyone else see Carmela after ten o'clock?"

"Wait," Romeo cried. "Where is Carmela now?"

"I had her remains taken to the ice house," Vincenzo replied gently. "Ernesto's wife will bathe her and dispose of her filthy garments. Before she's wrapped in her winding sheet, she must be examined more thoroughly than we were able to in the cantina."

Romeo sprang up. "I must protest. I won't have you pawing all over her."

"Simmer down, young man. I don't propose to examine her myself. In the absence of the official constable, I sent Alphonso to summon Mayor Bartoli. I've also requested that he bring back Doctor Gennari. It appears the unfortunate lady was struck with the pendulum, but I want to make certain there are no other wounds."

Gussie and I traded glances. In the privacy of our room, we had engaged in a heated debate over whether to reveal the true cause of the Russian's death. While it pained my usually forthright brother-in-law to remain silent, we finally agreed that Captain Forti was the only one we should tell. At this point, I trusted no one besides Gussie. The feeling was mutual.

Romeo sank back into his chair and seemed to drift into his private grief. As no one volunteered that they'd had contact with Carmela after Romeo left her at her door, Vincenzo demanded that everyone account for their whereabouts at the stroke of midnight.

Jean-Louis was the first to assert that he'd been in bed with his wife, fast asleep. Grisella agreed with a silent nod. As might be expected, we all made a similar report.

I thought Vincenzo's gaze hardened as Karl described drowsing over a pile of scores he was copying. The composer looked white and tense, but he stuck fast to his tale, and Vincenzo didn't challenge it openly. Instead, he announced his intention to descend to the servants' dining room off the kitchen.

Octavia stopped him with a high-pitched clearing of her throat. "Vincenzo, dear, I certainly hope this unfortunate business isn't going to interfere with my concert."

"Your concert?" Vincenzo repeated with a look of outright disbelief.

Karl's deep-set eyes were blazing like coals. "Octavia, you can't mean to go ahead with the concert after what happened to Carmela."

Octavia twisted uncomfortably. "Please don't think me harsh, but really, canceling my concert can't possibly help poor Signora Costa. Why not proceed as planned?"

"My dear, I should think all plans concerning the concert and even the opera itself are at a standstill for the present," Vincenzo said quietly.

"Impossible!" Octavia started from her seat and took a few running steps toward her husband. "The theater has been booked and the opera must be played."

"By all means," a new voice chimed in. Jean-Louis left Grisella and strode to Octavia's side. "Signora Dolfini is absolutely correct. Contracts are in force for all of us. If we hadn't come to Italy, my wife could have had a lucrative run in Paris. This neighborhood concert is of little importance to us one way or the other, but the production of *Il Gran Tamerlano* is a different matter. The opera must go on or..." He finished with a very Gallic shrug.

"Or what?" Vincenzo asked.

"I believe you have some excellent lawyers in Venice," the Frenchman replied, locking gazes with his host.

"You would bring suit against us?"

Jean-Louis nodded solemnly. "I must look out for my wife's interests."

Karl had been listening carefully, chewing at a thumb nail. He asked, "Without Carmela, how can we go on with rehearsals? Who will sing the part of Irene?"

Octavia hazarded a small smile. "Since that terrible scene in the cantina, I've thought of nothing else. One soprano has been cruelly taken from us, and of course, nothing must be spared to find her killer. My husband and the authorities will see to that, I have no doubt. But meanwhile, someone must fill Signora Costa's shoes..." Here she paused to strike a pose with one arm held aloft in a dramatic gesture. "Fortunately, a trained soprano stands before you."

I thought Karl's eyes might pop from his head. A strange choking noise between a growl and a cough issued from his throat. Finally he managed to spit out, "You're mad. Stark staring mad."

"What?" shrieked Octavia. "Really, Karl, you go too far. I may be an amateur, but my voice can be counted as first-rate. Maestro Vivaldi once heard me at a musical evening and couldn't stop talking about my performance."

Emilio sat up tall, curiosity piqued. "What did the great maestro say?"

"The red priest said he'd never heard a voice to equal mine. He seemed quite overcome," Octavia answered, smiling again.

Gussie leaned toward me with a mischievous twinkle in his eyes. He whispered, "Maestro Vivaldi must have been commenting on the volume."

Suppressing a smile, I put a finger to my lips. I'd been watching a struggle play out on Karl's face: the inherent honesty of the artist vied with the subterfuge forced on vassals of all sorts. The artist won out.

"My music," the composer stated, proudly facing Octavia, "is quite beyond your reach."

While Octavia gazed at her paramour like a dog who'd been kicked by a gentle master, Jean-Louis spread his hands in a conciliatory gesture. "Maestro Weber," he said smoothly, "I see a possible compromise here. Perhaps our talented hostess could oblige us until a professional singer can be summoned from Venice. Signora Dolfini would sing Irene's parts in the concert, the professional in the finished production."

"Now wait just a minute." Emilio was on his feet this time. "That means I'll have to rehearse all my pieces with two different sopranos. That's double the work. That's hardly fair. Tito, Romeo, Gabrielle, it will be the same for you. What do you say?"

I shook my head, scarcely able to believe that we had gone from grieving over a murdered colleague to fussing over casting in the space of a few minutes. But everyone else, even Romeo, felt the need to voice an opinion. In the general squabble that ensued, I was the only one to notice Vincenzo slip quietly from the salon.

♫♫♫

Several joyless days passed. Inside the villa, rehearsals proceeded. I thought Vincenzo might put a stop to them: each time our paths crossed, his expression had become grimmer. But Octavia was still keen on her concert, and her husband apparently lacked the fortitude for a pitched battle.

Since Karl was once again Octavia's "poppet," I assumed she had forgiven his traitorous remarks on her abilities. Striving to prove him wrong, she set about learning the part of Irene the rejected princess with fierce determination. She also worked through an hour of vocal exercises every morning before rehearsal, particularly concentrating on the rapid execution of allegros, which had been Carmela's stock-in-trade. I actually had to admire several of her more attractive efforts.

There was a new constraint among the rest of us. Romeo soldiered on with the role of Bazajet, but his heart wasn't in it. I felt the same. The workaday camaraderie that greased the company's relationships had been polluted by suspicion and doubt. Had one of our number harbored a secret hatred for Carmela? If not, who had summoned her to her death?

Work proceeded in the vineyard as well. With a heroic effort, Ernesto and his pickers got the remaining grapes in before an intermittent drizzle of several days duration set in. The rest of the stomping was a sad affair with none of the carnival atmosphere that usually accompanied the completed grape harvest. As persistently and anonymously as the buzzing of wasps under the eaves, the word went around that the vintage was anticipated to be the poorest in years.

Word also buzzed through the increasingly jumpy indoor servants, and thence to the company, that Vincenzo and Mayor Bartoli had finished questioning everyone on the estate. They had ascertained that a maid helped Carmela undress and unpin her hair at ten thirty, but despite their continuing efforts, they had turned up no suspects in either murder. On the evening leading up to Carmela's death, the workers had remained in the vineyard or cantina until the last glimmer of twilight faded. A communal dinner in one of the cleared-out threshing barns followed. With a day of stooping and carrying topped by a heavy meal, almost everyone had returned to their homes well before midnight. They were all accounted for by family and friends; there are no loners in the countryside.

Only Ernesto, Santini, and a few old graybeards had sat up smoking their pipes and comparing the grapes to those of years past. These men could vouch for each other until half past twelve.

One bright ray pierced the general gloom: letters. After a particularly gruesome rehearsal, musically speaking, Karl slammed out of the villa for a damp, solitary walk just as I happened upon Giovanni depositing the Post on the round table in the foyer. I scooped up those addressed to me or Gussie, leaving only one thin envelope for Karl. Giovanni immediately ran this out on the portico and hailed our departing maestro, but Karl must have been concentrating on a difficult melody. Instead of returning at the footman's call, he plowed ahead into the sodden landscape.

Unable to work outside, Gussie had started painting in the *barchessa* attached to the east wing of the main house. This farm building had been cleared of animals and plows and other equipment and set up as a studio. I headed there as fast as my feet would fly.

"I have a surprise," I sang out, concealing the letters under my jacket as I entered the lofty room lined with bulging hay racks.

Gussie looked up from his easel. He sat on a three-legged stool surrounded by boards pinned with dozens of sketches. Near at hand, a wooden crate served as a table for his paints and turpentine jars. Someone had done a nice job of clearing the *barchessa*. Except for a nest of straw in the opposite corner, the packed dirt floor had been swept clean. While my sensitive nose picked up a lingering scent of animal refuse, Gussie didn't seem to be bothered.

"Well, man, are you going to keep me in suspense forever?" Gussie brushed an unruly lock of hair from his forehead, at the same time depositing a bright smear of blue.

"No, but you'll have to come away from your canvas for a bit."

Sighing, he dipped his brush in turpentine and wiped it through a cloth. "I might as well. I'm not making much progress."

From my vantage point, in the weak light that Gussie had amplified with myriad candles, I could see only a faint outline of… what? Distant mountains poking into a cloud-swept sky?

"Oh, don't look at it. I'm barely started." He waved a hand toward the rain-spotted windows that topped the hay racks. "My spirits were already low, and now this miserable weather."

"These will cheer you up," I cried as I flashed the folded packets. "One from Annetta, one from Liya, and one from Benito that I'm hoping contains another message from Alessandro."

"It's about time. I was beginning to think everyone had forgotten us." He made a grab for his letter, and his eyes crinkled with cheer as soon as they lit on Annetta's writing. In great excitement, he broke the seal. I followed suit with my letter from Liya. A long silence fell as we both lost ourselves in news from home.

"Your Titolino slipped a lizard in Annetta's sewing basket," Gussie said after a moment.

I chuckled. "They must have heard her scream all the way to the Piazza. Annetta can't sing a note, but her voice was always twice as loud as mine or Grisella's.

"Oh, no," I continued as I scanned Liya's lines. "The boys were wrestling and broke the big milk pitcher."

Gussie shook his head in wonderment. "They were wrestling on the kitchen table?"

"She doesn't say," I replied distantly, tracing my wife's closing declaration of love with my forefinger. I could almost feel the smooth flesh of her cheek under my hand, the press of her lips against mine. At that moment, I missed Liya so badly I could have run the forty miles to Mestre, jumped in the lagoon, and swam home.

"I say, Tito." Gussie cleared his throat and slipped his letter in his waistcoat. "No matter how they squabble, Liya's son has been damned good for Matteo. Before Titolino came, Matteo was with women most of the time. Even when you and Liya move house, you'll still be close by, and they'll grow up together, testing each other as boys should."

"Don't look for us to be moving any time soon."

He cocked his head. "I'm not pushing you out, mind, but I thought you meant to use your earnings from *Tamerlano* to find a bigger place to live."

"I did, but I've been thinking. Grisella has been pressing me to confront Jean-Louis, but she's desperately afraid that he won't give her up without a fight." I tapped my last, unopened letter against my palm. "Perhaps the Frenchman can be bought off."

"Oh, Tito. No."

"Unfortunately, I've not come up with any other ideas for permanently removing Jean-Louis Chevrier or Fouquet or whatever he chooses to call himself from my sister's life. He's a businessman—we should be able to strike a deal. I just hope it's one I can afford."

Gussie was slowly shaking his head, his jaw set tightly, his lips compressed.

"Don't look at me like that, Gussie. It won't involve your finances. If I can't stretch to Jean-Louis' price, I'll approach Alessandro for it. He's been doing well these past years."

"It's not that, Tito. You know if you needed money, I'd help you in a heartbeat."

"What is it, then?"

"It's Grisella. We know she's not being entirely forthright about her escape from Constantinople."

"The other red-haired girl, you mean?"

"Well, yes, that. And this business of the pasha she's so afraid of, a Turkish nobleman so enamored that he'd have her followed all over Europe." Gussie fiddled with his brushes, wiping each one and then tossing the crumpled rag to the floor. As he laid out a clean cloth, he said, "By Jove, her story just doesn't wash. I know you don't want to hear it, but I think Grisella is hiding something that may bring trouble on all of us."

I shuffled my feet uneasily. Gussie was right about one thing: his doubts were anything but welcome. They too closely mirrored my own. Thoroughly unsettled, I tore into the letter addressed in Benito's hand. Perhaps it contained some news from Alessandro that could shed light on our quandary.

As Gussie rearranged the jars and candles on his makeshift table and set up stools for both of us, I read aloud. My man-servant's proud report of smuggling Alessandro's letter into the Post without our wives being any the wiser was amusing, but neither of us laughed, not with the pages from Constantinople holding who knew what revelations. I spread them in the puddle of candlelight, and we began to read.

Chapter Eleven

Constantinople, 2nd September 1740

Dearest family,

In my last letter, I spoke of The Red Tulip. I have now gained entry to that establishment, and a more disgraceful sewer of vice I could scarcely imagine. Yes, this is your sailor brother who once boasted he had visited every *taverna* from Cádiz to Corfu. Before I embraced the way of the Prophet, I did many things that shame me today. I was once as debauched as any of my shipmates. When a towering cliff of water stood over the deck or we lay becalmed, hungry, thirsty, and doubtful over our continued survival, then we entreated our creator with fervent prayers and promises. But when we reached land, God became a stranger once again, and we drank, whored, and gambled as before. Thanks to Zuhal and her family, I am now a changed man. With the noble example of Yusuf Ali as my daily guide, I keep on the straight path as completely as my weak will allows.

Enough preaching. I know I'm being insufferably tiresome. New converts always are. You want to know what happened at The Red Tulip, and thus I shall proceed.

Last night, I made my way to the brothel located in an alley that winds off Pera's Taksim Square. A black eunuch in a ridiculously large turban opened the door. With palms together, he gave my companion a deferential bow of recognition. To gain entrance, I had renewed my acquaintance with a friend from the wild days of my youth: Antonio Fosca. You may remember him, Tito. We used to roam the six quarters of Venice, inventing practical jokes that earned us no end of trouble. You always tried to follow us, but I chased you back home. It was better so.

We called Antonio "Signor Calamaro" because, like the squid, he always had his hands in numerous enterprises at the same time. The years have not been particularly good to my old friend. After failing to make his fortune in Venice, he traveled to Constantinople, attached himself to the Bailo, and now runs errands for the Venetian Consul. Calamaro is little changed, still charming, handsome, and dangerous to know. The doorkeeper conducted us to an anteroom painted with garish arabesques and invited us to take our ease on a low divan strewn with rugs and pillows. He clapped his hands at another eunuch, and a tray bearing sesame cakes and *boza*, a weak beer, was set before us. If we wanted something stronger, we would have to pay.

"My friend and I are not here for refreshment," said Calamaro. "Send Yanus in at once."

The doorkeeper bowed himself out, and the proprietor soon took his place. Yanus was a lithe, middle-aged man dressed in a European suit of plum satin. A snow white wig contrasted with his leathery skin and the dark eyes that darted hither and yon. He assessed my gold watch chain and the silver lace on my tricorne with the practiced squint of a pawnbroker. I was also garbed in Western dress, you see, just for the evening. Zuhal had found my white hose and the garters that held them up most entertaining.

"Ah, Signor Dolfin," Yanus said in tones of infinite regret. "We have missed you these past weeks, and now that you again favor us with your company, I must tell you that your favorite companion is indisposed."

"No matter. Lali is a cute little thing…" Here Calamaro elbowed me in the ribs. "Her breasts sport tits like thimbles, Alessandro. But tonight, I fancy something different."

Yanus nodded. "And your wishes, Signor… Alessandro… Might I have a proper name to call you by?"

"Let's just leave it at Alessandro. Show us the best you have and I'll be satisfied."

"Make mine a blonde," added Calamaro firmly.

Yanus disappeared behind a latticed screen, and three musicians slowly filed in. They carried fiddle, drum, and tambourine. To preserve the fantasy of the harem, they were all blindfolded. Once they had struck up a tune, Yanus returned with a young dancer.

The girl was white, probably Circassian or Greek, and her long tresses had been bleached to a pale gold. Yanus had prepared her well. She flashed a smile toward Calamaro and kept her gaze fixed on him as her body moved in a rhythmic pantomime of physical love. By the time she had fallen to her knees and bowed her back so that her hair rippled over the floor like a carpet of ripe wheat, my companion was fairly panting.

Yanus quoted a price and Calmaro jumped to his feet. As he cupped the girl's elbow and steered her across the floor, Yanus rubbed his hands and turned to me. He offered another young bud, "just as supple and luscious, only with hair like a raven's wing."

I'd been giving the matter some thought. "In truth," I said, "I prefer someone more experienced. Bring out the oldest woman you have."

Calamaro halted, one foot through the door. Sneering, he said, "The East must have changed you, old friend. In Venice, you were never the mother-loving type."

Yanus also wore an expression that suggested my tastes were not as adventuresome as he might have expected. "Are you certain? The very oldest?"

I answered with a firm nod.

Yanus once again dove behind the screen. Some minutes later, he reappeared with a woman of perhaps thirty-five. Her soft cheeks carried the impression of bedclothes and her tangled curls had been hastily gathered under a conical cap decorated with pearls and feathers. The rest of her simple costume consisted of rose damask drawers peeking from beneath a gauzy silk smock. As Yanus arranged its folds to best effect, the woman sent me a puzzled smile.

I didn't haggle over price, just ordered Yanus to ransack his cellar for a decent Italian wine. He bowed his agreement, not bothering to hide his increasingly speculative expression.

I followed the woman upstairs to her room. Her name was Sefa, which means pleasure in Turkish. Though obviously surprised to have been summoned, she was determined to please. Murmuring a string of compliments about my person, she removed her cap, shook out curls touched with black henna, and drew back the sheets of the bed she had most certainly just made up. A Western bed. Asking Europeans to take their pleasure on a mat that could be rolled up and stored in a closet was apparently too much authenticity for The Red Tulip.

I watched as Sefa fetched a silver perfume sprinkler wrought in the shape of the male appendage. With a coy smile, she traced it along the silky outline of her pendulous breasts, then drizzled lilac scent over the wrinkled bedclothes. I must have surprised her even more when I begged her to forget all that and simply sit at the foot of the bed.

Positioning a plump footstool so we could converse on the same level, face to face, I explained that I only wanted to put some questions to her. She made her eyes into slits, accentuating the wrinkles that spread from their corners.

"Do you know a man named Louis Chevrier?" I began.

The bright spots burning over her cheekbones told me I'd chosen the right woman, but Sefa merely cleared her throat and said, "Men come and go like leaves blown in the wind. They seldom give a name."

"This man would have been a frequent visitor, perhaps an associate of the proprietor."

"What makes you think so?"

I decided to take the plunge. "Chevrier asked my sister to contact him here. It's been a while, perhaps a year or more. She's Venetian, but can probably make herself understood in the local dialect and several other languages, as well. She's very pretty with long red hair. Known for her singing voice. Have you seen anyone of that description?"

Sefa cocked a graceful eyebrow. "Is that why you asked for me? You wanted to talk to someone who's been here a long time?"

I nodded. This was no time for flattery or dissimulation. If I wanted Sefa's cooperation, I saw I would have to be honest. "My sister's name is Grisella," I replied. "She may have been ill."

Staring at a rose painted on a wall panel, Sefa worked her jaw back and forth until a knock at the door startled us both. She crossed the room. Shiny black hands handed in a tray with a wine bottle and two glasses. Sefa poured herself a generous portion and drank deeply before handing me a glass. I touched my lips to the rim, but forbore swallowing.

Instead of returning to the bed, she crossed to a small window and told me I'd made a clever choice. She had belonged to Yanus for so many years that her usefulness has changed from entertaining his clients to training his new girls.

I put down my glass and joined her. The window was secured with not one, but two layers of wire grilling set in the frame an inch apart. Even Sefa's small hands would have been scraped raw if she tried to squeeze them through the grill. The outside was completely dark. The Red Tulip must back up to the solid wall of another building. Again I asked if Sefa had ever seen Grisella at the brothel.

"Perhaps," she replied, irritating me with an actressy attempt at mystery.

I ordered her to explain.

"Louis Chevrier popped up about eighteen months ago," she said. "He'd been traveling through Wallachia, collecting peasant girls to sell in Constantinople. Yanus bought three. One was Danika."

"Why do you mention this one? Was there something special about Danika?"

Before answering, Sefa took another long swallow of wine. "Danika was special in every way. Of course, Yanus only saw her natural red hair and the kind of milky skin that goes with it. That and her trim little figure."

Sefa had evidently seen more. To keep her talking, I fetched the bottle and topped off her glass. "What was Danika like?"

"A true innocent," she replied dreamily. "A child of the mountains who thought the streets of Constantinople were paved with diamond dust. Poor Danika actually believed Chevrier's lies. As they traveled south, he promised the girls that they would be trained as Karshilama dancers, perform in city-wide festivals for a few years, and then be married off to rich men who would spoil them with presents. Instead, she was locked up here and starved and beaten until her will was broken. Her red hair made her such a treasure that Yanus saved her for the clients that pay big, the ones that do a lot of damage."

Sefa wiped her mouth with the back of her hand, leaving a pink trail of wine across her cheek. "I tended Danika's bruises and held her while she cried, sometimes for hours. She clung to me, somehow believing I could protect her from Yanus. I couldn't, of course. All I could do was try to help her adjust to her new life. We became… special friends."

I stopped her there. Sefa's relations were her own affair. I wanted to know what Danika had to do with Grisella and how Chevrier fit into the picture.

In bitter words, Sefa described Chevrier and Yanus as two of a kind. Vigilant and merciless, like a pair of wolves that hunt together. Chevrier kept bringing girls until every room in The Red Tulip was full. The two men broke them in together, then prowled the city to entice more rich clients. Business had always been good, but with Chevrier around,

the girls were forced to work night and day to sat-
isfy a steady stream of men they hadn't seen before:
Russians with vodka on their breaths, moody Poles,
even Chinamen with squinty eyes.

Sefa's nose was growing pink and her words
slightly slurred. I took her glass, saying, "No more
of this until you get to Grisella."

She nodded gravely and replied thusly, "One
morning, Danika's room was empty when we arose
for the day. There was no word or message. She was
just gone. The next day, another red-haired woman
took her place. She didn't work on her back, just
stayed shut in for almost two weeks. I only know
she was a redhead because I took her dinner tray
in one day when the cook was busy."

Greatly interested, I urged Sefa to tell me more.
She complied, looking as if she might be sick at
any moment. "I asked the girl a hundred questions.
Where was Danika? What had Yanus done to her?
But she wouldn't say a word. She just smiled this hard
smile, even when I fell to my knees and begged."

"How long ago was this?"

Sefa took my hand and led me to her wardrobe,
slyly reclaiming her wine glass on the way. "Letters
and numbers are beyond me, but every morning I've
wakened without Danika, I've made a mark."

She opened the door of the wardrobe and pushed
brightly hued garments aside. Dots of kohl trailed
down the inside of the pine cabinet like black tears.
A hasty computation told me Danika had been gone
for slightly over a year's time.

"What happened to the silent red-haired girl?"
I asked.

"She stayed in Danika's old room until Chevrier
conducted some business with a foreign gentleman

in Yanus' office. After that I never saw the girl or Chevrier again."

"Where did they go?"

Sefa shook her head. "I don't know and I don't care. Danika is the only thing I care about. Over and over, I begged Yanus to tell me what happened. At first, he gave me the back of his hand or worse. When he saw I wouldn't give up, he told me... something."

Sefa's voice trailed off. She took a hasty swig of wine, thought for a moment, then nodded to herself. "Yanus could have been concocting a story meant to shut me up. Or he could have been speaking the truth. You will help me find out which.

"You want to know what Chevrier and his red-head were up to?" she continued in a new, confidant tone. "There's a passage that runs beside Yanus' office. It once led to the outside, but the door was bricked up years ago. Now the passage is curtained off and used to store broken furniture and suchlike. Some time ago, I found a place near the floor where the wall is thin and you can hear everything that is said next door. I crawled to that spot when Chevrier had his meeting with the foreign visitor. If you'll do something for me, I will tell you what I heard."

So, family, you may well imagine that I didn't like this turn of events one bit. I went to that disgusting brothel to discover information, not to become a whore's errand boy. But what could I do? Sefa might be hoodwinking me. Still, if there was one chance in ten that she had information about Grisella, I had to play her game. In this part of the world, two red-haired young women are too much of a coincidence. Especially when one is dead and one has disappeared.

I asked what she wanted me to do.

"Go to Danika's village. Ask for her," Sefa replied with a challenging nod. "Yanus told me that Danika's brother came to fetch her home to Wallachia. Yanus agreed to release her because her brother offered a generous ransom he'd raised from selling sheep."

I found that hard to believe, but Sefa assured me that such a thing had happened several times since she had been confined in The Red Tulip. "A Muslim family would never come after a dishonored girl," she said, "but Danika was a Christian. They have different ways. And Danika did tell me of an older brother who looked out for her."

I was still dubious. If this brother was so protective, why had he allowed her to be taken in the first place? Then I remembered how Grisella had once slipped through our grasp and hung my head in shame.

Much annoyed, I asked Sefa just where this village could be found. She named a place beyond the Balkan Mountains.

I paced her tiny room, figuring the journey in my head. I'd have to take a ship up the Bosphorus and north along the Black Sea coast to Varna. Once on land, I'd hire a horse to take me into the rocky uplands, a backward, bandit-infested area if there ever was one. Sefa was demanding a dangerous journey of at least ten days, even with the best of luck.

I must finish quickly, dear ones. The midday call to prayers has begun. I argued with Sefa, pointing out that Danika would hardly leave without a word of goodby for her dearest friend, but the woman was adamant. Before she will tell me what led up to the departure of Chevrier and the red-haired girl, I must travel to this godforsaken village. If Danika is there, she's to surrender a little silver ring that Sefa gave her as a present. If not, I'm to bring back the name of the brother as proof that I at least tried.

Seeing no honorable way to shake off this burden, I will leave for Wallachia as soon as possible and write again when I have news.

In haste,
Alessandro

Anger had started welling up inside me the moment I read of Grisella taunting Sefa at The Red Tulip. Out by the drive, my sister had looked into my eyes, thrown herself on my bosom, and described how Jean-Louis had given her into the care of his sweet, Christian landlady. She'd fed me a brazen falsehood, and I'd swallowed it as eagerly as a baby licking sugar off a spoon.

"I'm an idiot, Gussie, a full-fledged idiot." I jumped up, knocking my stool aside. "You are right to mistrust Grisella. Her entire story may be nothing more than a web of lies."

Gussie stared at me steadily. "It's no joy to be right in this case. I'm sorry, Tito."

"It's Alessandro that I'm sorry for. He's setting out on a fool's errand. No…" I bent over the letter and shuffled back to the first page. "He wrote this on the second of September and today is the thirtieth. He's actually had time to travel to Danika's village and return home. If only we could have gotten word to him. If only Constantinople were not so far away."

"What do you think really happened to Danika?"

"I think Jean-Louis, probably with Yanus' help, transported her to the *yali* to serve as a duplicate for Grisella. Perhaps they even murdered poor Danika at The Red Tulip, before they set out."

"That means the fire must have been planned well in advance. And…" he continued carefully, "that Grisella is not entirely innocent in this matter."

Giving a tense nod, I reached for Gussie's paint rag and molded it into a ball. I voiced my thoughts as I kneaded the cloth: "But why? Surely the fire at the *yali* was more than an elaborate plan for Jean-Louis to abscond with my sister."

"In the letter before this one, Alessandro mentioned that the Russians from the embassy were very interested in where Count Paninovich stored his valuables. What if Grisella and Jean-Louis made away with something—something the Russians prize highly?"

"You're right." I again consulted the papers before us. "And now, according to Alessandro's whore, we learn that Jean-Louis met with… here it is… 'a foreign gentleman' before he and Grisella left Constantinople for good. Was this a Russian, I wonder? And Sefa mentions business. Does that mean something was bought and sold?"

"We won't have any answers for several weeks. That's assuming Alessandro wasn't kidnapped by bandits and Sefa keeps her promise."

I tore at the ball of cloth in my hands. Ripping off stripes of fabric suited my mood precisely. "I'm not worried about Alessandro. He could outmaneuver a pack of bandits with one hand tied behind his back. Whether he can trust Sefa remains to be seen."

"What are you going to do in the meantime, Tito?"

"Do?"

Gussie bit his lower lip. "About Grisella. You hoped… I mean, you ventured a theory that the murder of the Russian stranger had something to do with Carmela's earrings. But now Carmela has been killed with her pearls in place. That poor lady has established her innocence rather conclusively, don't you think?"

"Yes…" My ominous tone might have stopped some people, but not Gussie.

"So, what are you going to do? Are you going to tell Grisella what we know about The Red Tulip?"

"No, not yet."

Gussie sighed. "Why?" he asked with a long-suffering look.

"I don't know," I answered miserably, twisting what remained of the paint cloth around my hand.

"I do." Gussie stood up and faced me squarely. "You can't stand to relinquish your dream. You've always wanted to see your family reunited. Everyone getting along—everyone happy. You've been longing for that ever since your father gambled away your manhood and banished you to the *conservatorio* in Naples."

I shuddered. Gussie had hit the nail squarely on the head. The first few months at the Conservatorio San Remo had been the most difficult of my life. The pain of being separated from my family had far eclipsed the physical pain the surgeon had wrought. For a time, I might have even gone a little mad. I developed a bizarre fantasy: real life existed only in Venice where my father and my brother and sisters were going about their daily activities. My life at the *conservatorio* was that of a ghost. I moved through my lessons like an insubstantial phantom. I sang, but no one heard. Or so I believed. How could a dead boy who had been cast out of his home produce any sounds? Half a year passed before I returned to a semblance of my old self.

I took a deep breath, staring down at the cloth I'd been torturing. "We'll never all be together again, will we?"

"That time is past. We have to look to the—"

"Gussie!" My hand shot out and grabbed his wrist.

"Tito?" My brother-in-law gazed at me as if I really had lost my mind.

"Don't you see what this is?"

"What?"

"This cloth! Where did you get it?"

"It's… just a paint rag…" he stammered. "I tore it off a larger piece. I have it somewhere around here…" Gussie pawed through his supplies and came up with a bundle of cloth.

I whisked it from his hands and unfurled a nightshift that had seen some rough times. The torn muslin was dirty and stained but not sufficiently to disguise its tiny yellow rosebuds.

"This is Carmela's nightshift!" I cried.

"Her shift was draped across her bed. We all saw it."

"That was only one of her nightshifts, a fresh one. I searched her room, remember? She had a stack of these in her chest of drawers. All identical, all cut from the same bolt of sprigged muslin." I peered at him intently, agog with curiosity. "What on earth are you doing with it?"

"I found it here." He crossed the *barchessa* in a few loping strides and dug into the hay bulging from the nearest rack. "I neglected to stock my painting case with rags. Rather than go back through the house and find a servant, I started looking around for something I could use. I spotted the tail end of the gown protruding from the feed. It was dusty, but once I'd shaken it out, it seemed like the very thing, a discarded garment that had somehow got misplaced."

Failing to find anything else tucked in the sweet-smelling fodder, Gussie joined me as I moved Alessandro's letter aside and spread what was left of the nightshift on the upturned crate. Besides the ruffles that Gussie had torn off to wipe his brushes, a side seam had ripped open and some lace at the neckline had come loose. The front was stiffened in a trail of dried, colorless patches, and the entire shift was liberally stained with purple splotches. One in the unmistakable shape of a handprint.

"Gussie," I said over a lump in my throat. "These are grape stains. Carmela must have left her room in her night clothes and come in contact with the grapes. Then she got back into the day garments she was discovered in."

Gussie's eyes went wide. "Or… maybe someone else dressed her."

"Maybe," I agreed slowly.

With a grim expression, my brother-in-law turned the shift back over and bent to scrutinize the patches on the front. He straightened and asked, "Was she violated, do you think?"

I took another look. "Quite possibly," I concluded, then fell silent, nodding. I was considering how easily a clock's hands can be changed and doubting that the note found in the cantina had ever been delivered to Carmela.

Chapter Twelve

The rest of that day and most of the next kept me busy with rehearsal. It was not until after dinner that I was able to set off for a damp stroll to Signor Luvisi's villa. The deluge had passed, but I was still glad for the beaver hat that sheltered my face against the raindrops blowing off the tree branches. I also reminded myself to add a few extra coins to Benito's next pay purse, a little reward for his insistence on packing my heavy cloak and knee-high boots.

Back at the *barchessa*, Gussie and I had spent some time pondering how Carmela's nightshift had arrived at that unexpected location. And when.

Someone had been very clever, we decided. The clock's hands frozen upward at the traditional witching hour had led everyone to assume that the pendulum had been removed just as it was about to strike midnight. The note that requested Carmela's presence in the cantina at that hour had amply reinforced that impression. But now we realized that it could all be a carefully constructed fiction. From eleven o'clock on, the pendulum could have been removed at any time and the hands reset. Eleven was the last hour that Gussie and I agreed we had heard the clock strike.

Nita's story of how her grieving young master had allowed his villa to pass into Dolfini hands had already piqued my curiosity. When I remembered that Vincenzo had proudly shown Gussie's *barchessa* studio to the Mayor's party that included

Signor Luvisi, curiosity turned to suspicion. I began to wonder just how much Signor Luvisi might resent his new neighbors. In all honesty, I must also admit that I was eager to follow any avenue of suspicion that pointed away from Grisella.

As I navigated the curving drive that led to the Villa Luvisi, I stopped for a moment and noted what close twins the two houses were. Except for different fencing and the horses grazing in a pasture where Vincenzo had planted a crop of wheat, I could have doubled back and been approaching the villa I had just left. The likeness extended even to the doorknocker, a gauntleted hand clenched in a fist.

I don't often manipulate my fame to advantage, but on that chilly afternoon I needed a plausible excuse to pay my address to Signor Luvisi. While the footman carried my card into the recesses of the house, I perfected my patter. When he returned to show me to a study made snug with a cheery fire and camlet window draperies that kept out the drafts, I was ready.

Signor Luvisi rose from an armchair upholstered in worn leather. A smile played over his aristocratic features. "Signor Amato, you favor me. I've often enjoyed your performances at the Teatro San Marco. You are truly one of Venice's greatest music makers." Though Luvisi's tone was polite, I could see that he didn't quite know what to make of my unexpected visit.

"I appreciate your seeing me, Signore. I hesitated before imposing myself on you, but since arriving at the Villa Dolfini, I've fallen in love with your part of the country. I'm most interested in acquiring a villa of my own and wonder if you might know of a suitable property."

He raised his shaggy eyebrows. "Surely you are not going to retire and deprive Venice of your fine talent."

"Not at all. At least, not yet. I merely want a place where I can retreat from the hubbub of the city and rest my voice for a few weeks at a time."

"I see," he replied. "I imagine the adulation of the crowds must turn onerous at times."

"It is a bit tiresome to be on constant view. In the country I'll be able to refresh myself in peace and tranquility."

"I'm afraid to say that the vicinity of Molina Mori has not been exactly tranquil of late."

"No, of course not." I kept my tone regretful but light. "But surely the tragedies at the Villa Dolfini are an aberration. This is such a beautiful place, far from the madness of the city. It's hard to believe that murder has intruded on this paradise."

"Now you're beginning to sound as wholeheartedly romantic as Vincenzo Dolfini."

"Am I?" My smile was innocent.

Luvisi invited me to take a seat by the fire, summoned the footman, and ordered coffee. A perfect choice. In this very masculine room hung with paintings of dogs and horses and smelling of tobacco, we could settle in over our warm cups like men who had known each other for years.

Once the footman had served us and withdrawn, the talk again turned to available estates. "I can think of nothing up for sale at present," Luvisi said. "Most families around here tend to hang onto their land."

"A pity. I thought that since Signor Dolfini had only recently acquired his property…" I took a sip of the pungent brew and let my words hang in the air, hoping Luvisi would feel compelled to elaborate. I wasn't disappointed.

"The sale of the neighboring estate was a singular occurrence. Perhaps you've heard that my cousin Annibale once owned it, before his wife died."

"Nita told me something of the sort."

"What Nita didn't tell you—because I kept the matter between myself and Vincenzo Dolfini—" My host set his cup and saucer back on the tray with a delicate rattle. "Is that I've made the man several offers for it."

"When?"

"The first was late last winter, before he had even taken residence. I appealed to his sense of justice. When my cousin lost the estate at the Ridotto, he was wild with grief and despair. If he had been himself, he would never have let the estate leave family hands. Given that a greedy foreigner won the lot, Annibale should have contacted me, confessed what he'd done in good time for me to buy it back. Unfortunately, that didn't happen. Events moved quickly and Dolfini became the owner. When the news reached me, I immediately offered Dolfini more than he had paid—the man deserved something for his trouble, after all."

"He refused you?"

Luvisi nodded, leaning forward. His lion's mane of hair was gathered back by a thin black ribbon, but enough light strands escaped to make a halo of silvered gold around his head. "Vincenzo Dolfini's concept of justice differs considerably from mine. Dolfini only understands the ruthless give and take of the marketplace, not the fair play of gentlemen."

"You must have been very disappointed, a blood relation cut off from land that by ancient tradition should be yours."

"Disappointed?" He gazed at me for a moment, head tilted. "Deeply wounded best describes my reaction. Annibale's former land curls within mine like a walnut in its shell. Now that nut has been crushed." He sat back to stare at the fire with his hands tented under his chin. If I wasn't mistaken, his eyes grew moist.

I bent to my coffee, suddenly uncomfortable with the emotions my questions were arousing. But then I reminded myself that I had come to gather information, not cultivate a friendship. I asked, "What was your next move?"

"I waited," he replied simply. A wan smile returned to his face as he topped off his coffee with a stream of warmer brew from the pot. "Will you join me?"

I held out my cup, all ears.

"Yes…" he continued. "I waited and watched. As I rode my fields, I watched wagons piled with the Dolfini household goods trundle down the road toward their new villa. They had brought a shocking load for a summer's stay—it must have required an entire fleet of barges to row it across the lagoon.

"And then I caught sight of Octavia Dolfini riding in an open carriage beside her husband. An unfortunate footman was risking his footing to cover her with an immense sunshade. The signora was corseted and painted in the latest French fashion, as proud as the Queen of Sheba, with a face like the hitching end of my old mule." He laughed, loudly and good-naturedly. "I'd already determined that Dolfini knew nothing about farming. He'll be ready to sell in a month, I thought."

"You approached him again?" I prompted.

He nodded slowly. "I sweetened my offer considerably, but I hadn't counted on Dolfini's resolve, and I'd neglected to consider the steward."

"Ernesto?"

"Ernesto." Luvisi nodded again. "On his own, he had already seen to the early spring planting, and once Dolfini arrived with his eager, featherbrained plans, Ernesto showed himself to be a master of diplomacy. Truly, the man has missed his calling. He should be carrying out missions of the greatest delicacy for the Doge's court. Somehow he managed to finish the planting, prune the grapes, and keep the entire farm on an even keel while convincing Dolfini that he was doing just as he'd directed. Of course Dolfini didn't want to sell. Everything was going swimmingly."

"Are you going to try again?"

"No." Luvisi shook his head emphatically. "I told Dolfini that my last offer was just that. If he turned me down, I would consider him a cad and a blackguard, but I would never again seek to rejoin the Luvisi estates. I now consider my legacy his to manage as best he can."

I sipped at my coffee, then began diffidently, "I just thought… Signor Dolfini might be feeling beleaguered… with two murders in the past week and no arrest of the killer in sight. The villa is practically in chaos. Everyone is so nervous, the bare footfall of a maid in the corridor causes shudders and squeals."

Luvisi was following me with absorption, but he merely said, "Dolfini seems convinced that he can handle the matter. For the sake of everyone on the estate, I wish him good luck."

"I must say, you seem quite reconciled to the division of the Luvisi holdings. Is there no trace of a lingering grudge?"

He shifted in his chair and sent me a peculiar smile. "An ill will creates good for no man, especially its bearer."

When I didn't answer at once, his smile grew wider and he said, "I'd heard you fancied yourself adept at solving mysteries. What are you going to ask me about next? My whereabouts on the nights of the murders?"

I forced myself to chuckle. "You caught me out, Signore. Once I'd heard the story of how Vincenzo Dolfini bought his estate, I couldn't help wondering if there was bad blood or if you might feel justified in causing trouble for him. So if you wouldn't mind... just to indulge my love for puzzles... where were you?"

I was relieved when Luvisi began to chuckle, as well.

"You'll have to look elsewhere for your murderer, Signor Amato. When both the stranger and the singer were killed, I was in bed with my good wife. If she hadn't gone into Molina Mori, she would tell you so herself."

It seemed a good time to take my leave; Signor Luvisi had suffered my impertinent questions with a generous forbearance that could only be stretched so far. Before the footman showed me out, I posed just one more. "Do you know of any household in the district that has guests from far away?" I went on to describe the woman I'd seen peering through the Dolfini gates.

"I know who you must be speaking of. I haven't seen the lady, but my wife has. A dull little bird putting up at the Post house with her two little ones. She claims to be awaiting her husband, a soldier who is leaving his regiment and is to meet her shortly, but it's most unusual."

"How so?"

"Well, a woman alone, waiting for a husband who never seems to come. She watches from the window in her room nearly all day, they say. And according to the old cats who make such things their business, the poor woman hasn't had so much as a letter from him. Seems a pity, doesn't it?"

"Indeed."

As I left the Villa Luvisi, I stepped off the circular drive and peeped in the windows of the *barchessa* that corresponded to the one where Gussie's studio had been set up. Instead of an easel and paint brushes, I saw a brown and white bull with horns that must have been a full yard wide. He was pulling wisps of hay from a rack just like the one where Gussie had found Carmela's nightshift.

Deep in thought, I continued toward the open gate. The sun had made a third-act appearance and was casting long shadows over the lawn. I could feel its warmth soaking through the cloak on my back. Once I'd reached the public road, I paused and cast an appraising glance in the direction of the village. For reasons I had yet to fully consider, I was interested in finding out more about the soldier's drab wife. But the walk into Molina Mori and back to the Villa Dolfini would throw me past my time. I had promised Karl I would return to rehearsal by five at the latest. With a sigh, I headed east.

I'd trudged a dutiful quarter mile or so when a farm wagon drew up alongside. Santini gazed at me from the driver's seat, slack-jawed and devoid of curiosity. Manuel and Zuzu rode on the bed of the wagon with some provision sacks.

"Signor Amato," the boy cried. "We'll give you a ride."

I hopped on the back. Manuel appeared head over heels with delight at having one of the players who had invaded the villa all to himself. As the wagon jolted along, he plied me with questions about my operatic travels. We made ourselves comfortable against some sacks of rice, and with Zuzu's head on my knee, I told Manuel about London and Madrid and the other great cities I had visited.

Santini didn't seem to be listening. He handled the reins in silence, never taking his eyes off the road. I sensed no dissatisfaction or resentment in the man, rather a void in the place where most people displayed their feelings. "Does he ever speak?" I asked Manuel, lowering my voice and jerking my head toward the front of the wagon.

"Once in a while, when he gets excited," Manuel replied, also in low tones. "There was an accident a few years ago, you see. When I was still young."

I suppressed a smile. If this boy no longer considered himself young, my twenty-eight years must seem positively ancient.

Manuel continued, "A horse trod on Santini's head. He lay as still as death for a good week or more. Finally he came to, but he's never been the same. He's strong in body, but his senses are still weak. Papa watches out for him, and if Papa is busy, he asks me or Basilio to take charge. Mostly me, even though Basilio is older. Papa says my head is tacked on straighter than Basilio's."

"Is your brother forgetful?"

"No..." The boy drew out the word, rubbing his nose thoughtfully. "Hotheaded, more like. It's just that you never know what Basilio is going to do."

"Ah, I see, he gets in trouble."

Manuel nodded vigorously. "He gets us both in trouble. He acts before he thinks, while I like to think things through."

As I smiled at Manuel's unassuming assessment, the boy surprised me by drawing a square of folded cream-colored paper out of his woolen waistcoat. "Before I forget, we stopped at the Post. This letter is addressed to you."

I immediately saw that Benito had forwarded another missive from Alessandro. My pulse quickened. Why was my brother writing again so soon? He had closed yesterday's letter with the intention of boarding a ship for Varna. With the unexpected missive burning like a hot coal in my pocket, I endured the rest of the ride to the villa, then another extended rehearsal.

Karl was in a particularly dark mood. He dismissed the others and drilled me through all six of my solo arias. Try as I might, I didn't seem to be able to produce the precise effects he intended. The more I taxed my throat, the more zealous his corrections. Threatening to recall me if he thought of anything further, he finally ended my torture and I was able to escape to my room. Gussie had not returned from his painting, but I could wait no longer. I tore into the letter.

Constantinople, 5th September 1740

My dear family,

Have I told you what a clever, sweet wife I have? Behind Zuhal's beautiful black eyes lies a brain that sometimes astonishes even me. She sends her greetings, by the way. Especially to you, Annetta. We have both been worrying over your condition, so much so that Zuhal consulted a wise woman well-known in our district. From her, she obtained the recipe for a cordial said to raise the spirits of women laid low by childbirth. I copied it into Italian and will enclose it in these pages. We pray it brings the roses back to your cheeks.

And what besides recipes, you may ask, makes Zuhal such a prize among women? Simply that she has saved me no end of time and trouble. The day after my visit to The Red Tulip, she was helping me pack my case for a departure on the morning tide. Cursing the bargain I'd made with Sefa, I had arranged passage on a sloop bearing grain to the Balkans. So you can see how my wife proposed her splendid plan, I will recount the scene in its entirety.

Zuhal began by observing that I had not told Sefa about the Frankish man who appeared at the *yali* to collect the body of the other red-haired woman. "Did you think that Danika's lover couldn't bear the truth?" she asked, handing me a woolen scarf to wear onboard ship.

I confess I was nonplused for a moment, surprised that Zuhal knew of such relationships between women. When will I learn? Though they watch the world from behind the veil, these Turkish women know everything.

"I didn't think that Sefa would believe me," I answered. "She has little reason to trust the word of any man. She demands tangible proof."

"The silver ring."

"Either the ring or the name of Danika's brother."

"Surely it is not an expensive piece—this ring. Not worth stealing, I mean."

"No, Yanus would never have allowed either of the women to keep anything of value. The ring is merely a trinket, probably more lead than silver. Sefa told me she'd scratched a crude drawing of entwined hearts into its soft metal."

"Then…" Zuhal bent to unpack my case.

"Wait! What are you doing, woman?" I was annoyed, you see, in no mood for delay.

She straightened, smiling. "We both know where the ring must be, husband. Retrieve it and save yourself a journey into the wilds of the mountains."

I stood astounded. Could my wife possibly mean what I thought? The ring likely encircled the finger of a rotting corpse sealed within the coffin beneath Grisella's grave marker. Did Zuhal mean for me to dig it up?

"Why not?" she said. "All manner of grief could overtake you on this journey. The ship could encounter foul weather or pirates, and once you've reached Varna, you still have to cross mountains and forests filled with runaway peasants who would kill a man for a pair of boots, much less a good horse."

"I'm not afraid. Before I met you, I traveled through worse places and lived to tell the tale."

Zuhal came to my side and pressed her head onto my shoulder. "I know how brave you are, but I would die of worry if you took off to the Balkans by yourself. I suffer badly enough when you sail to

Venice in a convoy protected by a military fleet."
She underscored her words with a fervent caress.

The rest of the evening would be of no interest
to you. Let me just say that I eventually came to
see the wisdom in Zuhal's plan. Though the idea
of opening the grave was distasteful, the sooner I
delivered proof of Danika's fate to Sefa, the sooner I
would know what devilment Grisella and Chevrier
had been up to. Happily, I had only one day to wait
until the dark of the moon. Plenty of time to make
the necessary arrangements.

Christians have been buried in the cemetery
behind the church of St. Anthony since the days
of Byzantine rule, protected by an iron fence and
a hedge of interlocking evergreens. It is fortunate
that the Greek churches follow the practice of the
Roman in leaving the transept open so their faithful can offer up prayers at any time they feel the
need. Abusing their generosity made me feel like
a scoundrel, but as our Aunt Carlotta used to say,
"Needs do as needs must."

So, one hour past midnight, stealing myself to
the shame of idolatry and reciting the most beautiful
names of Allah in my head, I entered a side chapel
and made a show of kissing St. Anthony's feet. I lit a
candle and fell to my knees, straining my ears for the
step of a priest or sacristan. I needn't have bothered.
The church was deserted and utterly quiet. After a
few minutes I made my way through a back door,
crossed to the cemetery gate, and undid the bolt.
Yusuf Ali and several loyal workers from our warehouse awaited me, all clad in black robes.

The rest was a vile business. I had provided our
party with sharp spades, but the ground was hard
from the dry summer and the sexton had buried
the coffin deep. Taking turns, the workers and I dug

for what seemed like hours. Yusuf Ali kept watch in a sliver of light emitted by a lantern with a sliding shade. Just when I was coming to the conclusion that the grave must be empty after all, my spade clunked on wood.

At my muffled cackle of success, my father-in-law jumped down into the pit and opened the lantern's shade to its fullest. He helped me scrape dirt from the coffin lid and then produced a hammer and chisel from beneath his robes. After working the blade beneath the lid, Yusuf Ali paused to question me with his loving gaze. "My son," he asked, "are you prepared for whatever we may find?"

Covering my nose with the sleeve of my jacket, I urged him to proceed.

Nails ripped through wood, and a sickening miasma enveloped us. Dust to dust, the priests say, but this once lovely girl had yet to become one with the earth. Strands of rusty red hair surrounded a face that had melted into a nightmare mask of teeth, bone, and blackened hide. A shroud stained with the fluids of corruption covered what was left of the body. In truth, family, if it had been Grisella, I would never have recognized her.

Yusuf Ali discovered the ring that told the tale. As he tried to wrest it from the little finger of the corpse's left hand, that appendage snapped like a dry twig. He handed it to me. With bile rising in my throat, I removed the slim circle and held it to the lantern. The metal was dull and dark, but the design inscribed on it was still visible: two overlapping hearts.

By the time I reached home, pink streaks shone in the eastern sky, and the crescent sails of fishing boats bobbed atop the waters of the Golden Horn. I thought I might never sleep again, certain I would see Danika's grotesque skull whenever

I closed my eyes, but I was wrong. I had barely told Zuhal all that had occurred when I sank into dreamless oblivion with my head in her lap. That night, refreshed in body and spirit, I set out for Pera. Without Calamaro.

Yanus raised his eyebrows when he found me sitting on his anteroom divan, but his surprise didn't cripple his bargaining skills. To gain admittance to Sefa's chamber, I had to give nearly twice what I'd paid before. The woman jumped up from her bed the minute I'd shut the door behind me.

"What are you doing here?" Trembling with anger, Sefa threw a shawl over her gauzy nightshift and faced me squarely. Her voice rose to a shriek. "You're supposed to be on your way to Wallachia."

Promising news, I insisted that she quiet down. As she scanned my solemn features, her anger quickly turned to fright. She seemed to steel herself for the worst.

I began by placing the ring in her hand. By the time I had finished recounting our foray to the cemetery, Sefa had stumbled backward to the bed and covered her face with her hands. Sobbing mightily, she asked me questions I couldn't answer. How was Danika killed? Had she suffered?

I will never understand women. I wanted to help, I truly did. I tried to comfort Sefa with words, then produced a handkerchief and started to wipe her cheeks. She twisted angrily away. "Get out," she cried. "Just go. I need to be alone." In case I didn't fully understand, she grabbed a candlestick from the bedside table and threw it at my head.

I hopped backward, dodging. "I can't go," I said firmly. "I've kept my part of our bargain, and you owe me some information. I won't leave until I have it."

Sefa pushed herself up on one hand. Her dark hair streamed over her shoulders, making a frame for the pale face harshened by grief. She answered in a guttural whisper. "Not now, damn you. Some other time."

I'm not proud of my next words, but the prospect of returning to The Red Tulip turned my stomach. "I've paid for your time, and dearly, too. Do you want me to call Yanus and demand he return my money? Tell him you're less than satisfactory?"

Sefa wasn't a woman to be trifled with. She hissed like a cornered cat, then lay back and pulled the bedclothes over her head. I slowly counted to twenty, then clicked the door open and called for a servant. In low tones, I told the boy what I wanted.

A whisper escaped the satin quilt. "You bastard. Yanus will beat me until I can't stand."

I crossed the floor and jerked her cover off. "I ordered wine, but if you don't start talking, Yanus will be next."

Sefa called me every vile name the Turkish language contains, adding a few Arabic and Italian for good measure. She was starting on her stock of Greek curses when the wine arrived. Red-eyed and resentful, Sefa clutched her glass and drained it dry before she would consent to talk sensibly. Even then, the facts of the matter were liberally mixed with outbursts of grief-distraught anger. I will endeavor to summarize.

On her knees in the passage beside Yanus' office, ear glued to the wall, Sefa had listened in on a conversation. She had risked sneaking away from her work because she had observed Yanus ushering in "a very tall Russian gentleman of military bearing." Apparently, it was Yanus' bowing and scraping that had aroused her curiosity. Sefa couldn't remember when her owner and tormentor had bent his knee to anyone.

Yanus addressed the Russian only as Your Illustrious Highness. Over and over, the brothel owner begged his pardon for the necessity of arranging the meeting in such squalid conditions and apologized for being part of such an appalling business. For his part, the Russian replied in frosty tones and refused offers of food or drink as if Yanus were offering him the dog's dinner. The Russian soon wearied of Yanus' fawning and declared that he would depart if Chevrier was not brought to him immediately. This was followed by scurrying steps and a door opening and closing.

That part of the conversation was conducted in Turkish, but once Yanus had delivered Chevrier and departed, French became the order of the day. Sefa had only a smattering of that language, but she understood the most important point: Chevrier had come by the property of some very exalted person named Anna and was holding it for ransom. The Russian gentleman was furious, but willing to pay handsomely for its return.

Sefa believed that Grisella must have stolen a casket of fabulous jewels from this Anna and was using Chevrier as her middleman. I was beginning to form another idea.

I asked if anyone had uttered a word about gems or jewelry.

She admitted not.

Then I exhorted the unhappy woman to think back to anything that might help me piece the puzzle together.

Sefa's swollen eyelids drooped. She drove her fingers along her scalp and pulled at her hair. "I've told you everything. Something was handed over. Money was exchanged. I don't know what it was for."

"Did they mention a sum?"

"No. I heard clinking sounds, like coins pouring out on a hard surface and being gathered up again. Chevrier said, 'We have a bargain.' That's when I slipped away. I'd been in the passage far too long."

"Did you see the Russian leave?" I asked.

"Yes," She replied with a drawn out sigh. "I was pretending to sweep the stairs. The gentleman couldn't wait to get out of here. Yanus tried more flattering words, but he pushed him aside, grabbed his cloak and hat from the doorkeeper, and marched out without a backward glance."

"Was the Russian carrying anything?"

"Like what?"

"A box or a bag."

"Oh." Sefa squeezed her eyes shut. "No. Whatever Chevrier sold him must have fit in a pocket."

There was nothing else to be learned at The Red Tulip. I left Sefa to her grief, disappearing as fast as the Russian gentleman.

You have probably come to the same conclusion that I have, family. "This Anna" is undoubtedly Anna Ivanova, Empress of All the Russias, and the Russian gentleman is her consul in Constantinople. Grisella's association with Count Paninovich must have embroiled her in some very nasty business indeed.

Constantinople is not known as "city of the world's desire" for nothing. Sitting on a crucial waterway that links the Mediterranean to the Black Sea, it controls all trade from that quarter. If the city were in Russian hands, they would gain southern access and be free to sail from ports that aren't frozen with ice six months of the year. A very attractive prospect.

Though Russian traders and envoys are tolerated here, no one in the Sultan's court ever forgets
Russia's continuing designs on the Bosphorus.
Military skirmishes have broken out on the Russo-
Turkish border several times in the last few years,
and I predict that out-and-out war looms in our
future. I shudder to think what intrigue Count
Paninovich had embarked on. I would really rather
not know. It's safer that way.

And so I must tell you, I have no intention of
investigating this matter further. In my efforts to
find our sister, I have neglected our business at the
warehouse most shamefully. My father-in-law would
never complain, but my absence has put a burden
on him. That must stop. Grisella has again taken
up with the blackest of rogues, and I will no longer
make excuses for her. Tito or Gussie, if you want
to comb Europe for Grisella and her Frenchman,
more power to you, but I am finished!

Forgive my bitterness, family. It stems from disappointment. Though Allah forgives those who repent,
I never knew our little sister to repent of anything.

Please write. I hope for a letter on every mail
coach, and I embrace you all in my heart.

Ever your loving,
Alessandro (or Iskender, if you would care
to know the Muslim name that Zuhal has
bestowed on me)

The image of Danika's corpse lingered in my mind for some
minutes, even after I had crossed to the wash basin and splashed
bracingly cold water on my cheeks. I tried to will the horror
away by rereading the last part of the letter and pondering what
Jean-Louis could have sold to the Russian consul. When Gussie
burst into our room, he found me deep in thought.

Chapter Thirteen

"Tito," my brother-in-law cried, "you're wanted. You must come down to the salon at once!"

I slowly raised my head from the letter. "Karl will have to simmer for a bit, Gussie. Alessandro has written again, and I'm not budging an inch until you've read this."

"No, it's not Karl who wants you. Everyone in the house has been summoned." He continued in breathless tones, "The constable Captain Forti has arrived, and he's belching fire and brimstone."

Not surprising—a drenching rain was hardly favorable weather for hunting boar. Still, I had begun to think the high constable would never make an appearance. The rigors of rehearsal, the company drawing together in the face of violence, and the pressure to keep my own family secrets had all combined to make the Villa Dolfini seem as isolated as an Alpine fortress. But now that Captain Forti had breached our defenses, Gussie and I needed to reach a decision.

Heaving a sigh, I deposited Alessandro's neatly written pages on the table. I weighed them down with the unlit lamp, then tilted my gaze toward my brother-in-law. "What do you think? Do we tell Captain Forti what we've found?"

Grim and white-faced, Gussie replied, "He doesn't appear to be a man we'd like to cross. I'm for giving him the bullet and the nightshift and washing our hands of the whole matter."

He continued in that vein all the way downstairs. I'd seldom known Gussie's customary good humor to be so thoroughly dampened.

In the salon, we found the opera company, Jean-Louis, Octavia, Vincenzo, and the entire household staff already assembled. Ernesto also stood in attendance, occupying an awkward space between the servants lined up against the wall and the villa's higher ranking residents, who were seated in closer proximity to the constable's formidable gaze.

Captain Forti was a little under six feet in height, with a florid complexion and a gray campaign wig that stood up like a bristle brush on top. His dark eyes were close-set and sharp, and his thin lips stretched over a bulging set of artificial teeth. Like many old soldiers, he walked with a slight limp. The constable's entire person contrived to give the impression of a man who is bothered by his teeth, short on tolerance at the best of times, and a whisker away from dressing down anyone who had the temerity to get in his way.

Gussie and I tucked ourselves behind Vincenzo's wing chair as Captain Forti rapped out a steady stream of commentary in front of the crackling fire. Evidence of dried mud on his boots and brown cord breeches made me think he had not even stopped to change his clothing before hastening to the villa. Indeed, as his summary of our tragic events unfolded, we learned that Captain Forti had been on the estate for several hours and had lost no time initiating his investigation.

The ice house had been his first stop, and of course this battlefield veteran had recognized a gunshot wound to the head of the murdered stranger. This fit very well with information he'd wrested from a tenant who lived beyond the vineyard. He'd been outside seeing to a sick donkey and recalled hearing a loud shot and seeing a flash of powder sometime before midnight on that fatal night.

"I'm surprised he hadn't mentioned it before." The Captain swept his gaze over the assembled company, baring his outsize teeth in a grimace.

"We get a lot of rabbit poachers in the woods this time of year," Ernesto replied, "so a stray gunshot wouldn't be likely to cause comment. Especially as no one knew the stranger had been shot."

Captain Forti gave a brisk nod. "It's the disappearance of the bullet that should have lain within the victim's deteriorating skull that I find of paramount interest. Lead doesn't dissolve into thin air. Someone interfered with the corpse and I want to know who and why."

Gussie sent me an anxious look. I nodded quickly.

"Captain," Gussie announced as he fished the little ball of lead from his waistcoat pocket, "I have the bullet here."

Vincenzo sprang from his chair with a gasp of astonishment.

Captain Forti crossed the rug to stand beside him. "Who are you?" he asked curtly.

"Augustus Rumbolt, Captain, at your service."

"You're English." The constable's bristly eyebrows arched in surprise. "You can't be a singer. Everyone knows the English can't sing. What are you doing here at the villa?"

"Signor Rumbolt is an artist of great repute," answered Vincenzo. "I've hired him to paint scenes of my estate."

"Then how did you come by this?" Captain Forti demanded as he snatched the bullet from my brother-in-law's open palm. Tact was required. Fortunately, Gussie possessed that virtue in abundance. Introducing me and making our visit to the ice house seem the most natural activity in the world, he related how we had come upon our discovery and carefully put it aside until the proper authorities arrived to take charge of it.

Over the chair that separated us, Captain Forti eyed us with cold disdain. "I hope you two don't consider yourselves more capable of solving these crimes than the Doge's appointed representative."

"Certainly not!" Gussie wore an expression of abject innocence.

"Because there's no one who can hunt down a criminal faster than I can. See here—" With a confident nod, the constable dug in a capacious pocket and removed the stranger's pistol. "Signor

Dolfini has furnished this clue that's been sitting on the shelf in his study, completely unnoticed."

Vincenzo cringed as Forti waved the pistol about.

"I instantly identified it to be of Russian make," the constable continued, "and I'm certain that the identity of the first victim can't be far behind. That's where experience gets you."

"Of course." I bowed my head in what I hoped he would interpret as shame. "You must excuse our clumsy efforts, Captain. We were merely trying to be of assistance."

Captain Forti rocked back on his heels. "Is there any other way you upstart bloodhounds have tried to be of assistance."

"Well, I did find one small thing…" Gussie said, shuffling his feet uneasily. While he fidgeted, I noticed Jean-Louis casually drape an arm over Grisella's shoulder. It had begun to twitch, and her mouth was drawing to one side.

"Out with it, man," commanded Captain Forti.

"I have one of Carmela Costa's nightshifts—"

"You dog! You were with my Carmela?" That was Romeo, struggling to lift his bulk from the low couch. He sank back down as Emilio jerked on the back of his jacket.

"No!" said Gussie. "I simply came across it. I was tearing off paint rags without even knowing what it was. It was Tito who recognized the shift. I'm afraid it shows some signs of… a struggle."

Puzzled looks flew around the salon. Jean-Louis hugged Grisella more tightly.

"Where is this garment?" asked the constable.

"In the *barchessa*, where I found it."

"Then that is where we will continue." Captain Forti's teeth clicked decisively. "Signor Dolfini, conduct us, if you please."

Vincenzo stood tall and smoothed out his waistcoat as if grateful for any small task that acknowledged him as master of the villa. He offered his arm to Octavia, but she ignored him and took Karl's instead. Under Captain Forti's inquisitive gaze, our embarrassed host moved out of the salon and started down the corridor. The musicians followed, crowding through the entryway, then the steward and a clot of curious servants.

"Aren't you coming?" Gussie whispered, clearly anxious to join the rush.

I returned his whisper. "You go on and keep your eyes open. I'll be there in a moment." I nodded my chin toward Grisella and Jean-Louis, who were tarrying in the salon.

The Frenchman approached Captain Forti. "My wife is not well. All this excitement has given her a terrible headache. I beg your leave for her to withdraw to our room."

The constable eyed Grisella narrowly. With drooping shoulders, my sister raised a pale hand to her brow and parted her lips with a sigh. It was a classic operatic gesture; she struck just such a pose at the end of one of Asteria's more pathetic arias. But Captain Forti was clearly impressed.

"You may take your ease, Signora," he said with a curt nod.

"*Merci, Capitaine*," Grisella responded in a wan whisper, with a flutter of her eyelashes.

Jean-Louis gave her a gentle push in the direction of the staircase and then stepped toward the straggling line of servants headed toward the *barchessa*.

"You're not going up to tend to your wife?" an obviously surprised Captain Forti asked. "You have my permission."

Jean-Louis halted, and for once the Frenchman's characteristic sang-froid deserted him. His looked everywhere except at the constable. "Ah, no… Madame Fouquet will be fine once she lies down… it wouldn't be fair to the others if I stayed behind." Without waiting for a reply, he ducked his head and hurried to fall in behind the rest of the party.

Captain Forti and I followed, catching up to the group as they left the warmth of the house to traverse the breezy colonnade that led to the *barchessa*.

Night had fallen. A wash of yellow light from a hanging lamp outlined the columns and railings but barely extended into the low shrubbery on either side. In the darkness, wet leaves dripped and a night bird sounded a low call. Captain Forti took great interest in the door that led to this passage. He opened and shut it several times and gave the handle a good rattle.

Once inside the stable-turned-studio, the constable ordered the footmen to light Gussie's candles and everyone else to gather in one corner and hold their tongues. The household sorted themselves out as before: servants in back, then Ernesto and the opera company, the Dolfinis in front, with Karl plastered to Octavia's right shoulder. In the dim, smoky light, their flesh-and-blood faces took on an unsettling resemblance to wax dummies.

Following Captain Forti's instructions, Gussie pulled the soiled shift from his satchel and demonstrated how he had found it in the hay rack.

The constable took possession of the garment. With the shift folded over one arm, he dug a steel spectacle case out of his waistcoat, flipped the top, and balanced the lenses on his nose. After examining the muslin for some minutes, front and back, he whipped off the spectacles and pronounced only one word: "Rape."

On a chorus of gasps, the still faces suddenly came alive. One of the maids threw her apron over her head, and the other started to cry. Everyone, singer and servant alike, began whispering to his neighbor.

"Silence," Captain Forti barked. His obsidian gaze swept our group and lit on Vincenzo. "I'm told you do not share a bed with your wife, Signor Dolfini. Were you sleeping alone on the night Signora Costa was murdered?"

"What an impertinent question."

"It is still a question that must be answered."

"Yes," said Vincenzo, staring at Gussie's easel as if he longed to jump straight into the peaceful vineyard captured on canvas. "I was alone in my suite from eleven o'clock until Alphonso woke me with the news that the clock had been tampered with. I admit that Octavia and I sleep in separate rooms, but I'm hardly the only man in the villa."

The constable's head ratcheted to the left a fraction of an inch. "You Maestro Weber, you were the only other man lodged in a room of his own that night, were you not?"

Octavia had folded her arms tightly across the front of her bright blue gown. She opened her mouth to speak, but Karl stopped her with a subtle nudge. "I was at my scores all night," the composer said. "I'd decided that a passage we would rehearse on the morrow was… unacceptable. After making the necessary changes, I had to copy new scores for the singers and accompanists." Karl spoke with conviction, but his very words told me how nervous he was. I'd noticed that his "s" turned to a very German "z" whenever he was tense or excited.

"Your room shares a wall with Signora Costa's," the constable observed. "Did you hear any noise from that quarter?"

"Nothing." Karl shook his head firmly.

"You must have heard the clock strike," I broke in, determined to ask at least one question before I was silenced. "I mean, since you were awake most of the night, and it's only a few steps from your door. What was the last hour it chimed?"

"I hardly think—" began Captain Forti.

"Don't you see?" I rushed on. "The pendulum could have been removed at any time and the hands reset."

The constable raised his eyebrows and thought a moment. "Well?" he asked Karl.

The composer seemed genuinely puzzled. "I hadn't really thought about it." He cupped his hand and stroked his hollow cheeks. "I may remember drowsing off and being awakened by the two o'clock chimes, but then, it could have easily been another night. When I first came to the villa, the clock tended to keep me awake, but after a week or so, my ears became accustomed." He spread his hands. "I'm sorry, I can't be certain about the clock, but I'm telling you that I didn't leave my room. Besides, why would I want to do away with Carmela? Her rendition of the role of Irene was crucial for the success of my opera. With Carmela gone, I'm still not sure what I'm going to do."

Octavia had been taking agitated breaths and twisting the large topaz on her forefinger. She could keep silent no longer. "Why do you single out my husband and Maestro Weber? Just because the other men share a room doesn't mean that one of them couldn't have slipped out unnoticed. In truth, I find it ridiculous that you suspect anyone from the house at all. It doesn't make sense that someone from inside would come to this outbuilding to hide a nightshift."

"It doesn't make sense that this garment even exists." The constable shook the muslin clasped in his fist. In the flickering light, the shredded fabric danced like a capering specter. "Why keep an incriminating piece of evidence that could so easily be burnt to ashes or torn to bits? Without this gown I would believe that the woman had only been bashed on the head. Now it appears she was raped, as well. Though—" he shrugged his shoulders "—it may be of little matter in the end. A criminal can only be hanged once."

I thought Octavia turned a little pale at that. Perhaps we all did.

Captain Forti spent a few moments pacing the perimeter of the *barchessa*. We had all been intimidated back into silence, so the only sound was the uneven stumping of his boot heels on the packed dirt. "Is this entrance locked at night?" he finally asked, creaking open a set of double doors wide enough for animals to be driven through.

The constable was obviously expecting an answer from Vincenzo, but our host looked perplexed. With a gesture, he transferred the question to his steward.

Ernesto took a deep breath. "The stable doors are secured with a bar from the inside."

"And that one?" Captain Forti pointed toward the door to the colonnade.

"It has a lock, but in my lifetime it's never been used."

"Why not?"

"My grandfather Ilario lost the key when he was a young man. Since someone always sleeps here to guard the cattle, no one's ever bothered to have another made."

"What about the door to the house at the other end of the open passageway?"

"I lock that when I close the shutters."

Captain Forti took a few deliberate steps toward a loose pallet of straw in the opposite corner. Kicking at the bedding, he uncovered a ragged blanket I'd not noticed before. "Someone sleeps here?" he asked.

"Yes," answered Ernesto.

"Every night? Even since the painter has set up shop?"

"Yes."

"Who is it that is content with such a mean resting place?" Captain Forti's tones were silky, but dangerous.

"One of my workers—Santini, by name. He's simple in the head, but I believe him to be absolutely trustworthy. He—"

"Don't tell me what you believe," Captain Forti interrupted brusquely. "I will determine who is trustworthy and who is not. I want to question this Santini. Tell me where he can be found and I'll send a deputy to fetch him here."

"I'll go," Ernesto said quickly. "He could be one of several places."

Receiving a curt nod, the steward lit a lantern and left by the double doors. He returned in a few minutes, urging Santini along with a hand at the small of his back. The rustic's lank mane dripped from a beat-up tricorne, and his slack jaw was covered with several days' worth of stubble. When he realized the entire household was watching him, his eyes started rolling.

Captain Forti had been waiting in the soldier's at-ease posture of spread legs and crossed arms, fingering his watch chain impatiently. Pursing his lips as if he'd just sucked on a lemon, he looked Santini up and down. "Do you know who I am?" he thundered.

Santini replied with a barely perceptible quiver of his chin.

"Can you not remove your hat in the presence of the law?"

Ernesto palmed the tricorne's crown and shoved the dusty hat into Santini's midriff. The man responded with a proper nod and opened his mouth. The cords of his neck stood out as he struggled to form the first words I had ever heard him speak: "Pl... please... excuse... Captain."

Captain Forti unfurled the soiled nightshift. He spit out the words: "Do you recognize this?"

Santini shook his head violently.

"You do." The ivory teeth came together with a sharp crack. "You hit Signora Costa over the head with the brass pendulum, but not until you'd forced yourself on her. To cover your shameful deed, you stripped off this nightshift and put her in clean clothing. Then you hid this in the hay rack right beside your pitiful bed."

Santini had been shaking his head throughout. Now a painful rasp emerged from his throat: "No, no." His eyes squeezed shut, and tears spilled down his weather-beaten cheeks.

"Please, Captain," Ernesto said. "I know this man. I'm the closest thing to family that he has. Santini isn't capable of such an act. As you can see, his mind is but a child's. He could never have planned the deceptions involved in the two murders.

"So far, I'm only accusing him of one."

"Even so, with all due respect, there was a note found beside the vat in the cantina."

Captain Forti nodded briskly. "I've seen it."

"Santini is no longer able to read or write." Ernesto allowed a triumphant smirk to conform his lips.

The constable met it with an even uglier grin. He asked, "Was the note addressed to Signora Costa? Did it mention her name at all?"

"Well… no," Ernesto faltered. "But, it was obviously meant for her."

"Was it? How can you be sure? Perhaps the lady wrote it herself, and its recipient turned out to be more than she bargained for," Captain Forti shot back.

I bit my lip, annoyed that I hadn't considered that possibility. The constable must have a more subtle mind than I'd judged.

Ernesto wasn't finished yet. He dug a claw-like hand into Santini's filthy shoulder and asked, "But would a worldly, beautiful singer have ever sent such a note to this man?"

Captain Forti opened and closed his mouth like a fish out of water. In the tense silence, the snap of his dentures resounded like shots. Eventually he said, "All right, I'll give you that, but my nose tells me this man knows more about the nightshift than he's telling. Perhaps some time in a jail cell will loosen his tongue."

"But it's harvest time and Santini is one of my most willing workers." Ernesto addressed the constable, but his eyes sent Vincenzo a silent plea.

The master of the villa dipped his chin and took a sudden interest in his boots. The rest of the party traded nervous looks.

"I implore you, Captain," Ernesto continued, "Santini is no danger to anyone, and he wouldn't be able to tell you any more if he rotted in jail for a year. Let the man stay on the estate where he's needed."

"And what if he should make a break for the mountains?"

"He won't. I'll supervise him at his work during the day and lock him in the stable tack room at night."

Captain Forti stared at the trembling Santini, dark eyes glinting like they must when he had a magnificent boar at the end of his rifle. The constable had just opened his mouth—to order Santini's arrest I was certain—when he was interrupted.

"Yes, Captain." Vincenzo had found his voice and, perhaps, a small segment of backbone. "We still have crops to get in and every hand is needed. If you agree, I'll stand as Santini's bondsman. I'll produce him whenever you want or forfeit one hundred *zecchini*."

Looking as surprised as I felt, Captain Forti replied, "Will you put your signature to that pledge?"

"Of course, right now if you like."

"All right." The constable nodded slowly, grinding his jaws from side to side. "The rest of you may return to the house, but don't even think of leaving the estate. There will be more questions later, I assure you."

As we filed out onto the colonnade, I cast a brief look back. Vincenzo scribbled out a chit for the constable while Santini stared at the ground with sweat rolling down his cheeks. Ernesto hovered near, clenching and unclenching his fists.

♫♫♫

Our parade down the hall to the central foyer was slow and somber. With the arrival of Captain Forti, the enormity of the villa's murders had finally pierced the tough skin of all our individual problems and concerns. Emilio, who usually carried himself with such dignity, was slumping along as if he bore the weight of the world on his shoulders. His young friend Romeo seemed to have aged ten years. The two went in the salon, threw themselves on the sofa, and sat silently shaking their heads.

Instead of following the singers, the Gecco brothers veered off toward the stairs, whispering between themselves. If not for the constable's ban on travel, I would have bet my last *soldo* that they were planning to pack their bags and seek conveyance to the Brenta. Even Nita, generally so calm and efficient, seemed at a loss for what to do next. She stared at the big front door, nervously fingering something shiny that she held in her clenched fist. Moving closer, I saw she held a rosary.

"Signora?" Nita's gaze sought Octavia. "What should I do about supper? It's already past the time."

The lady of the villa plucked at the lace fichu that decorated her shallow bosom. Gingery strands had escaped her chignon and brushed about her flushed cheeks. Her flat, emotionless gaze swept the group as if we were all complete strangers, even Karl. "They will want something, I suppose. Are there eggs in the larder?"

"*Si*, Signora. Plenty."

"Then we'll have *frittate* with onions and mushrooms. And perhaps some cold chicken if there's any left… and cheese…" Octavia took Nita's elbow and propelled her toward the kitchen. The still blubbering maids brought up the rear.

Octavia might be preoccupied, but Karl had hardly forgotten his patroness; his hooded eyes followed her until she disappeared down a side corridor. Then he made a beeline for the harpsichord. After a few exploratory chords, he launched into a plodding D minor melody that I'd never heard before. He paused, repeated, and tinkered with the bass as if he were having a wordless conversation with the keyboard. Was he was composing on the spot? If so, I thought our maestro must be feeling very melancholy indeed.

Vincenzo had returned. I'd seen him give the footmen orders that sent the boys in three different directions. Now he was asking Alphonso about the condition of the clock. "Can you put it right again?"

The old valet shrugged his bony shoulders. "I could if I had the pendulum, but Captain Forti's men took it away. Who knows when they'll see fit to return it?"

"Don't worry about it then." Vincenzo's tone sagged as wearily as his seamed cheeks and the pouches beneath his reddened eyes. "I'll be in my study. Bring some brandy."

Alphonso trotted off, and Vincenzo started down the hall. Gussie was tugging at my sleeve, urging me to retire to our room, but I put a finger to my lips. I'd noticed Jean-Louis watching Vincenzo with his hawk-like gaze. Now he bolted after the man and raised his voice. "A word, Signor Dolfini, if you please."

Vincenzo paused. I expected Jean-Louis to harangue our host on the need for the opera to proceed despite the arrival of the law, but the Frenchman surprised me. He was concerned over Santini running loose. I heard Jean-Louis strenuously advise Vincenzo to withdraw his bond, but a series of crashing arpeggios from Karl drowned out any further conversation. The two men entered Vincenzo's study and closed the door.

I felt another tug on my sleeve.

"Tito, I'm dying to read the latest letter." Gussie had regained some of his good humor. His blue eyes were alight with curiosity, and while the expression on his face couldn't precisely be called a smile, he looked more cheerful than anyone else in the villa.

My hand sprang to the jacket pocket where I kept my calfskin wallet containing the letters, then I remembered I'd left the latest spread out on the table. "It's upstairs, let's go. You won't believe what Alessandro got himself in the middle of…"

We took the stairs quickly, conversing as we went. Once in the upper corridor, I looked toward the stricken clock. Someone had closed the door where the pendulum should have hung, but the arrow-shaped hands were still frozen at midnight. How fitting, I thought. It seemed like the entire villa had been caught in the snare of that mournful hour.

I was turning our doorknob when Gussie stayed my hand. "There's someone in there," he whispered. "Crying—don't you hear it?"

I put my ear to the polished wood. Yes. Someone sobbing, a woman most like.

Our eyes met in an instant of foreboding. Then I flung the door open, and Grisella sprang up from the table, clutching Alessandro's letter.

"Tito!" she cried, her voice high and shrill, her eyes swollen and red.

I stretched out a trembling hand, barely containing my vexation. "That letter belongs to me."

She tightened her hold on the pages, crumpling and pressing them to her bosom. Her lips twisted like writhing earthworms as she stared wildly from me to Gussie. Spittle escaped one corner of her mouth, and her shoulder jerked violently. The pages rattled and tore.

"Grisella…" I faltered, unsure how to proceed, my anger dribbling away. This was just how my sister had looked before her girlhood fits exploded in flailing arms and growling epithets. Back then Annetta or Berta had administered her elixir and she calmed at once, but I had no medicine. Should I go next door to search for a bottle in her room? Or run downstairs for Jean-Louis?

Gussie was more decisive. He darted forward and delivered a smart slap. Giving a little yelp, Grisella wheeled around and fell back onto my bed. We quickly moved to her side.

"Allow me to thank you, esteemed brother-in-law." Grisella spoke through clenched teeth, pushing up with one hand and rubbing her blazing cheek with the other. "You have restored me to myself as deftly as my so-called husband ever did."

"Forgive me." Gussie's brow puckered, and his eyes shone with concern. "It was the quickest remedy that occurred to me. I've heard your full-blown fits can be deadly."

"Not so far," she replied dryly. "These days, they are never so vicious as the ones Annetta must have described. I'm sure my sister has told you a great deal about me. I would ask a thousand questions about her, except that I will soon see Annetta for myself. Won't I, Tito?"

To cover my discomfort, I retrieved the pages of Alessandro's letter. Several had torn, but they were still readable. I handed them to Gussie, who immediately smoothed them out and began to skim the lines.

Grisella slid off the bed and came to me. She curled her fingers around my hand and placed my palm on her still red cheek. "You're going to take me home, aren't you, Tito? Surely you can't hold me responsible for the death of the poor girl that Alessandro unearthed."

"Who should I hold responsible?"

"Jean-Louis, of course. You have no idea what a brute he is."

"I do. You've told me."

She pressed her lips in a thin line, then said provocatively, "It's worse than you think. You don't know everything."

I refused to rise to the bait. Tired to death of Grisella's dramatics, I removed my hand from her cheek and said, "I know what I need to know about Jean-Louis."

Grisella wasn't out of cards to play. Drawing back with a wounded look, she asked, "Would you rather it had been me in that coffin?"

"Of course not."

"Well then, show some brotherly feeling."

I shook my head, sighing. "What do you want of me?"

"What I've always wanted. Take me home. You'll keep your promise, won't you?"

I felt hot and cold at the same time. My stomach roiled like I'd swallowed an eel, but I couldn't let Grisella go on thinking I would serve as her champion.

I spoke quickly, before my longing to reunite my family could destroy my resolve: "Based on what Alessandro has discovered, I don't see how I can take you back to Venice."

Her startled face swam before my eyes. Every bit of strength I had went into forcing the next words through my dry throat. "You're a liar, a thief—you may have even committed murder."

"No, Tito, no." The cry exploded from her lips. "I admit I made up a story about Jean-Louis' landlady. But only because I didn't want you to think badly of me. I didn't want you to know I'd stayed at that brothel. You have no idea how ashamed I was to find myself in such a place. It was filthy—the sounds and the smells. That's why I wouldn't leave my room or talk to the other women."

"And Danika's disappearance that coincided so conveniently with your arrival?"

"I never even saw the girl, knew nothing about her. That was Jean-Louis, I tell you."

"Besides Danika, your escape from Turkey involved the death of Count Paninovich."

She tossed her head. "So *you* say."

"So Alessandro says. Our brother went to great lengths to follow your trail."

"Oh, Tito, I expected more from you. Alessandro was always hard. He thought he could do no wrong and no one else could do any right. He expected the worst of everyone, especially me, and apparently that hasn't changed. But you—you were different. You always understood. You used to take up for me with Papa and Alessandro, remember?"

I shut my eyes for an instant, trying mightily *not* to remember.

Grisella twisted her fingers into a prayerful gesture. "Please, you must understand. I didn't steal anything from Vladimir—it was Jean-Louis, all Jean-Louis. He thought Vladimir possessed something of great value—I don't even know what—"

"Are you telling me you don't know what item changed hands at The Red Tulip?"

She shook her head wildly.

"I find that hard to believe."

"I wasn't at that meeting—Alessandro's whore confirms it." She jerked her chin toward the letter in Gussie's hands. "Jean-Louis kept me entirely in the dark. He promised to get us both to Paris, and I went along with him because he was my only chance to get out of that accursed Turkish hell. I didn't steal anything from Vladimir. I didn't start the fire. I didn't kill anybody. I just unlocked the back gate of the *yali* at the appointed time, and Jean-Louis did the rest."

I stole a glance at Gussie. His head was still bent to the letter. "Grisella," I began. "I can't—"

"Tito, you must listen." Her voice was a moan. "Every woman has her little ruses. Annetta, Zuhal, and yes, even your Liya. We do what we must when we have only our own wiles to save us. My only sin is lying when circumstances demanded. For the love of Heaven, tell me your promise still stands." With a tearful sob, she threw herself on my chest and clasped her arms around my back.

A knock sounded at the door, causing Grisella to squeeze me even more tightly. Twisting in her grasp, I saw Gussie quickly fold the letter and slip it in his waistcoat. Then he picked up the lamp and crossed to the door. My brother-in-law is tall and broad, much broader than the slit he creaked open.

"What is it?" Gussie asked. I noticed he held the lamp at eye level to further blind our visitor.

The response was muffled.

Hoping it was a footman that Gussie could quickly send on his way, I broke Grisella's hold. I could only sigh in frustration as she sank to the floor and, reaching up from her nest of taffeta skirts, glued herself to my knees.

"By Jove," Gussie exclaimed as Jean-Louis shouldered the door wide open. The Frenchman stumbled into our room, face twisted in a scowl.

"Gabrielle," he rapped out. "I've been searching everywhere. What are you doing in here?"

My sister jumped to her feet, jaw quivering. "*Mon cher*, I was just talking to my… colleague."

"*Zut*! You call this talking?" His dark brows slashed down toward his beaked nose. "Do you think I'm a fool? Return to our room at once."

Grisella met his sharp gaze with her own. I thought she might challenge him, but I was wrong. My sister simply raised her chin and sailed from our chamber with a swish of her hips.

Jean-Louis waited until she had passed into the corridor before stepping close enough for me to smell the brandy on his breath. "Don't think I've not noticed her working on you. My wife likes your kind—you soft half-men—she'd love nothing more than to scoop you up like a choice morsel. But hear me well, if I catch you together again, I'll make you both very sorry."

I mustered as much dignity as I could manage. "You are quite mistaken, Monsieur. I hold no amorous attraction for your wife, nor she for me."

Jean-Louis gave a derisive snort of the type that only the French are able to produce, but he did retreat a step as Gussie came to my side and loomed as a silent, forbidding presence.

"Just know this, my friend," Jean-Louis drawled as he strolled toward the door. "The woman you believe to be a legitimate singer would be nothing more than a whore without me. Before I secured her position at the Paris Opera, she wasn't above warbling her tunes while stripped to her corset. Be that as it may, Gabrielle is my whore and will be governed by me in this and all other matters. I refuse to be made a laughing stock while she dallies with a capon who can barely get a rise out of his cock."

I watched Jean-Louis leave with a heavy heart. Never had a man taken umbrage at such severely crossed purposes.

Part Three

"Now more than ever seems it rich to die,
To cease upon the midnight with no pain."

—John Keats

Chapter Fourteen

Where opera is concerned, nothing succeeds like scandal. Several years ago, I sang Orfeo at the Teatro Regio in Torino. The prima donna who sang Euridice, my operatic bride, was seven months gone with child. A very special child. As every Savoyard from nine to ninety was well aware, the soprano was the Duke's mistress. Torino audiences couldn't get enough of the nightly spectacle: from the royal box that overlooked the stage, the Duke caressed Euridice with tender gazes while the Duchess stared daggers. Instead of the customary two week run, we played for two months. I feared my poor Euridice would be forced to have her baby in the middle of the River Styx.

Octavia's concert profited from a similar notoriety. Not one of the citizens of Molina Mori who were favored with an invitation refused it. The Villa Dolfini was already colored with the tragic history of Francesca Luvisi's sudden death and her young husband's self-imposed banishment; now two murders added an alluring tint of danger and mystery. The belated funeral Mass that Padre Romano finally conducted for our unlikely pair of victims only fanned the flames of the public's curiosity. Those who had been excluded in the first round of concert invitations besieged Octavia with notes and afternoon calls. We were, as the saying went, *il furore*.

Despite the base motives that raised Molina Mori's interest in her concert, Octavia was determined to provide her neighbors with the musical experience of a lifetime. No idleness was tolerated in any quarter. Every worker not involved with gathering grain or winemaking was set to help with the building of a temporary stage which would jut out from the front portico and cover the steps. Benches to accommodate the burgeoning audience also had to be knocked together. Thus, the rasp of the saw and the banging of the hammer pervaded our rehearsals as thoroughly as the delicious smells wafting from the kitchen. After the singing, the audience would be invited inside for coffee or sparkling wine and every sort of elegant pastry that Nita's repertoire could rise to.

Considering that we had replaced a seasoned soprano with an amateur who possessed more vigor than talent, rehearsals went remarkably well. The pressure of the impending performance forced Karl from his melancholy and honed his musicianship to a fine edge. Somehow he found the right words to help us all overcome our weaknesses and prevent our strengths from becoming our downfalls.

From the beginning, I had struggled with the character of Tamerlano. Now, with patience and prodding from the maestro, I gradually learned to surrender my civilized philosophy to the ways of the despotic tyrant who saw every city and woman as his for the taking. My arias became more believable, and my confidence grew with every practice session.

As far as I knew, Vincenzo ventured only a token protest against the concert. One day I chanced upon him and Octavia in the corridor and overheard a snatch of conversation:

"My dear," he started diffidently, "I know you want to be well thought of... so I feel I really must point out... I seldom see women of the rank you seek to emulate putting themselves about in quite the brash manner you intend."

Octavia responded with a frosty smile. "I'm certain that our friends will find my performance charming. Besides, I've sung at many musical evenings, in our home and others."

"But that was in the company of other ladies who were only obliging with a bit of after-dinner entertainment. Throwing your lot in with singers who make their living from the stage is a different thing altogether."

"As a true devotee of music, I am willing to make any sacrifice. Maestro Weber is pleased with the way I handle the part, and in the end, that is all that matters."

"Of course the German is pleased, Octavia. You're paying an exorbitant sum for him to be pleased…"

As I passed from earshot, I had a sudden thought. Octavia had originally plucked Karl from the anonymity of a Swiss spa to compose an opera which would boost her social standing, but somewhere along the way, her girlhood dream of conquering the stage had returned in full. Though others did not share her inflated opinion of her voice, it seemed to me that Octavia was being gradually seduced by her own wishful thinking. Karl had proposed several well-known sopranos to rehearse the role of Irene for the Venetian debut of *Il Gran Tamerlano*, but Octavia had found an excuse to reject each one. Did she imagine herself singing Irene in Venice? Did she actually believe that she could leap over the chasm separating the amateur from the professional?

Still seeking to untangle the knotted threads of our midnight murders, I wondered if it was just possible that Octavia might have killed Carmela to leave a hole in the cast that she could conveniently fill. Octavia was certainly large enough to over-power the petite Carmela once she had lured her to the cantina with the tantalizing note. But our hostess' ambition could not explain the change of the soprano's clothing and the lust-stained nightshift. I shook my head as I returned to rehearsal and picked up my assigned score. My theories were getting wilder and wilder. Perhaps I should bow to Captain Forti's dictum and focus on opera instead of murder.

When the concert day finally arrived, all was in readiness. Even the weather had bent to Octavia's stalwart will, bringing dry air and clear skies. If the temperature was not as warm as could be desired, at least the audience would be comfortable in their shawls and cloaks.

At dusk, Giovanni and the other footmen lowered the huge lantern that hung from the portico's ceiling, lit its four wicks, and hauled it up again. Torches set on iron spikes surrounding the makeshift stage further illuminated the musician's stands and the harpsichord that the footmen had carried out earlier in the afternoon.

The instrument's polished lid had been propped open, giving the audience a full view of the lovely mythological scene painted on its underside. I knew its sound would be just as lovely. Karl had spent over an hour plunking out scales and adjusting the tuning pins. Though Karl's zeal displayed itself more quietly than Octavia's, we all understood that the composer's career was riding on the success of *Tamerlano*. In some ways, this concert was a dress rehearsal for Venice. If our rural audience turned up their noses at his composition, Karl would be crushed.

At the appointed hour, I joined the other performers in the darkened foyer. Romeo was booming out fast sets of scales, and Emilio sounding "ahs" and "ohs" on his favorite note. I'd already warmed up in my room, so I drifted over to an unshuttered window to watch a steady stream of carriages pour through the front gates. After they had deposited their occupants, who made up an interesting assortment of impeccably dressed aristocrats, pompous village dignitaries, and shopkeepers in ancient finery, the drivers circled onto the lawn where Manuel and his brother Basilio directed them to park in neat rows.

The crowd appeared expectant and full of high spirits as Vincenzo directed Mayor Bartoli and his wife to take seats on the front bench. The master of the villa then took the arm of a dignified woman who had arrived with Signor Luvisi. Vincenzo looked around expectantly, but the lady gestured to something out of my sight and shook her head in confusion. I quickly moved down the corridor to another window.

Behind a patch of shrubbery that shielded them from the audience, Ernesto was conversing with Signor Luvisi. If the steward's strained expression was any indication, he was bending the nobleman's ear over a matter of some import. Several times, Luvisi shook his head, appearing more resistant with each negative gesture. I was wondering what they could possibly be discussing when the steward abruptly shut his mouth. Vincenzo came into view. Luvisi welcomed him with an affable smile and allowed himself to be led away. Ernesto watched them leave with a grim jaw and cold stare, then stalked off toward the strip of lawn where the boys were parking the carriages.

I pondered what I'd seen for a several minutes. When I drifted back to the first window, the guests of lesser prominence were crowding onto the benches behind their betters. Over the greasy smoke of the torches, I spotted Gussie's blond haystack bobbing along one of the back rows. Captain Forti was also very much in evidence. Declining to sit, he stomped about the perimeter of the benches with his gaze trained on the audience rather than the stage.

The performance began with an enthusiastic welcome from Octavia and a brief outline of the opera's plot from Karl. The composer barely looked like himself. Though we were playing without scenery or full costumes and skipping many of the recitatives, Octavia had insisted that Karl get himself up as he would for the premiere at the Teatro San Marco. The German who usually favored plain woolens and unbound hair wore a coat of ivory silk encrusted with gold embroidery and a formal wig whose curls soared to an uncommon height. His hollow cheeks were powdered, rouged, and graced with a mouse-skin patch below his right eye.

After our transformed maestro had settled himself at the harpsichord and the fiddlers had taken their places, Romeo and Emilio passed through the front door to the stage. Knowing I couldn't be seen by the audience and anxious to see how *Tamerlano* fared, I remained at the dark window. Octavia had stationed herself at the window on the opposite side of the door.

Grisella waited just inside the dim salon, staring down at the tiles with heavy-lidded eyes. Jean-Louis hovered close by. Since our confrontation, the man had behaved more like a jailer than a husband. I'd managed no private words with my sister, as Jean-

Louis kept her in their chamber except for rehearsals and meals, both of which he monitored with a keen eye.

Out front, the audience greeted Romeo and Emilio with a tumult of applause. Romeo was dressed in black velvet breeches, a jacket of purple silk threaded with silver, and a regrettably tight waistcoat the color of a canary bird. To convey the impression of a captured sultan, a coil of white linen sat atop his periwig and a shiny link of chains spanned his wrists. Emilio had used more restraint in his concert garb. His entire suit was of gosling green, decorated only by gold buttons polished to a high shine. A jeweled crown twinkled on the neat bob wig that framed his thin face.

My colleagues' voices contrasted as sharply as their persons. As Romeo sang of Bajazet's shameful defeat, his mellow basso throbbed with tragic swells, echoed by tremolos from Lucca's violoncello. Like a slow-moving river of exquisite pathos, Romeo's aria flowed over the gaily dressed ladies and gentlemen and drenched them in sorrow. Such an ill-treated captive! Such agony!

The audience was enraptured. Women inclined their heads and pursed their lips in distress. Signor Luvisi was so overcome, he had to reach for a handkerchief to wipe his eyes.

Emilio followed Romeo's lament with an aria cantabile meant to comfort the now swooning prisoner, just the sort of lyrical piece that showed Emilio's silvery soprano to best advantage. I was impressed with his trills, more so with his never-ending notes that seemed to echo off the starry dome above. Karl was pleased, as well; his profile displayed a grin as his fingers hammered the keys and his gaze bobbed between his instrument and the divine castrato.

But when it came time for bows, who did the audience cheer to the skies? Romeo! For once, a basso scored a triumph over a castrato. Cries of "Bravo" swelled over the applause. Mayor Bartoli's wife even tossed Romeo a nosegay of posies under her husband's astonished eyes.

As I stepped away from the window, a frisson of premonition ran up my spine. The many-headed monster of fashion had been fascinated with my kind for some time now. We castrati were the darlings of the public, the acknowledged princes of the stage. But nothing lasts forever. Were tastes about to change? Were more natural voices finally coming into their own?

I had no time to consider the matter; Grisella and I were on next. As we waited at the door, Emilio blew past, then Romeo, all smiles.

The audience welcomed Grisella and me with the same fervor as our two colleagues, and I was relieved to see my sister's sullen expression change to joy. The air between us had been heavy with unspoken hurts and disappointments, but all tension dissolved as we took on the mantles of our characters.

Grisella made a lovely Asteria. She had costumed herself more thoroughly than the rest of us, and I wondered if her ensemble had traveled with her from Turkey. Baggy trousers peeked from under a close-fitting white robe topped with a damask jacket stiff with brocaded silver flowers and accented with wide, drooping sleeves. A scarf of glossy white silk confined her bright curls and hung down her back. Metallic spangles glittered along the hem of the scarf, which was held in place with a golden band wound round her head.

Grisella's first aria presented her as a fragile creature, worried almost to death by the fate of her sultan papa. Her notes were true and brilliant, her acting wistful and tender. Every gesture, even the crook of her little finger, proclaimed her a captive princess.

Which only made me seem all the more terrible as I threatened to make her father food for my scimitar if she refused to become my queen. The audience booed and hissed, but I wasn't worried. They were hissing the evil Tamerlano, not my singing abilities.

Grisella launched into her answering aria with flashing eyes and roulades so impassioned that several spangles popped off her costume. Beneath the princess' wounded butterfly exterior lurked a steely resolve. Singing from the very front of the little stage, she let the audience in on her secret: she did intend to wed Tamerlano, but only so that she could stab him with a dagger smuggled into their wedding bed. In typical opera fashion, I had to stalk around in the background, stroking my trailing fake mustache while pretending I didn't hear a word of her plan. Grisella outdid herself, ending with a crescendo di forza which brought the crowd to their feet. Flowers and excited cries of "Brava" rained down on the boards.

My sister was a true prima donna. Without a particle of modesty, she retrieved her flowers, signaled Karl, and repeated the aria not once, but twice. I must admit that I got out of character sufficiently to join my own applause with the tempestuous clapping that greeted each of her encores. My time would come. In our next round, I had an aria that would also astound.

When every last drop of praise had been milked from the crowd, we retreated back to the foyer and traded places with Octavia. Bursting with pride and excitement, I turned to offer my sister a congratulatory embrace. But Jean-Louis grabbed her by the elbow and whisked her into the salon, scattering her flowers across the terracotta tiles. I picked up one red rose and inhaled its sweet aroma. Feeling oddly jealous, I took up my place by the window once again.

Octavia's entrance occasioned uncertain smiles, raised eyebrows, and only fragmentary applause from the benches. I had a good view of her face as she turned toward Karl and nodded her readiness. Octavia wasn't dismayed by the tepid welcome. On the contrary, her countenance shone with the classic signs of a stage-struck soprano. This middle-aged woman in the ridiculously low-cut gown was as infatuated with performing as any young nymph promoted from the chorus to her first solo role.

Karl struck the keynote, and his paramour's voice rose in determined song. This was Octavia's stellar moment.

But something was wrong. In the audience, heads turned away from the stage, men murmured, women tittered. As a wave, the assembly stirred and rose to its feet.

Karl played doggedly on. Mario and Lucca scraped out a few dissonant chords, then let their bows fall silent and stretched up out of their seats to search for the cause of the commotion. As Octavia's eyes bulged at the errant fiddlers, her voice also faltered to a halt. Karl's hands finally sank away from the keyboard, leaving a silent void that glorious music had filled only a moment before.

Insisting that we must see what was going on, Emilio jerked the door open. All of us, even Grisella and Jean-Louis, ran out to join Octavia.

On the graveled drive, at the edge of the stage, stood a young woman. I recognized her at once. She was the little blonde who had peered at me from the front gates a few days ago. The soldier's wife, if Signor Luvisi's information was correct. She was dressed in the same drab cloak, and a little boy grasped her hand. In the crook of her arm she held a baby about six months old, a girl by the look of its pink filet cap.

Under the amazed gaze of Octavia's guests and the players on the platform, she dropped the boy's hand and hoisted her petticoats. Climbing clumsily onto the stone lip of a flower bed and thence onto the boards of the stage, she made herself and her infant as much a part of the show as any of us. The boy scrambled after her, looking like he was about to burst into tears. The woman's face was blank, her stare unblinking as she walked straight toward the harpsichord.

Octavia ran forward and flapped her hands as if she were driving a goose back to its pen. "Go away!" our hostess cried, cheeks glowing brick-red in the torchlight. "Get off the stage! You have no business coming up here while I'm singing."

The expressions of my fellow performers showed varying degrees of bewilderment and curiosity. Except for Karl. He had risen from the harpsichord and was staring down at the keys as though memorizing the pattern of cracks in the ivory.

Our diminutive intruder's gaze never wavered as she moved her brood in the composer's direction. A pink flush ascended from her neck to her pale face. "We do have business here," she stated in a meek voice accented with German. "We have come to ask Maestro Weber a question."

The composer's shoulders slumped even lower, and Octavia threw up her hands. Catching Vincenzo's eye, she mouthed,

"Do something." Vincenzo hurried along the space between the stage and the audience. At the juncture where the woman had climbed up, he joined forces with Captain Forti and one of his deputies.

Impending capture spurred the little woman to continue. In shaky, but perfectly audible tones, she asked, "Karl, *mein lieb*, how long are you going to let us starve and wither away in that horrible room?"

Octavia shrieked out a question of her own: "Karl, don't tell me you know this woman?"

Whatever depths Karl's spirit had sunk to in those few moments, it now rose on wings tipped with starlight. The composer seemed to throw off his melancholy like a worn-out cloak. He ripped off his ridiculous wig, brushed his sandy hair from his brow, and straightened his narrow shoulders. Wearing the expression of an ancient knight setting out on a sacred quest, he strode to the woman's side. His strong arm encircled her waist, and he spoke so all could hear: "Of course I know her. Signora Dolfini, allow me to present my wife, Frau Weber."

Octavia threw her head back and roared like a wounded lioness.

♫♫♫

Our audience had decamped in confusion, Karl and his family had been banished to the Post house in Molina Mori, and Octavia was in her room having hysterics. What was left of the opera company had gathered in the dining room to tuck into Nita's buffet of delicacies.

"I always thought Karl was hiding a secret," I mused, licking a dollop of cream filling off my thumb.

"You never said," Gussie replied between bites of a shiny plum tart. "What made you think so?"

"It was those letters he received and never seemed to answer. They made me curious. I meant to get to the bottom of them one day, but since I didn't think they had anything to do with our murders..." I finished with a shrug of my shoulders and reached over the table for another pastry.

My nose recognized the heavy scent of jasmine and musk a second before someone bumped me from behind. "Sorry, Tito," Romeo said as we whirled to face each other. Despite his plate heaped with sweets, Romeo's expression was as sour as vinegar.

"So," he continued, "I suppose the little mouse and her pups have put an end to our grand show. Who would have thought that *Tamerlano* would meet such a shameful defeat?"

I nodded. "Not only shameful, but premature. Now we'll never know what Venice would have made of it."

Emilio had been in earnest conversation with the Gecco brothers. Looking far from happy, he joined us, saying, "It's one thing for a performance to be booed from the pit or ignored by the box holders, but to be denied even the opportunity to bring our efforts to the theater... maddening." The castrato pacified his ire by popping several honeyed dates in his mouth.

"What are you going to do, Tito?" Romeo asked.

"Do? When?"

"After Captain Forti finds Carmela's murderer and releases us."

"Don't forget about the first murder," I said.

Romeo shook his head doubtfully. "Surely the killers are one and the same. It's hard enough to imagine one murderer in our midst, much less two."

Emilio's hand fluttered to his lips. He plucked out a date pit with thumb and forefinger, then asked, "Two? Come now, Tito, you don't really believe that, do you?"

"It's possible," I replied carefully. "We still have no idea why the stranger and Carmela were murdered."

Emilio snorted, unconvinced. "What does it matter why? Both deaths occurred at midnight and both involved the clock. We obviously have a killer with a mania for timepieces." He lowered his voice. "I haven't wanted to say—after all, it's no business of mine as long as he doesn't come after me—but I favor Vincenzo's valet."

"Old Alphonso?" I asked. "Whyever for?"

"I've noticed him rooting around inside the clock several times."

"Alphonso knows clocks," I replied. "He once valeted for a clockmaker, so Vincenzo relies on him to keep this one in good running order. The little man barely has the strength to carry a full laundry basket, much less heave corpses hither and yon."

Emilio gave a peevish shrug. "Well, when Captain Forti makes his arrest, don't forget that I mentioned Alphonso first."

Romeo made an effort to smile. "I'm sure Captain Forti will get his man, whoever he his. My concern is the damage this infernal stay in the country has done to my career. Before I left Venice, Maestro Porta talked of reviving his opera *Numitore*. He dangled a small part for me, but I turned it down on the spot because I'd just been offered the role of Bazajet." Sadness rushed into every crevice of the basso's face. "Now my role of a lifetime has gone up in smoke, and I have no prospects in sight. Do either of you have any engagements lined up?"

While Emilio boasted that he had "something quite astounding in the offing," I paused in thought, momentarily perplexed by how completely life at the Villa Dolfini seemed to have swallowed up my past and my future. Giving myself a mental shake, I answered, "Nothing certain, but I suppose something will turn up. I never go without work for long."

"Yes, it's different for you castrati," Romeo answered sourly. "You don't know what it is to worry about bread on the table." His accompanying look clearly stated that despite my favorable prospects for employment, he wouldn't be me for all the gold in the Doge's treasury. "By the way," he continued. "Do you think there will be any problem collecting our pay for the time we've already put in on *Tamerlano*?"

Gussie had been listening to our conversation in silence. Now he smiled in sympathy. "I'm having similar doubts about my paintings. Octavia appears to want to turn her back on the opera completely. I wonder if Signor Dolfini will also give me the boot."

Emilio rolled his eyes. "Mario just told me Octavia threatened to plunge a dagger into any impertinent rascal who so much as mentions the opera."

"That's all we need," replied Romeo glumly. "One more murder and we'll never get out of this villa."

"We shouldn't worry overmuch," I said. "Octavia will calm down eventually. She may never want to sing another note, but she'll give us our fair compensation."

Emilio brought his face close to mine and said in a whisper, "The Frenchman isn't so sure. He's still talking of bringing suit if his wife's contract isn't honored."

I cast a glance toward Jean-Louis and Grisella across the room at the buffet. Earlier, I'd noticed that while she sipped at a coffee, Jean-Louis seemed intent on consuming the value of Grisella's pay in cakes and pastries. Now he patted his midsection, and with a crook of his finger, summoned one of the footmen who were waiting to take the uneaten food back to the kitchen.

"Is the fire in our room made up?"

"Yes, Signore, it's good and warm," answered the youngest footman. Adamo, by name.

"I'll have a bath then, with plenty of hot water."

The boy's dismay was palpable. At the end of this long day, with many duties left to be done, the last chore he wanted was fetching the tin bath and carrying pails of water to fill it. Grisella seemed to share my concern. She laid a timid hand on Jean-Louis' arm, but he shook it off.

"Get to it then," the Frenchman said. "I'll be up in a few minutes."

"Yes, Signore." Adamo left the dining room with leaden steps.

Jean-Louis ran a bilious eye over the offerings on the sideboard. He must have found an empty crevice in his stomach, for he reached for one more chocolate éclair. After giving it a lingering inspection, he put one end in his mouth and employed a forefinger to shove it in whole. Jaws working, he jerked his head at Grisella.

Murmuring a few words, she took a step back and raised her coffee cup.

Quick as the flick of an eyelid, Jean-Louis whipped the cup from her hand. Splashing a streak of brown liquid down her white Turkish robe, he poured the remaining coffee into the vase of belladonna lilies that decorated the sideboard.

His words carried on a burst of irritation: "Now you're finished. Come on."

♫♫♫

I didn't expect to see my sister again that night. The singers and musicians, accepting Gussie as one of their own, moved from the dining room to the salon. Keyed up from the evening's surprises and no doubt feeling a little sorry for ourselves, we congratulated each of our concert performances with a series of liberal toasts from the brandy decanter.

I confess that I then grabbed centerstage by recounting several stories from my extensive travels. Never one to accept second billing, Emilio rose from the sofa and announced his intention to retire.

I pulled him back down with a tug on the tail of his jacket. "Don't rush off," I said, "you'll have your turn."

The castrato complied by allowing Gussie to fill his glass, but he stared moodily into the fire and crossed his arms as if he meant to block any and all convivialities. Romeo eagerly stepped into the breach with some scandalous gossip about the Papal Nuncio and a certain soprano who was well-known in Venetian circles.

We were all reaching that muzzy, golden state where the cares of the day seem to evaporate like soap bubbles in the sun when Grisella entered.

"Gabrielle, my pretty," slurred Romeo. "How did you slip your lead?"

My sister giggled like a child at a marionette show and whipped off her head scarf to let her brazen curls spill down her back. Smoothing out her coffee-stained robe, she dropped down beside me on the sofa and said, "Jean-Louis has been at the brandy, too. He fell asleep in his bath, and I wanted some company."

Emilio raised his glass. "A toast to Gabrielle. Never one to miss an opportunity."

"To Gabrielle," we echoed.

Mario fetched a glass for the only lady that remained in our dwindling company, and we whiled away another hour in reminiscing over our greatest triumphs and most spectacular failures. Grisella laughed, pink-cheeked, at the tales of the men and offered a few Parisian theater stories of her own.

Why couldn't it be like this forever, I thought. I could just conveniently forget all Grisella's troubles in Constantinople, pretend that Danika and Count Vladimir Paninovich had never existed. Grisella and I could make a new start. We could sing together in Venice, at the Teatro San Marco. With our perfectly blended voices, we could make operatic history.

As I was losing myself in that wonderful fairy tale, the harbinger of truth was trotting through the door, white-faced and terrified.

"Signori," cried the young footman Adamo. "Help, please. Upstairs."

Chapter Fifteen

From the door of the chamber, nothing in the lamp-lit room looked amiss. The room's one bed was several steps away; its bedspread of Lombardy lace held an untidy pile of men's clothing, and Jean-Louis' jacket hung over a bedpost. Across the room, before the flickering fireplace, a hip bath sat in a nest of Turkish toweling. Jean-Louis filled the tub. He had his back to the door and his feet stretched toward the warmth of the flames. A rolled up towel supported his head against the lip of the tin tub. Quite comfortable, it appeared, as Jean-Louis was very still. Asleep, Grisella had said.

But Adamo hadn't summoned us because Jean-Louis was sleeping.

I turned back toward the corridor, intent on intercepting Grisella, but didn't see my sister. Instead Vincenzo was rushing toward me with Alphonso on his heels. Master and valet quickly moved to the tub to gaze down on Jean-Louis. Vincenzo stared with eyes bulging and mouth agape. Alphonso turned the color of a fish's belly and made a run for the door. I took his place, dimly aware of Gussie and the others bunching in behind me.

I must have been becoming accustomed to corpses, because I trembled only slightly at this one. Jean-Louis' usual cool stare had changed to round-eyed surprise, probably at the weapon that had punctured his throat. From near his jaw, a strange object protruded at an acute angle. It was a brass shaft that ended in a round disk with a hole in its center. Blood trailed from the place where it met Jean-Louis' white neck, changed course at his collar bone, and meandered through the black hairs sprinkled over his chest. It seemed a very small trickle, but it was enough to make the tub water glisten like liquid rubies.

"What is that thing sticking out of his throat?" Vincenzo shivered despite his quilted dressing gown. "Some sort of dagger?"

"It's one of the hands from the clock in the hall." To my horror, I heard laughter welling out of my throat but couldn't seem to stop it. "Our murderer couldn't find his pendulum, so he was forced to pillage the clock for another weapon."

Vincenzo sent me a dark glance. "Adamo, go check the clock," he ordered.

As the slap of energetic footfalls sounded down the corridor, I forced myself to calm down and take a cooler look. The crimson water had overflowed the tub and soaked into the margins of the white toweling, and a puddle had formed around the soap and scrub brush that lay near Jean-Louis' flaccid right hand. At his left hand, an overturned brandy glass caught the firelight.

The footman returned, bursting through the door. "Signor Amato is right about the clock. The big hand is gone."

Grisella followed Adamo into the room. Clutching her spangled scarf to her stomach, she breathed in shallow gasps. "You all ran out of the salon so fast, I couldn't keep up with you." She took hold of a bedpost for support and searched our grim faces. "What has happened? Is Jean-Louis ill?"

As she pushed away from the bed, I sprang to block her path. "You mustn't see this," I said. "He's been stabbed. He's dead."

"No, not my husband!" With a wail of anguish, she put her hands to her face and doubled over. I embraced her, and she leaned her weight against me like a trusting child. As we crept from the chamber together, I dimly heard Vincenzo ask, "Is Captain Forti still about the place?"

I steered Grisella next door to my room. As soon as I had her in the chair, she collapsed with head thrown back and eyelids flickering. Gussie quickly fetched another glass of brandy from the decanter downstairs. Little by little, taking small sips from the glass in my hand, she soon revived sufficiently to converse. First I gently described the method by which the Frenchman had been killed, then I asked a few questions.

"When did you leave Jean-Louis?"

"I don't know exactly. So much has happened this evening, I've lost track of the time." Twin daubs of color stained Grisella's pale cheeks, and her dark eyes seemed as round as saucers. "He made me scrub his back and talk to him while he soaked. He nodded off gradually... Jean-Louis drinks wine like mother's milk, but brandy always puts him to sleep... at least, it did..." She sighed and continued, "Once I saw he was snoring, I came straight down to the salon."

I thought back. "That must have been around eleven o'clock."

She nodded miserably.

"Was anyone else upstairs?"

"Some servants were moving around earlier, but I didn't see anyone on my way down."

"Octavia?"

My sister shook her head gravely. "All was quiet in her corridor."

"Vincenzo gave her a sleeping powder," said Gussie, shrugging. "I heard Nita say while we were still eating."

I considered, gnawing at a knuckle. I already suspected my sister of being more involved with the deaths in Constantinople than she would admit, and from her own mouth, I had heard how Jean-Louis misused her. Now he was dead. I had to ask the question.

"Grisella, did you stab Jean-Louis?"

A wary light flashed in her eyes, but she answered without hesitation. "No, Tito. I swear on my soul that Jean-Louis was sleeping peacefully in his bath when I left our room."

One thing made me believe her. Death must have been nearly instantaneous for Jean-Louis, but the damp stains that soaked the toweling around the tub indicated he had churned up a few splashes in his death throes. I saw no way that Grisella could have committed that murder without getting a drop of blood-red water on her white clothing, and a red stain would have been even more evident than the brown coffee spill that trailed down the front of her robe.

"Don't think ill of me." She lifted trembling hands to her brow, and her mouth pulled to one side. "Have pity on me, brother. I need your help now more than ever."

"Why do you need me? You are an accomplished soprano. You can go back to Paris and make your own arrangements. You are well known there, and the theater managers are sure to embrace you."

"I can't, Tito. Don't you see? I've never been on my own. I don't know how to make travel arrangements or negotiate contracts. Besides, I need someone to look after me when the fits are at their worst."

"You could hire a companion," I suggested. "Or find a manager who won't abuse you as Jean-Louis did. Someone worthy of your trust."

"Trust?!" She sprang from the chair, wringing her scarf in her hands. Her shoulders were shaking. "How do I know who to trust? I left my home and my family for a man who promised his eternal love. Instead, he tired of me in the space of a year and gave me to his brothers to use at their pleasure. The last of them sold me off to a Russian who treated me no better. Vladimir always promised to take me back to St. Petersburg, but he lied, too. When his work in Constantinople was finished, he meant to pass me off to a Turk. Monsters! All of them!"

Swaying on her feet, Grisella burst into wild, convulsive sobs. Gussie patted her shoulder while murmuring, "There, there," and I fetched her scarf that had fallen to the floor. When I pressed it into her hand, she embraced me with all her might.

My own arms seemed to tighten around her trembling body with a will of their own.

Grisella whispered, voice brimming with entreaty, "Don't you understand, Tito? You are the only one I trust—the only person in the world who can help me. There was never a woman more wretched than I—never a woman more in need of her family. You must take me home." She tilted her head back and looked me in the eye. "Please, you must. I promise you will never be sorry. I'll be the meekest, most biddable sister that ever was. I'll let myself be guided by you and Annetta in all things."

How could I refuse her? With her husband in all but name dead a few paces away? Only a brother with a heart of ice could betray her as so many others had done.

♫♫♫

It was my turn to be questioned. At long last.

Once Captain Forti had arrived, official wheels had begun to turn. Everyone in the villa had been herded into the salon under the watchful eyes of a pair of deputies stationed between the fluted entrance columns. One by one, we had been summoned. I'd watched as singers and servants had returned from Captain Forti with expressions that spanned anxiety to relief. After giving her statement, Grisella had curled herself into the corner of the sofa with head bowed and hand to her brow.

Now I was the last but one. Gussie was the only other person who hadn't been questioned.

"Signor Amato," a deputy announced in a flat tone.

Heartened by a flashing smile from my brother-in-law, I rose and followed the man out of the salon. If he knew he was escorting a singer who had entertained kings and princes, he didn't show it. Like the other deputies, he was merely a peasant who had traded a lifetime tied to another man's land for a uniform with shiny buttons. Our footfalls echoed down the long corridor and challenged the oppressive silence that pervaded the villa. The air was so tense and still, the very house might have been holding its breath.

The deputy delivered me to Vincenzo's study. Bookshelves covered the walls, punctuated here and there by maps of the estate and its environs. Captain Forti had installed himself behind Vincenzo's desk as if he were the master of the villa or perhaps the entire territory. In the lamplight, the varnished walnut desktop glowed like a watery expanse. Floating on its surface was one lone sheet of paper turned writing side down.

The constable rubbed his jaw as he gave me a cold, silent assessment. He did not invite me to sit. He had brought a black-clad secretary who was stationed at a smaller clerk's desk with quill and ink pot ready to take notes.

"Statement of Tito Amato," Captain Forti barked at the secretary.

The particulars were quickly disposed of. Under rapid-fire questioning, I accounted for my whereabouts all evening and named the people who had been eating and drinking together for the several hours leading up to Jean-Louis' murder.

"So," the constable continued more slowly. "While the opera company was drowning its disappointment in spirits, the only persons unaccounted for were a few servants, Signor and Signora Dolfini... and your sister."

It was not a question, but a statement of fact. Grisella must have told Captain Forti of our true relationship. Why? My mouth had gone dry and the pause was reaching an uncomfortable length when I simply answered, "Yes."

"Why didn't you inform me that you and Madame Fouquet are related?" The constable's teeth clicked impatiently.

"I didn't think it had any bearing on the murders."

"You think, eh?"

There was the scratch of the secretary's pen, then another silent pause.

Captain Forti continued, "Once again, you're trespassing on my territory. Your wrong-headed deductions are becoming a nuisance. Just give me the truth and I'll interpret it."

"Yes, Captain. I understand."

"Good. Now we might get somewhere." He nodded tersely. "Did your sister and her husband have a contented marriage?"

"Sticking strictly to the truth, Jean-Louis Fouquet was not Grisella's husband—that's my sister's given name—Grisella."

He nodded again.

I went on, "She and Jean-Louis merely lived together as man and wife without the blessing of a priest. Did Grisella tell you that, as well?"

"She did not, but somehow I'm not surprised. You opera people are steeped in false identities and stage deceptions. The principles of decent folk mean nothing to you."

I felt my face reddening. "Don't paint us all with the same brush, Captain."

"No? Do you deny that you have a renegade Jewess living in your home as your mistress?"

The constable pressed on before my astonished tongue could respond. "When I was first informed of the nasty business here at the Villa Dolfini, I sent a man to make a few inquiries in Venice. I like to know who I'm dealing with, you see. It's quite a menagerie you have there on the Campo dei Polli." He showed his unnaturally white teeth in a grimace. "Now, I ask you again. Did your sister and her so-called husband get on well?"

"Before coming to prepare Maestro Weber's opera, I had not seen Grisella for many years," I answered carefully. "But from what I've gathered in the past few days, they had differing ideas about how her career should be conducted."

"Did Fouquet treat her cruelly?"

"Surely that's for her to say."

"She admits that he beat her."

"Well, then—"

"But only after I confronted her with the statements that others had given. According to your fellow singers, she sometimes had bruises."

I wet my lips. "That is true."

"Had you offered to intercede between your sister and... Monsieur Fouquet."

"We had discussed the possibility of her returning to the family home in Venice."

"Without Monsieur Fouquet."

"That's right."

The secretary penned frantically.

Captain Forti nodded grimly. "Was the Frenchman included in that discussion?"

"No. If it came to Grisella leaving Jean-Louis, we were going to inform him when it seemed judicious to do so."

"And when would that be? Surely you and your sister had some understanding between you."

I gaped at the man, more than a little disconcerted by the tack the constable's questions were taking. The last thing I wanted was to be pushed into discussing Alessandro's letters and the strains they had caused between Grisella and me. "I can't really say," I answered vaguely. "We hadn't decided on a definite course of events, but I was thinking we should wait until the end of rehearsals here, when the opera was ready to be taken to the theater in Venice."

"Why?"

"Well, such a discussion was bound to cause a bit of unpleasantness…"

"More than a bit, I should think." Captain Forti slowly rose to his feet. Using one forefinger, he gave the paper on the desk a push. It sailed toward me, and I made a grab for it.

"Look it over," he continued.

Greatly puzzled, I ran my eyes over a standard theatrical contract notarized with an embossed seal. I'd signed many of these in my time, including one for *Tamerlano*, but this wasn't my contract. Madame Gabrielle Fouquet was named as the artist, and Jean-Louis had signed as her representative. The thing that made me gulp was the salary. For her role as Asteria, Grisella would receive half again what I'd been promised. Either Karl or Octavia must have been absolutely determined to tempt Grisella away from Paris.

Captain Forti was staring at me, grinding his teeth.

"Where did you get this?" I asked.

"Signor Dolfini supplied it from his records. A generous sum is it not?"

I had to agree that it was.

"Exactly." Captain Forti leaned forward, fingers splayed on the shiny desktop. "Not a sum that Jean-Louis Fouquet would simply wave goodby to as you and your sister skipped down the road to Venice without him."

"He was entitled to a percentage. We could have made some suitable arrangement."

"Why should he agree to forfeit any of what he expected? Indeed—why should you?"

I drew a long shuddering breath. "What are you implying?"

"That perhaps the easiest way to rid yourselves of the Frenchman was to kill him."

My jaw dropped. "You can't suspect me. After the concert broke up, I was in the dining room or salon the entire evening."

"So I've been told—your fellow castrato was most forthcoming. You regaled the company with one story after another, and when Emilio Strada tried to leave, you used force to restrain him. All the better to insure that your sister had adequate time to dispense with the lover who had become painfully tiresome."

I couldn't believe what I was hearing. A few exaggerated words from Emilio and Captain Forti believed that I had schemed with Grisella to kill Jean-Louis. My temples began to throb; the blood drummed in my ears.

Meeting the constable's uncompromising gaze, I said, "You're on the wrong track, Captain. I had nothing to do with the man's death, and I don't see how Grisella could have either. She came down from their room without a drop of blood on the Turkish costume she'd been wearing all evening and joined in our talk without the slightest sign of distress."

"I've yet to work it all out, Signor Amato, but I will in time. My method is simple and sure. I come upon something that doesn't smell right and follow its trail wherever it leads. The secrecy over your relationship, the story your sister just told me about her flight from Constantinople—it all smells to high heaven. Why would a decent Italian woman consent to live among infidels? Or pretend to be French? Upon my soul, I don't know which is worse."

I took an involuntary step back. I wanted to scream at the constable's stupidity but forced myself to be silent. Captain Forti was a man on a mission, hot on the trail of his latest quarry. He was so convinced that he was right, anything I might say would only make things worse. I was certain his next words would order my arrest, but a brisk rapping intervened.

Displaying a toothy scowl, Captain Forti shifted his eyes to the door. "Come in," he ordered in a raised voice.

The same deputy who had conducted me to the study entered, clutching Ernesto in an iron grip. He pushed the sweating, rumpled steward forward and announced, "The peasant Santini has escaped, and this man refuses to answer any questions. We just barely stopped him from going after Santini himself."

Ernesto dusted off his jacket and faced the constable. "I'll answer any question you would care to put to me, Captain. But I can't tell you how Santini got out of the tack room, because I don't know."

Forti's scowl deepened. "When was he shut up?"

"I locked Santini in after dinner, at about five o'clock. With tonight's concert, I had too many things to do to supervise him as well."

"Was that the last time you saw him?"

"Yes, Captain." Ernesto nodded uneasily.

"When was his escape discovered?"

The deputy answered, "Just a few minutes ago, during a search of the outbuildings."

A new light came into the constable's eyes, and he grinned with cold satisfaction. "I thought that mute had a rank smell about him. And I never did get to the bottom of the business with the nightshift." Captain Forti hit the desk with a closed fist. "So, our Santini was locked in, stewing and sweating over his guilt until fright got the better of him. He broke out and ran, but we'll soon have him. The man can't have got far."

Captain Forti came around the desk in limping bounds. Moving faster than I would have thought the old soldier capable, he crossed the study and clapped Ernesto on the back. "You'll have your chance to track him. We'll make up several search parties, blanket the area. You'll come with me—you must know all the man's haunts."

Ernesto protested, but for naught. He was swept along in the constable's headlong rush to begin the hunt.

For a moment, I stood in the book-lined study forgotten and bemused. Captain Forti had changed his focus to a new quarry. I wouldn't be clapped in irons that night, but I couldn't rejoice. Even if the constable managed to capture Santini, I sincerely doubted that justice would be served. Sighing, I shot a glance toward the only other person remaining in the room.

The secretary merely shrugged and took out his penknife to sharpen his quill.

♫♫♫

For once Gussie awakened before me. I had passed a dreamless night, so deep in sleep that I forgot where I was. When Gussie shook my shoulder, I kept my eyes glued shut. "No, Liya," I insisted with a groan. "I don't have to go to the theater for hours. Slip back under the sheets for a bit."

"Tito, wake up," Gussie's deep voice replied with an exasperated sigh.

My eyes flew open. I took in the lofty bed chamber as different from the confined room under the eaves that I shared with Liya as the surrounding fields were from the city of stone and water that was Venice.

Everything suddenly came flooding back: Gussie and I were in the midst of a bucolic paradise that had been invaded by a clever, merciless killer. And for all Captain Forti's bluster, the chief lawman had no more clue to the murderer's identity than I did.

"Tito!" Gussie's expression and tone were both urgent. Fully dressed, he waved a sheaf of papers under my nose. "You must read this letter at once."

I rolled over and propped myself up on one elbow. My brother-in-law pressed the missive into my hand. "Where did this come from?" I asked with a dry, thick tongue.

"Giovanni brought it from the Post yesterday, but in all the commotion, it slipped his mind. He gave it to me when I went down to breakfast. It contains urgent news from Alessandro."

I scooted to a sitting position and unrolled the pages on my crimson coverlet. The morning sunlight fell on shaky and uneven characters quite unlike my brother's usual bold script.

Constantinople, 15th September 1740

Dear family,

I write to you from bed, a bit battered and sore, but do not be alarmed. By Allah's mercy, I am now safe at home. My writing arm is propped up on a pillow, so you must excuse my scrawl, as well as my brevity. I send you a warning. Pray don't ignore it as I did mine.

A few days after I told Sefa of Danika's death, the city was abuzz with rumors about a whore who had murdered her keeper in the middle of Taksim Square. Every person who came through the doors of the warehouse had a more fantastic story to tell. Fearing the worst, I sent one of our more capable workers out to discover the truth.

Ahmet returned with news that the proprietor of The Red Tulip had been bloodied, but the wound was not mortal. Wielding a broken wine bottle, one of his women had chased him from the brothel into the busy square. Bypassers tried to restrain her, but she struggled and screamed like a mad woman. A pair of Janissaries finally wrestled her to the ground and took her to a nearby guardhouse. According to the descriptions that Ahmet gathered, the attacker was most surely Sefa.

Nothing is ever simple in Constantinople. Predictable, yes. Simple, no. All officials expect a small present as compensation for attending to their assigned duties. To induce them to go out of their way, a bigger present is required. And it must be the right present, not an outright money bribe. To visit Sefa, I had to work my way through a series of wardens and jailers with astonishingly varied tastes. Fortunately, the bazaar was close at hand; practically any item can be found in its stalls.

You may ask why I went to such trouble, especially as I had intended to wash my hands of the entire matter. It comes down to simple justice. Yusuf Ali and I agreed that my visits to The Red Tulip set this train of unfortunate events in motion. Sefa had been arrested because of my search for Grisella. I owed it to her to see how she fared.

Sefa was surprised to see me. They had placed her in a cell with a score of other women, all of whom drew veils over their faces when I approached the bars. Sefa and I talked in a corner, as far from curious ears as possible.

"With Danika dead, there was no reason for me to go on living," she whispered between sobs. "I meant to cut my own throat right after I sent Yanus to the firepots of Hell. I would have done the same for Chevrier and your Grisella, but they are long gone."

Realizing that I might take exception to the murder of my sister, Sefa lowered her eyes, keened softly, and pummeled her chest with her fist. There was no real comfort I could offer. Instead, I sought to turn her mind to practical matters. I asked if she'd had sufficient food. When she shook her head, I promised I would leave enough piastres with her jailer to purchase dinners for many days. Then I inquired about an attorney. Of course, she had none.

Ottoman justice is quite different from that of Venice. Turkish courts sit uneasily on the crossroads of imperial law, religious teaching, and tribal custom. The forfeit of blood money is the usual penalty for causing bodily injury. Since Sefa has nothing of her own and no family to provide for her, she could end up in prison for a very long time. Still, if Yanus fails to press his claim with the court, she may well be turned loose. I believe that a skilled attorney stands a decent chance of persuading Yanus that he is hardly in a position to call attention to himself or his activities. As I recounted all this to the unhappy woman, she stopped sniffling and a slight trace of hope brightened her face. I told her that my father-in-law and I were willing to provide counsel for her.

"But why would you do this for me?"

Sefa didn't really understand my explanation, but she did want to show her gratitude in some way. Before I left, she clutched my sleeve through the bars.

"Please. You must be very careful," she urged. "I'm sure Yanus has figured out that you were the one who told me about Danika's death."

"And who am I?" I replied, smiling.

Sefa knew me only as Alessandro the Venetian. She had no idea of my surname, my business, or my place of residence. Even so, when I reminded her that Yanus knew no more, she bit her lip anxiously.

"Yanus has ways and means that you could only dream of," she said. "Mark my words. If he wants to find you, he will."

"For what purpose?" I asked. "Yanus is no fool. His best course of action is to forget this incident completely. I will certainly never return to The Red Tulip to remind him."

Back at the warehouse, I reported this conversation to Yusuf Ali and left the legal arrangements to him. So confident that his attorney would prevail, my father-in-law spent the afternoon musing about what could be done with Sefa after she was freed. I did a good afternoon's work among the bales and, after stopping at the mosque for sunset prayers, set off for home. Without a care in my idiotic skull, I took the short way through a doglegged alley bounded by high walls on both sides. By this time it had grown dark, but I knew this passage like the back of my hand.

A trio of men stood at the entrance, dressed in plain caftans with nothing to set them apart. One faced the wall and had pulled his robe aside as if to make water. The others waited quietly and shuffled aside as I passed. I paid them no heed until I sensed the nearness of someone directly at my back. Running was no good, dear ones. I turned to fight, but they brought me down before I could even reach for my stiletto. A vicious blow left me insensible to the world.

I awoke in a tiny room with metal shutters over the windows and straw heaped in the corner as a crude bed. The only light came from a barred slit in the door. Manacles and chains pinioned me to the wall. After many hours of being nearly eaten alive by bugs and lice, I was removed to a larger room to face my interrogator.

I will not distress you with details of my abuse. Suffice to say, a man can learn much from the questions put to him, even in such extraordinary circumstances. My captors were Russian and their chief goal was to learn where Chevrier and Grisella had got to. They obviously blamed them for the fire at the *yali* which they believed was set for the purpose of covering up the murder of Count Paninovich.

Apparently, they discovered that the count's jugular vein had been cut before the *yali* was set ablaze. I know this because they threatened me with the same fate, even holding a stiletto to my neck while they pummeled me with questions about Grisella's whereabouts. "An eye for an eye," they explained.

Count Paninovich must have been very dear to someone with great power. His murder provoked ten times more anger than the theft of whatever Chevrier and Grisella stole from the *yali* and sold back at great price. Try as I might, I could inveigle no hint of what that might be.

Here is my warning, family. Agents from St. Petersburg have been dogging Chevrier and Grisella around Europe, intent on taking revenge. So far, the pair must have managed to stay one step ahead of their pursuers. But now that the Russians know who I am, that Grisella is my sister, and all about our house on the Campo dei Polli, they will surely send a man to our house. No, I didn't break and supply that information, but they know.

You must be on the alert. And if Grisella returns, alone or with Chevrier, you must not let her in. Do you understand? It is of prime importance that you provide no refuge. The Russians are out for blood! Harden your tender heart, Annetta. If you shelter our evil sister, you may well condemn everyone in the house to execution.

I am at the end of my strength for now and must close so that this letter will catch the mail coach. I know you have questions; one more I will answer quickly. It was Calamaro who furnished the information about my identity that set my captors on my trail. Yanus sought him out because he remembered it was he who had first introduced me to The Red Tulip. Together they made hay by selling me off to the Russians.

Fortunately, Yusuf Ali also remembered what I'd told him of Calamaro. When I failed to return home, he sought out Calamaro at the Bailo's residence. That feckless wastrel was no match for my formidable father-in-law. Once confronted, Calamaro revealed his scurvy bargain as quickly as an apprentice seaman threatened with the cat-o'-nine-tails. Yusuf Ali then alerted his confidants at the Sultan's court who called at the Russian embassy and secured my release with their well-polished combination of courtesy and menace.

Ah, here comes Zuhal with a steaming tureen. To restore my strength, she has made my favorite sheep's foot soup. She doesn't seem to realize that the sight of her lovely face will heal me faster than any tasty dish.

Be on guard, dear family, and keep yourselves safe. More than ever, I wish I could cross the miles in a twinkling and deliver this warning in person. I kiss each of you a hundred times!

Your devoted brother,
Alessandro

Chapter Sixteen

"I must leave at once." Gussie had been pacing in tight circles while I'd read Alessandro's letter. Now he retrieved his boots from the wardrobe and sat down to unbuckle his shoes.

"I don't dare wait until nightfall," he continued as he exchanged his stockings of white silk for warmer wool. "At the very moment this letter reached Venice, a message from the Russians might have been delivered to who knows how many of their agents."

My heart dropped to my stomach. Gussie was right—someone had to get home and quickly. At that moment, our entire household consisted of our wives, three small children, an infant, several female servants, and a manservant recovering from broken ribs and a fractured skull. Even when Benito was at his best, his skills ran more to pressing the lace frills of my neckcloths than fighting off intruders.

"We should both go." I leapt out of bed and reached for my breeches.

"Don't be daft, Tito. Captain Forti had stationed deputies around the house and at the gates. The only way off this estate is to ride over the fields and intercept the public road that leads back to Padua. You can barely keep your seat on a horse."

I bleakly agreed. Gussie was the horseman, not I. While I had been singing my first hymns in the parish choir, this son of English gentry had been galloping his pony over fields and streams.

"Are you going to take one of Vincenzo's horses?"

Gussie nodded as he struggled into his boots. "He has a chestnut mare named Alfana—fifteen hands, sleek, with a steady gait. That horse will suit me perfectly. I'll leave her at the stable where we hired the carriage that brought us here. For a fee, I'm sure the stableman will see that she gets back to the estate."

"With luck, you may reach Padua in time to catch the Burchiello."

"That's my plan. The boat stops at every landing along the canal, but that can't be helped. It's still the fastest way home." He stood up, looking as stalwart as any operatic hero that I had ever played.

"You'll be in Venice by tomorrow," I said wistfully, tying my shirt front. The thought of our snug house had me fighting back sudden tears. I abandoned the laces and grasped Gussie by both shoulders. "Keep our family safe, old friend. If harm comes to any one of them, how will we forgive ourselves?"

Gussie reached up to cover my hands with his and brought them together between us. Still enclosing them in a tight grip, he replied in a fevered tone. "Don't worry, Tito. Once I get home, the door will be barred to anyone we haven't known for years, and I'll hire six-foot bravos to accompany Annetta and Liya to the market. The Devil himself won't be able to penetrate my defenses."

I nodded in a series of jerks. "I know you'll take care of everything… I just wish there was something I could do."

"There is," said Gussie, dropping his hands. "You can create a diversion while I saddle Alfana and start off. I've already had a look round outside. The grooms were pressed into joining Captain Forti's hunting parties, so the stable is deserted except for one boy."

"The deputies?"

"The pair at the gate presents no problem. The house hides the stable from their view, and I'll be riding in the opposite direction. But there's one more man patrolling the house. Earlier, he was flirting with one of the maids at the kitchen door. Who knows where he'll be when the time comes?"

I thought quickly. The situation called for something simple, a brief distraction that would shift the focus from the stable for a few minutes and then die down. I could manage that. After all, as Captain Forti had so disparagingly remarked, I was steeped in stage deceptions of all sorts. Later, I would have to explain both Alfana and Gussie's absence to Vincenzo, but I thought I could handle that, too. The master of the villa was a reasonable man.

I finished dressing while Gussie hurriedly packed a few essentials in a pouch he could sling over his shoulder. We agreed on the time of his departure as thirty minutes hence, and set our watches accordingly. Once Gussie was away, I wouldn't see him again until I'd also reached home. With decidedly mixed emotions, I cautioned him about a hundred dangers of the road and wished him one last Godspeed.

My brother-in-law stood stiffly without returning my farewell. I detected something unsaid in his glittering blue eyes.

"What is it?" I asked quietly.

"Tito," he replied in a voice heavy with sorrow and worry. "You can't bring Grisella home. Not now, not ever. Do you understand?"

I nodded, smiling faintly. I'd known that since I laid eyes on the first lines of Alessandro's latest letter.

♫♫♫

The house seemed strangely quiet without the tinkle of the harpsichord and warbling of the singers wafting from the salon. I paused for a moment in the foyer, listening intently, trying to ascertain where the inhabitants of the villa had got to. A low chatter and the clink of silverware on china came from the dining room. Keeping out of sight, I drew near enough to identify the voices.

"Has anyone checked on Gabrielle?" Romeo was asking.

"She was still asleep when I came down." Octavia answered with more warmth than I would have expected, given the humiliating conclusion to her concert the night before. "I put her in Signora Costa's old room. It has unhappy associations, but at least Signora Costa's things have been packed up and the room cleaned. One of the maids is sitting with Madame Fouquet so she won't wake up alone."

"Well, if you ask me," said Emilio. "That bloodthirsty peasant's last murder was very convenient for Gabrielle. Her husband was one of the nastier bit of goods I've ever come across, arrogant, sly, selfish. Once Gabrielle recovers from the shock of his death, she should do very well on her own."

Good, I thought. Word still hadn't got round the villa that Gabrielle Fouquet was really Grisella Amato. I wasn't ready to face the questions that revelation would bring just yet.

A new voice chimed in, and I recognized Mario's bald tones. "I just hope the constable and his men catch that madman soon. I'm tired of looking over my shoulder all the time. Besides, we need to get back to Venice."

"Just so," his brother Lucca added. "We'll have to hustle to find positions for the new opera season. I suppose our old chairs at the San Moise are already filled."

A loud rattle followed, and I pictured coffee slopping over the rim of a delicate cup. "Don't speak to me of the new season," Octavia thundered. "I won't hear a word about arias or librettos or composers. Especially not lying, deceiving, snake-in-the-grass composers."

A moment of strained silence.

Romeo spoke up warily. "I suppose you'll be glad to get us all out of your hair."

Octavia must have signaled her agreement in no uncertain terms, because Emilio instantly turned peevish.

"We're certainly not here for our health," the castrato complained. "Captain Forti has made prisoners of us, and now that the peasant's flight proves his guilt, I don't understand why. The murders are solved. It's just a matter of bringing the man in to face justice."

Romeo's bass rumbled, "I suppose the constable wants to be certain he acted alone. After all…"

I heard soft footfalls on carpet an instant before a subdued male voice murmured behind me: "Good morning, Tito."

A hand fell on my shoulder. Hoping I didn't appear as furtive as I felt, I turned to face Vincenzo. His face was haggard, the skin gray and loose as a husk.

"Are you coming in to breakfast?"

I shook my head. "I was just thinking that my appetite seems to have deserted me."

He smiled weakly. "We must keep our strength up, though, mustn't we. It won't do to let events beat us down."

"Just now, a bit of air would do me more good than food. I'm going for a walk."

"Suit yourself." He sighed and entered the dining room as if girding himself for battle.

So much for above stairs, but what about the servants? Since Vincenzo had just come down, his valet would be clearing up his bath and shaving gear. The footmen would be waiting at table, perhaps ferrying dishes to or from the kitchen by the back stairs. If I could be sure that Nita or the other maid wasn't out in the kitchen garden, I could proceed in the direction of the stable undetected.

After retrieving my outdoor attire from the cloakroom, I took the stairs that led down to the kitchen and hurried along the narrow passage. The minutes seemed to be flying by, and I cursed myself for listening too long outside the dining room. At the kitchen, I paused with my cloak slung over my arm. Pots bubbled over the fire, releasing billows of steam that shrouded the smoke-stained bricks. Nita was standing at the long table with her back to me. She seemed totally engrossed in plucking feathers off a goose, and her helper was nowhere in sight.

I continued along the passage more slowly, nosing my way through the unfamiliar warren of larders and work rooms. Soon a rhythmic thumping met my ears, accompanied by unmistakable gasps and moans. Ah, the other maid. But who was sharing her pleasure?

Creeping silently, I peered around the edge of a dingy curtain at the entrance to a long, narrow storage room. Enough light filtered down from a dirty window near the ceiling for me to make out oil jars, baskets of potatoes, pails, and sacks of other provisions stacked along the wall. At the far end of the space was a heaving tangle of bare flesh atop some folded sacks. The thinner of the two maids had her skirt bunched around her waist. One of Captain Forti's deputies was taking her from behind, and she winced with each thrust. Yes, I was certain the man was a deputy. His blue coat with the bright brass buttons lay discarded on the tiles.

Running on tiptoe, I tried first one passage and then another until I located an outside door. Once on the sunny path that ringed the back lawn, I pulled my watch from a waistcoat pocket. Only ten minutes until Gussie planned to slip into the stables.

Though the blood was coursing through my veins, I forced myself to saunter like a man with no particular destination. I passed the sprawling vegetable garden, several barrows piled with orange pumpkins, the shed that held the olive press, and finally reached the stable yard.

The yard formed a stone quadrangle open on one end with carriage bays to my left, empty kennels before me, and the building that housed the horses forming the other side. In the center of the yard was a hitching post, and against this leaned a boy on a backless chair, cracking hazelnuts for all he was worth.

I hailed the fellow with a cheery greeting and a twiddle of my fingers. "Going for a little walk," I announced, exaggerating my already high speaking voice. I pointed my stick at the grove of elm and hazel that spread out on a gentle incline beyond the stables. "Can't get lost in these woods, can I?"

He turned a rum eye on me, seeing just what I wanted him to. The infamous exploits of many of my fellow singers had led people, even stable boys, to expect certain things of a castrato: refined manners, extravagant impulses, a delicate sensibility, and above all, more talent than brains.

Not ceasing his nutcracking, the boy called back, "No one is supposed to go off the estate."

"Oh, yes, I know." I tittered a high laugh as I continued on toward the trees. "I'm not going far, just a morning stroll on a beautiful day."

I found the grove perfect for my purpose. Under the trees, its lush soil nurtured a thicket of small bushes, ferns, and thick vines. Above, the hazels' broad leaves were turning brown, and higher still, the elms were shriveled and yellow. Enough foliage remained on the branches to throw great patches of undergrowth into dusky shadow. As I leaned on my stick, envisioning my next move, a bird hooted, mellow and throaty. I took it as my clarion call.

With a carefully modulated shriek designed to carry no farther than the stable yard, I turned and ran back down the path. My feet churned up dust and small rocks went flying. The boy darted out of the stable yard, and I called, "Help me, please. For the love of God."

Under a tangle of dark hair, the boy's broad face registered surprise and irritation. Swiping his hair from his eyes, he half-turned toward the villa.

"No, don't run off." I spoke in a terrified whisper as I skidded to a halt. "You must come with me. That mad murderer is loose in the wood. I saw him."

"Then I must fetch a deputy, Signore."

The boy was poised to flee, so I seized him by the collar of his faded jacket.

"No, no. You mustn't leave me here alone. The killer that Captain Forti is chasing is hiding in the woods. He's stalking me, I'm certain, but I can't run another step." I huffed and puffed and, for good measure, patted my heart dramatically. "You can't run off with that monster loose."

The boy curled his lip. "It's only that crazy old mute, Santini," he replied with the arrogance of the young and healthy. "I'm not afraid of him."

"You can catch him, then. Come—" I tugged at his collar. "I'll show you where I saw him. It's just into the wood, not far."

The boy dug in his heels, casting a glance back into the stable yard. I used the silver knob on my stick to turn his face squarely back toward me. I'd seen something he hadn't: Gussie peering around the corner of the building.

"Think what a hero you can be. If you capture Santini, the older fellows will come back and be forced to hang their heads in shame."

His dark eyes glowed. "Will there be a reward?" he asked as he shifted energetically from foot to foot.

"I shouldn't be surprised. If you can bring Santini in, I'll contribute a *zecchino* myself."

He thought less than a moment before grabbing a hay fork and taking off for the wood. As he brandished his makeshift weapon, his excited treble rang out, "Hurry, Signore, show me where you saw him."

Cleto, as the boy was known, turned out to be a tireless tracker. He poked his long fork in every bush and weedy hillock of the grove, and I suffered more than a few pangs of guilt as he insisted on searching far longer than I knew to be necessary. When we finally headed back to the stable yard, Cleto looked so dejected that I gave him his *zecchino* anyway. I held another in reserve if he got in trouble over Alfana's disappearance.

♫♫♫

I passed the next several hours in the most acute state of anxiety, believing that Gussie was speeding toward Venice, but not certain. What if Alfana stepped in a rabbit hole? What if Gussie reached the Brenta too late for the Burchiello? Grisella also caused me a good deal of grief.

My sister rose in the late morning. Pale and listless in one of her plainer gowns of midnight blue, she shakily installed herself on a chaise in the salon and took a steady stream of condolences. Mario surprised me by giving her an impromptu concert on his violin, and Octavia set up her embroidery frame near at hand. Thus, Grisella was never alone and that suited me just fine. She kept sending me timorous smiles and once or twice suggested that a walk might lift her spirits. I ignored her by keeping my nose buried in some month-old gazettes. Just then, I didn't care to engage in another emotional scene with my sister.

Near dinner time, Vincenzo wandered in and crossed the salon to gaze wistfully out toward his back lawn. The musicians were clustered around the harpsichord talking among themselves, and Octavia was gamefully trying to demonstrate a new embroidery stitch for the unheeding Grisella. There wouldn't be a better time to catch Vincenzo alone, so I joined him at the glass doors and asked him to step out on the loggia. He agreed with a disinterested nod.

The day had grown warmer than October had a right to be, and a light breeze had sprung up. For a moment, Vincenzo and I stood at the loggia rail drinking in the fine weather that was quite capable of turning bitter within a matter of hours. Then I explained that we'd had a letter about an emergency at home and confessed to Gussie's theft of Alfana. I ended with the assurance that the horse would be returned forthwith.

Vincenzo sighed. "I don't suppose I'll ever get my paintings of the estate, will I?"

His question silenced me for a moment. The master of the villa was more concerned over paintings than the unintended loan of a good horse? "Signor Dolfini," I said haltingly, "I confess that the news from Venice was so dire that Gussie didn't even consider his work. I'm sure he'll make some arrangement to finish your scenes once this crisis has passed."

"It doesn't matter."

"Why do you say that?"

Vincenzo shrugged his broad shoulders. "Six months ago, I came here with the highest hopes you could imagine—a peaceful retreat from the city, crops and animals flourishing under my care, a veritable paradise. I thought this was where I belonged, but I was a fool. What a mess I've made of it all."

"Running a farm is difficult. You must give yourself time to learn the ways of the country."

"I could live here for ten years and not be a successful farmer. I believed the grape harvest wouldn't be harmed by a few days either way. Ernesto warned me, but I pressed forward, and now we're stuck with a vintage they tell me will taste no better than horse piss." He shook his head and his hands tightened on the railing. "My instincts are for manufacturing, not agriculture, and it appears that I'm too old to change."

The sorrow in his voice made me forget my own worries for the moment. "Signor Dolfini, you condemn yourself too severely. You are hardly old, and you have an excellent steward to guide you in your new pursuit."

"Ernesto must think I'm a terrible meddler. I try to put what I've read into practice, but apparently you can't learn farming from a book. I get in Ernesto's way more than anything else. If only I had been born on the land as he was, instead of on our crowded island."

"Think of it this way—once the casting of iron implements must have been a complete mystery to you, but gradually you came to know that trade like the back of your hand. You can learn farming the same way. I know many singers who were forced to master another calling when their voices could no longer support them. One of them now runs a very prosperous vineyard."

"Truly?" he asked, a hopeful smile hovering on his lips.

I nodded vigorously, but his smile died.

"But that singer hasn't had three people murdered on his estate, has he?"

"No," I admitted, "but unless you're the murderer, you can hardly blame yourself for that, can you?"

As my companion stared mournfully toward the distant hills, Octavia fluttered her handkerchief at the salon door. "Vincenzo," she screeched. "You're wanted. Santini has been captured."

The master of the estate whirled and hurried across the sun swept tiles.

I followed, feeling a prickle of dread along my spine.

♫♫♫

"We found him up in the hills, hiding in a deserted charcoal burner's hut." Ernesto jumped down from a black wagon driven by one of Captain Forti's deputies. "Now they're holding him in the lock-up at Molina Mori."

The front drive was crowded with laborers who must have been working close enough to the road to see the wagon trundle up from the village. They clustered around Ernesto, and their excited questions seemed to bedevil the steward as sorely as a swarm of mosquitoes. Batting his hands in front of his face, Ernesto climbed the steps to the columned portico.

Vincenzo and Octavia waited at the top, surrounded by musicians and servants. Grisella hovered near me until I sidestepped away and planted myself beside a waist-high jardinière of vines and geraniums.

"Captain Forti sent the wagon to fetch his deputies," Ernesto said. He swayed on his feet, face gray with fatigue. "He's called them back in and says the singers are free to go."

A loud cheer arose from the Gecco brothers and they both scrambled back inside the house. To pack their trunks, I presumed. Romeo and Emilio nodded cheerfully, but stayed outside to hear the rest of the news. I glanced at Grisella just long enough to see her eyes also light up.

"Forti didn't come with you?" Vincenzo asked.

"No, we found Santini early this morning and the constable questioned him as soon as we returned to Molina Mori. It took Captain Forti several hours, but he finally got the confession he wanted. Now he's gone to secure a warrant to have Santini moved to the jail in Padua."

Vincenzo swallowed hard. "Did they hurt him badly?"

"How else would Captain Forti get Santini to admit to the three murders? Only hours before, after I was forced to help those brutes take him, Santini swore to me that he'd had nothing to do with any of the deaths."

Several voices, mostly those of my fellow musicians, chimed in with support for Captain Forti. Emilio's scathing soprano carried more loudly than the others: "Of course, the peasant would say he was innocent once he's been arrested. But Carmela's nightshift was practically in his bed. And he ran, for God's sake."

In brusque tones, Vincenzo ordered everyone to be silent, then placed a hand on the exhausted steward's shoulder. "Tell us how he was captured."

Ernesto shuddered and passed a hand over his brow. He began in a level voice, "I used to take Santini with me when I went up into the hills to secure fuel for the stoves. A charcoal burner maintained a kiln there for many years, but when the timber began to run out, he moved on and the kiln went cold. It's been several years, but I thought Santini might remember and seek refuge there. Sure enough, we found tracks leading to the hut. Captain Forti wanted to burst in with pistols cocked, but I convinced him to let me risk only myself. Calling Santini's name, I pushed the door open and found him huddled in the corner. He was in a pitiful state, filthy, cold, hungry."

Ernesto heaved a sigh and continued, "He trusts me, so I was able to keep him calm and allow himself to be put in the manacles. I rode in the wagon beside him all the way back to Molina Mori, surrounded by deputies. In his hoarse whispers, Santini swore his innocence over and over... by the Blood of the Savior, by the bones of Saint Mark... on his dear mother's salvation..."

Ernesto trembled violently. His voice rose. "When we reached the village, I begged Forti to listen to reason. But the constable was too busy showing off his prize to Mayor Bartoli and every lazy *facchini* who gathered round. The deputies dragged Santini into the lock-up and barred the door to me. I found my way to an alley behind the building and listened to him scream while they did their worst. I beat on the bricks... trying somehow to make them stop... but there was nothing I could do..."

Ernesto's voice faltered. He hung his head and gazed at his hands, which I now saw were bruised and swollen. All at once, the steward's sturdy shoulders began to shake in gasping sobs. He twisted his neck, fighting the tears that engulfed him.

Vincenzo's eyes went wide with shock, but he soon collected himself and encircled the smaller man in a solid embrace. Pounding Ernesto on the back, he said, "You've done everything a man of honor could do. Now you must rest and tend to yourself."

The steward shook his head wildly, but Vincenzo continued in masterful tones, "You're no good to Santini or me in this condition, and we both need you at your best. Ah, here is your good wife. Let her take you home…"

I hadn't noticed Pia joining the group of workers who had hung on every word of Ernesto's story, but now many hands pushed her forward. After a shy curtsy to Vincenzo, she took charge of her husband and led him away.

The black wagon, bearing the full complement of deputies, was already halfway down the drive. The crowd began drifting away, the laborers and servants shaking their heads and muttering among themselves. I thought I knew why. They had worked alongside Santini for many years, knew his character and his limitations through and through. Like me, they understood he was no more capable of carrying out the elaborate midnight murders than an African ape.

Vincenzo might share my qualms. On the loggia, he'd had the look of a sad, beaten man. His face was still ashen, but his flared nostrils and clenched jaw told me that his disappointment had turned to anger. Without further conversation, Vincenzo strode down the portico stairs, and set off in the direction of the *barchessa* with new determination.

Octavia was a different story. For the first time since Karl's wife had intruded on the concert, Octavia was her old, high-handed self. Beaming a broad smile, she gave instructions that dinner be hastened so that we could all make plans to leave the villa. A carriage could be provided, baskets of food for the road. She trotted inside—to make a list, no doubt. Romeo and Emilio trailed in her wake.

A few steps away, Grisella stood with pale hands crossed over her dark mourning clothes. She had listened to Ernesto's tale in wide-eyed wonder; now she narrowed her gaze to slits and glided toward me. Her skirts made a dry rustle on the portico tiles, and a smile thinned her lips. "When will we be leaving for Venice, Tito?"

The question was asked softly, but it burned my ears like acid.

I don't think I answered with so much as a grunt. Suddenly filled with panic, I felt my heart hammering in my chest and every sinew in my legs taut as a bow string. Without conscious thought, I turned and ran.

My flying steps took me around the house in the opposite direction from that Vincenzo had taken. Past the stables where Cleto looked up from his nutcracking with a puzzled grimace. On and on until I lost myself in the woods I had used for my play-acting only that morning.

Chapter Seventeen

Somewhere on the hillside, I slowed to a walk. Sweat soaked my neckcloth, and my raspy breath was the loudest sound in the grove. I trudged on, acutely aware that I was only putting off the inevitable. Before the day was over, I would have to break my sister's heart, but just then I needed to close my mind to everything except simply moving forward.

The woods became thicker, closing in with the odor of dying vegetation. Mushrooms configured in obscene shapes sprouted from fallen branches, and above, the ragged orange and gold leaves changed to a uniform brown. The dwindling path grew steeper, leading me on until it split at the summit of a ridge.

The left-hand fork plunged into deep gloom that would have made a wonderful stage-set for a descent to the underworld. Lichen-furred rocks fell away in natural stairsteps, and shoulder-high bushes fingered thorny branches across the path. The other fork appeared to continue a short way before emerging into a sunlit clearing. Being no fool, I directed my steps in that direction, paused for a moment in the last of the cool shade, then narrowed my eyes as I stepped into the light.

An outcropping of limestone made a natural vantage point for the plain below. Marveling at the view, I found a convenient boulder and sat down to catch my breath. The air was so clear, the distant cone-shaped hills appeared to be within a mere ten minutes' walk. Their slopes flamed with autumn glory, but the estate that spread out directly below held greater interest for me.

The Villa Dolfini inhabited the land in a harmonious sweep of avenue, house, lake, and gardens. Farther from the main house, at the heart of the estate, tenant workers' cottages sat at the border of vineyards and fields. Merely tracing the paths that wandered between red-roofed buildings and ripe crops was a balm to my burning brain. From this distance, all appeared tranquil, lush, productive. It was almost impossible to believe that three murders had occurred within those peaceful confines.

With chin in hand and elbow on knee, I tried to picture the villa as it must have been two centuries ago, newly built. From then until now, its people had toiled in mutual dependence and put down roots as deep as the trees in the woods behind me. One man alone cannot cultivate the land and tend the animals. It requires many hands, each bringing different skills and talents. And over it all the landowner must reign as a benevolent ruler. Grapes and grains and olives cannot be bullied. Especially grapes, as Vincenzo had found to his sorrow.

Vincenzo. I scratched my chin. Poor Vincenzo, so well-meaning and enthusiastic, yet so ineffective. According to Nita, life at the villa had been good until the grief-stricken Annibale Luvisi allowed it to pass into the hands of the iron merchant and his ambitious, opera-mad wife. Vincenzo might understand every last detail of iron working, but the nurturing relationship of the landowner to his estate eluded him. He had allowed Octavia to squander extravagant sums on famous singers while the basic needs of the farm were ignored. No wonder he and his steward had clashed.

At the thought of Ernesto, my gaze lit on his neat cottage drowsing under the bright blue sky. A thread of white smoke ascended from its chimney. A woman, the magnificent Pia I presumed, came out of the house and crossed to the garden with a basket on her hip. I watched as she bent to pick something for Ernesto and the boys' supper. I didn't find Pia nearly as entrancing as Gussie did, but I had to agree with his theory that she was one of the prime reasons Vincenzo resented having to leave the countryside for Venice.

Pia's husband must be within, still smarting over Captain Forti's arrest of the hapless Santini. Ernesto fretted over the mute like his own flesh and blood. Even accounting for the excellent care that the steward lavished on everything connected with the estate, his shielding of Santini seemed oddly out of proportion. But that was Ernesto, as proud of the Villa Dolfini as if it were his own.

Ernesto. I sat up tall, brushing away a bee that buzzed near my ear. Observing the villa from this height, letting my mind rove back through my stay, I began to examine the steward from a fresh perspective. Suddenly, separate incidents that had seemed unrelated began to arrange themselves into an orderly flow.

At the beginning of the planting season, the Dolfinis had arrived to upset the time-tested balance that kept the Villa Dolfini running smoothly. Who would have been most discomfited by the new regime? Ernesto, of course. To protect the people and animals and crops that depended on him, the steward had extended himself to the utmost. Still, Vincenzo's meddling and Octavia's whims had undermined his efforts.

How perplexed Ernesto must have been to see a troupe of singers invade the villa, how frustrated to have his grape harvest threatened. In addition to those insults, the new master might be bedding his own wife. How much could the conscientious steward be expected to endure? Ernesto must have wanted the Dolfinis off the estate more than anything else in the world.

That must be it! I slapped my palm on my thigh. Ernesto committed the murders to send Vincenzo and Octavia running straight back to the city where they so obviously belonged. A warm rush of relief suffused me. Grisella was most certainly a liar, but she wasn't an outright killer. Ernesto was our midnight murderer. He had to be.

I shifted excitedly on my rocky seat, staring down at the steward's house as if my eyes could bore a hole straight through the roof tiles. Why had I not suspected Ernesto before? The man had a sense of nobility about him, it was true, but he also had convenient access to the villa. Opening and closing the shutters gave him a perfect opportunity to plot and spy. And to help him execute his plans, he took the key to the villa's front door away with him every night.

Following my trail of thought, I could see why Santini's arrest had thrown Ernesto into such turmoil. The steward was not a monster; he was more like a madman who appears perfectly sane until someone innocently mentions the topic that sparks his mania. In fact, Ernesto probably believed committing murder was no more a sin that culling weak animals from the herd, merely a distasteful part of his overall duty. But his well-laid scheme had come to a bad end. The innocent Santini had been accused of Ernesto's crimes, and now the steward's guilt knew no bounds.

I had many questions left to answer. Thanks to Alessandro's letter that I had read only that morning, I was now certain that the Russian stranger had been one of the Empress' agents trailing Grisella and Jean-Louis, but how had Ernesto come to put a bullet in his brain? I could see why Carmela had been killed and immersed in the grapes; it was fitting revenge for the concert that threatened the vintage. But why had Jean-Louis been chosen as a victim? What did the prominent use of the clock signify? And perhaps most important, had Ernesto acted alone?

I recalled what the steward had said at our first meeting, when he discovered our carriage wheel bouncing over the field: *Signor Luvisi and I have an understanding.* He had been talking about invading Luvisi's land to retrieve the loose sow, but what if there was more to this understanding? My curiosity had been aroused by the intense conversation the two men had been having before the concert last night. Jean-Louis' murder had driven it from my head. Now it returned in full force.

I sprang up and trotted to the other side of the limestone outcrop. Peering down, I saw a wooded stream separating the two estates. Beyond that thread of silver, the domed Villa Luvisi shimmered in the sunlight like the phantom twin of the Villa Dolfini. If I judged correctly, the dark path that continued over the ridge would be the quickest route to the neighboring villa.

In two minutes, I was hammering down the lichen-covered stones, dodging the thorns that plucked at the fabric of my jacket.

♫♫♫

Despite my disheveled appearance, Signor Luvisi received me in his study with the same grace as before. Thanks to the ever-grinding gossip mill that flourishes in country places, he had already been informed of Jean-Louis' murder and Santini's capture.

"It saddens me to my core," he said, shaking his noble head. "Never has such wickedness invaded our peaceful corner of the country. Men have killed each other in the heat of anger, that's to be expected now and again. But planned, deliberate murder? Three within the span of a few days? It's... unthinkable."

"Signor Dolfini seems equally affected," I replied. "He isn't looking at all well."

Luvisi leaned forward in his leather chair and sent me a speculative look. "Does he agree with Captain Forti? Does he believe that Santini committed these murders?"

"I don't think so, but Octavia and my fellow musicians seem to accept it. The shaggy peasant is such a convenient culprit. He is completely unable to defend himself, and though the peasants on the estate seem troubled by his arrest, no one is brave enough to speak up for him except Ernesto. Indeed, the steward takes his part to an astonishing degree. I find that... puzzling."

Luvisi's gaze turned flinty. "Puzzling or suspicious?"

"Both, I suppose."

"Hmm, still investigating, I see." He gave my stained breeches and torn jacket a searching glance. "What have you been up to? You look as though you've been dragged behind a cart."

"Actually, I've been up on the ridge that lies between the two estates, taking in the view and... studying the problem."

"Have you eaten?"

"No, not today," I answered, suddenly ravenous.

Signor Luvisi went to the door and called to a footman. Before resuming his seat, he fetched a glass of wine from a carafe and removed the lid from a china box that contained sweet biscuits. Serving me with an intimate kindness that I scarcely deserved, he said, "These will do until they bring something more substantial."

My host watched as I refreshed myself, then continued, "If you suspect Ernesto Verdi of having anything to do with these murders, let me assure you that you are quite wrong. I've seldom had the pleasure of knowing a finer man, and I can only wish that my own steward were as capable."

"Yes," I admitted, downing a mouthful of biscuit. "Ernesto has many good qualities, but I fear that his sense of responsibility has been his undoing."

"What are you talking about?"

"Before I explain, I must request some information. I observed you and Ernesto in a heated conversation before the concert last night. Will you tell me what was said?"

Luvisi pursed his lips and narrowed his eyes. An aristocrat was not in the habit of having his private conversations questioned.

"Please," I added. "It may prove important."

"Very well." His deep-set eyes glowed with strong emotion. "Secrecy would serve no purpose in this case. Ernesto begged me to make another attempt to persuade Vincenzo Dolfini to sell me the estate."

"Just last week, you told me that no one besides Vincenzo knew you had made an offer in the first place."

"So I thought. I tend to forget that a man who is surrounded by servants is surrounded by spies." His mouth pulled to one side in a rueful grin. "Well-meaning spies in my case, but still… not something a man likes to dwell on."

"What did you tell Ernesto?"

"The same as I told you. For reasons that elude my humble understanding, the Lord has seen fit to put the farm in Vincenzo Dolfini's hands. That finishes the matter as far as I'm concerned."

"Ernesto must have been disappointed."

"I suppose he was." Luvisi shrugged. "Ernesto is very obser-vant. He's noticed how all the troubles have worn Dolfini down and thought he might be more receptive to an offer. I was flattered that Ernesto judges me to be an exemplary landowner, but my mind is made up and I told him so."

I took a swallow of wine. "Ernesto is not the only observant man."

The nobleman cocked his head in question.

"When you called at the Villa Dolfini with Mayor Bartoli and Padre Romano, I saw you gaze around the foyer as if you were mourning a long-lost treasure. Do you expect me to believe that you would allow Providence to snatch your ancestral villa away without so much as a whimper?"

He gazed at me for a moment, round-eyed, then burst out laughing. "Now really, Signor Amato, is this your theory? You think Ernesto killed those people to induce Dolfini to sell me the estate? That I encouraged him?"

"Perhaps," I replied cautiously. Up on the ridge, it had all made perfect sense. In the face of Luvisi's laughter, I began to have doubts.

Luvisi sighed. "You're partly right. If truth be told, I would like nothing better than to see the two estates reunited, but I have resigned myself to that impossibility."

It was my turn to silently question.

He rose and moved to prop an elbow on the mantle above the crackling fire. "I'll tell you something I'm not proud of, Signor Amato. And as none of my servants accompanied me into Venice last month, I think it will be actual news, not picked-over gossip."

He stared into the flames for a moment, then continued. "I have a touch of Annibale's mania. In short, I like to gamble. But I am not one for the Ridotto. There, who knows who one is playing against? Any man with a mask and silk coat is admitted, and many a varlet learns to rig a faro game at his mother's knee. No. I prefer to cast my lot onto the sea. The sea is merciless, but the sea doesn't cheat."

"You staked a great sum?"

He nodded. "I took an enormous share in a ship-load of rare goods—the finest silks, mosaics, and glassware—traveling west to recoup some of our lost trade from the Spanish and Portuguese. It was a daring enterprise. If the ship wasn't captured by Barbary corsairs, it could go down in the stormy Gibraltar Strait or founder on the rocks. But if it reached its destination… ah, if only… then I would realize a tenfold return."

"What happened?"

Luvisi strode to his desk. Using a small brass key from a waistcoat pocket, he opened a drawer and removed a sheet of paper. Frowning, he brought it to me. "The ship went down, but of course, I am still liable for my share. This is the statement of account I picked up at the shipping office on my last trip into Venice."

I scanned the document and whistled under my breath, quite sure I would never see such a sum no matter how famous I might become. "Are you ruined?" I asked quietly.

He waved his hand airily. "Not ruined, no. I never wager more than I can afford. Though the debt pinches, I will settle the account over time. But I'll not be taking on another such risk anytime soon. And I cannot make offers for property that is now beyond my means. Vincenzo Dolfini is safe from my persuasions for… oh, five years, at least."

"Does Ernesto know about this?"

"Besides my creditors and my good wife, you are the only person who knows of my misfortune. I'd appreciate it if you kept it to yourself."

"You have my word. But…" I paused to think.

"But what?"

"If Ernesto didn't know about your financial reversal, he may have assumed that all he had to do was create enough horror and turmoil at the Villa Dolfini to send Vincenzo begging you to take it off his hands."

"I'll never believe that Ernesto committed cold-blooded murder."

"If he is not the guilty party, why is he so tremendously affected by Santini's arrest?"

Luvisi scratched his chin. "Santini wasn't always... like he is. Five years ago, he was trusted to take excess produce to market and keep the accounts himself. My cousin Annibale thought quite highly of him, and Ernesto depended on him as his right-hand man."

"Manuel told me there was an accident. Santini was trampled by a horse."

"That's right. Did Manuel also tell you Ernesto was riding that horse?"

I shook my head slowly.

"It happened in an instant. Ernesto had ridden out to one of the back fields to inspect some work that Santini was supervising. After they finished their talk, Ernesto wheeled his mount around, thinking that Santini was clear. But the man had turned back with something else on his mind. Exactly what, he's never been able to recall. The horse reared and came down on his head."

Yes, that explained a great deal. A man like Ernesto would carry the responsibility of Santini's condition for the rest of his life. That's why the steward looked after the peasant like a mother hen.

Luvisi slanted a speculative glance my way. "Signor Amato, I don't presume to tell you your business, but I can't help noticing that you have a pressing reason for wanting these murders solved. Perhaps even more pressing than you are willing to acknowledge."

I sat up straighter, my interest pricked.

"For Santini's sake, Ernesto is just as keen to find the true killer. I think it is high time you and he joined forces. You must have a talk with him—I'm sure you will find it fruitful." He nodded judiciously, then glanced toward the door where the footman entered with a steaming tray. "Ah, your meal has arrived. Eat your fill, and I'll send you back to the villa in my carriage."

Signor Luvisi's cook had produced a delicious mound of risotto simmered with buttered mushrooms and chicken livers. I ate the warm food gratefully, as quickly as decency allowed, not for pleasure, but to keep my strength up. I anticipated a long night, for I doubted that my talk with Ernesto would proceed as smoothly as my generous host thought it might. I had held something back as I talked with Luvisi: while on the ridge, I'd noted one particular thing about the layout of the Dolfini estate that didn't tally with information Ernesto had supplied about the night of the first gruesome murder.

♫♫♫

Signor Luvisi's driver let me off at the steps of the Villa Dolfini. I saw a flutter of movement at a front window, perhaps a hand raised in greeting, but I didn't go in. Instead, I dashed around the house and set off across the back lawn toward Ernesto's cottage. Dusk was falling, the long, lazy dusk of a perfect autumn day. The sky was pink behind the dark hills and the smoke from burning leaves and field waste hung in the still air.

The cottage windows were dark, but I knocked anyway. "It's Tito Amato," I called.

The door opened so quietly, I knew it must be Pia before she came into view. She gave me a brittle smile at odds with the soft curves of her face. "Still here, Signor Amato? I saw the rest of your troupe going down the drive this afternoon. The wagon was weighed down with their trunks and fiddle cases."

"There are a few things I must do before I leave. One of them is to settle a certain matter with your husband."

"Ernesto and the boys are at the stables, checking on the horse that was returned from Padua."

My heart leapt beneath my ribs. Alfana was back! That meant that Gussie was well and away. Halfway to Venice on the river barge, I hoped. Halfway home to look after our loved ones.

"This pleases you?" Pia asked.

"Very much." I felt like spinning her around in a joyful dance, but contented myself with a small bow of thanks.

At the entrance to the stable yard, Zuzu met me with a few waves of her plumed tail. She must have decided that I had a right to be there because she gave only a soft woof to let her young masters know that a friend had arrived. Manuel appeared at the door to the horse stalls, then trotted across the yard.

"Signor Amato," he said in greeting, "everyone up at the house has been worried about you, asking where you ran off to."

"They'll know soon enough." I shrugged. "Tell me something, Manuel. Is Zuzu the only dog on the estate?"

Sending me an odd look, the boy bent to scratch the dog's shaggy head. "Yes. Why?"

"Just something I've been wondering about," I mumbled as I crossed the yard.

Inside the stable, a groom was exchanging Alfana's bridle for a halter. A sullen Basilio was fetching water, and Ernesto was running his palm down the back of one of the mare's hind legs. She acknowledged his concern by craning her neck and blowing a fluttering breath through soft nostrils. She looked dusty, but none the worse for her unexpected journey.

"When did she get back?" I asked.

Ernesto cocked an eyebrow, scowling. "A few minutes ago. The stableman in Padua had a carriage coming this way, so he put her on a lead."

"Is she all right?"

The steward picked up her foot and examined the hoof before answering. He seemed to be struggling to control his temper. "Looks like it. No thanks to that young buck who took off with her."

"It was necessary," I said. "And Gussie is an expert horseman."

Ernesto made a grudging nod. "He saw that Alfana was properly cooled and wiped down before they sent her back, I'll give him that." The steward patted the horse's chestnut rump as she lowered her head to take a long drink of water from Basilio's bucket. "Well, now that you've seen her, you had best go back to the house. They've been asking about you every ten minutes, especially the Frenchwoman."

I shuffled my feet on the packed dirt of the stable floor. "Actually, I came looking for you. I've just had a very illuminating talk with Signor Luvisi. He thinks we can help each other, you and I."

Manuel and Basilio traded baffled glances while their father pulled his chin back in outright disdain. I could almost read his thoughts: How could a less than robust, decidedly unmanly castrato singer help him in any way?

"It's about the murders," I continued. "I spent some time up on the ridge today, thinking things through. Like you, I suspect that Santini has been unjustly accused."

"I don't suspect, I know," he answered gruffly.

"And yet, he escaped on the same night that another midnight murder occurred. Terribly convenient. You have to ask—why would an innocent man run for the hills?"

The steward frowned, but I detected a new gleam in the eyes under his knotted brow.

If Ernesto could provide no other information, I at least expected him to solve the mystery of Santini's flight. Ernesto had ridden cheek by jowl with Santini as the constable's wagon had carried the escapee back to Molina Mori. Santini had protested his innocence along the way. If he had not also furnished a few details about his escape, I was the King of France.

The steward continued to press his fingers into Alfana's sleek muscles and tendons. "Get me a curry brush," he ordered the groom. After the man did as instructed, Ernesto sent him away. Then he told his sons to go home. Basilio's sullen look instantly turned to a devil-may-care smile. Whistling through his teeth, he left the stable at a loping run.

Manuel tarried behind. "I'll bed down Alfana's stall, Papa. Get some hay in her rack."

"I told you to go, boy." Ernesto's tanned face was as inscrutable as a mask fashioned of wrinkled leather. "Tell your mother I'll be along after I talk with Signor Amato."

"*Sì*, Papa," said Manuel under his breath. Aiming a long, curious glance toward me, he slunk through the door with his thumbs in his pockets.

The steward and I faced each other over a mountain of horseflesh.

Chapter Eighteen

Starting at the top of Alfana's neck, Ernesto moved the curry brush in a smooth, circular motion. I kept quiet, hoping he would start talking on his own and perhaps tell me more than I could glean with questions. Unfortunately, Ernesto was one of those rare men who are not discomfited by silence. He simply concentrated on loosening the dust and dirt imbedded in the horse's coat, and when he reached her tail, exchanged the flat curry brush for one with longer, softer bristles.

As his sure strokes sent loose hair and dust flying toward the floor, he asked, "What's on your mind, Signor Amato?"

"Tell me about Santini," I replied, trying to appear at ease by slouching against a wooden post.

"Not much to tell. It's my fault he's at Captain Forti's mercy, and I mean to put it right somehow."

"Yes, Signor Luvisi told me you were riding the horse that caused Santini's accident."

He lowered the brush and studied me for a moment. Alfana swung her head around in displeasure; she evidently enjoyed her brushing. Ernesto gave her a distracted pat, keeping his eyes on me. "That's a very old story. I was speaking of something more recent. The singer's nightshift that was stuffed in the hay rack put Forti on Santini's scent, and the responsibility for that lies squarely on my shoulders."

I straightened. "You hid the nightshift in the *barchessa*?"

"No." He went back to brushing, but more slowly now. His voice was stiff. "That was Santini, but if I'd been on my toes, he wouldn't have had Signora Costa's night clothing in the first place. I like to keep him near me—since Signor Luvisi opened his mouth, I guess you understand why. Making Santini my shadow has never been a problem, but when the opera company moved in, I would have been smart to put the house off limits for my old friend."

"Why is that?"

Ernesto stopped brushing. His shoulders drooped wearily. "Because Santini thought Signora Costa was the loveliest sight he'd ever laid eyes on. A theatrical beauty of her like rarely strays far from her adoring public, certainly not as far as our remote hills. Santini was enchanted. For him, she was Venus, Cleopatra, and the Queen of Sheba rolled into one. Each time we came inside to secure the shutters, I would catch him lingering around whichever room she happened to occupy, staring at her as if his heart was ready to burst. One night, after we'd made the rounds of the second floor, I saw him stuffing something down the front of his shirt."

"What was it?"

"A lace shawl that she'd worn over her shoulders the day before. He'd lifted it from one of her baskets while I'd been leaning out a window. I returned it to her room—after I'd given Santini the devil and made him promise not to touch another of Signora Costa's things."

"He broke his promise, I take it."

Ernesto nodded as he ran his fingers through Alfana's glossy mane. Silently, he gathered hay onto a wicked-looking fork and filled her feed rack. Only after he had settled the horse in her stall did he elaborate.

Still grasping the three-pronged fork, he said, "When your painter friend showed Captain Forti where he'd discovered the nightshift, I immediately guessed what had happened. I thought my heart would stop beating then and there. I volunteered to bring Santini before Captain Forti so that I'd have a chance to question him first, and it didn't take long to worm the story out of the poor fellow. Several days before Signora Costa's death, Santini stole one of her shifts from the laundry hamper. He hid it in the *barchessa* thinking it would never be missed."

"I see. He had no hope of ever possessing his beloved, so he assuaged his passion with her clothing instead."

Ernesto nodded grimly.

"Then how do you explain the grape stains on the fabric? Isn't it possible that the soprano's night clothing so inflamed Santini's lust that he was driven to abduct her from her bed and assault her in the cantina?"

"No, that's not possible."

"Why? That thick-walled chamber is built right into the ground, far from the villa's sleeping quarters. Signora Costa could have screamed all night without being heard."

"No." The steward's tone was adamant. "Santini would never have dared to touch the lady herself. He was never a particularly brash or violent man. Since the accident, he's been even more peaceable. The grape stains on the nightshift didn't come from the cantina, but from the juice that covered his hands and arms after tipping the harvest baskets all day. You were out in the vineyard. You saw what a mess he was."

I nodded, remembering.

"Unfortunately, Santini's accident also left him with an aversion to soap and water that is almost as strong as his difficulty speaking." Ernesto sighed and picked at the dirt floor with the hay fork. "I had to insist that he deny any knowledge of the nightshift—I saw no other way to keep him safe. If he admitted he'd stolen it, Captain Forti would have jumped to the same conclusion that you just did and arrested him on the spot. I needed to delay the constable so that I could shift suspicion away from Santini for good and all. Mainly I wanted to take another look at the note that was left beside the stomping vat."

Ernesto made good sense. The brain-addled peasant could not have been responsible for Carmela's death. The note, as well as the use of the clock pendulum, pointed to the work of a more cunning brain.

"Have you made any headway there?"

He shook his head. "Signor Dolfini stashed the note in his desk. I've managed to study it several times—on the sly—but it tells me nothing. The handwriting is obviously disguised."

"What about the paper itself?"

He pondered a moment, chin pressed into the hands clasping the wooden shaft of the hay fork. I couldn't help noticing how big those hands were, how hardy and reddened, like baby hams with sausages for digits. "It wasn't regular writing paper," he said. "I hoped I might be able to match it to stationery belonging to a guest or someone from the house, but it was too thick for stationery. And one of the long edges had been torn—very carefully—like the writer had taken pains to press it into a sharp fold before ripping it from a larger piece."

I thought of the reams of paper that Karl used to copy scores. "Could it have been music paper?" I asked quickly.

"No, I compared it to the maestro's scribblings, along with every other length of paper in the villa." He exhaled with a snort. "I even checked the drawings your painter friend has hanging up in the *barchessa*. Nothing even came close to matching."

I nodded slowly, turning my thoughts to the murder of Jean-Louis that had occurred when Santini had been so conveniently at large. "Where is the tack room?"

"Along here. Right down the aisle."

Relieved to see Ernesto return the hay fork to its place, I followed him past several more stalls to a roughly paneled room filled with trunks, wooden saddle horses, and racks for bridles and carriage reins. In the dim light, I saw several hooks suspended from the ceiling; their sharp, curving prongs were designed to hold tack while it was being cleaned. In one corner, a cot had been neatly made up with several striped horse blankets. A heady mix of oil and leather and horse liniment filled my nose. There were no windows. The only way in or out was through a solid planked door that now stood open. "How is this door secured?"

I asked. "And who took charge of imprisoning Santini on the night of the concert?"

"I did. With that." Ernesto indicated a large key on an iron ring that hung from a hook outside the door. "I got him settled and locked the door at about five o'clock."

"This arrangement isn't much of a barrier to thievery—the key hangs within arm's reach of its lock."

"If I had any reason to expect that saddles might walk away, I would take the key back to the cottage. But that hasn't been necessary. Until recently, the estate was blessedly free from crime of any sort."

I closed the door and pounded on the oak planks. The door fit flush in the frame. I squatted low. Barely a finger's breadth separated the hard-packed floor and the bottom of the planks. "How did Santini manage to get out?"

Shrugging, Ernesto grasped one of the tack hooks and idly set it swinging back and forth. I gulped and took a few steps to my right. If the steward sent that implement swinging in my direction, it could cause considerable damage.

"Come now," I prompted warily, "you and Santini had plenty of time to talk while he was being taken into Molina Mori. You are his trusted confidant. Surely he told you how he escaped."

Ernesto caught the swinging hook in his large fist. "Oh, he told me, but you wouldn't believe it. I don't believe it—it's impossible—only a fancy produced by his poor diseased brain. But still…"

I supplied the unspoken words. "…he broke out some way."

When the steward merely nodded, I added, "Can it hurt to tell me what he said?"

Ernesto frowned in the manner of a man who wants help but isn't accustomed to asking for it.

"Back home, I'm known for solving several impossible puzzles," I said.

"Well… here it is then. Santini claims that an angel opened the door of the tack room and told him to run away as far and as fast as he could."

"An angel?" I repeated in a baffled tone. I don't know what I expected, certainly not a tale of supernatural intervention.

"I know it sounds fantastic, but that's his story and I couldn't shake him from it. He was sleeping on that cot when the noise of a key rattling in the lock woke him. As he turned to look, the door swung open and a shining presence floated into the room. He threw the covers over his head, horrified, sure the end of the world was at hand. But the angel came right up to the cot. Raising her lamp, she spoke in a sweet voice. 'You're free,' she said, 'run like the wind or they'll hang you for sure.' Santini was still too frightened to move, so she jerked the covers from his shaking hands, pulled him to his feet, and pushed him toward the door."

"Hardly the work of a disembodied spirit. Why did he describe her as an angel?"

"Her garb was pure white, like the heavenly host in the big stained glass window at church. He also said that as she moved, she sparkled like sunlight on the lake. And around her head, a halo glowed with the brightness of the noontime sun."

"What, no wings?" I spoke flippantly, but a very bad feeling was uncurling in the pit of my stomach.

Ernesto shook his head. "Not that he mentioned."

A shining woman in white. Who was eager to free Santini from his prison. Could it be? The sickening sensation climbed to my throat. I stepped toward the cot, my gaze quickly sweeping the area around it. "Ernesto, could we get some more light in here?"

The steward disappeared and returned with a lantern.

"Hold it close," I ordered, falling to my knees. Patting the blankets yielded nothing, so I whisked them from the cot and shook each one.

"What are you looking for?"

"That," I cried as a pinpoint of light arced toward the floor like a miniature shooting star. The steward stepped back as I retrieved my prize. For an instant, a silver spangle floated on my palm like an anonymous scrap of carnival debris. Then I was forced to acknowledge the truth. I recognized the tiny bauble; it had decorated Grisella's Turkish costume.

Since Ernesto had locked Santini up before the concert began, the peasant hadn't seen Grisella sing in the diaphanous Turkish robe and head scarf wound with a golden band. Throughout her stay at the villa, Jean-Louis had kept her so confined that Santini had probabaly barely laid eyes on her. When an exotic vision glided into the tack room, he jumped to an understand-able, but totally erroneous conclusion.

Grisella as a heavenly messenger? What a farce! I made a tight fist around the spangle and squeezed my eyes shut, fighting a bitter surge of anger.

"You know who Santini's angel was," Ernesto whispered.

I let my fingers relax and stared down at the glittering circle of silver, so innocent in itself, so horrible to find in this particular setting. I harbored no trace of admiration for Jean-Louis; if I had been in Grisella's shoes—goaded, beaten, selfishly exploited—I might also find myself slitting the vile Frenchman's throat. But my sister went out of her way to dump the blame on an inno-cent. That was the true evil that sent anger coursing through my veins like a corrosive poison.

"May I?" Without waiting for an answer, Ernesto took the spangle and examined it by the lantern's glow. "It looks like it belongs on a stage costume."

I nodded stiffly. "You saw it earlier tonight."

"Then it must be Madame Fouquet who let Santini out," he replied on a sharp intake of breath. "She must have killed her husband and intended my poor friend to take the blame."

"Not Madame Fouquet." I forced the words through an aching throat. They sounded almost as guttural as Santini's speech. "I mean, that is not her real name. The woman the villa knows as Gabrielle Fouquet is really my sister, Grisella Amato."

"Your sister?" His eyes blinked several times. "Why do you tell me this?"

"I'm giving you the truth because I want the truth in return."

"The truth about what?"

"The first midnight murder."

He raised a wary eyebrow. "But I know nothing more than anyone else."

"Not from what I've observed." I spoke more easily now. The truth was coming out, and no matter where it led, I wanted more of it. "Today I went up on the ridge, Ernesto. The entire estate stretched out before me like a vast map. According to Captain Forti, one of the tenant farmers heard a loud shot and saw a flash of powder before the body of the stranger was discovered. You blamed poachers in the woods, but the woods are nowhere near the tenants' cottages. That shot was fired much closer—at the intruder that Zuzu alerted the boys to."

Ernesto clenched huge fists. His tense jaws bulged.

"Yes, I heard a dog bark that night, right after the clock had chimed eleven, and Manuel just confirmed that Zuzu is the only dog on the estate." I paused for breath and then delivered my final blow. "Wherever Zuzu roams, the boys are never more than one step behind. One of your sons killed the stranger—Basilio, I'll wager, because he is the hothead."

I stepped back, unsure how Ernesto would react. My heart was beating like a drum, and my hand hovered over the pocket that housed the Turkish dagger that Alessandro had given me some years ago. My brother had also taught me how to use it.

But Ernesto didn't erupt in violence. In fact, the man remained perfectly controlled. "You see very clearly, Signor Amato," he said.

"Some things."

"You want to know the rest, I take it."

I barely dared to breathe. "That's right."

The steward ran his tongue over his teeth. "Come with me, then."

♫♫♫

I followed Ernesto out of the stable. It was fully dark now. The moon hadn't risen, but thousands of stars twinkled against a blue-black sky. Nearer to the earth, mist clung to the surrounding hills like white smoke.

Bearing the lantern, Ernesto marched in the direction of the house. Past the olive press, past the garden, until he veered left onto the path that led toward the vineyard. He stopped when he reached a point that overlooked the ornamental lake. Across dark, lapping water, the stone footbridge stood out as a graceful arch.

"Here's where it happened," he announced matter-of-factly.

"What led up to the shooting?"

"It was as you said. We were all in bed, Pia and I, and in the cottage loft, Manuel and Basilio. When Zuzu began barking with the frenzy that signals unaccounted strangers, I thought it must be a poacher taking the easy route from the woods on the ridge to those farther north. I threw the covers back, but the boys were way ahead of me. Before I even had a candle lit, they had pulled on their breeches and boots and scrambled down the ladder. They were both keen to put the intruder to flight, so I sent them out—" Ernesto's voice broke for the first time "—God save my soul, I allowed Basilio to take the long gun."

"Loaded?"

"Of course," he replied with irritation. "What use would a gun be if it wasn't loaded? If they ran into trouble, there'd be no time to wrap the shot, tamp it down, prime the pan."

"Yes, I see."

He continued on a more subdued note. "Basilio is the better shot, but Manuel has always been the faster runner, so he arrived first. Zuzu had the stranger cornered. He was crouching in the bushes by the water, right here." The steward raised the lantern to illuminate a thick clump of shrubbery. "It was either dive into the lake or face Zuzu's bared teeth. Perhaps he couldn't swim—who knows. When Manuel tried to drag him from the bushes, he fought like a tiger. Lagging behind, Basilio saw him flatten Manuel with a powerful punch, then leap on his body and grab his throat like he meant to squeeze the life out of him." A note of pride crept into the steward's voice. "Basilio didn't hesitate. He shot the stranger to save Manuel."

We were both silent for a moment, gazing at the spot where the stranger had met his end.

"Do you have a brother, Signor Amato?"

"Oh, yes."

"Then perhaps you understand."

I nodded slowly, then asked, "Did the boys come to you immediately?"

"I heard the shot and met them halfway. They were shocked, terrified. So was I when they showed me the body."

"Why did you move the body to the villa instead of burying him in some desolate place?"

"If the stranger had been some wayfaring beggar, I would have done just that. But the man was clearly a gentleman—people would be looking for him, a hue and cry would be raised. If he was discovered in a hasty grave with a bullet in his head, my sons would have been in serious trouble. We had to move quickly. I made my decision in a flash—dump the corpse among the singers who were descending on the estate like a plague of locusts."

I silently raised my eyebrows. Critics and rivals had called me many things, but no one had ever compared me to a biblical plague.

"I could never make you understand," he continued. "You're a Venetian."

"What does that have to do with it?"

"Almost every square inch of your island has been paved with stone. Scarcely a patch of fertile ground has been saved, and the straggly things you call trees are a pitiful sight to behold. How can you comprehend how much this land means to me?"

"I may see more than you think. Since the day you fixed our carriage wheel, I've understood that you are much more than a simple steward. Another man may own this land, but you've been groomed to be its caretaker from the time you were born. You're a true guardian. The welfare of the farm and its people depends on you."

Ernesto's shoulders began to shake. I couldn't see his eyes in the darkness, but I suspected they were full of tears. He said,

"The old master, Annibale Luvisi—he understood the traditions, the proper relationships. He kept to his place and allowed me to keep to mine."

"And then Vincenzo Dolfini bought the estate," I prompted.

He moaned. "I'll never forget the day they arrived. It was worse than an artillery barrage. Signor Dolfini and I rode over the fields, him firing questions, quoting self-styled experts who probably never set foot on a working farm, ordering me to do this, undo that—all to the ruin of the vines and crops. Things were bad enough, but once the signora conceived her plan to host the opera company, it went from bad to worse. She was sucking the estate dry, and I was desperate to be rid of all of you. I thought a murder in your midst would send you locusts flying back to Venice at first light. Once I'd made my decision, I got the boys calmed down and we carried the stranger's body to the house. I unlocked the front door with the big key. We rushed him upstairs, and I made it look like he'd been hit over the head. Then we opened a shutter as if someone from the inside had given him entrance, and I locked the front door."

"Why did you use the clock pendulum?"

"It was handy." He shrugged and elaborated, "I wound that clock everyday. More than once, I'd thought what a formidable weapon the pendulum could make in the wrong hands."

"And why midnight?"

The lantern bobbed as he shrugged again. "I didn't even notice the time. I was just trying to complete our unhappy task as quickly as possible. The last thing I wanted was someone coming out of their room to surprise us."

I shook my head; so much for hidden meanings in the midnight scenario that Gussie and I had pondered so deeply. "And what if someone from the opera company had been arrested for the murder?"

Ernesto answered simply and sadly, "Better one of you than my sons."

"And now," I said, gazing up at the luminous crescent moon rising over the hills, "you have a dilemma. It wasn't one of your hated locusts that was arrested, but someone you feel deeply responsible for, someone you have pledged to safeguard and protect."

He nodded solemnly. "And it seems that you also have a dilemma. Your sister released Santini for her own ends. What shall we do?"

I felt a cold weight on my chest. Before the night was out, I would have to face Grisella. The first midnight murder no longer remained a mystery, and the spangle that I'd tucked in my breeches pocket told me what I needed to know about the third. It was Carmela's murder that I still didn't understand. Had Grisella committed that unspeakable horror as well? Surely not. My sister didn't possess the strength to tip Carmela into the stomping vat. At least, not alone, I thought fiercely, pushing and pummeling the facts I knew into some semblance of understanding that could eventually lead to true justice. To his credit, Ernesto remained silent, a lumpy silhouette just out of the lantern's glare.

"If you'll trust me," I finally said. "I may be able to convince Captain Forti that Santini is innocent."

"I won't go along with anything that puts my sons at risk," he responded quickly. "I've already made up my mind about that. If it comes to it, I'll say that I shot the stranger and dumped his body in the villa entirely on my own."

"That won't be necessary." I shook my head firmly, trying to instill us both with more confidence than I felt.

"What do you want me to do?" he asked.

"First, a question. Where is the note that was found by Signora Costa's body?"

"In the top right hand drawer of Signor Dolfini's desk," he answered quickly. "If he hasn't moved it."

I nodded grimly. "Then all I want you to do is have the carriage ready with lamps lit and harnessed with fresh horses."

"And where is the carriage going?" he asked in a voice heavy with suspicion.

His tone surprised me at first, then I realized that he thought I would be trying to arrange Grisella's escape. I answered, "If things turn out as I expect, it will be taking me to Molina Mori to lay evidence against my sister before Captain Forti."

"You would turn your sister in to the *Capitano?*"

Grisella's misdeeds marched through my head. All the people she had wreaked misery on made a long line that stretched back to the time when I'd returned to Venice to make my stage debut. Many of those faces I could clearly picture; Count Paninovich and Danika, I had to imagine. It was time for Grisella to accept the sad consequences of her actions. In halting words, I explained this to Ernesto as best I could.

When I'd finished, the steward promised to have the carriage waiting in the stable yard.

We sealed our pact as brothers would: an embrace, followed by a kiss on each cheek. Ernesto's grasp was warm and strong.

Chapter Nineteen

I meant to enter the villa quietly and have a private search of Vincenzo's desk, but the footman Giovanni spotted me the moment I set foot on the tiles of the foyer.

"Signor Amato has returned," he cried, and the three remaining occupants of the house hurried out of the salon.

Octavia was in the lead, square-jawed and assertive. "Finally! We'd nearly concluded that you'd decided to walk back to Venice."

Fortunately, she didn't pause for an explanation. "Madame Fouquet has been telling us the most amazing stories." Octavia raised painted eyebrows. "She says she is your sister Grisella who was carried off to Constantinople against her will years ago. I can't think why you two were keeping your relationship a secret. Did you know she once sang for the Grand Turk himself?"

"There are many things I don't know about my sister," I replied in an ice-water voice.

Grisella, still garbed in her somber widow's gown, ran toward me on light feet. She clutched my arm and sent me a fervent, eager smile. "Tito and I are just beginning to get reacquainted. Once he's taken me home, we'll have plenty of time to share stories."

Octavia continued in intrigued speculation. "My dear, I can't help but wonder whether your late husband was in on the secret?"

Grisella shook her head gravely. "Jean-Louis was rather... jealous."

"Jealous?" The eyebrows drew up one more notch. "Of a brother?"

"I suppose you think it strange, but Jean-Louis was so used to having my full attention, you see. We planned to tell him… when the time was right." Grisella allowed a grimace of grief to contort her features, then buried her face in my jacket.

Her touch filled me with sorrow and loathing. Though I had lost all patience with her deceits, I resisted the impulse to shirk away. I would soon confront my sister. But the moment was not yet. Not yet.

Vincenzo had been following this exchange in silence. Studying his unassuming tradesman's face, I came to a spontaneous decision. More than anyone, I wished Gussie were at my side to see the rest of this night through. That was not to be, but here before me stood a man of an upright and dependable nature. "Signor Dolfini," I asked with a pointed look. "Could I speak with you a moment in your study?"

He opened his mouth, but Octavia broke in. "If you're worried about your pay. I'll have a purse prepared for both of you before you leave in the morning."

Ignoring Octavia, I kept my gaze locked on Vincenzo's.

"Certainly." The master of the villa motioned toward the right-hand corridor. "Come along."

Grisella was clearly nervous about being separated from me again. She clung to my arm with the strength of a blacksmith until I gave my word that I would not disappear and that I would most certainly talk with her before she retired. Thus assured, she reluctantly followed Octavia back into the salon with only one or two wistful glances.

Vincenzo and I were soon in his study with the door shut. He took up a position behind his desk; I faced him from the opposite side and didn't mince words. "Are you satisfied with Captain Forti's arrest of Santini?"

"Hardly! I spent the afternoon questioning the servants and the tenant workers again. I was hoping to pick up some new fact or just-remembered observation—anything that would shed light on the murders."

I inclined my head. "I salute you, Signore. I hoped you wouldn't be taken in by Captain Forti's hasty conclusion."

"Um, yes. Cooler heads and all that." He nodded, pushing some papers around his desk. "But where have you been? I've never seen you in quite such a mess."

"I've been investigating in my own way. Unless I miss my guess, a solution is near at hand."

"In truth?"

I nodded.

"Well, I must say, you don't seem very pleased about it."

"There's not a particle of joy in what I've learned. The killer is not who you might expect."

I must have gazed in the direction of the salon without meaning to, for Vincenzo replied in shocked tones, "Not that pretty child?"

"Grisella is hardly a child. In her twenty-two years, she's witnessed more low, sneaking deeds than most men see in a lifetime."

"But she's your sister, man."

As if I hadn't been repeating that to myself ever since I found Grisella's telltale spangle in the tack room. As if the murderous prima donna hadn't once been the copper-haired toddler who learned to walk while grasping my fingers. I found myself swaying on my feet, gripping my head with both hands. The enormity of my sister's guilt pressed on me like a physical weight, squeezing my brain, constricting my chest.

Vincenzo hurried around the desk. He placed both hands on my shoulders and shook me for all I was worth.

Snatching a deep breath, I returned to my senses. At least for a while.

"Tell me how this is possible." Vincenzo slung questions right and left. "How did Madame Fouquet commit three murders that baffled us all? Why would she kill her own husband? And who was the stranger that nearly putrefied in my ice house?"

I responded carefully. Though the motives and methods underlying the villa's murderous events were becoming clearer, I was still feeling my way like a man crossing a swollen stream on underwater rocks. "I can enlighten you about the identity of the stranger. My sister lived with a Russian gentleman in Constantinople. He died in violent circumstances, and one of his countrymen was sent to take revenge for Grisella's part in the tragedy. The rest of the details will have to wait. I need you to help me with something that will complete my understanding."

"What is it?"

"I want to see the note that was found by the stomping vat."

"Certainly—anything to help." Vincenzo stepped behind the desk, opened a drawer, and removed the purple-daubed rectangle of thick, creamy paper.

I took it from his outstretched hand. Yes, I thought, something in Ernesto's description had seemed very familiar. I glanced at the writing, but its intentionally anonymous hand was of no import. It was the paper that mattered.

"There's an item I must compare this to. While I search for it, I'd like you to keep Grisella in the salon."

"I'll do my best." Vincenzo's tone was shaky, but he underscored his agreement with a determined nod.

I was halfway across the study when I stopped and spun around. "Oh, yes. I've taken the liberty of ordering Ernesto to have the carriage ready. If I find what I expect, I will need to lay my evidence before Captain Forti."

Vincenzo nodded. "You have my blessing. Earlier today, I was ready to chuck it all—simply find a buyer, return to Venice, and forget that I was ever master here. But as I made my rounds of the fields and cottages this afternoon, spoke with all the workers, I realized that I would never be happy without a piece of ground to call my own. My neighbors have been putting down roots for centuries, but their families all started as tender shoots at some point. Octavia and I have not been blessed with children, but perhaps it's not too late. And then there are my nephews. If I persevere, I can start my own dynasty."

I met his determination with a smile. "Imagine, in not too many years, people will forget that this house was ever called anything other than the Villa Dolfini."

"Go on, then." Vincenzo drew himself up proudly, gazing into the distance as if he could see through the walls to the fields beyond. For the first time, he reminded me more of a nobleman than an ironmonger. "Do what you must to bring this terrible business to an honest end, Signor Amato. Then Ernesto and I can get on with the completion of the harvest."

I left the study and quietly headed upstairs, all the while wondering if the magnificent Pia had contributed to Vincenzo's new resolve. I shook my head as I stood at the door of Carmela's old room, the chamber now given over to Grisella. Whatever tangle Vincenzo's desire for Pia had created, the three affected parties would have to unravel it themselves. I had more pressing matters to address.

♫♫♫

I stepped inside the chamber, pulling the door shut behind me, and paused for a moment to let my eyes adjust to the dim light. Ernesto had not yet closed the shutters; the weak moonlight streamed through the casement window and made two bluish pools on the carpet. I located a three-branched candlestick and tinderbox on the tripod table. Once I had the wicks burning brightly, I made a quick survey of the room.

Octavia had directed Nita to pack up Carmela's things to await the settlement of her estate. Brass-bound trunks and boxes secured with twine made a tower in the corner by the wardrobe; nestling somewhere in that neat stack were the spectacular Russian pearls. Carmela had never married or had children, but I'd heard her mention an elderly mother and a host of brothers and sisters that still lived in a Friulian village northwest of Venice. I had to smile as I pictured a tiny woman with a face like wrinkled parchment proudly donning her daughter's earrings and lace shawl to wear to Sunday Mass. Throughout the commodious chamber, Grisella's possessions had taken the place of

Carmela's. In one day, my sister had strewn every horizontal surface with stays, petticoats, fans, scent bottles, and more. One of the items I sought had been carelessly tossed on the back of a chair. I placed the candlestick on the table and retrieved the spangled scarf that Grisella had worn for the concert.

A pier-glass hung between the windows. On impulse, I fluttered the length of white silk over my head. Holding it tight with one hand at the back of my neck, I postured in front of the mirror. As I turned this way and that, I saw a tall eunuch with hollow cheeks and worried eyes making a spectacle of himself in a ridiculous headdress. But I had to admit that its spangles did reflect the candle's rays like tiny bursts of celestial starlight, and I could understand how the weak-minded Santini had allowed his imagination to run away with him.

Spurred by the thought of the mute afraid and alone in his jail cell, I dug in my pocket for the spangle I'd found in the tack room and compared it to those on the scarf. As I expected, it was a perfect match. Squinting at the delicate silk, I even managed to find a frayed thread that had allowed several of the ornaments to work loose. I carefully folded the silver disk into the scarf and placed the lot in my pocket. If I was going to convince Captain Forti that Santini was not his man, I would have to present solid evidence.

For the moment, I closed my mind to the implications of that course of action and turned my attention to Grisella's bedside table. On it sat the book I'd seldom seen Grisella without, a volume about the size of the palm of my hand with a red leather spine and marble paper covered boards. It was hardly great literature. *Amalia, or the Memoirs of an Errant Lady* read the title page. I opened the back cover. For reasons unknown to me, printers generally left a few blank pages at the end of such books. *Amalia* was no exception. There were two blank leaves. And the stub of one more. The last page had been carefully torn away.

I carried the book over to the candle and laid the note that Vincenzo had supplied against the torn page, pressed my thumb along its folds. Another perfect match.

A hot flush sprang to my face. My sister was a murderer two times over, four if I wanted to count her complicity in the deaths of Danika and Count Paninovich. How could a sister of my own blood come to such a pass? Had she been flawed from birth, her palsies only the most visible sign of an evil humor that circulated in her marrow? Or had Grisella been scarred by coming to womanhood in our unhappy household?

With our mother dead and our father a bitter, critical taskmaster, each of us had sought the world's approbation in a different way. Alessandro had thrown himself upon the sea, amassing goods and monetary success with the tenacity of a badger. Annetta had cultivated a sunny disposition and attempted to please everyone who came across her path. Grisella was probably more like me than the others. We both loved crawling in the skin of an operatic character and being rewarded with applause and adulation for our efforts. Back at the *conservatorio*, something flamed up inside me the day I first performed on the stage. It was like kindling touched by a glowing torch. Grisella burned with the same fire, but hers was a destructive blaze.

Sharp regret pricked at my heart when I thought of what might have been. What if the young Grisella had never caught Domenico Viviani's eye? What if she had been allowed to complete her vocal studies at the Mendicanti and found her place on the stage as I did? What if Father had never—

Enough!

I had my evidence. I knew what I must do, but my feet seemed to be rooted to the carpet. In my mind's eye, I saw Annetta's mild face and heard her words as if she whispered in my ear: "Look, Tito, the fireplace. It's well laid, ready for lighting. One touch from your candle and it will blaze to life. You can burn the book and the scarf, burn them to ashes so we can have our Grisella home with us where she belongs."

Just as quickly, out of nowhere, came Alessandro's deep baritone. "What are you waiting for, little brother? I combed Constantinople to get to the bottom of Grisella's misdeeds, exposed her black heart as clearly as the sun at midday. You can't let her get away with murder. Go for the constable! Now!"

I stood in an agony of indecision, breathing in deep, heaving gasps. Family first? Forgive murder? Let an innocent man hang? Then the latch on the door clicked.

"Tito? What are you doing?"

I whirled. My sister stood in the doorway, framed by the brighter light of the corridor. She saw the book still open on the table, saw the note that lay upon it.

I expected endless excuses and lamentations. I never imagined that Grisella would charge at me like an enraged lioness, spitting oaths while her nails tore at my cheeks.

My hands flew up to protect my face. I stumbled backward. Her raking fingers clutched my hair, and she knocked my head into the bedpost. Rolling and tumbling with stars flashing before my eyes, I somehow managed to pin the struggling woman to the bed.

"Get out of my room," she cried on a snarl from some deep animal place. "Leave me be."

"It's too late for that, Grisella. I know you killed Carmela and Jean-Louis. I can't just walk away."

"I didn't kill Carmela. Far from it. I tried to save her."

"What are you talking about?" Gingerly, I released her arms but kept my position astride her narrow hips.

"Jean-Louis was determined to get rid of Carmela," she cried.

"Why?"

"When she boasted of performing for the court in St. Petersburg, Jean-Louis convinced himself that Carmela had heard about Vladimir's death and later realized that I was his mistress who was supposed to have died with him."

Yes, that might be, I thought silently. Carmela had been singing in Paris just before she came to the Villa Dolfini. Who knows what scraps of backstage gossip she could have picked up concerning Grisella and Jean-Louis, then knit in with other news she'd heard in St. Petersburg? Blood trickled from a gash on my cheekbone and reached the corner of my lips. I stanched it with my ruffled cuff, never taking my eyes off Grisella's face.

Her words continued to pour out. "Jean-Louis recognized the body Carmela discovered in the corridor right away. He was a Russian agent who had been following us off and on for months. We'd changed our names and thought we'd lost him before I appeared in Paris. Then, one night, there he was in the audience—with the audacity to hand me a bouquet over the footlights. It went on like that for weeks. He was stalking us, taunting us, biding his time until he struck."

"Why didn't you run away? Go into hiding far from Paris?"

"We were desperate to leave, but Jean-Louis' high living had left our purse as thin as a pauper's. Maestro Weber's offer seemed heaven sent. Without telling a soul where we were going, we came to the Villa Dolfini only to find Carmela in the cast. I knew her for a first-rate gossip, and Jean-Louis was wary of her from the outset. When she boasted of hobnobbing with Empress Anna Ivanova's inner circle in St. Petersburg, he decided that she was the one who had alerted our pursuer to our whereabouts."

"The Russian's murder must have been quite a surprise—your enemy dead at your door without either of you lifting a finger."

"We thought Carmela had killed him, perhaps because he refused to pay as much as they'd agreed on." She gazed up at me with a scowl, calmer now. "But when Captain Forti announced that the stranger had been shot, none of that made sense anymore."

I held my tongue about Manuel and Basilio, instead asking, "You say you tried to save Carmela. How?"

She twisted under me, her mouth and shoulder tensing rhythmically. "Let me up. If I'm going to explain, I'll need a few drops of my medicine."

I studied her for a long moment. Slowly I eased back. One foot found the floor, and then the other. Grisella moved more quickly, springing up and fetching her bottle of elixir from a dresser drawer. The brown liquid nearly reached the stopper. She returned to sit on the edge of the bed, tipped her head back, and consumed several gulps.

I also sank down on the mattress, turning to face her.

"Jean-Louis was determined to get rid of Carmela," she went on, her voice low and dreamlike, the muscles of her face and shoulders going slack. "We fought nonstop for two days. What a shame to consign Carmela's wonderful voice to an early grave, I argued. The Russian who had pursued us so intently was dead, and I was sure that Carmela could be persuaded to forget who we really were. The very thought of murdering a fellow singer sent shivers up my spine. But Jean-Louis said he could never feel safe as long as Carmela was alive. He decided to duplicate the first murder—use the pendulum, strike at midnight, all of it."

"Why?"

"Last year a killer terrified Paris for weeks—people were still talking about him when we arrived. He was a lunatic who murdered prostitutes in a particularly gruesome way—always the same weapon, the same park by the Seine, the same hour of the night. Jean-Louis thought making Carmela's murder appear to be the work of such a demented soul would cast suspicion away from him. Besides, at midnight I could quite believably insist that he was in bed with me."

"Had Jean-Louis already identified Santini as a convenient scapegoat?"

"No, I'll wager he hadn't even noticed that filthy mute until Carmela's nightshift was found in the *barchessa*. Why should he, after all?" She tossed her brassy curls. "But if my plan had worked, the man would not have been accused because Carmela would have packed her bags and left. I meant to warn her. That's why I sent that message." Grisella pointed toward the table where the candles burned brightly over the book and the note. "I first tried to pass it to her during that silly game of blind man's bluff, but Jean-Louis watched me like a hawk. It wasn't until the next evening at supper that I managed to tuck it into her shawl that had slid off the back of her chair. Once Jean-Louis and I had gone up to bed, I doctored his brandy with a few drops of my elixir. He fell asleep at once, and I was able to sneak downstairs to keep our appointment in the cantina."

"Why did you choose the cantina? Why not just have a talk in her room?"

"I wanted a private place where we wouldn't be interrupted. With Romeo around, Carmela's room might as well have had a swinging door on it."

I nodded. "What happened in the cantina?"

She dropped her chin, no longer able to look me in the eye. "I'd barely started to explain what danger she was in when Jean-Louis rushed in like a raging bull. I'd misjudged his plow-horse constitution. To lay him low, I should have used half a bottle."

"So he hit her with the pendulum?"

"Yes, when he woke in an empty bed and found Carmela's room empty, too, he grabbed the pendulum from the clock and started searching for us. He began with the cantina because he'd made a point of telling me about watching the grape stomping that afternoon. It all happened so fast. When Jean-Louis swung the pendulum, Carmela didn't even have a chance to scream. I heard her skull crack and watched her crumple to the stone floor."

Looking up, Grisella wrapped her arms around her midsection and swayed from side to side. "It was terrible, Tito."

I nodded, sick. "You must have helped Jean-Louis arrange her body in the stomping vat."

"Yes, I suppose I did. I don't know why he insisted on it, but he did. Oh, don't give me that accusing look. What was I to do? Carmela was already dead, and Jean-Louis was furious with me. If I hadn't cooperated, I would have been floating in the grapes, too."

"Why did you leave the note where it would be found?"

She shook her head. "I didn't. I thought I'd cast it into the vat to dissolve in the slurry."

"I see," I answered dully, wondering how much of my sister's tale was the truth.

"Tito?" Grisella reached out to curl her fingers around mine. "Do you understand now?"

"Understand?"

"Why I had to kill Jean-Louis…"

Chapter Twenty

The stark memory of Jean-Louis' corpse in his bloody bathwater flashed through my mind. Then I pictured the man I had grown to know during our stay at the villa: a greedy ruffian with a craving for luxury who wasn't ashamed to live off the earnings of his pretend wife. "I understand why you wanted to get rid of him, Grisella. But plunging the clock hand into his jugular? Do you really expect me to condone that?"

Her eyes glimmered brightly. "But I had to kill him. You made me do it."

"Grisella!"

"You did! When you promised to take me home, you became my protector. I was saved! Saved from the cruel Frenchman who'd taken me in with honeyed words, then used me in the most shameful ways imaginable. Finally everything was going to be all right. But then Alessandro had to stick his long nose into our business. He convinced you that I was at fault for what happened in Constantinople. What does he know? He wasn't there the night of the fire. He didn't see Jean-Louis cut Vladimir's throat and carry in that lifeless girl's body. He didn't see how I threw myself at Jean-Louis, trying to stop him catching the curtains on fire from the lamp's flame. No, Alessandro turned you against me so that you refused to take me home even though you knew what a monster Jean-Louis was. What else was I to do? I had to kill him."

"You could have told me that Jean-Louis killed Carmela. I would have seen that he faced the law for his crime."

She shook her head stubbornly. "If I told anyone, he assured me that I would also be implicated. He would swear that I wrote the note to lure Carmela to the slaughter, not to warn her."

I sighed, running a hand over my face. What frustration! My sister had an answer for everything and took blame for nothing. "Grisella," I said. "Jean-Louis stole something from Count Paninovich. The woman Alessandro met at The Red Tulip was a witness to Jean-Louis selling something of great price to the Russian Envoy. Can you honestly tell me you had no part in that?"

She narrowed her eyes. "Vladimir owed me that. I'd been with him for two years, and he was making plans to cast me aside like an old stocking that isn't even worth darning. While I waited and worried, he was smiling and happy because he was going back to Russia, back to Anna Ivanova's court to be given a hero's welcome. Every time I looked at him, the unfairness made my blood boil."

"You took this valuable item to get some of your own back," I observed, keeping my tone gentle in hopes that she would tell me more.

"I did and I'm proud of it, no matter how much trouble that damnable list has caused."

"List?"

She nodded fervently. "The list was the reason that Vladimir had been dispatched to Turkey in the first place. He'd been given unlimited funds to become friendly with the staff of all the embassies and as many Turkish military officers as would extend their courtesies. Vladimir was full of dash and quite liberal with his purse, so he gathered a substantial set of hangers-on, mostly young men with more vigor than brains. The Turks hold themselves above many of our pleasures, but when someone else is paying, you'd be surprised what they get up to."

"It was a list of corruptible officials?"

She raised an eyebrow. A smile cold as mountain frost split her lips. "That would have been an excellent idea. But no,

Vladimir used his naïve young men to develop a complete list of the boundary forts around the Black Sea, including their manpower and artillery stocks."

Aha! Based on what Alessandro had told us of Russia's continuing designs on Turkish waterways, Count Paninovich's list would have been very valuable indeed.

"I saw the list as my safe passage back to Italy," she continued. "I knew where Vladimir kept the key to the box that secured all of his important papers, but what could I do with the list once I had it in my hand? To transform this document into gold, I needed a man who knew his way around the underside of Constantinople, a man who wasn't afraid to take a chance. Jean-Louis popped up at just the right moment..." She paused, shrugging. "I truly didn't expect him to be so ruthless—there was no need to kill Vladimir, no need for the substitution of the red-haired girl. We could have simply run away, sold the list back to the Russians through a safe intermediary, and lived on the proceeds.

"But Jean-Louis wouldn't have it, and once we'd left Turkey behind, he gobbled up our gold like a pig at a trough. We visited every grand city in Europe, always the best accommodation, the finest clothing, food, drink. With no vice beyond the reach of his purse, he fell into deeper and deeper depravity. If he wasn't at the faro table, he was bedding another woman, sometimes two and three at a time. If I so much as whispered a word of caution, I felt the back of his hand. Within six months, the money we'd received for Vladimir's list was totally gone. To keep us from starving, Jean-Louis put me on the stage. I was just starting to enjoy a bit of success when we realized that the Russian had caught up with us again.

"Do you understand now?" Grisella regarded me with her hands on her hips, radiating the same self-satisfaction that followed one of her stupendous arias. "Jean-Louis was a pig, and I slit his throat like a pig at slaughtering time. Why not?"

I gazed at her in wonder, my breath constricting in my throat as I tried to detect one particle of shame. There was none. Finally,

I asked, "How did you manage without getting any blood on your caftan?"

She giggled brightly. "How would you manage it, Tito?"

"I wouldn't."

"Well, my dear brother, if you ever find yourself in a similar predicament, you must strip down to your skin..." She nodded heartily. "Yes, I removed every stitch. After I dealt with the clock, of course. Being spotted running naked through the hall might have attracted unwanted attention. After I'd dispatched Jean-Louis, I cleaned myself up and slipped back into my Turkish costume."

Shaking my head at that discomfiting revelation, I rose to my feet. "And what are we to do now?"

"I don't suppose I can rely on you to take me back to Venice," she replied disparagingly. "You've become a harsh judge, Tito. Even with the wrong that's been done to me, you find your little sister too soiled to take her place on the Campo dei Polli with the sainted Annetta and her English buffoon."

"No, I can't take you home, not while a man sits in jail unjustly accused."

"That's hardly my fault. The peasant must have been guilty of something or he wouldn't have broken out of the stable. No wonder Captain Forti arrested him."

"I have no way of knowing if most of what you've told me is the truth or more of your deceit, but I am certain of one thing." My voice was thick with anger as I removed the spangled scarf from my pocket and shook it just out of her reach. "You let Santini out of the tack room intending for him to be blamed for the murder you committed. You left one of your baubles from this scarf behind, and I'm taking it to Captain Forti."

After an instant of paralysis, Grisella made a grab for the gauzy fabric. I was ready. I whisked my prize behind my back and plunged toward the table where the volume and note rested.

Grisella did her best to stop me. With her entire face twitching, she tugged at my arms and the tail of my jacket, grunting, barking, and uttering curses as vile as any I'd ever heard. I pushed her away only to be assaulted anew. In the midst of our struggle, Vincenzo and two footmen burst into the chamber.

"What's this?" Vincenzo cried, with the boys frozen wide-eyed behind him. "Madame Fouquet excused herself for the water closet some time ago. We only just realized that she'd slipped upstairs."

"Help me!" I begged. "Quickly! She killed Jean-Louis."

At Vincenzo's nod, both footmen laid hold of Grisella and wrestled her up against the stout wardrobe. She spat at them.

Panting, I slid the note between the volume's pages and crammed it and the scarf into a deep pocket. I clasped Vincenzo's shoulder. "There's no time to explain everything that's happened. I promise I won't leave you in the dark any longer than need be, but right now, I must get to Captain Forti. Keep Grisella in this room. Lock the door, and for God's sake, don't let her out no matter what she tells you."

"Yes, yes. We have her now. She won't fool us again."

"I'm depending on you," I cautioned sternly.

"Trust her to us, Signore."

I shot one more glance at Grisella. Squirming and twisting in the footmen's grasp, she could have been a savage attired in a lady's gown. Her eyes bulged from their sockets, her hair hung in frowsy clumps, and spittle covered her chin.

I ran from the chamber as if pursued by the Furies of Hell.

♫♫♫

The carriage bucked and bounced over the rutted lane. Ernesto was on the driver's seat, pushing his team as fast as the terrain and darkness allowed. As we sped on, the coach lamps illuminated the margin of the fields bordering the road. Heartsick and exhausted, I saw sinister forms where daylight would have revealed a gentle, prosaic landscape. Shocks of grain became phantoms in the mist. Hanging vines, gibbets. And twisted tree trunks, hulking giants.

Finally, I closed my eyes, sank back against the leather cushion, and rehearsed what I would say to Captain Forti. I could give a coherent account of the murders of Carmela and Jean-Louis; it was the first death that presented problems. I had already decided that true honor did not demand that a pair of boys defending themselves from a Russian assassin should face the hangman. And Ernesto's noble determination to sacrifice himself for his sons' sake would be a mockery of justice, as well as a tragic waste. I couldn't allow either. In this case, truth must be forced to bow to justice.

I pondered uneasily. I would have to convince Captain Forti that Jean-Louis shot the Russian. Not an impossible task. After all, the Russian had come to the villa to exact revenge from Grisella and Jean-Louis, giving one of them more reason to kill him than anyone else. Only a few rough details might need to be smoothed over. Had Jean-Louis possessed a pistol? Would the impetuous Captain Forti even think to search through his belongings?

The carriage drew to an abrupt halt. It was quite late and the village of Molina Mori had put itself to bed. I saw a shuttered house through the carriage window, and rising behind it, the black profile of the church tower blotting out the stars.

Ernesto jumped to the ground and pounded on the door. By the time I joined him, Captain Forti had appeared in dressing gown and nightcap. Grey tufts of hair surrounded owl eyes in a countenance that seemed oddly shrunken. It took me a moment to realize that the man hadn't stopped to put his teeth in. At first, the constable refused to admit us, but once I started spilling out my tale on the doorstep, he opened the door and allowed us to pass into his drafty hall.

Forti wasn't at all happy with my revelations, but he was a sworn officer of justice and possessed enough integrity to hear me out. After listening to my story and duly examining the exhibits I'd brought forth from my pockets, he sent for a pair of mounted deputies with torches. He then found his teeth, dressed, and joined me in the carriage.

As our entourage set off for the villa, the bell in the church tower sounded a deep-throated note. One, then two, then three. I counted the mournful strikes for a total of twelve. Midnight.

The bell may as well have been tolling Grisella's death knell. I shivered miserably as Captain Forti peppered me with questions I could barely answer.

The Villa Dolfini had never gone to bed: when we came up the drive, yellow light poured from every window. My anxieties multiplied as I led the constable and his deputies to Grisella's room. Had my desperate sister been throwing herself against the door the whole time I'd been gone? Would she go with the deputies quietly? If not, how would they subdue her? And further afield, would Annetta ever forgive me for giving Grisella up?

Vincenzo met us at the top of the stairs. He gestured toward the door that Giovanni and Adamo were flanking like sentries. "She's been very quiet for a half hour or so. At first she begged me to let her speak with Octavia, but once she saw that I was deaf to her pleas, she went completely silent."

"You've done well," I replied with a nod. Relief began to unfurl within me, but then a new horror jerked it away. Grisella's elixir! I'd had my sister locked in with nearly a full bottle of her powerful medicine. What if she was silent because she'd swallowed the lot? Just as quickly, another thought came on the heels of the first: Would the gentle death of the apothecary's potion not be her best course of action?

Vincenzo was handing the room key to Captain Forti. I swiped it from his fingers. Under their startled gazes, I drove the key into the lock, turned until I felt it click, and threw open the door.

I blinked, struggling to get my bearings in the dim light. Two candles had burned themselves out. By one wavering flame, we all saw… nothing. The room was empty. Grisella had disappeared.

I whirled on Vincenzo. "You let her escape."

"No, not at all. The boys and I haven't left the corridor since you set off for Molina Mori. Madame Fouquet hasn't set a foot through the door."

"You must have stepped away at some point," rumbled Captain Forti.

"No. Not for a second," Vincenzo insisted with a raised chin.

"Then…" I suddenly realized that cool, damp night air filled the room. One of the windows stood open, and in the shadows beneath it, a stool had been overturned.

Captain Forti and I reached the window at the same moment. He tried to shoulder me aside, but I squeezed my head through beside his. Peering down, I saw a ledge that separated the first level of the villa from the second. It was a lip of stone barely four inches wide. By hanging full-length out of the window opening, Grisella's toes would have just made contact with it.

"Impossible," Captain Forti murmured.

"Surely not," I agreed, trying to picture a woman in a full skirt clinging to the smooth side of the building, inching her way along. Even a rope dancer would have thought twice before embarking on such a daring feat. And yet.

"What's that?" I whispered, wiggling my arm through to point down the side of the building to a sinuous shadow that climbed from ground to roof. "A vine?"

Captain Forti sneered in disbelief, but led us all outside to examine the area. By the light of the footmen's lanterns and the deputies' torches, we found a vine roughly the thickness of my arm. Some of its branching tendrils had torn loose from the wall, and fresh leaves littered the ground at its base. Nearly bent double, nose to the dirt, the constable proved his worth as a hunter by discovering faint imprints of a woman's shoe.

"By damn, the little woman did it. She climbed down the side of the villa." Forti straightened with a gleam of admiration in his eyes.

In my heart, hope exploded like a festival skyrocket. Grisella still had a chance! I'd brought the law as duty demanded, but my daring sister had outfoxed us all. Despite everything she'd done, I couldn't be sorry.

"But she can't have got far," Forti finished. On a shout, he urged his men to their horses, and furious activity ensued.

The constable gave me a push and chivvied me along. "You're with me in the carriage. Now, where to? Toward the river? Doesn't really know the country, does she? How fast can she run?"

Yes. No. I don't know. With my mind reeling, I'm not sure whether the words passed my lips or not. Our party pulled away from the Villa Dolfini with a pounding of horseshoes and rattle of wheels on gravel. We turned left at the gate and sped along the road in the opposite direction from Molina Mori. After just a few minutes, I heard a shout and Ernesto whipped up the horses. I leaned out, gripping the window's edge for all I was worth.

"There she is," someone cried.

The rays of the carriage lamps lit on a limping figure making her determined way along the road: a woman with a dark cloak trailing behind her, brassy curls spilling from its hood. At the sound of our commotion, she stumbled into an uneven run, but with our greater speed, we soon overtook her.

The deputies jumped from their horses. Grisella whirled this way and that, still seeking escape from certain capture. For a heartbeat, her wild gaze fastened on me. With a terrible wrench of sorrow, I looked upon her dark eyes glittering with rage and her mouth contorted in a slash of misery and pain.

♫♫♫♫

Venice, Feast of All Souls 1740

Dear Alessandro,

Grisella is gone. Her lovely face, her intriguing smile, and most elusive of all, the crystalline voice that could make an entire opera house shiver.

You know this, of course, because Gussie has written. He's been stronger than I, the rock of our entire household. Though I returned to Venice several weeks ago, I've been too dispirited to compose a letter. This day set aside to pray for the souls of our beloved departed seems like a fitting time to take up my pen and relate a few things I think you would like to hear straight from me.

I stayed with our sister throughout her trial, until the very end, as close as I could get. Grisella was held in the guardhouse at Padua. Nearby, I found a tiny room usually rented out to university students, and I visited her whenever the authorities would permit. She suffered with her palsies during the trial, but once she knew her fate was certain, she turned as calm as the lagoon on a windless day. Her twitching and writhing disappeared entirely.

Grisella and I didn't speak of recent events during the last days, but spent our time recounting memories of our childhood on the Campo dei Polli, dissecting them like the corpses of small animals on a naturalist's slab. Grisella only became angry with me when I did not recall events in the same light that she did. Then she instructed me in the particulars, extracting the promise that I would never forget again.

Our sister's end was mercifully quick. To insure that she would not die by slow suffocation, I had arranged for men who excel at the sport of leaping up to pull on the legs of jerking bodies to wait near at hand. Their services weren't needed. When the trap gave way, her slender neck broke with a sharp crack.

I saw that she was buried in a churchyard outside Padua, for good this time. Given Grisella's history, the priests at first denied her a sanctified resting place. It took my entire purse from *Tamerlano* to change their minds. No matter, I can soon earn the sum back when I'm ready to take up my work again.

When that will be I cannot say. Liya and Titolino are the bright spots in my life, but even they cannot lift this gloom that has settled upon me. Some days I wander the streets, numbly absorbing the sights and smell of the canals. Other days I sit with Annetta. She has forgiven me, I think, but this tragedy has set her back. For a while, Gussie had hoped to bring her to Padua to see Grisella one more time, but she wasn't strong enough to make the journey. Now Annetta rocks endlessly as she stares at that last drawing Gussie made of Grisella. We took it away once, but Annetta's unquenchable tears were even worse.

You say you often visit your mosque. When you are at your prayers, don't forget Annetta. Don't forget any of us. On top of our grief, we still live in fear of a steely-eyed Russian showing up at our door.

Perhaps after Christmas I will be ready to return to the stage. It is rumored that a production of *Il Gran Tamerlano* is to be mounted with all the pomp and splendor the opera deserves. But not in Venice. Maestro Weber found a generous patron at the court of Naples. A castrato fresh from my old conservatory will play the cruel tyrant. I have no regrets. As Gussie so candidly observed, I am completely unsuited for the role. I must find something that fits me better.

Wherever my travels take me, brother, I will never return to Terrafirma in autumn. Perhaps in the spring, when the trees are bursting with feathery green leaves and young buds. Or summer in its flower-strewn glory. Or even winter, with its Alpine blasts and bare tree branches. But never in autumn when the dying earth is shrouded in red and gold. That season now belongs exclusively to Grisella, and I would not for the world intrude on her solitude.

Ever your loving,
Tito

Author's Note

As a young reader, I cut my teeth on English country house mysteries. From *The Moonstone* of Wilkie Collins to the later versions penned by Agatha Christie and her fellow Golden Age authors, the archetypes of the genre enchanted me. An isolated manor, a body in the library, and a cast of suspicious characters could provide hours of entertainment. The taste never really left me. I think I was curled up on my sofa watching a rented copy of Robert Altman's *Gosford Park* when it occurred to me that Tito could have his own country house adventure, with a Venetian twist.

Venetian Villas

At its height, the Venetian Empire took in a vast arc of mainland territory that swept from the Po River in the south to the mountains that form a natural barrier between Italy and Slovenia in the northeast. Its people would not have been Venetian if they hadn't transferred their comfortable way of living to this fertile land, which they called Terrafirma. Villas designed by the Renaissance architect Andrea Palladio and his disciples sprang up all over Terrafirma. Serving as both peaceful retreats and working farms, the villas featured classical motifs adapted to residential and agricultural use. Many of the most beautiful still exist and are dotted along the Brenta, a river which was made into a canal between the Venetian lagoon and the city of Padua in the sixteenth century.

While the Villa Dolfini is a fictional structure, it owes parts of its layout to the Villa Rotunda at Vicenza and to the Villa Cornaro. This last is lovingly described by Sally Gable in *Palladian Days*, her account of restoring this sixteenth century home. For an American take on the theme, think of Thomas Jefferson's Monticello. Our third president was a keen student of architecture whose own house was built according to Palladio's pleasing, symmetrical designs.

The Opera and Its Backer

Of course, I had to populate my villa and find a reason for Tito and Gussie to visit. An ambitious patroness gathering an opera company fit the bill. In mid-eighteenth-century Venice, the noble class was confined to a few hundred ancient and distinguished families from the so-called Golden Book. Music provided one of the few entrées into their rarified society. Octavia's character contains undertones of Georgina Weldon, an eccentric, Victorian-era Englishwoman famous for taking up Charles Gounod when the composer of *Faust* was down on his luck. Her biography is entertainingly chronicled in *The Disastrous Mrs. Weldon* by Brian Thompson.

Tamerlano, the Italian name for Timur the Lame who sought to establish a fourteenth-century Mongol empire, had become a popular literary character by Tito's time. The English playwright Christopher Marlowe used the tyrant as a subject, and a play by Nicolas Pradon served as a basis for several opera libretti. Many composers put Timur's story to music, the most famous being George Frederick Handel. In the eighteenth century, the borrowing of storyline and characters was not regarded with the same disfavor as it is today. A lovely DVD of the Halle Festival's production of Handel's *Tamerlano* directly inspired the descriptions of the musical passages in *The Iron Tongue of Midnight*.

Tourette Syndrome

Since the publication of *Interrupted Aria*, the first novel in the Baroque Mystery series, readers often inquire about Grisella's condition. Today she would be diagnosed with Tourette Syndrome, a neurological disorder characterized by motor and vocal tics that first manifest during childhood. The most dramatic feature of the disease is the compulsion to voice disturbing words and phrases, not only swear words, but also racial epithets and other socially inappropriate material. A broad range of impulse control difficulties may also be present. The course of the disease waxes and wanes over time, with adults often learning to control their symptoms to a great degree.

The current treatment involves medication and psychotherapy. Grisella's elixir was compounded of substances available at the time, primarily opiates dissolved in alcohol, to which Grisella became addicted. In its analgesic value, it would have been similar to the more familiar laudanum, an opiate tincture sometimes sweetened with sugar.

Further Reading

I'd also like to direct the interested reader to several excellent histories of Constantinople. I enjoyed getting up to speed on Alessandro's world, sometimes having to force myself to put the books aside and get back to writing. His Constantinople was a complex society, all the more so for a new convert to Islam. These volumes helped me envision what Alessandro experienced: *Osman's Dream: The Story of the Ottoman Empire* by Caroline Finkel and *Constantinople, City of the World's Desire* by Philip Mansel.

Readers' Guides

For the use of teachers, librarians, and book clubs, a Readers' Guide is available for each of the novels in the Baroque Mystery series. These may be obtained by contacting the author through her website at www.beverlegravesmyers.com.

Acknowledgments

My heartfelt thanks to Joanne Dobson, Kit Ehrman, and my husband, Lawrence, for reading *The Iron Tongue of Midnight* in manuscript and offering wise suggestions. And to everyone who provided technical details about early opera, painting, architecture, or other specific matters: Flavio Ferri Benedetti, Kit Ehrman, Benjamin Hufbauer, Ann Lee, Megan McKinney, Janine Volkmar, Mark Windisch, and Luci Hansson Zahray. As always, the efforts of the staff at the Louisville Free Public Library were invaluable in gathering the materials necessary for the extensive research that made this book possible. Thanks are also due to my agent, Ashley Grayson, for his encouragement and support, and to my editor at Poisoned Pen Press, Barbara Peters, for her patience and attention to detail.

To receive a free catalog of Poisoned Pen Press titles, please contact us in one of the following ways: